J.G. BALLARD was born in 1930 in Shanghai, China, where his father was a businessman. Following the attack on Pearl Harbor, Ballard and his family were placed in a civilian prison camp. They returned to England in 1946. After two years at Cambridge, where he read medicine, Ballard worked as a copywriter and Covent Garden porter before going to Canada with the RAF. He started writing short stories in the late 1950s, while working on a scientific journal. His first major novel, *The Drowned World*, was published in 1962. His acclaimed novels include *The Crystal World*, *The Atrocity Exhibition*, *Crash* (filmed by David Cronenberg), *High-Rise*, *The Unlimited Dream Company*, *The Kindness of Women* (the sequel to *Empire of the Sun*), *Cocaine Nights*, *Super-Cannes*, *Millennium People* and, most recently, *Kingdom Come*. J.G. Ballard's memoir, *Miracles of Life*, is published in 2008.

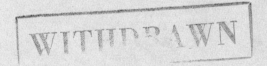

By the same author

J.G. BALLARD

Empire of the Sun

HARPER PERENNIAL
London, New York, Toronto and Sydney

This edition produced for The Book People Ltd,
Hall Wood Avenue, Haydock, St Helens, WA11 9UL

Harper Perennial
An imprint of HarperCollinsPublishers
77–85 Fulham Palace Road
Hammersmith
London W6 8JB

www.harperperennial.co.uk

This edition published by Harper Perennial 2008
1

Previously published in paperback by Harper Perennial 2006, Flamingo 1994
(reprinted thirteen times) and by
Grafton 1985 (reprinted seven times)

First published in Great Britain by Victor Gollancz Ltd 1984

A catalogue record for this book
is available from the British Library

ISBN 978-0-00-781544-9

Set in Plantin

Printed and bound in Great Britain by Clays Ltd, St Ives plc

Mixed Sources
Product group from well-managed
forests and other controlled sources
www.fsc.org Cert no. SW-COC-1806
© 1996 Forest Stewardship Council

FSC is a non-profit international organisation established to promote the
responsible management of the world's forests. Products carrying the FSC
label are independently certified to assure consumers that they come
from forests that are managed to meet the social, economic and
ecological needs of present and future generations.

Find out more about HarperCollins and the environment at
www.harpercollins.co.uk/green

Empire of the Sun draws on my experiences in Shanghai, China, during the Second World War, and in Lunghua C.A.C. (Civilian Assembly Centre) where I was interned from 1942–45. For the most part this novel is based on events I observed during the Japanese occupation of Shanghai and within the camp at Lunghua.

The Japanese attack on Pearl Harbor took place on Sunday morning, 7 December 1941, but as a result of time differences across the Pacific Date Line it was then already the morning of Monday, 8 December in Shanghai.

J. G. Ballard

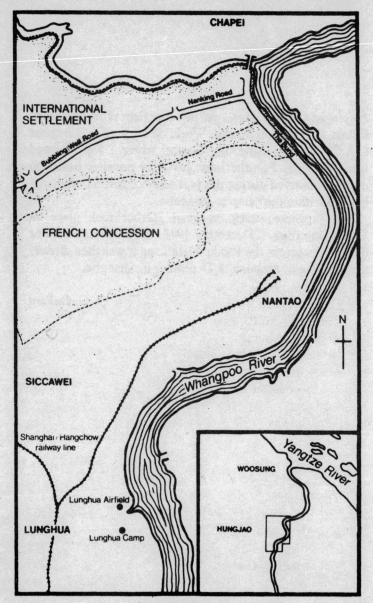

Shanghai in 1941

Contents

Part I

1

The Eve of Pearl Harbor

Wars came early to Shanghai, overtaking each other like the tides that raced up the Yangtze and returned to this gaudy city all the coffins cast adrift from the funeral piers of the Chinese Bund.

Jim had begun to dream of wars. At night the same silent films seemed to flicker against the wall of his bedroom in Amherst Avenue, and transformed his sleeping mind into a deserted newsreel theatre. During the winter of 1941 everyone in Shanghai was showing war films. Fragments of his dreams followed Jim around the city; in the foyers of department stores and hotels the images of Dunkirk and Tobruk, Barbarossa and the Rape of Nanking sprang loose from his crowded head.

To Jim's dismay, even the Dean of Shanghai Cathedral had equipped himself with an antique projector. After morning service on Sunday, 7 December, the eve of the Japanese attack on Pearl Harbor, the choirboys were stopped before they could leave for home and were marched down to the crypt. Still wearing their cassocks, they sat in a row of deck-chairs requisitioned from the Shanghai Yacht Club and watched a year-old *March of Time*.

Thinking of his unsettled dreams, and puzzled by their missing sound-track, Jim tugged at his ruffed collar. The organ voluntary drummed like a headache through the cement roof and the screen trembled with the familiar images of tank battles and aerial dogfights. Jim was eager to prepare for the fancy-dress Christmas party being held that afternoon by Dr Lockwood, the vice-chairman of the British Residents' Association. There would be the drive through the Japanese lines to Hungjao, and then Chinese conjurors, fireworks and yet more newsreels, but Jim had his own reasons for wanting to go to Dr Lockwood's party.

Outside the vestry doors the Chinese chauffeurs waited by their Packards and Buicks, arguing in a fretful way with each other. Bored by the film, which he had seen a dozen times, Jim listened as Yang, his father's driver, badgered the Australian verger. However, watching the newsreels had become every expatriate Briton's patriotic duty, like the fund-raising raffles at the country club. The dances and garden parties, the countless bottles of Scotch consumed in aid of the war effort (like all children, Jim was intrigued by alcohol but vaguely disapproved of it) had soon produced enough money to buy a Spitfire – probably one of those, Jim speculated, that had been shot down on its first flight, the pilot fainting in the reek of Johnnie Walker.

Usually Jim devoured the newsreels, part of the propaganda effort mounted by the British Embassy to counter the German and Italian war films being screened in the public theatres and Axis clubs of Shanghai. Sometimes the Pathé newsreels from England gave him the impression that, despite their unbroken series of defeats, the British people were thoroughly enjoying the war. The *March of Time* films were more sombre, in a way that appealed to Jim. Suffocating in his tight cassock, he watched a burning Hurricane fall from a sky of Dornier bombers towards a children's book landscape of English meadows that he had never known. The *Graf Spee* lay scuttled in the River Plate, a river as melancholy as the Yangtze, and smoke clouds rose from a shabby city in eastern Europe, that black planet from which Vera Frankel, his seventeen-year-old governess, had escaped on a refugee ship six months earlier.

Jim was glad when the newsreel was over. He and his fellow-choristers tottered into the strange daylight towards their chauffeurs. His closest friend, Patrick Maxted, had

12

sailed with his mother from Shanghai for the safety of the British fortress at Singapore, and Jim felt that he had to watch the films for Patrick, and even for the White Russian women selling their jewellery on the cathedral steps and the Chinese beggars resting among the gravestones.

The commentator's voice still boomed inside his head as he rode home through the crowded Shanghai streets in his parents' Packard. Yang, the fast-talking chauffeur, had once worked as an extra in a locally made film starring Chiang Ching, the actress who had abandoned her career to join the communist leader Mao Tse-Tung. Yang enjoyed impressing his eleven-year-old passenger with tall tales of film stunts and trick effects. But today Yang ignored Jim, banishing him to the back seat. He punched the Packard's powerful horn, carrying on his duel with the aggressive rickshaw coolies who tried to crowd the foreign cars off the Bubbling Well Road. Lowering the window, Yang lashed with his leather riding crop at the thoughtless pedestrians, the sauntering bar-girls with American handbags, the old amahs bent double under bamboo yokes strung with head-less chickens.

An open truck packed with professional executioners swerved in front of them, on its way to the public strang-lings in the Old City. Seizing his chance, a barefoot beggar-boy ran beside the Packard. He drummed his fists on the doors and held out his palm to Jim, shouting the street cry of all Shanghai:

'No mama! No papa! No whisky soda!'

Yang lashed at him, and the boy fell to the ground, picked himself up between the front wheels of an oncoming Chrysler and ran beside it.

'No mama, no papa . . .'

Jim hated the riding crop, but he was glad of the Packard's horn. At least it drowned the roar of the eight-gun fighters, the wail of air-raid sirens in London and

Warsaw. He had had more than enough of the European war. Jim stared at the garish façade of the Sincere Company's department store, which was dominated by an immense portrait of Chiang Kai-Shek exhorting the Chinese people to ever greater sacrifices in their struggle against the Japanese. A faint light, reflected from a faulty neon tube, trembled over the Generalissimo's soft mouth, the same flicker that Jim had seen in his dreams. The whole of Shanghai was turning into a newsreel leaking from inside his head.

Had his brain been damaged by too many war films? Jim had tried to tell his mother about his dreams, but like all the adults in Shanghai that winter she was too preoccupied to listen to him. Perhaps she had bad dreams of her own. In an eerie way, these shuffled images of tanks and dive-bombers were completely silent, as if his sleeping mind was trying to separate the real war from the make-believe conflicts invented by Pathé and British Movietone.

Jim had no doubt which was real. The real war was everything he had seen for himself since the Japanese invasion of China in 1937, the old battlegrounds at Hungjao and Lunghua where the bones of the unburied dead rose to the surface of the paddy fields each spring. Real war was the thousands of Chinese refugees dying of cholera in the sealed stockades at Pootung, and the bloody heads of communist soldiers mounted on pikes along the Bund. In a real war no one knew which side he was on, and there were no flags or commentators or winners. In a real war there were no enemies.

By contrast, the coming conflict between Britain and Japan, which everyone in Shanghai expected to break out in the summer of 1942, belonged to a realm of rumour. The supply ship attached to the German raider in the China Sea now openly visited Shanghai and moored in the river, where it took on fuel from a dozen lighters – many of them, Jim's father noted wryly, owned by American oil companies. Almost all the American women and children had been evacuated from Shanghai. In his class at the Cathedral School, Jim was surrounded by empty desks. Most of his friends and their mothers had left for the safety of Hong Kong and Singapore, while the fathers closed their houses and moved into the hotels along the Bund.

At the beginning of December, when school ended for the day, Jim joined his father on the roof of his office block in Szechwan Road and helped him to set fire to the crates of records which the Chinese clerks brought up in the elevator. The trail of charred paper lifted across the Bund and mingled with the smoke from the impatient funnels of the last steamers to leave Shanghai. Passengers crowded the gangways, Eurasians, Chinese and Europeans fighting to get aboard with their bundles and suitcases, ready to risk the German submarines waiting in the Yangtze estuary. Fires rose from the roofs of the office buildings in the financial district, watched through field-glasses by the Japanese officers standing on their concrete blockhouses across the river at Pootung. It was not the anger of the Japanese that most disturbed Jim, but their patience.

As soon as they reached the house in Amherst Avenue he ran upstairs to change. Jim liked the Persian slippers, embroidered silk shirt and blue velvet trousers in which he resembled a film extra from *The Thief of Bagdad*, and he was eager to leave for Dr Lockwood's party. He would endure the conjurors and newsreels, and then set off for the secret rendezvous which the rumours of war had prevented him from keeping for so many months.

By way of a happy bonus, Sunday was Vera's free afternoon, when she visited her parents in the ghetto at Hongkew. This bored young woman, little more than a child herself, usually followed Jim everywhere like a guard dog. Once Yang had driven him home – his parents were to stay on for dinner at the Lockwoods' – he would be free to roam alone through the empty house, his keenest pleasure. The nine Chinese servants would be there, but in Jim's mind, and in those of the other British children, they remained as passive and unseeing as the furniture. He would finish doping his balsa-wood aircraft, and complete another chapter of the manual entitled *How to Play Contract Bridge* that he was writing in a school exercise book. After years spent listening to his mother's bridge parties, trying to extract any kind of logic from the calls of 'One diamond', 'Pass', 'Three Hearts', 'Three No Trumps', 'Double', 'Redouble', he had prevailed on her to teach him the rules and had even mastered the conventions, a code within a code of a type that always intrigued Jim. With the help of an Ely Culberston guide, he was about to embark on the most difficult chapter of all, on psychic bidding – all this and he had yet to play a single hand.

However, if the task proved too exhausting he would set off on a bicycle tour of the French Concession, taking his airgun in case he ran into the group of French twelve-year-olds who formed the Avenue Foch gang. When he returned home it would be time for the Flash Gordon radio serial on station XMHA, followed by the record programme when he and his friends telephoned requests under their latest pseudonyms – 'Batman', 'Buck Rogers', and (Jim's) 'Ace', which he liked to hear read out by the announcer though it always made him cringe with embarrassment.

As he flung his cassock to the amah and changed into his party costume he found that all this was threatened. Her head muddled by the rumours of war, Vera had decided not to visit her parents.

'You will go to the party, James,' Vera informed him as she buttoned his silk shirt. 'And I will telephone my parents and tell them all about you.'

'But, Vera – they want to see you. I know they do. You've got to think of them, Vera . . .' Baffled, Jim hesitated to complain. His mother had told him to be kind to Vera, and not to tease her as he had done the previous governess. This moody White Russian had terrified him as he recovered from measles by telling him that she could hear the voice of God in Amherst Avenue, warning them from their ways. Soon afterwards Jim had impressed his school friends by announcing that he was an atheist. By contrast, Vera Frankel was a calm girl who never smiled and found everything strange about Jim and his parents, as strange as Shanghai itself, this violent and hostile city a world away from Cracow. She and her parents had escaped on one of the last boats from Hitler's Europe and now lived with thousands of Jewish refugees in Hongkew, a gloomy district of tenements and faded apartment blocks behind the port area of Shanghai. To Jim's amazement, Herr Frankel and Vera's mother existed in one room.

'Vera, where do your parents live?' Jim knew the answer, but decided to risk the ruse. 'Do they live in a house?'

'They live in one room, James.'

'One room!' To Jim this was inconceivable, far more bizarre than anything in the Superman and Batman comics. 'How big is the room? As big as my bedroom? As big as this house?'

'As big as your dressing-room. James, some people are not so lucky as you.'

Awed by this, Jim closed the door of the dressing-room and changed into his velvet trousers. His eyes measured the little chamber. How two people could survive in so small a space was as difficult to grasp as the conventions in contract bridge. Perhaps there was some simple key which would solve the problem, and he would have the subject of another book.

Fortunately, Vera's pride made her rise to the bait. When

she had left for her parents', setting off on the long walk to the tram terminus in the Avenue Joffre, Jim found himself still pondering the mystery of this extraordinary room. He decided to raise the matter with his mother and father, but as always they were too distracted by news of the war even to notice him. Dressed for the party, they were in his father's study, listening to the short-wave radio bulletins from England. His father knelt by the radiogram in his pirate costume, leather patch pushed on to his forehead and spectacles over his tired eyes, like some scholarly buccaneer. He stared at the yellow dial embedded like a gold tooth in the mahogany face of the radiogram. On a map of Russia spread across the carpet he marked the new defensive line to which the Red Army had retreated. He stared at it hopelessly, as mystified by the vastness of Russia as Jim had been by the Frankels' minute room.

'Hitler will be in Moscow by Christmas. The Germans are still moving forward.'

His mother stood in her pierrot suit by the window, staring at the steely December sky. The long train of a Chinese funeral kite undulated along the street, head nodding as it bestowed its ferocious smile on the European houses. 'It must be snowing in Moscow. Perhaps the weather will stop them . . .'

'Once every century? Even that might be too much to ask. Churchill must bring the Americans into the war.'

'Daddy, who is General Mud?'

His father looked up as Jim waited in the doorway, the amah carrying his airgun like a bearer, this member of a volunteer infantry in velvet blue ready to aid the Russian war effort.

'Not the BB gun, Jamie. Not today. Take your aeroplane instead.'

'Amah, don't touch it! I'll kill you!'

'Jamie!'

His father turned from the radiogram, ready to strike him. Jim stood quietly by his mother, waiting to see what happened. Although he liked to roam Shanghai on his bicycle, at home Jim always remained close to his mother, a gentle and clever woman whose main purposes in life, he had decided, were to go to parties and help him with his Latin homework. When she was away he spent many peaceful hours in her bedroom, mixing her perfumes together and idling through the photograph albums of herself before her marriage, stills from an enchanted film in which she played the part of his older sister.

'Jamie! Never say that . . . You aren't going to kill Amah or anyone else.' His father unclenched his hands, and Jim realized how exhausted he was. Often it seemed to Jim that his father was trying to remain too calm, burdened by the threats to his firm from the communist labour unions, by his work for the British Residents' Association, and by his fears for Jim and his mother. As he listened to the war news he became almost lightheaded. A fierce affection had sprung up between his parents, which he had never seen before. His father could be angry with him, while taking a keen interest in the smallest doings of Jim's life, as if he believed that helping his son to build his model aircraft was more important than the war. For the first time he was totally uninterested in school-work. He pressed all kinds of odd information on Jim – about the chemistry of modern dyestuffs, his company's welfare scheme for the Chinese mill-hands, the school and university in England to which Jim would go after the war, and how, if he wished, he could become a doctor. All these were elements of an adolescence which his father seemed to assume would never take place.

Sensibly, Jim decided not to provoke his father, nor to mention the Frankels' mysterious room in the Hongkew ghetto, the problems of psychic bidding and the missing soundtrack inside his head. He would never threaten Amah again. They were going to a party, and he would try to cheer his father and think of some way of stopping the Germans at the gates of Moscow.

Remembering the artificial snow that Yang had described in the Shanghai film studios, Jim took his seat in the Packard. He was glad to see that Amherst Avenue was filled with the cars of Europeans leaving for their Christmas parties. All over the western suburbs people were wearing fancy dress, as if Shanghai had become a city of clowns.

2

Beggars and Acrobats

Pierrot and pirate, his parents sat silently as they set off for
Hungjao, a country district five miles to the west of
Shanghai. Usually his mother would caution Yang to avoid
the old beggar who lay at the end of the drive. But as Yang
swung the heavy car through the gates, barely pausing
before he accelerated along Amherst Avenue, Jim saw that
the front wheel had crushed the man's foot. This beggar had
arrived two months earlier, a bundle of living rags whose
only possessions were a frayed paper mat and an empty
Craven A tin which he shook at passers-by. He never moved
from the mat, but ferociously defended his plot outside the
taipan's gates. Even Boy and Number One Coolie, the
houseboy and the chief scullion, had been unable to shift
him.

However, the position had brought the old man little
benefit. There were hard times in Shanghai that winter, and
after a week-long cold spell he was too tired to raise his tin.
Jim worried about the beggar, and his mother told him that
Coolie had taken a bowl of rice to him. After a heavy
snowfall one night in early December the snow formed a
thick quilt from which the old man's face emerged like a
sleeping child's above an eiderdown. Jim told himself that
he never moved because he was warm under the snow.

There were so many beggars in Shanghai. Along Amherst
Avenue they sat outside the gates of the houses, shaking
their Craven A tins like reformed smokers. Many displayed
lurid wounds and deformities, but no one noticed them that
afternoon. Refugees from the towns and villages around
Shanghai were pouring into the city. Wooden carts and

rickshaws crowded Amherst Avenue, each loaded with a peasant family's entire possessions. Adults and children bent under the bales strapped to their backs, forcing the wheels with their hands. Rickshaw coolies hauled at their shafts, chanting and spitting, veins as thick as fingers clenched into the meat of their swollen calves. Petty clerks pushed bicycles loaded with mattresses, charcoal stoves and sacks of rice. A legless beggar, his thorax strapped into a huge leather shoe, swung himself along the road through the maze of wheels, a wooden dumb-bell in each hand. He spat and swiped at the Packard when Yang tried to force him out of the car's way, and then vanished among the wheels of the pedicabs and rickshaws, confident in his kingdom of saliva and dust.

When they reached the Great Western Road exit from the International Settlement they found a queue of cars on both sides of the checkpoint. The Shanghai police had given up any attempt to control the crowds. The British officer stood on the turret of his armoured car, smoking a cigarette as he gazed over the thousands of Chinese pressing past him. Now and then, as if to keep up appearances, the Sikh NCO in a khaki turban reached down and lashed the backs of the Chinese with his bamboo rod.

Jim gazed up at the police. He was fascinated by the gleaming Sam Brownes of these sweating and overweight men, by their alarming genitalia that they freely exposed whenever they wanted to urinate, and by the polished holsters that held all their manliness. Jim wanted to wear a holster himself one day, feel the enormous Webley revolver press against his thigh. Among the shirts in his father's wardrobe Jim had found a Browning automatic pistol, a jewel-like object resembling the interior of his parents' cine-camera which he had once accidentally opened, exposing hundreds of feet of film. It was hard to imagine those miniature bullets killing anyone, let alone the tough communist labour organizers.

By contrast, the Mausers worn by the senior Japanese NCOs were even more impressive than the Webleys. The wooden holsters hung to their knees, almost like rifle-scabbards. Jim watched the Japanese sergeant at the check-point, a small but burly man who used his fists to drive back the Chinese. He was almost overwhelmed by the peasants struggling with their carts and rickshaws. Jim sat beside Yang in the front of the Packard, holding tight to his balsa aircraft as he waited for the sergeant to draw his Mauser and fire a shot into the air. But the Japanese were careful with their ammunition. Two soldiers cleared a space around a peasant woman whose cart they had overturned. Bayonet in hand, the sergeant slashed open a sack of rice which he scattered around the woman's feet. She stood shaking and crying in a sing-song voice, surrounded by the lines of polished Packards and Chryslers with their European pas-sengers in fancy dress.

Perhaps she had tried to smuggle a weapon through the checkpoint? There were Kuomintang and communist spies everywhere among the Chinese. Jim felt sorry for the peasant woman, whose sack of rice was probably her only possession, but at the same time he admired the Japanese. He liked their bravery and stoicism, and their sadness which struck a curious chord with Jim, who was never sad. The Chinese, whom Jim knew well, were a cold and often cruel people, but in their superior way they stayed together, whereas every Japanese was alone. All of them carried photographs of their identical families, little formal prints, as if the entire Japanese Army had been recruited only from the patrons of arcade photographers.

On his cycle journeys around Shanghai – trips of which his parents were unaware – Jim spent hours at the Japanese checkpoints, now and then managing to ingratiate himself with a bored private. None of them would ever show him their weapons, unlike the British Tommies in the sandbagged blockhouses along the Bund. As the Tommies lay in their hammocks, oblivious of the waterfront life around them, they would let Jim work the bolts of their Lee-Enfields and ream out the barrels with the pull-throughs. Jim liked them, and their weird voices full of talk about a strange, inconceivable England.

But if war came, could they beat the Japanese? Jim doubted it, and he knew that his father doubted it too. In 1937, at the start of the war against China, two hundred Japanese marines had come up the river and dug themselves into the beaches of black mud below his father's cotton mill at Pootung. In full view of his parents' suite in the Palace Hotel, they had been attacked by a division of Chinese troops commanded by a nephew of Madame Chiang. For five days the Japanese fought from trenches that filled waist-deep with water at high tide, then advanced with fixed bayonets and routed the Chinese.

The queue of cars moved through the checkpoint, carrying groups of Americans and Europeans already late for their Christmas parties. Yang edged the Packard to the barrier, whistling with fear. In front of them was a Mercedes tourer emblazoned with swastika pennants, filled with impatient young Germans. But the Japanese searched the interior with the same thoroughness.

Jim's mother held his shoulder. 'Not now, dear. It might frighten the Japanese.'

'That wouldn't frighten them.'

'Jamie, not now,' his father repeated, adding with rare humour: 'You might even start the war.'

'Could I?' The thought intrigued Jim. He lowered his aircraft from the window. A Japanese soldier was running the bayonet of his rifle across the windshield, as if cutting an invisible web. Jim knew that he would next lean through the passenger window, venting into the Packard's interior his tired breath and that threatening scent given off by all

Japanese soldiers. Everyone then sat still, as the slightest move would produce a short pause followed by violent retribution. The previous year, when he was ten, Jim had nearly given Yang a heart attack by pointing his metal Spitfire into the face of a Japanese corporal and chanting 'Ra-ta-ta-ta-ta . . .' For almost a minute the corporal had stared at Jim's father without expression, nodding slowly to himself. His father was physically a strong man, but Jim knew that it was the kind of strength that came from playing tennis.

This time Jim merely wanted the Japanese to see his balsa aircraft; not to admire it, but to acknowledge its existence. He was older now, and liked to think of himself as the co-pilot of the Packard. Aircraft had always interested Jim, and especially the Japanese bombers that had devastated the Nantao and Hongkew districts of Shanghai in 1937. Street after street of Chinese tenements had been levelled to the dust, and in the Avenue Edward VII a single bomb had killed a thousand people, more than any other bomb in the history of warfare.

The chief attraction of Dr Lockwood's parties, in fact, was the disused airfield at Hungjao. Although the Japanese controlled the open countryside around the city, their forces were kept busy patrolling the perimeter of the International Settlement. They tolerated the few Americans and Europeans who lived in the rural districts, and in practice there was rarely a Japanese soldier to be seen.

When they arrived at Dr Lockwood's isolated house Jim was relieved to find that the party was not going to be a success. There were only a dozen cars in the drive, and their chauffeurs were hard at work polishing the dust from the fenders, eager for a quick getaway. The swimming-pool had been drained, and the Chinese gardener was quietly removing a dead oriole from the deep end. The younger children and their amahs sat on the terrace, watching a troupe of

25

Cantonese acrobats climb their comical ladders and pretend to disappear into the sky. They turned into birds, unfurled crushed paper wings and danced in and out of the squealing children, then leapt on to each other's backs and transformed themselves into a large red cockerel.

Jim steered his balsa plane through the verandah doors. As the adults' world continued above his head he made a circuit of the party. Many of the guests had decided not to appear in costume, as if too nervous of their real rôles to cast themselves in disguise. The gathering reminded Jim of the all-night parties at Amherst Avenue which lasted to the next afternoon, when distracted mothers in crumpled evening gowns wandered by the swimming-pool, pretending to look for their husbands.

The conversation fell away when Dr Lockwood switched on the short-wave radio. Glad to see everyone occupied, Jim stepped through a side door on to the rear terrace of the house. He watched the line of weeding women move across the lawn. There were twenty Chinese women, dressed in black tunics and trousers, each on a miniature stool. They sat shoulder to shoulder, weeding knives flashing at the grass, while keeping up an unstoppable chatter. Behind them Dr Lockwood's lawn lay like green shantung.

'Hello, Jamie. Cogitating again?' Mr Maxted, father of his best friend, emerged from the verandah. A solitary but amiable figure in a sharkskin suit, who faced reality across the buffer of a large whisky and soda, he stared down his cigar at the weeding women. 'If all the people in China sat in a line they would stretch from the North to the South Pole. Have you thought of that, Jamie?'

'They could weed the whole world?'

'If you want to put it like that. I hear you've resigned from the cubs.'

'Well . . .' Jim doubted if there was any point in explaining to Mr Maxted why he had left the wolf-cubs, an act of

26

rebellion he had decided upon simply to test its result. To his disappointment, Jim's parents had been surprisingly unmoved. He thought of telling Mr Maxted that not only had he left the cubs and become an atheist, but he might become a communist as well. The communists had an intriguing ability to unsettle everyone, a talent Jim greatly respected.

However, he knew that Mr Maxted would not be shocked by this. Jim admired Mr Maxted, an architect turned entrepreneur who had designed the Metropole Theatre and numerous Shanghai nightclubs. Jim often tried to imitate his raffish manner, but soon found that being so relaxed was exhausting work. Jim had little idea of his own future – life in Shanghai was lived wholly within an intense present – but he imagined himself growing up to be like Mr Maxted. Forever accompanied by the same glass of whisky and soda, or so Jim believed, Mr Maxted was the perfect type of the Englishman who had adapted himself to Shanghai, something that Jim's father, with his seriousness of mind, had never really done. Jim always enjoyed the drives with Mr Maxted, when he and Patrick sat in the front seat of the Studebaker and embarked on unpredictable journeys through an afternoon world of empty nightclubs and casinos. Mr Maxted drove the Studebaker himself, a trick of behaviour that seemed exciting and even faintly disreputable to Jim. He and Patrick would play the untended roulette wheels with Mr Maxted's money, under the tolerant smiles of the White Russian bar-girls darning their silk stockings, while Mr Maxted sat in the office with the owner, moving around other piles of banknotes.

Perhaps, in return, he should take Mr Maxted on his secret expedition to Hungjao Airfield?

'Don't miss the film show, Jamie. I rely on you to keep me up to date with the latest news in military aviation . . .'

Jim watched Mr Maxted sway along the tiled verge of the

empty swimming-pool, curious to see if he would fall in. If Mr Maxted was always accidentally falling into swimming-pools, as indeed he always was, why did he only fall into them when they were filled with water?

3

The Abandoned Aerodrome

Pondering the answer, Jim stepped from the terrace. He ran across the lawn past the weeding women, sailing his aircraft over their heads. The women ignored him, their knives stabbing at the grass, but Jim always felt a faint shiver of horror when he strayed too close to them. He could visualize what would happen if he fainted in their path.

At the south-west corner of the estate was Dr Lockwood's radio mast. A section of the wooden fence had been displaced by the stay-wires, and Jim stepped through the gap on to the edge of an untended field. A burial tumulus rose from the wild sugar-cane at its centre, and the rotting coffins projected from the loose earth like a chest of drawers.

Jim set out across the field. As he passed the tumulus he stopped to peer into the lidless coffins. The yellowing skeletons were embedded in the rain-washed mud, as if these poor peasants had been laid out on pallets of silk. Once again Jim was struck by the contrast between the impersonal bodies of the newly dead, whom he saw every day in Shanghai, and these sun-warmed skeletons, every one an individual. The skulls intrigued him, with their squinting eye-sockets and quirky teeth. In many ways these skeletons were more alive than the peasant-farmers who had briefly tenanted their bones. Jim felt his cheeks and jaw, trying to imagine his own skeleton in the sun, lying here in this peaceful field within sight of the deserted aerodrome.

Leaving the burial mound and its family of bones, Jim crossed the field to a line of stunted poplars. He climbed a wooden stile on to the floor of a dried-out rice-paddy. The leathery carcass of a water buffalo lay in the shade under the hedge, but otherwise the landscape was empty, as if all the Chinese in the Yangtze basin had left the countryside for the refuge of Shanghai. Holding the balsa aircraft over his head, Jim ran along the floor of the paddy towards an iron building that stood on a ridge of higher ground a hundred yards to the west. Overgrown by nettles and sugar-cane, the remains of a concrete road passed a ruined gatehouse and then gave way to an open sea of wild grass.

This was the aerodrome at Hungjao, a place of magic for Jim, where the air ran with dreams and excitements. There was the galvanized hangar, but little else remained of this military airfield from which Chinese fighters had attacked the Japanese infantry columns advancing on Shanghai in 1937. Jim stepped into the waist-high grass. Like the water in the sea at Tsingtao, below the warm surface was a cool world touched by mysterious currents. The bright December wind buffeted the grass, patterns swirled around him like the slipstreams of invisible aircraft. Listening carefully, Jim could almost hear the sounds of their engines turning.

He launched the balsa model into the wind, and caught it as it returned to his hand. Already he was bored with this model glider. Where he now played, Chinese and Japanese pilots had stood in their flying suits, fastened their goggles over their eyes before taking off for the attack. Jim waded through the deeper grass that rose to his shoulders. The thousands of blades seethed around his velvet trousers and silk shirt, as if trying to identify this miniature aviator.

A shallow ditch formed the southern edge of the airfield. Lying in the deep nettles was the fuselage of a single-engined Japanese fighter, perhaps shot down while trying to land on the grass runway. The wings, propeller and tail section had been removed, but the cockpit remained intact, the rusting metal of the seat and controls blanched by the rain. Through the open radiator shutters Jim could see the cylinders of the engine that had pulled this aircraft and its pilot through the sky. The once burnished metal was now as rough as brown pumice, like the hulls of the rusting U-boats beached in the cove below the German forts at Tsingtao. But for all its rust this Japanese fighter still belonged to the sky. For months Jim had been trying to devise a way of persuading his father to take it back to Amherst Avenue. At night it could lie beside his bed, lit by the newsreels inside his head.

Jim rested his balsa model on the engine cowling, climbed over the windshield and lowered himself into the metal seat. Without the parachute that provided a cushion for the pilot, he was sitting on the floor of the cockpit, in a cave of rusting metal. He gazed at the instrument dials with their Japanese ideograms, at the trim wheels and undercarriage lever. Below the instrument panel he could see the breeches of the machine-guns mounted in the windshield cowling, and the interrupter gear that ran towards the propeller shaft. A potent atmosphere hovered over the cockpit, the only nostalgia that Jim had ever known, the intact memory of the pilot who had sat at its controls. Where was the pilot now? Jim pretended to work the controls, as if this sympathetic action could summon the spirit of the long-dead aviator.

Below one of the clouded dials a metal tape bearing a row of Japanese characters had been punched into the dashboard, a list of manifold pressures or pitch settings. Jim peeled the tape from its worn rivets, then stood up and slipped it into the pocket of his velvet trousers. He lifted himself from the cockpit and climbed on to the engine cowling. His arms and shoulders were trembling with all the confused emotions that this ruined aircraft invariably set off in his mind. Giving way to his excitement, he picked up his model glider and launched it into the air.

Caught by the wind, the model banked steeply and soared

across the perimeter of the airfield. It skidded along the roof of an old concrete blockhouse and fell into the grass beyond. Impressed by the model's speed, Jim jumped from the engine cowling and ran towards the blockhouse, arms outstretched as he machine-gunned the flitting insects.

'Ta-ta-ta-ta-ta . . . Vera-Vera-Vera . . . !'

Beyond the overgrown perimeter ditch of the airfield was an old battleground of 1937. Here the Chinese armies had made one of their many futile stands in the attempt to halt the Japanese advance on Shanghai. Ruined trenches formed zigzag lines, a collapsed earth palisade linked a group of burial mounds built on the causeway of a disused canal. Jim could remember visiting Hungjao with his parents in 1937, a few days after the battle. Parties of Europeans and Americans drove from Shanghai, and parked their limousines on country roads covered with cartridge cases. The ladies in silk dresses and their husbands in grey suits strolled through the debris of a war arranged for them by a passing demolition squad. To Jim the battlefield seemed more like a dangerous rubbish tip – ammunition boxes and stick grenades were scattered at the roadside, there were discarded rifles stacked like matchwood and artillery pieces still hitched to the carcasses of horses. The belt ammunition of machine-guns lying in the grass resembled the skins of venomous snakes. All around them were the bodies of dead Chinese soldiers. They lined the verges of the roads and floated in the canals, jammed together around the pillars of the bridges. In the trenches between the burial mounds hundreds of dead soldiers sat side by side with their heads against the torn earth, as if they had fallen asleep together in a deep dream of war.

Jim reached the blockhouse, a concrete fort whose gun slits let a faint light into their damp world. He climbed on to the roof and walked across the open deck, searching the nettle banks for his aircraft. The plane lay twenty feet away, caught in the rusting barbed wire of an old trenchwork. The paper was torn from its wings, but the balsa frame was still intact.

He was about to jump from the blockhouse, when he noticed that a face was looking up at him from the trench. A fully armed Japanese soldier squatted by the broken earth wall, his rifle, webbing and ground sheet laid out beside him as if ready for inspection. No more than eighteen years old, with a passive and moon-like face, he stared at Jim, unsurprised by the apparition of this small European boy in his blue velvet trousers and silk shirt.

Jim's eyes moved along the trench. Two more Japanese soldiers sat on a wooden beam that protruded from the ground, rifles held between their knees. The trench was filled with armed men. Fifty yards away a second platoon squatted under the parapet of an earth bunker, smoking cigarettes and reading their letters. Beyond them were groups of other soldiers, their heads barely visible among the nettles and wild sugar-cane. An entire company of Japanese infantry was resting in this old battlefield, as if re-equipping itself from the dead of an earlier war, ghosts of their former comrades risen from the grave and issued with fresh uniforms and rations. They smoked their cigarettes, blinking in the unfamiliar sunlight, their faces turned towards the skyscrapers of downtown Shanghai whose neon signs flashed across the empty paddy fields.

Jim looked back to the fuselage of the fighter aircraft, expecting to see its dead pilot standing in his cockpit. A Japanese sergeant was walking through the deep grass between the blockhouse and the aircraft. His strong legs left a yellowing gully behind him. He finished the stub of his cigarette, drawing the last of the smoke into his lungs. Although the sergeant ignored him, Jim knew that he had decided what to do next with this small boy.

'Jamie . . . ! We're all waiting . . . there's a surprise for you!'

Jim's father was calling to him. He stood in the centre of the airfield, but could see the hundreds of Japanese soldiers in the trenchworks. He wore his spectacles, and had thrown away his eye-patch and the jacket of his pirate costume. Although out of breath after running from Dr Lockwood's house, he forced himself to stand still, in the way that least unsettled the Japanese. The Chinese, who would cry at moments of stress and wave their arms, never understood this.

Nonetheless, Jim was surprised that this small token of deference seemed to satisfy the sergeant. Without a glance at Jim, he threw away his cigarette and jumped the perimeter ditch. He plucked the balsa aircraft from the barbed wire and threw it among the nettles.

'Jamie, it's time for the fireworks . . .' His father walked quietly through the grass. 'We ought to go now.'

Jim climbed from the roof of the blockhouse. 'My plane's down there. I could get it, I suppose.'

His father watched the Japanese sergeant walk along the parapet of the trenchworks. Jim could see that it was an effort for his father to speak. His face was as strained and bloodless as it had been when the labour organizers at the cotton mill threatened to kill him. Yet he was still thinking about something. 'We'll leave it for the soldiers – finders keepers.'

'Like kites?'

'That's it.'

'He wasn't very angry.'

'It looks as if they're waiting for something to happen.'

'The next war?'

'I don't suppose so.'

Hand in hand, they walked across the airfield. Nothing moved except for the ceaselessly rippling grass, rehearsing itself for the slipstreams to come. When they reached the hangar his father tightly embraced Jim, almost trying to hurt him, as if Jim had been lost to him forever. He was not angry with Jim, and seemed glad that he had been forced to visit the old aerodrome.

But Jim felt vaguely guilty and annoyed with himself. He had lost his balsa plane and lured his father into a dangerous meeting with the Japanese. Solitary Europeans who strayed into the path of the Japanese were usually left dead on the roadside.

When they returned to Dr Lockwood's house the guests were already leaving. Rounding up the children and amahs, they climbed hurriedly into their cars and drove in convoy back to the International Settlement. Wearing the trousers of his Father Christmas suit and a beard of surgical cotton Dr Lockwood waved to them as Mr Maxted drank his whisky by the drained swimming-pool and the Chinese conjurors climbed their ladders and transformed themselves into imaginary birds.

Still grieving over the loss of his plane, Jim sat between his parents in the back of the Packard. Were they frightened that he might get up to some new mischief if he sat in the front beside Yang? He had managed to spoil Dr Lockwood's party and make it unlikely that he would visit Hungjao Aerodrome again. He thought of the crashed fighter in which he had invested so much of his imagination, and of the dead pilot whose presence he had felt in the rusting cockpit.

Despite the setbacks, Jim was delighted when his mother told him that they would leave the house in Amherst Avenue for a few days and instead would stay in the company's suite at the Palace Hotel. The end-of-term examinations at the Cathedral School began the next day, with geometry and scripture. Since the cathedral was only a few hundred yards from the hotel he would have ample time the next morning for revision. Jim was keen on scripture, especially now that he was an atheist, and always enjoyed receiving the Reverend Matthews' traditional accolade ('The first, and the biggest heathen of the lot, is . . .').

Jim waited in the front seat of the Packard while his parents changed and their suitcases were loaded into the trunk. When they set off through the gates he looked down at the motionless figure of the beggar on his frayed mat. He could see the pattern of the Packard's Firestone tyres in the old man's left foot. Leaves and shreds of newspaper covered his head, and already he was becoming part of the formless rubbish from which he had emerged.

Jim felt sorry for the old beggar, but for some reason he could think only of the tyre patterns in his foot. If they had been driving in Mr Maxted's Studebaker the pattern would have been different: the old man would have been stamped with the imprint of the Goodyear Company . . .

Trying to distract himself from these thoughts, Jim switched on the car radio. He always looked forward to the evening drives through the centre of Shanghai, this electric and lurid city more exciting than any other in the world. As they reached the Bubbling Well Road he pressed his face to the windshield and gazed at the pavements lined with nightclubs and gambling dens, crowded with bar-girls and gangsters and rich beggars with their bodyguards. Six thousand miles away, across the International Dateline, the Americans in Honolulu were sleeping through the early hours of Sunday morning, but here, a day ahead in time as in everything else, Shanghai was ready to begin a new week. Crowds of gamblers pushed their way into the jai alai stadiums, blocking the traffic in the Bubbling Well Road. An armoured police van with two Thompson guns mounted in a steel turret above the driver swung in front of the Packard and cleared the pavement. A party of young

Chinese women in sequinned dresses tripped over a child's coffin decked with paper flowers. Arms linked together, they lurched against the radiator grille of the Packard and swayed past Jim's window, slapping the windshield with their small hands and screaming obscenities. Hundreds of Eurasian bar-girls in ankle-length fur coats sat in the lines of rickshaws outside the Park Hotel, whistling through their teeth at the residents who emerged from the revolving doors, while their pimps argued with the middle-aged Czech and Polish couples in neat, patched suits trying to sell the last of their jewellery. Nearby, along the windows of the Sun Sun department store in the Nanking Road, a party of young European Jews were fighting in and out of the strolling crowds with a gang of older German boys in the swastika armbands of the Graf Zeppelin Club. Chased by the police sirens, they ran through the entrance of the Cathay Theatre, the world's largest cinema, where a crowd of Chinese shopgirls and typists, beggars and pickpockets spilled into the street to watch people arriving for the evening performance. As they stepped from their limousines the women steered their long skirts through the honour guard of fifty hunchbacks in mediaeval costume. Three months earlier, when his parents had taken Jim to the première of *The Hunchback of Notre Dame*, there had been two hundred hunchbacks, recruited by the management of the theatre from every back alley in Shanghai. As always, the spectacle outside the theatre far exceeded anything shown on its screen, and Jim had been eager to get back to the pavements of the city, away from the newsreels and their endless reminders of war.

After dinner, as Jim lay in his bedroom on the tenth floor of the Palace Hotel, he tried not to sleep. He listened to the drone of a Japanese seaplane landing on the river at the Nantao Naval Air Base. He thought of the crashed fighter at Hungjao Aerodrome, and of the Japanese pilot whose seat he had filled that afternoon. Perhaps the spirit of the dead aviator had entered him, and the Japanese would join the war on the same side as the British? Jim dreamed of the coming war, of a newsreel in which he stood in his flying suit on the decks of a silent carrier, ready to take his place with those lonely men from the island nation in the China Sea, borne with them across the Pacific by the spirit of the divine wind.

4

The Attack on the Petrel

A field of paper flowers floated on the morning tide, clustered around the oil-stained piers of the jetty and dressed them in vivid coloured ruffs. A few minutes before dawn Jim sat at a window of his bedroom at the Palace Hotel. He wore his school uniform and was keen to start an hour's revision before breakfast. As always, however, he found it difficult to keep his eyes from the Shanghai waterfront. Already the odour of fish heads and bean curd sizzling in peanut oil rose from the pans of the vendors outside the hotel. Tung-stained junks with eyes painted on their bows sailed past the opium hulks beached on the Pootung shore. Thousands of sampans and ferry-boats were moored along the Bund, a city of floating hovels still hidden by the darkness. But between the factory chimneys of Pootung the first sunlight was diffusing across the river, illuminating the square profiles of the USS *Wake* and HMS *Petrel*.

The American and British gunboats were anchored in midstream opposite the banking houses and hotels of the Bund. Jim watched a motorboat carrying two British officers back to the *Petrel* after their parties ashore. He had met the captain of the *Petrel*, Captain Polkinhorn, at the Shanghai Country Club, and knew all the naval ships on the river. Even in the pearly light he noticed that the Italian monitor *Emilio Carlotta*, which had been berthed beside the Public Gardens on the Bund, provocatively in front of the British Consulate, had slipped anchor during the night. Her place had been taken by a Japanese gunboat, a squat and war-stained craft with dirty guns and stark camouflage patterns on the funnel and superstructure. Rust leaked from the anchor vents on either side of her bows. The steel shutters were still locked over the bridge windows, and sandbags protected the barbettes of the forward and rear gun turrets. Looking at this powerful ship, Jim wondered if it had been damaged during its patrol of the Yangtze gorges. Sailors and officers moved about the bridge house, and a signal lamp flashed a message across the river.

Two miles upstream, beyond the Naval Air Base at Nantao, was a boom of sunken freighters which the Chinese had scuttled in 1937, in an attempt to block the river. The sunlight shone through the holes in their steel masts and funnels, and the incoming tide washed across their decks, swilling through the staterooms. As he rode back in the company launch after visiting his father's cotton mill Jim always longed to climb aboard the freighters and explore their drowned cabins, a world of forgotten voyages overgrown by grottoes of rust.

He watched the Japanese gunboat by the Public Gardens. The signal lamp flickered insistently from the bridge. Was this weary gun-platform about to sink on to its own anchors? Although Jim had a deep respect for the Japanese, their ships were always being disparaged by the British in Shanghai. The cruiser *Idzumo*, moored alongside the Japanese Consulate at Hongkew half a mile downstream, looked far more impressive than the *Wake* and the *Petrel*. In fact the *Idzumo*, flagship of the Japanese China Fleet, had been built in England and served in the Royal Navy before being sold to the Japanese during the Russo-Japanese War in 1905.

The light advanced across the river, picking out the paper flowers that covered its back like garlands discarded by the admirers of these sailors. Every night in Shanghai those Chinese too poor to pay for the burial of their relatives would launch the bodies from the funeral piers at Nantao, decking the coffins with paper flowers. Carried away on one tide, they came back on the next, returning to the waterfront of Shanghai with all the other debris abandoned by the city. Meadows of paper flowers drifted on the running tide, and clumped in miniature floating gardens around the old men and women, the young mothers and small children, whose swollen bodies seemed to have been fed during the night by the patient Yangtze.

Jim disliked this regatta of corpses. In the rising sunlight the paper petals resembled the coils of viscera strewn around the terrorist bomb victims in the Nanking Road. He turned his attention to the Japanese gunboat. A launch had been lowered and was setting out across the river towards the USS *Wake*. A dozen Japanese marines sat facing each other, their rifles raised like oars. Two naval officers in full formal dress stood in the bows, one with a megaphone in his gloved hands.

Puzzled that they should be paying a ceremonial visit so early in the morning, Jim climbed on to the window ledge and pressed himself against the plate glass. Two picket-boats had set out from the *Idzumo*, each carrying fifty marines. The three craft met in the centre of the river and cut their engines. They wallowed among the paper flowers and old packing cases. A motorized junk powered past them, the bamboo cages on its deck loaded with barking dogs on their way to the Hongkew meat market. A naked coolie stood at the helm, drinking a bottle of beer. He made no attempt to alter course as the junk's wash drenched the launch from the gunboat. Ignoring the spray, the Japanese officer called to the *Wake* through his megaphone.

Laughing to himself, Jim drummed his palms against the window. None of the American officers were on board, as everyone in Shanghai well knew. All would be sleeping soundly in their rooms at the Park Hotel. Sure enough, a drowsy Chinese crewman in shorts and vest emerged from the fo'c'sle. He shook his head at the Japanese picket-boat coming alongside, and began polishing the brass rail as the marines clambered on to the gangway and moved swiftly to the deck. Carrying rifles with bayonets fixed, they ran the length of the ship, searching for any American members of the crew.

Followed by the second picket-boat, the motor-launch approached HMS *Petrel*. There was a terse exchange with the young British officer on the bridge, who dismissed the Japanese in the offhand way that Jim had seen his parents refuse to buy the Java heads and carved elephants from the dugout salesmen who surrounded the cruise ships in Singapore harbour.

Were the Japanese trying to sell something to the British and Americans? Jim knew that they were wasting their time. Standing against the window with his arms outstretched, he tried to remember the semaphore he had learned so reluctantly in the cubs. The Japanese officer in the launch was signalling with a lamp to the gunboat by the Public Gardens. As the light stuttered across the water Jim noticed that hundreds of Chinese were running past the British Consulate. Billows of smoke and steam pumped from the gunboat's funnel, as if the ship was about to burst.

The barrel of the forward gun turret exploded in a single flash that scorched the bridge and deck. Six hundred yards away there was an answering explosion as the shell struck the superstructure of the *Petrel*. The pressure wave of this detonating round cracked against the hotels of the Bund, and the heavy plate glass hit Jim on the nose. As the gunboat fired a second shell from its rear turret he jumped on to the bed and began to cry, then stopped himself and crouched behind the mahogany headboard.

From its moorings beside the Japanese Consulate the cruiser *Idzumo* had also opened fire. Its guns flashed through the smoke that rose from its three funnels and curled along the water like a black feather boa. Already the *Petrel* was hidden within a pall of steam, below which a series of raging fires were reflected in the water. Two Japanese fighter aircraft flew along the Bund, so low that Jim could see the pilots in their cockpits. Crowds of Chinese scattered across the tramway lines, some towards the quayside, others sheltering on the steps of the hotels.

'Jamie! What are you doing?' Still in his pyjamas, his father burst barefoot into the bedroom. He stared uncertainly at the furniture, as if unable to recognize this room in his own suite. 'Jamie, keep away from the window! Get dressed and do what your mother tells you. We're leaving in three minutes.'

He seemed not to notice that Jim was wearing his school uniform and blazer. As they shielded their eyes from the point-blank shellfire there was a huge explosion from the centre of the river. Like rockets in a firework display, burning pieces of the *Petrel* soared into the air and then splashed into the water. Jim felt numbed by the noise and smoke. People were running down the corridors of the hotel, an elderly Englishwoman screamed into the lift shaft. Jim sat on the bed and stared at the burning platform that settled into the river. Every few seconds there was a steady flicker of light from its centre. The British sailors on the *Petrel* were fighting back. They had manned one of the guns and were returning fire at the *Idzumo*. But Jim watched them sombrely. He realized that he himself had probably started the war, with his confused semaphores from the window that the Japanese officers in the motor launch had misinterpreted. He knew now that he should have stayed in the cubs. Perhaps the Reverend Matthews would cane him in front of the whole school for being a spy.

'Jamie! Lie on the floor!' His mother knelt in the communicating doorway. In a pause between the salvoes of shells she pulled him from the vibrating windows and held him to the carpet.

'Am I going to school?' Jim asked. 'It's the scripture exam.'

'No, Jamie. Today there'll be a school holiday. We're going to see if Yang can take us home.'

Jim was impressed by her calm. He decided not to tell her that he had started the war. As soon as his parents had dressed they set out to leave the hotel. A crowd of European and American guests surrounded the lifts. Refusing to take the stairs, they pounded on the metal grilles and shouted down the shafts. They carried suitcases, and wore their hats and overcoats, as if deciding to take the next steamer to Hong Kong. His mother joined them, but his father took her arm and forced their way to the staircase.

Knees knocking with the effort, Jim reached the entrance lobby before them. Chinese kitchen staff, guests from the lower floors and White Russian clerks crouched behind the leather furniture and potted palms, but Jim's father strode past them to the revolving doors.

All firing had ceased. Throngs of Chinese ran along the Bund between the stationary trams and parked cars, old amahs hobbling in black trousers, coolies pulling empty rickshaws, beggars and sampan boys, uniformed waiters from the hotels. A pall of grey smoke as large as a fogbound city lay across the river, from which emerged the topmasts of the *Idzumo* and the *Wake*. By the Public Gardens clouds of incandescent soot still pumped from the funnel of the Japanese gunboat.

The *Petrel* was sinking at her moorings. Steam rose from her stern and midships, and Jim could see the queue of sailors standing in the bows, waiting to take their places in the ship's cutter. A Japanese tank moved along the Bund, its tracks striking sparks from the tramlines. It swivelled jerkily around an abandoned tram, and crushed a rickshaw against a telegraph pole. Sprung loose from the wreckage, a warped wheel careened across the roadway. It kept pace with the Japanese officer who commanded the assault troops, his sword raised as if whipping the wheel ahead of him. Two fighter aircraft streaked along the waterfront, the wash from their propellers stripping the bamboo hatches from the sampans and exposing hundreds of crouching Chinese. A battalion of Japanese marines advanced along the Bund, appearing like a stage army through the ornamental trees of the Public Gardens. A platoon with fixed bayonets raced to the steps of the British Consulate, led by an officer with a Mauser pistol.

'There's the car . . . we'll have to run!' Taking Jim and his mother by the hand, his father propelled them into the street. Immediately Jim was knocked to the ground by a coolie striding past. He lay stunned among the pounding feet, expecting the bare-chested Chinese to come back and apologize. Then he picked himself up, brushed the dust from his cap and blazer and followed his parents towards the car parked in front of the Shanghai Club. A group of exhausted Chinese women sat on the steps, sorting their handbags and choking on the diesel fuel that drifted across the river from the capsized hull of the *Petrel*.

As they set off along the Bund the Japanese tank had reached the Palace Hotel. Surrounding it were the fleeing staff, Chinese bellboys in their braided American uniforms, waiters in white tunics, and the European guests clutching their hats and suitcases. Two Japanese motorcyclists, each with an armed soldier in the camouflaged side-car, pushed ahead of the tank. Standing on their pedals, they tried to force a way through the rickshaws and pedicabs, the horse-carts and gangs of coolies tottering under the bales of raw cotton hung from yokes over their shoulders.

Already a sizeable traffic jam blocked the Bund. Once again the crush and clatter of Shanghai had engulfed its invaders. Perhaps the war was over? Through the rear window of the Packard, itself now stalled in the traffic, Jim watched a Japanese NCO screaming at the Chinese around him. A dead coolie lay at his feet, blood pouring from his head. The tank was trapped in the press of vehicles, its path blocked by a white Lincoln Zephyr. Two young Chinese women in fur coats, dancers from the nightclub on top of the Socony building, struggled with the controls, laughing into their small jewelled hands.

'Wait here!' Jim's father opened his door and stepped into the road. 'Jamie, look after your mother!'

Machine-gun fire was coming from the Japanese marines who had captured the USS *Wake*. Riflemen on the bridge were shooting at the British sailors swimming ashore from the *Petrel*. The ship's cutter, loaded with wounded men, was sinking in the shallow water that covered the mud-flats below the quays of the French Concession. The sailors slipped to their thighs in the black mud, arms streaming with blood. A wounded petty officer fell in the water, and drifted away towards the dark piers of the Bund. Clinging to each other, the sailors lay helplessly in the mud, as the quickening tide rippled around them. Already the first funeral flowers had found them and begun to gather around their shoulders.

Jim watched his father push through the sampan coolies who crowded the wharf. A group of British men had run from the Shanghai Club and were taking off their overcoats and jackets. In waistcoats and shirt-sleeves they jumped from the landing stage on to the mud below, arms swinging as they sank to their thighs. The Japanese marines on the USS *Wake* continued to fire at the cutter, but two of the Britons had reached a wounded sailor. They seized him under the arms and dragged him towards the mud-flat. Jim's father waded past them, his spectacles splashed with water, scooping the black ooze out of his way. The tide had risen to his chest when he caught the injured petty officer drifting between the piers of the wharf. He pulled him into the shallow water, dragging him by one hand, and knelt exhausted beside him on the oily mud. Other rescuers had reached the sinking cutter. They lifted out the last of the wounded sailors and fell together into the water. They began to swim and crawl towards the shore, helped on to the mud-flat by a second party of Britishers.

The cloud of burning oil from the *Petrel* crossed the Bund and enveloped the stalled traffic and the advancing Japanese. As Jim wound up his window the Packard was thrown forward, and then shaken violently from side to side. Broken glass fell from the windshield and showered the seats. Jim lay on the rear floor of the passenger cabin as the door pillar struck his mother's head.

'Jamie, get out of the car . . . Jamie!'

Dazed, she opened her door and stepped on to the road, taking her handbag from the swaying seat. Behind them the Japanese tank was forcing its way past the Lincoln Zephyr abandoned by the Chinese dancers. The metal tread crushed the rear fender around its wheel and then rammed the heavy car into the back of the Packard.

'Get up, Jamie . . . we're going home . . .'

A hand to her bruised face, his mother was pulling at the warped rear door. The tank stopped, before making a second pass at the Lincoln. Japanese marines moved between the cars and rickshaws, lunging with their bayonets at the crowd. Jim climbed on to the front seat and opened the driver's door. He jumped into the road and ducked below the shafts of a rickshaw laden with rice bags. The tank moved forward, smoke throbbing from its engine vents. Jim saw his mother pushed into the throng of Chinese and Europeans whom the marines were forcing across the Bund. A second tank followed the first, then a line of camouflaged trucks packed with Japanese soldiers.

A final rifle shot rang out from the USS *Wake*. The last of the wounded British sailors were pulled on to the mud-flat below the Bund. Oil leaking from the swamped *Petrel* lay in an elongated slick across the river, calming this place of battle. The British civilians who had helped to rescue the sailors sat in their greasy shirt-sleeves beside the wounded men. Jim's father was dragging the injured petty officer on to the mud-flat. Exhausted, he lost his grip and collapsed in a shallow stream that ran through the oily bank from a sewer vent below the pier.

The Japanese soldiers on the Bund were driving the crowd away from the quay, forcing the Chinese and Europeans to step from their cars and rickshaws. Jim's mother had disappeared, cut off from him by the column of military trucks. A wounded British sailor, a sandy-haired youth no more than eighteen years old, climbed the steps from the landing stage, hands outstretched like bloody ping-pong bats.

Straightening his school cap, Jim darted past him and the watching sampan coolies. He ran down the steps and jumped from the landing stage on to the spongy surface of the mud-flat. Sinking to his knees, he waded through the damp soil towards his father.

'We brought them out – good lad, Jamie.' His father sat in the stream, the body of the petty officer beside him. He had lost his spectacles and one of his shoes, and the trousers of his business suit were black with oil, but he still wore his white collar and tie. In one hand he held a yellow silk glove like those Jim had seen his mother carrying to the formal receptions at the British Embassy. Looking at the glove, Jim realized that it was the complete skin from one of the petty officer's hands, boiled off the flesh in an engine-room fire.

'She's going . . .' His father flicked the glove into the water like the hand of a tiresome beggar. A hoarse, throttling explosion sounded across the river from the capsized hull of the *Petrel*. There was a violent rush of steam from the risen decks, and the gunboat slipped below the waves. A cloud of frantic smoke seethed across the water, surging about as if hunting for the vanished craft.

Jim's father lay back against the mud. Jim squatted beside him. The noise of the tanks' engines on the Bund, the shouted commands of the Japanese NCOs and the drone of the circling aircraft seemed far away. The first debris from the *Petrel* was reaching them, life jackets and pieces of planking, a section of canvas awning with its trailing ropes, that resembled an enormous jellyfish, dislodged from the deep by the sinking gunboat.

A flicker of light ran along the quays like silent gunfire. Jim lay down beside his father. Drawn up above them on the Bund were hundreds of Japanese soldiers. Their bayonets formed a palisade of swords that answered the sun.

5

Escape from the Hospital

'Mitsubishi . . . Zero-Sen . . . ah . . . Nakajima . . . ah . . .'

Jim lay in his cot in the children's ward, and listened to the young Japanese soldier call out the names of the aircraft flying over the hospital. The skies above Shanghai were filled with aircraft. Although the soldier knew the names of only two types of plane he found it difficult to keep up with the endless aerial activity.

For three days Jim had rested peacefully in the ward on the top floor of St Marie's Hospital in the French Concession, disturbed only by the young soldier's furtive smoking and his amateur plane-spotting. Alone in the ward, he thought about his mother and father, and hoped that they would soon come to visit him. He listened to the seaplanes flying from the Naval Air Base at Nantao.

' . . . ah . . . ah . . .' The soldier shook his head, stumped again, and searched the immaculate floor for a cigarette end. In the corridor below the landing Jim could hear the French missionary sisters arguing with the Japanese military police who now occupied this wing of the hospital. Despite the hard mattress, the whitewashed walls with their unpleasant icons above each bed – the crucified infant Jesus surrounded by Chinese disciples – and the ominous chemical smell (something to do, he surmised, with intense religious feelings), Jim found it difficult to believe that the war had at last begun. Walls of strangeness separated everything, every face that looked at him was odd.

He could remember Dr Lockwood's party at Hungjao,

and the Chinese conjurors who turned themselves into birds. But the bombardment of the *Petrel*, the tank that had crushed the Packard, the huge guns of the *Idzumo* all belonged to a make-believe realm. He almost expected Yang to saunter into the ward and tell him that they were part of a technicolour epic being staged at the Shanghai film studios.

What was real, without any doubt, was the mud-flat to which his father had helped to drag the wounded sailors, and where they had sat for six hours beside the dead petty officer. It was as if the Japanese had been so surprised by the speed of their assault that they had been forced to wait before they fully grasped any sense of their victory. Within a few hours of the attack on Pearl Harbor the Japanese armies which encircled Shanghai had seized the International Settlement. The marines who captured the USS *Wake* and occupied the Bund celebrated by parading in force in front of the hotels and banking houses.

Meanwhile, the wounded survivors of the *Petrel* and the British civilians who had helped to rescue them remained on the mud-flat beside the sewer. An armed party of military police stepped from the landing stage and walked among them. Captain Polkinhorn, wounded in the head, and his first officer were taken away, but the others were left to sit under the sun. A Japanese officer in full uniform, scabbard held in his gloved hand, moved among the injured and exhausted men, peering at each in turn. He stared at Jim as he sat in his blazer and school cap beside his exhausted father, obviously puzzled by the elaborate badges of the Cathedral School and assuming that Jim was an unusually junior midshipman in the Royal Navy.

An hour later Captain Polkinhorn was taken in a motor-launch to the site of the sunken *Petrel*. Before abandoning ship the captain had been able to destroy his codes, and for days afterwards the Japanese sent divers down to the wreck in an unsuccessful attempt to retrieve the code-boxes.

Soon after ten o'clock the Japanese reopened the Bund, and thousands of uneasy Chinese and European neutrals were ushered along the quay. They looked down at the wounded crew of the *Petrel*, and stood silently as the Rising Sun was ceremonially hoisted to the mast of the USS *Wake*. Shivering beside his father in the cold December sun, Jim gazed up at the expressionless eyes of the Chinese packed together on the quay. They were witnessing the complete humiliation of the Allied powers by the empire of Japan, an object lesson to all those reluctant to enter the Co-Prosperity Sphere. Fortunately, some hours later a party of officials from the Vichy French and German embassies forced their way through the crowd. They protested volubly about the treatment of the wounded British. Impelled by one of their abrupt changes of mood, the Japanese relented and the prisoners were on their way to St Marie's Hospital.

Once there, Jim's sole thought was to leave the hospital and return to his mother at Amherst Avenue. The French doctor who mercurichromed his knees and the sisters who bathed him saw immediately that Jim was a British school-boy, and tried to have him released. The Japanese, however, had taken over a complete wing of the hospital, cleared out the Chinese patients and installed a guard on each floor. A young soldier was posted outside the children's ward on the top floor, and passed the time asking the nuns for cigarettes and calling out the names of the aircraft overhead.

A Chinese nun told Jim that his father was with the other civilians in a ward below, still recovering from the effects of heart strain and exposure, but would be ready to leave in a few days. Meanwhile, for reasons of their own, the Japanese High Command had begun to eulogize the bravery of Captain Polkinhorn and his men. On the second day the commander of the *Idzumo* sent a party of uniformed officers to the hospital, who paid tribute to the wounded sailors in

the best traditions of bushido, bowing to each one of them.
The English-language *Shanghai Times*, British-owned but
long sympathetic to the Japanese, carried a photograph of
the *Petrel* on its front page, and an article extolling the
courage of its crew. The main headline described the
Japanese attack on Pearl Harbor and the bombing of Clark
Field at Manila. Pencil drawings supplied by a neutral news
agency showed apocalyptic scenes of smoke rising from the
slumped American battleships.

Now that the Japanese had won the war, Jim mused,
perhaps life in Shanghai would return to normal. When the
young soldier showed him the newspaper he carefully
studied the photograph of fighter-bombers taking off from
the Japanese carriers, scenes that he seemed to remember
from his own dreams in his bedroom at the Palace Hotel on
the eve of the war.

Lounging on the bed beside him, the soldier pointed to
the assault aircraft, keen to impress Jim with this staggering
feat of arms.

'. . . ah . . . ah . . .'

'Nakajima,' Jim said. 'Nakajima Hayabusa.'

'Nakajima . . . ?' The soldier sighed deeply, as if the
subject of military aviation was far beyond the grasp of this
small English boy. In fact Jim recognized almost all the
Japanese aircraft. British newsreels of the Sino-Japanese
War openly derided the Japanese planes and their pilots,
but Jim's father and Mr Maxted always spoke of them with
respect.

Jim was wondering how he could see his father when the
guard corporal bellowed a command up the stairwell. The
young private was terrified of this small and unpleasant
corporal, clearly the most important rank in the Japanese
Army. He put away his cigarette butt, picked up his rifle
and dashed from the ward, waving a warning finger at Jim.

Glad to be alone, Jim immediately climbed out of bed.

Through the window he could see a group of convalescent Chinese orphans on the balcony of the adjacent wing. In their European dressing-gowns – like Jim's, donated by a local French charity – they spent all day staring at him. A metal fire-escape linked the two wings, blocked by heaps of sandbags packed against the windows in 1937 to protect them from stray shells fired across the river.

Bare-footed, Jim crossed the ward to its rear door. A narrow catwalk led between the sandbags, and the loose sand was littered with hundreds of cigarette ends thrown down by the bored French doctors. Picking his way through the pieces of broken glass, he set off along the fire-escape. A metal staircase ran to the opposite wing, linked by a rusting bridge to the ward below Jim's.

Jim moved swiftly down the steps and crossed the bridge. Somewhere on this floor were his father and the survivors of the *Petrel*. The windows of the wards overlooking the gangway had been painted with blackout tar. Watched by the wide-eyed orphans, he followed the gangway around the wing. The rear door into the ward was bolted, but as he pulled at the handle the Chinese children ducked below their balcony. An armed Japanese soldier stood on the roof, shouting down into the well between the wings. Soldiers with fixed bayonets ran across the courtyard of the hospital, and a motorcycle with armed side-car swung through the entrance. Jim could hear boots and rifle butts ringing on the stone stairways, and a French nun's voice raised in protest.

He crouched between the sandbags outside the locked door. Soldiers were moving along the gangway of the children's ward, and sand poured through the rusting grilles. A klaxon sounded in the Avenue Foch, and Jim was convinced that the entire Japanese occupation forces in Shanghai were searching for him.

A bolt clattered, and the door opened into the darkened ward. In the brief glare of sunlight Jim saw the cave-like

54

room crowded with bandaged men, some lying on the floor between the beds, and the nuns being pushed aside by Japanese soldiers with rifles and canvas stretchers. As the blanched faces of young British sailors turned towards the sun, a stench of sickness and wounds emerged from the dark chamber and enveloped him.

The Japanese corporal stared at Jim, crouching in his pyjamas among the cigarette ends. He slammed the door, and Jim heard him shout as he slapped one of the Japanese soldiers with his fist.

An hour later they had all gone, leaving Jim alone in the children's ward. As the klaxons sounded from the Avenue Foch, he watched a military truck reverse into the hospital compound. The crew of the *Petrel* and the eight British civilians who had helped to rescue them were bundled down the staircases and loaded into the truck. Wounded men on stretchers lay under the legs of others barely able to sit.

Jim did not see his father, but the French sister told him that he had walked to the truck taking them to the military prison in Hongkew.

'This morning one of your sailors escaped. It's very bad for us.' The sister stared at Jim with the disapproving gaze of the Japanese corporal. She was angry with him in that new way he had noticed in the past weeks, not for anything he had done but because of his inability to change the circumstances in which he found himself.

'You live in Amherst Avenue? You must go home.' The sister beckoned to a Chinese nun, who laid Jim's freshly laundered clothes on the bed. He could see that they were eager to be rid of him. 'Your mother will look after you.'

Jim dressed himself, fastened his tie and carefully straightened his school cap. He wanted to thank the sister, but she had already left to look after her orphans.

6

The Youth with the Knife

Wars always invigorated Shanghai, quickened the pulse of its congested streets. Even the corpses in the gutters seemed livelier. Throngs of peasant women packed the pavements of the Avenue Foch, outside the Cercle Sportif Français the vendors locked wheels as they jostled their carts against each other, lines of pedicabs and rickshaws ten abreast hemmed in the cars that edged forward behind a continuous blare of horns. Young Chinese gangsters in shiny American suits stood on the street corners, shouting the jai alai odds to each other. In the pedicabs outside the Regency Hotel the bar-girls sat in fur coats with their bodyguards beside them, like glamorous wives waiting to be taken for a ride. The entire city had come out into the streets, as if the population was celebrating the takeover of the International Settlement, its seizure from the Americans and Europeans by another Asian power.

Yet when Jim reached the junction of the Avenue Pétain and the Avenue Haig a British police sergeant and two Sikh NCOs of the Shanghai police force still directed the traffic from their cantilever bridge above the crowd, watched by a single Japanese soldier standing behind them. Armed Japanese infantry sat like sightseers in the camouflaged trucks that moved along the streets. A party of officers stood outside the Radium Institute, adjusting their gloves. Pasted over the Coca Cola and Caltex billboards were fresh posters of Wang Ching-Wei, the turncoat leader of the puppet regime. A column of Chinese soldiers overtook Jim in the Avenue Pétain, shouting slogans into the noisy air. They stamped away, clumsily marking time below the baroque façade of the Del Monte Casino, and then ran on past the greyhound stadium, a coolie army in pale orange uniforms and American-style sneakers.

Outside the tram station in the Avenue Haig the hundreds of passengers were briefly silent as they watched a public beheading. The bodies of a man and woman in quilted peasant clothes, perhaps pickpockets or Kuomintang spies, lay by the boarding platform. The Chinese NCOs wiped their boots as the blood ran into the metal grooves of the steel rails. A tram crowded with passengers approached, its bell forcing the execution party aside. It clanked along, connector rod hissing and throwing sparks from the overhead power line, its front wheels a moist scarlet as if painted for the annual labour union parade.

Usually Jim would have paused to observe the crowd. On the way home from school Yang would often drive by the Old City. The public stranglings were held in a miniature stadium with a scrubbed wooden floor and rows of circular benches around the teak execution posts, and always attracted a thoughtful audience. The Chinese enjoyed the spectacle of death, Jim had decided, as a way of reminding themselves of how precariously they were alive. They liked to be cruel for the same reason, to remind themselves of the vanity of thinking that the world was anything else.

Jim watched the coolies and peasant women staring at the headless bodies. Already the press of tram passengers was pushing them aside, submerging this small death. He turned away, tripping over the charcoal brazier in which a pavement vendor was frying pieces of battered snake. Drops of fat splashed into the wooden bucket, where a single snake swam, thrashing itself as it leapt at the hissing oil. The vendor lunged at Jim with his hot ladle, trying to cuff his head, but he slipped between the parked rickshaws.

He ran along the blood-smeared tramlines towards the entrance of the depot.

He pushed through the waiting passengers and squeezed himself on to a concrete bench with a group of peasant women carrying chickens in wicker baskets. The women's bodies reeked of sweat and fatigue, but Jim was too exhausted to move. He had walked over two miles along the crowded pavements. He knew that he was being followed by a young Chinese, probably a pedicab tout or a runner for one of Shanghai's tens of thousands of small-time gangsters. A tall youth with a dead, boneless face, oily black hair and leather jacket, he had noticed Jim outside the greyhound stadium. Kidnappings were commonplace in Shanghai – before his parents learned to trust Yang, they insisted that Jim always drove to school with the governess. He guessed that the youth was interested in his blazer and leather shoes, in his aviator's watch and the American fountain pen clipped to his breast pocket.

The youth stepped through the crowd and walked up to Jim, his yellow hands like ferrets. 'American boy?'

'English. I'm waiting for my chauffeur.'

'English . . . boy. You come now.'

'No – he's over there.'

The youth reached forward, swearing in Chinese, and seized Jim's wrist. His fingers fumbled at the metal strap, trying to release the watch-clasp. The peasant women ignored him, chickens asleep on their laps. Jim knocked away the youth's hand, and felt fingers grip his forearm. Inside his leather jacket he had drawn a knife, and was about to sever Jim's hand at the wrist.

Jim wrenched his arm away. Before the youth could seize him again, Jim hurled the wicker basket from the knees of the peasant woman on his right. The youth fell back, flailing with his heels at the squawking bird. The women jumped to their feet and began to scream at him. He ignored them and put away his knife. He followed as Jim ran through the queues of tram passengers, trying to show them his bruised wrist.

A hundred yards from the depot Jim reached the Avenue Joffre. He rested in the padlocked entrance to the Nanking Theatre, where *Gone with the Wind* had been playing for the past year in a pirated Chinese version. The partly dismantled faces of Clark Gable and Vivien Leigh rose on their scaffolding above an almost life-size replica of burning Atlanta. Chinese carpenters were cutting down the panels of painted smoke that rose high into the Shanghai sky, barely distinguishable from the fires still lifting above the tenements of the Old City, where Kuomintang irregulars had resisted the Japanese invasion.

The youth with the knife was still behind him, skipping and side-stepping through the crowd in his cheap sneakers. In the centre of the Avenue Joffre was the police checkpoint, its sandbagged emplacement marking the western perimeter of the French Concession. Jim knew that neither the Vichy police nor the Japanese soldiers would do anything to help him. They were watching a single-engined bomber that flew low above the racecourse.

As the plane's shadow flashed across the road Jim felt the Chinese youth snatch his cap and grip his shoulders. Jim pulled himself away, and ran across the crowded street towards the checkpoint, ducking in and out of the pedicabs and shouting: 'Nakajima . . . ! Nakajima . . . !'

A Chinese auxiliary in a Vichy uniform tried to strike him with his stave, but one of the Japanese sentries paused to glance at Jim. His eye had caught the Japanese characters on the metal tag that Jim had taken from the derelict fighter at Hungjao Aerodrome and was now holding in front of him. Briefly tolerating this small boy, he continued his patrol and waved him away with the butt of his rifle.

'Nakajima . . . !'

Jim joined the crowd of pedestrians moving through the checkpoint. As he guessed, his pursuer had vanished among the beggars and loitering rickshaw coolies on the French side of the barbed wire. Not for the first time Jim realized that the Japanese, officially his enemies, offered his only protection in Shanghai.

Nursing his bruised arm, and angry with himself for having lost his school cap, Jim at last reached Amherst Avenue. He pulled his shirt-sleeve over the dark weals that marked his wrist. His mother worried constantly about the danger and violence in the streets of Shanghai, and knew nothing of his long cycle rides around the city.

Amherst Avenue was deserted. The throngs of beggars and refugees had vanished. Even the old man with his Craven A tin had gone. Jim ran up the drive, looking forward to seeing his mother, sitting on the sofa in her bedroom and talking about Christmas. Already he assumed that they would never discuss the war.

A long scroll covered with Japanese characters had been nailed to the front door, the white cloth stamped with seals and registration numbers. Jim pressed the bell, waiting for Number Two Boy to open the door. He felt exhausted, as worn down as his scuffed shoes, and noticed that the sleeve of his blazer had been slashed from the elbow by the thief's knife.

'Boy, hurry . . .!' He began to say: 'I'll kill you . . .' but checked himself.

The house was silent. There was no sound of the amahs arguing over the laundry vat in the servants' quarters, or the clip-clip of the gardener trimming the lawn around the flower-beds. Someone had switched off the swimming-pool motor, though his father made a point of running the filter all winter. Looking up at the windows of his bedroom, he saw that the shutters of the air-conditioner had been closed.

Jim listened to the bell drill through the empty house. Too tired to reach again for the button, he sat on the polished steps and blew on his bruised knees. It was difficult to imagine how his parents, Vera, the nine servants, chauffeur and gardener could all have gone out together.

There was a muffled explosion from the bottom of the drive, the coughing exhaust box of a heavy engine. A Japanese half-track had entered Amherst Avenue, its crew standing among their radio aerials. They moved along the centre of the road, forcing a Mercedes limousine from the German estate to climb the pavement.

Jim jumped from the porch and hid behind a pillar. A high wall faced with terracotta tiles ran around the house, topped with broken glass. Gripping the tiles with his fingertips, he climbed the wall below the barred cloakroom window. After pulling himself on to the concrete ledge, he crawled on his knees through the glass blades. During the past year, unknown to the gardener and the nightwatchman, he had climbed the wall a score of times, always removing a few more of the sharp spears. He lowered himself over the edge and jumped into the dark branches of the cedar tree behind the summer house.

In front of him was the enclosed and silent garden, even more Jim's true home than the house itself. Here he had played alone with his imagination. He had been a crashed pilot on the roof of the rose pergola, a sniper sitting high in the poplars behind the tennis court, an infantryman racing across the lawn with his airgun, shooting himself down into the flower-beds and rising again to storm the rockery below the flagpole.

From the shadows behind the summer house Jim looked up at the verandah windows. An aircraft overhead warned him not to run too suddenly across the lawn. Although undisturbed, the garden seemed to have darkened and

61

grown wilder. The uncut lawn was beginning to billow, and the rhododendrons were more sombre than he remembered them. Ignored by the gardener, his bicycle lay on the terrace steps. Jim walked through the thickening grass to the swimming-pool. The water was covered with leaves and dead insects, and the level had fallen by almost three feet, draping a scummy curtain on the sides. Cigarette ends lay crushed on the white tiles, and a Chinese packet floated under the diving board.

Jim followed the pathway to the servants' quarters behind the house. A charcoal stove stood in the courtyard, but the kitchen door was locked. He listened for any sound from within the house. Beside the kitchen steps was the enclosed hood of the garbage compactor. A chute ran from the compressor into the kitchen wall beside the sink. Two years earlier, when he was younger, Jim had terrified his mother by climbing through the chute as she arranged a dinner party menu with the houseboy.

This time there was no danger of the motor being switched on. Jim lifted the metal hood, climbed between the scythe-like blades and edged his way through the greasy chute. The metal flap swung back to reveal the familiar white-tiled kitchen.

'Vera! I'm home! Boy!'

Jim lowered himself on to the floor. He had never seen the house so dark before. He stepped through the pool of water around the refrigerator and entered the deserted hall. As he climbed the staircase to his mother's bedroom the air was stale with the smell of strange sweat.

His mother's clothes were scattered across the unmade bed, and open suitcases lay on the floor. Someone had swept her hairbrushes and scent bottles from the dressing-table, and talcum covered the polished parquet. There were dozens of footprints in the powder, his mother's bare feet whirling within the clear images of heavy boots, like the

62

patterns of complicated dances set out in his parents' foxtrot and tango manuals.

Jim sat on the bed, facing the star-like image of himself that radiated from the centre of the mirror. A heavy object had been driven into the full-length glass, and pieces of himself seemed to fly across the room, scattered through the empty house.

He fell asleep at the foot of his mother's bed, rested by the scent of her silk nightdress, below this jewelled icon of a small exploding boy.

7

The Drained Swimming-Pool

Time had stopped in Amherst Avenue, as motionless as the
wall of dust that hung across the rooms, briefly folding itself
around Jim when he walked through the deserted house.
Almost forgotten scents, a faint taste of carpet, reminded
him of the period before the war. For three days he waited
for his mother and father to return. Every morning he
climbed on to the sloping roof above his bedroom window,
and gazed over the residential streets in the western suburbs
of Shanghai. He watched the columns of Japanese tanks
move into the city from the countryside, and tried to repair
his blazer, impatient for the first sight of his parents when
they returned with Yang in the Packard.

Large numbers of aircraft flew overhead, and Jim passed
the hours plane-spotting. Below him was the undisturbed
lawn, a little darker each day now that the gardener no
longer trimmed the hedges and cut the grass. Jim played
there in the afternoons, crawling through the rockery and
pretending to be one of the Japanese marines who had
attacked the *Wake*. But the games in the garden had lost
their magic, and he spent most of his time on the sofa in his
mother's bedroom. Her presence hung on the air like her
scent, holding at bay the deformed figure in the fractured
mirror. Jim remembered their long hours together doing his
Latin homework, and the stories she told him of her
childhood in England, a country far stranger than China
where he would go to school when the war was over.

In the talcum on the floor around him he could see the
imprints of his mother's feet. She had moved from side to
side, propelled by an over-eager partner, perhaps one of the

Japanese officers to whom she was teaching the tango. Jim tried out the dance steps himself, which seemed far more violent than any tango he had ever seen, and managed to fall and cut his hand on the broken mirror.

As he sucked the wound he remembered his mother teaching him to play mah-jong, and the cryptic coloured tiles that clicked in and out of the mahogany walls. Jim thought of writing a book about mah-jong, but he had forgotten most of the rules. On the drawing-room carpet he heaped a pile of bamboo stakes from the greenhouse, and began to build a man-lifting kite according to the scientific principles his father had taught him. But the Japanese patrols in Amherst Avenue would see the kite flying from the garden. Putting it aside, Jim ambled about the empty house, and watched the water level almost imperceptibly falling in the swimming-pool.

The food in the refrigerator had begun to give off an ominous smell, but the pantry cupboards were filled with tinned fruit, cocktail biscuits and pressed meats, delicacies that Jim adored. He ate his meals at the dining-room table, sitting in his usual place. In the evenings, when it seemed unlikely that his parents would come home that day, he went to sleep in his bedroom on the top floor of the house, one of his model aircraft on the bed beside him, something Vera had always forbidden. Then the dreams of war came to him, and all the battleships of the Japanese Navy sailed up the Yangtze, their guns firing as they sank the *Petrel*, and he and his father saved the wounded sailors.

On the fourth morning, when he came down to breakfast, Jim found that he had forgotten to turn off a kitchen tap and all the water had flowed from the storage tank. The pantry was amply stocked with siphons of soda water, but by now he had accepted that his mother and father would not be coming home. He stared through the verandah windows at the overgrown garden. It was not that war changed every-

65

thing – in fact, Jim thrived on change – but that it left things the same in odd and unsettling ways. Even the house seemed sombre, as if it was withdrawing from him in a series of small and unfriendly acts.

Trying to keep up his spirits, Jim decided to visit the homes of his closest friends, Patrick Maxted and the Raymond twins. After washing himself in soda water he went into the garden to fetch his bicycle. During the night the swimming-pool had drained itself. Jim had never seen the tank empty, and he gazed with interest at the inclined floor. The once mysterious world of wavering blue lines, glimpsed through a cascade of bubbles, now lay exposed to the morning light. The tiles were slippery with leaves and dirt, and the chromium ladder at the deep end, which had once vanished into a watery abyss, ended abruptly beside a pair of scummy rubber slippers.

Jim jumped on to the floor at the shallow end. He slipped on the damp surface, and his bruised knee left a smear of blood on the tiles. A fly settled on it instantly. Watching his feet, Jim walked down the sloping floor. Around the brass vent at the deep end lay a small museum of past summers – a pair of his mother's sun-glasses, Vera's hair clip, a wine glass, and an English half-crown which his father had tossed into the pool for him. Jim had often spotted the silver coin, gleaming like an oyster, but had never been able to reach it.

Jim pocketed the coin and peered up at the damp walls. There was something sinister about a drained swimming-pool, and he tried to imagine what purpose it could have if it were not filled with water. It reminded him of the concrete bunkers in Tsingtao, and the bloody handprints of the maddened German gunners on the caisson walls. Perhaps murder was about to be committed in all the swimming-pools of Shanghai, and their walls were tiled so that the blood could be washed away?

Leaving the garden, Jim wheeled his bicycle through the

66

verandah door. Then he did something he had always longed to do, mounted his cycle and rode through the formal, empty rooms. Delighted to think how shocked Vera and the servants would have been, he expertly circled his father's study, intrigued by the patterns which the tyres cut in the thick carpet. He collided with the desk, and knocked over a table lamp as he swerved through the door into the drawing-room. Standing on the pedals, he zigzagged among the armchairs and tables, lost his balance and fell on to a sofa, remounted without touching the floor, crash-landed into the double doors that led into the dining-room, pulled them back and began a wild circuit of the long polished table. He detoured into the pantry, swishing to and fro through the pool of water below the refrigerator, scattered the saucepans from the kitchen shelves and ended in a blaze of speed towards the mirror in the downstairs cloakroom. As his front tyre trembled against the smudged glass Jim shouted at his excited reflection. The war had brought him at least one small bonus.

Happily Jim closed the front door behind him, smoothed the Japanese scroll and set off towards the Raymond twins in the nearby Columbia Road. He felt that all the streets in Shanghai were rooms in a huge house. He accelerated past a platoon of Chinese puppet soldiers marching down Columbia Road, and swerved away showily as the NCO let loose a volley of shouts. Jim sped along the suburban pavements, in and out of the telephone poles, knocking aside the Craven A tins left behind by the vanished beggars.

He was out of breath when he reached the Raymonds' house at the German end of the Columbia Road. He freewheeled past the parked Opels and Mercedes – curious, gloomy cars which gave Jim all too much of an idea of what Europe was like – and came to a halt outside the front door.

A Japanese scroll was nailed to the oak panels. The door opened, and two amahs appeared, dragging Mrs Raymond's dressing-table down the steps.

'Is Clifford here? Or Derek? Amah . . . !'

He knew both the amahs well, and waited for them to reply in their pidgin English. But they ignored him, and heaved at the dressing-table. Their deformed feet, like clenched fists, slipped on the steps.

'It's Jamie, Mrs Raymond . . .'

Jim tried to step past the amahs, when one reached out and slapped him in the face.

Stunned by the blow, Jim walked back to his bicycle. He had never been struck so hard, either in school boxing matches or in fights with the Avenue Foch gang. The front of his face seemed to have been torn from the bones. His eyes were smarting, but he stopped himself from crying. The amahs were strong, their arms toughened by a lifetime of washing clothes. Watching them with their dressing-table, Jim knew that they were paying him back for something he or the Raymonds had done to them.

Jim waited until they reached the bottom step. When one of the amahs walked up to him, clearly intending to slap him again, he mounted his cycle and pedalled away.

Outside the Raymonds' drive two German boys of his own age were playing with a ball as their mother unlocked the family's Opel. Usually they would have shouted German slogans at Jim, or thrown stones at him until stopped by their mother. But today all three stood silently. Jim cycled past, trying not to show them his bruised face. The mother held her sons' shoulders, watching Jim as if concerned for what would soon befall him.

Still shocked by the anger he had seen in the amah's face, Jim set off for the Maxteds' apartment house in the French Concession. His whole head felt swollen and there was a loose tooth in his lower jaw. He wanted to see his mother and father, and he wanted the war to end soon, that afternoon if possible.

Dusty, and suddenly very tired, Jim reached the barbed-wire checkpoint on the Avenue Foch. The streets were less crowded, but several hundred Chinese and Europeans queued to pass the Japanese guards. A Swiss-owned Buick and a Vichy French gasoline truck were waved through the gates. Usually the European pedestrians would have gone to the head of the queue, but now they took their turn among the rickshaw coolies and peasants pushing handcarts. Gripping his cycle, Jim barely held his ground as a barefoot coolie with diseased calves laboured past him under a bamboo yoke laden with bales of firewood. The crowd pressed around him, in a sweat of stench and fatigue, cheap fat and rice wine, the odours of a Shanghai new to him. An open Chrysler with two young Germans in the front seat accelerated past, horn blaring, the rear fender grazing Jim's hand.

Once through the checkpoint Jim straightened the front wheel of his cycle and pedalled to the Maxteds' apartment house in the Avenue Joffre. The formal garden in the French style was as immaculate as ever, a comforting memory of the old Shanghai. As he rode the elevator to the seventh floor Jim used his tears to clean his hands and face, half expecting Mrs Maxted to have returned from Singapore.

The door to the apartment was open. Jim stepped into the hall, recognizing Mr Maxted's leather overcoat on the floor. The same tornado that had whirled his mother's bedroom in Amherst Avenue had swept in and out of every room in the Maxteds' apartment. Drawers full of clothes had been thrown on to the beds, ransacked wardrobes hung open above piles of shoes, suitcases lay everywhere as if a dozen Maxted families had been unable to decide what to pack at five minutes' notice.

'Patrick . . .' Jim hesitated to enter Patrick's room without knocking. His mattress had been hurled to the floor, and the curtains drifted in the open windows. But Patrick's model aircraft, more carefully constructed than Jim's, still dangled from the ceiling.

Jim pulled the mattress on to the bed and lay down. He watched the aircraft turning in the cold air that moved through the empty apartment. He and Patrick had spent hours inventing imaginary air battles in the sky of that bedroom above the Avenue Joffre. Jim watched the Spitfires and Hurricanes circling above his head. Their motion soothed him, easing the pain in his jaw, and he was tempted to stay there, sleeping quietly in the bedroom of his departed friend until the war was over.

But already Jim realized that it was time to find his mother and father. Failing them, any other Britons would do.

Facing the Maxteds' apartment building on the opposite side of the Avenue Joffre was the Shell Company's compound, almost all of its houses occupied by British employees. Jim and Patrick often played with the children, and were honorary members of the Shell gang. As Jim pushed his bicycle from the Maxteds' drive he could see that the British residents had gone. Japanese sentries stood in the entrance to the compound behind a box fence of barbed-wire. Supervised by a Japanese NCO, a gang of Chinese coolies were loading furniture from the houses into an army truck.

A few feet from the barbed-wire box an elderly man in a shabby coat stood under the plane trees and watched the Japanese. Despite his threadbare suit, he still wore white cuffs and a starched shirt front.

'Mr Guerevitch! I'm over here, Mr Guerevitch!'

The old White Russian was the Shell Company caretaker, and lived with his aged mother in a small bungalow beside the gate. A Japanese officer now stood in the front room, cleaning his nails as he smoked a cigarette. Jim had always liked Mr Guerevitch, although the elderly Russian remained unimpressed by him. Something of an amateur artist, in the right mood he would draw elaborate sailing ships in Jim's autograph album. His grey cupboard of a kitchen was filled with starched collars and their miniature front panels, and Jim was sorry that Mr Guerevitch could not afford a real shirt. Perhaps he would come back to live with him in Amherst Avenue?

Jim checked this thought as Mr Guerevitch waved him across the road with his newspaper. His mother might like the old Russian, but Vera would not – the Eastern Europeans and White Russians were even more snobbish than the British.

'Hello, Mr Guerevitch. I'm looking for my mother and father.'

'But how could they be here?' The old Russian pointed to Jim's bruised face and shook his head. 'The whole world is at war and you're still riding your bicycle around . . .' As the Japanese NCO began to abuse one of the coolies, Mr Guerevitch drew Jim behind a plane tree. He opened his newspaper to reveal an extravagant artist's sketch of two immense battleships sinking under a hail of Japanese bombs. From the photographs beside them Jim recognized the *Repulse* and the *Prince of Wales*, the unsinkable fortresses which the British war newsreels always claimed could each defeat the Japanese Navy single-handed.

'Not a good example,' Mr Guerevitch reflected. 'The British Empire's Maginot line. It's right that you have a red face.'

'I fell off my bicycle, Mr Guerevitch,' Jim explained patriotically, though he disliked having to lie to defend the Royal Navy. 'I've been busy looking for my mother and father. It's rather a job, you know.'

71

'I can see.' Mr Guerevitch watched a convoy of trucks speed past. Japanese guards with fixed bayonets sat by the tailboards. Behind them, their heads resting on each other's shoulders, groups of British women and their children huddled over their cheap suitcases and khaki bedrolls. Jim assumed that they were the families of captured British servicemen.

'Young boy! Ride your bicycle!' Mr Guerevitch pushed Jim's shoulder. 'You follow them!'

'But Mr Guerevitch . . .' The shabby luggage unsettled Jim as much as the strange wives of the British privates. 'I can't go with them – they're prisoners.'

'Go on! Ride! You can't live in the street!'

When Jim stood firm by his handlebars, Mr Guerevitch solemnly patted him on the head and set off across the road. He resumed his vigil behind his newspaper, watching the Japanese strip the houses in the compound as if itemizing his lost world for the Shell Company.

'I'll come and see you again, Mr Guerevitch.' Jim felt sorry for the old caretaker, but during his return journey to Amherst Avenue he was more concerned about the two battleships. The British newsreels were filled with lies. Jim had seen the Japanese Navy sink the *Petrel*, and it was obvious now that they could sink anything. Half the American Pacific Fleet was sitting on the bottom at Pearl Harbor. Perhaps Mr Guerevitch was right, and he should have followed the trucks. His mother and father might already have arrived at the prison to which they were being taken.

So, reluctantly, he decided to give himself up to the Japanese. The soldiers guarding the Avenue Foch checkpoint waved him on when he tried to speak to them, but Jim kept his eyes open for one of the corporals in charge of everything.

For some reason, that day there seemed to be a shortage

of Japanese corporals in Shanghai. Although he was tired, Jim took the long route home, along the Great Western and Columbia Roads, but no Japanese at all were there. However, when he reached the entrance to his house in Amherst Avenue he saw that a Chrysler limousine had parked outside the front door. Two Japanese officers stepped from the car and surveyed the house as they straightened their uniforms.

Jim was about to pedal up to them and explain that he lived in the house and was ready to surrender. Then an armed Japanese soldier stepped from behind the stone gatepost. He seized the front wheel of the cycle with his left hand, his fingers gripping the tyre through the spokes, and with a coarse shout propelled Jim backwards into a heap on the dusty road.

8
Picnic Time

Unable to surrender, Jim returned with his broken bicycle to the Maxteds' apartment in the French Concession. From then on he lived alone in the abandoned houses and apartments in the western suburbs of the International Settlement. Most of the homes had been owned by British and American nationals, or by Dutch, Belgian and Free French residents, all of whom had been interned by the Japanese in the days after the attack on Pearl Harbor.

The Maxteds' apartment house was owned by rich Chinese who had fled to Hong Kong in the weeks before the outbreak of war. Most of the apartments had been empty for months. Although the family of Chinese janitors still lived in their two basement rooms beside the elevator well, they had been completely cowed by the squad of Japanese military police who had seized Mr Maxted. As the uncut lawns grew deeper and the formal gardens deteriorated, they spent their time cooking small meals on a charcoal stove which they set up beside the cement statuary on the floor of the ornamental pond. The smell of bean curd and spiced noodles drifted among the disrobing nymphs.

During the first week Jim was free to come and go. He wheeled his cycle into the lift, rode to the seventh floor and let himself into the Maxteds' apartment through an un-latched mosquito window on the servants' balcony. The front door was fitted with a spyhole and a complex set of electrical locks – Mr Maxted, a prominent member of the pro-Chiang China Friendship Society, an organization of local businessmen, had once been the victim of an assassination attempt. Once Jim closed the door he was unable to open it again, but no one called apart from an elderly Iraqi woman who lived in the penthouse. When she rang the bell Jim watched her grimacing into the spyhole, parts of her ancient face semaphoring a mysterious message. She then stood thinking for ten minutes in the stationary lift, immaculately dressed and bejewelled in this abandoned apartment house.

Jim was glad to be left alone. After being knocked from his bicycle by the Japanese soldier he had barely managed to return to the Maxteds', and he slept on Patrick's bed for the rest of the day. He woke the next morning to the sound of trams clanking down the Avenue Foch, klaxons hooting from the Japanese convoys entering the city, and the thousands of continually blaring horns that were the anthem of Shanghai.

The bruise on his cheek had begun to subside, leaving his face thinner than he remembered it, his mouth a tighter and older shape. Looking at himself in the mirror of Patrick's bathroom, at his dusty blazer and grimy shirt, he wondered if his mother and father would still recognize him. Jim wiped his clothes with a wet towel – like Mr Guerevitch, many of the passing Chinese stared at him in a curious way. Nonetheless, Jim realized that there were certain advantages in being poor. No one could be bothered to cut off his hands.

The Maxteds' pantry was filled with cases of whisky and gin, an Aladdin's cave of gold and ruby bottles, but there were only a few jars of olives and a tin of cocktail biscuits. Jim ate a modest breakfast at the dining-room table, and then set about repairing his bicycle. He needed the machine to get himself around Shanghai, to find his parents and surrender to the Japanese.

Sitting on the dining-room floor, Jim tried to straighten the twisted forks. His hands fretted at the dusty metal, unable to clench themselves. He knew that he had been

75

badly frightened the previous day. A peculiar space was opening around him, which separated him from the secure world he had known before the war. For a few days he had been able to cope with the sinking of the *Petrel* and the disappearance of his parents, but now he felt nervous and slightly cold all the time, even in the mild December weather. He dropped and broke crockery in a way that he had never done before, and found it difficult to concentrate on anything.

Despite all this, Jim managed to repair his cycle. He unscrewed the front wheel and straightened the forks by bending them against the balcony railing. He tested the cycle in the drawing-room and then took the lift down to the foyer.

As Jim rode along the Avenue Foch he saw that Shanghai had changed. Thousands of Japanese soldiers patrolled the streets. Sandbagged sentry posts had been set up within sight of each other down the main avenues. Although the streets were filled with pedicabs and rickshaws, with trucks commandeered by the puppet militia, the crowds were subdued. The Chinese who thronged the pavements outside the department stores in the Nanking Road kept their heads down, avoiding the Japanese soldiers who sauntered through the traffic.

Pedalling fiercely, Jim followed a heavily laden tram that clanked along the Avenue Edward VII. Morose Chinese clung to its sides, and a crop-headed youth in a black mandarin suit spat at Jim, then leapt down and ran into the crowd, nervous that even this small act would set off a train of retribution. Bodies of Chinese lay everywhere, hands tied behind their backs in the centre of the road, dumped behind the sandbag emplacements, half-severed heads resting on each other's shoulders. The thousands of young gangsters in their American suits had gone, but at the Bubbling Well Road checkpoint Jim saw one youth in a blue silk suit being beaten by two soldiers with staves. As the blows struck his head he knelt in a pool of blood that dripped from his lapels.

All the gambling parlours and opium houses in the side-streets behind the racecourse had closed, and metal grilles sealed the entrances to the pawn shops and banks. Even the honour guard of hunchbacks outside the Cathay Theatre had deserted their posts. Their absence unsettled Jim. Without its beggars the city seemed all the poorer. The sullen rhythms of the new Shanghai were set by the endless wailing of the Japanese klaxons. The roads felt harder than he remembered them from his previous jaunts around the city, and already he was tired. His hands felt colder than the handlebars. Trying to keep up his spirits, he decided to visit all those places in Shanghai where his parents were known, starting with his father's office. The senior Chinese staff had always made a great fuss of Jim, and would be eager to help him.

However, the Szechwan Road had been closed by the Japanese. Barbed-wire barricades sealed off both ends of the street, and hundreds of Japanese civilians moved in and out of the foreign banks and commercial buildings, carrying typewriters and boxes of files.

Jim cycled down to the Bund, dominated now by the grey bulk of the cruiser *Idzumo*. It was moored four hundred yards from the quayside, its antique funnels freshly painted, canvas awnings flared over its gun turrets. A short distance upstream was the USS *Wake*, now flying the Rising Sun, with vivid Japanese characters on its bows. An elaborate christening ceremony was taking place in front of the Shanghai Club. Scores of senior Japanese civilians in frock coats, Germans and Italians in extravagant fascist uniforms, watched a march past of Japanese sailors and officers. Two tanks, several artillery pieces and a cordon of marines ringed the temporary parade ground on the tracks of the tramways terminal. The circling steel rails rang beneath their boots, the diagram of their victory over the British and American gunboats.

Resting his chin on the handlebars, Jim looked at the soldiers with fixed bayonets guarding the entrance to the Palace Hotel. None of them would speak any English, or have any idea that this European boy with his twisted bicycle was an enemy national. If he approached them in full view of the press-ganged Chinese audience the sentries would throw him to the ground.

Jim pedalled away from the Bund and began the long journey back to the Maxteds' apartment. By the time he crossed the Avenue Joffre checkpoint he was too tired to cycle, and pushed the small machine through the begging peasant women and the dozing rickshaw coolies. After climbing into the apartment he sat at the dining-room table and ate a few cocktail biscuits and olives, washed down with soda water from the siphon. He fell asleep on his friend's bed, under the endlessly circling aircraft that swam below the ceiling like fish seeking a way out of the sky.

During the next days Jim again tried to give himself up to the Japanese. Like his school friends, he had always despised anyone who surrendered – he accepted without question the stern morality of the *Chums Annuals* – but surrendering to the enemy was more difficult than it seemed. By now Jim was tired most of the time, as he cycled around the uncertain streets of Shanghai. The Japanese soldiers guarding the Country Club and the forecourt of the cathedral were too dangerous to approach. In the Bubbling Well Road he chased the Plymouth car belonging to a Swiss driver and his wife, but they shouted at him to go away and threw a coin on to the road, as if he were one of the Chinese beggar boys.

Jim went in search of Mr Guerevitch, but the old Russian caretaker was no longer watching the Shell compound –

perhaps he, too, was trying to surrender. Jim thought of the German mother who had watched him leave the Raymonds' house. She had seemed worried for him, but when he cycled all the way down to the Columbia Road he found that the gates of the German estate were closed. The Germans were drawing into themselves, just as nervous of the Japanese as everyone else. Jim was almost knocked from his cycle in the Nanking Road by two Japanese staff cars which swerved across the street. They stopped a truck filled with Germans from the Graf Zeppelin Club on their way to beat up the Jews in Hongkew. The Japanese NCOs ordered the Germans from the truck. They took away their clubs and shotguns, ripped off their swastika armbands, and sent them packing.

A week after his arrival at the Maxteds' apartment the electricity and water supplies were switched off. Jim bumped his cycle down the stairs to the foyer, where he found the old Iraqi woman arguing with the Chinese janitor. They both turned on Jim, screaming at him to leave the apartment house, though they had known all week that he was there.

He was glad to go. He had eaten the last of the cocktail biscuits, and his only meal the previous day had been a musty packet of Brazil nuts which he found in the sideboard. He felt tired but curiously light-headed – the last trickle of water from the bathroom taps had made him almost drunk, the same sensation he had known before the war when he was about to go to a party. He reminded himself of his mother and father, but already their faces were beginning to fade in his memory. He was thinking of food all the time, and he knew that there were a great many unoccupied houses in the western suburbs of Shanghai, with unlimited supplies of cocktail biscuits and soda water, enough to last him until the war ended.

Mounting his cycle, Jim left the French Concession and

pedalled along the Columbia Road. Quiet residential avenues ran between the trees, and the empty houses stood in their overgrown gardens. The rain had washed the ink from the Japanese scrolls, and the scarlet streaks ran down the oak panels, as if all the Americans and Europeans had been murdered against their front doors.

The Japanese occupation forces were too busy with their takeover of Shanghai to bother with these abandoned houses. Jim chose a crescent-shaped cul-de-sac hidden from the main road, where a half-timbered house rose behind high walls. A fading scroll hung between its brass coach lamps. Jim listened to the silence within the house, and then hid his cycle in the unswept leaves beside the steps. On his third attempt he climbed the wall of the Tudor garage and scaled its gabled roof. He lowered himself into the dense foliage of the garden, which clung to the house like a dark dream refusing to be woken.

Carrying a loose tile from the garage roof, Jim walked through the deep grass to the terrace. He waited until an aircraft flew overhead, and then broke the glass pane of a window housing the air-conditioning unit. He let himself into the house, opening the shutters of the air vent in order to hide the broken pane.

Quickly Jim moved through the shadowy rooms, a series of tableaux in a forgotten museum. The house was filled with photographs of a handsome woman posing like a film star. He ignored the framed portrait on the grand piano, and the huge globe of the earth beside the bookshelf. In the past Jim would have stopped to play with the globe – for years he had nagged his father for one – but now he was too hungry to waste a moment.

The house had been the property of a Belgian dentist. In his study, below the framed certificates, were white cabinets containing dozens of sets of teeth. Through the darkness they grimaced at Jim like ravenous mouths.

Jim walked through the dining-room to the kitchen. He side-stepped the pool of water around the refrigerator, and expertly ran his eye over the pantry shelves. To his annoyance this Belgian dentist and his glamorous companion had developed a taste for Chinese food – something his own parents rarely touched – and the pantry was hung like the store-room of a Chinese compradore with lengths of dried intestines and shrivelled fruit.

But there was a single can of condensed milk, of a richness and sweetness Jim had never remembered. He drank the milk, sitting at the desk in the dentist's study as the teeth smiled at him, and then fell asleep in a bedroom upstairs, between silk sheets scented by the body of the woman with the face of a film star.

9

An End to Kindness

Ever searching for food, Jim left the dentist's house the next morning. He found another temporary home in a nearby mansion owned by an American widow whom his parents had known before her departure for San Francisco. From there he moved on, staying for a few days in each house, shielded from the distant, ugly city by the high walls and deepening grass.

The Japanese had confiscated all the radios and cameras, but otherwise the houses were intact. Most of them were far more lavish than his own home – although a rich man, Jim's father had always been spartan – and were equipped with private cinemas and ballrooms. Abandoned by their owners, Buicks and Cadillacs slumped in the garages on their flattening tyres.

Yet their pantry cupboards were bare, leaving Jim to feed on the few leftovers of cocktail food from the fifty-year-long party that had been Shanghai. Sometimes, after finding an intact box of chocolates in a dressing-table drawer, Jim would revive and remember his parents dancing to the radiogram before lunch on Sunday, and his bedroom in Amherst Avenue now occupied by the Japanese officers. He played billiards in the darkened games rooms, or sat at a card table and laid out hands of bridge, playing each one as fairly as he could. He lay on the oddly scented beds, reading *Life* and *Esquire*, and in the house of an American doctor read the whole of *Through the Looking Glass*, a comforting world less strange than his own.

But the toy cupboards in the children's rooms made him feel ever more empty. He leafed through photograph albums, filled with images of a vanished world of fancy-dress parties and gymkhanas. Still hoping to see his parents, he sat by the bedroom windows, as the water drained from the swimming-pools of the western suburbs, draping their white walls with veils of scum. Although he was too tired to think of the future, Jim knew that the small stocks of food would soon be exhausted, and that the Japanese would turn their attention to these empty houses – already the families of Japanese civilians were moving into the former Allied premises in Amherst Avenue.

Jim scarcely recognized his long hair and grey cheeks, the strange face in a strange mirror. He would stare at the ragged figure who appeared before him in all the mirrors of the Columbia Road, an urchin half his previous size and twice his previous age. Much of the time Jim was aware that he was ill, and often he would have to lie down all day. The mains supply to Columbia Road had been turned off, and the water dripping from the roof tanks had an unpleasant metallic tang. Once, as he lay sick in an attic bedroom in the Great Western Road, a party of Japanese civilians spent an hour walking around the downstairs rooms, but Jim had been too feverish to call to them.

One afternoon Jim scaled the wall of a house behind the American Country Club. He jumped into a wide, over-grown garden and was running towards the verandah before he realized that a group of Japanese soldiers were cooking a meal beside the empty swimming-pool. Three men squatted on the diving-boards, feeding sticks to a small fire. Another soldier was down on the floor of the pool, poking through the debris of bathing caps and sun-glasses.

The Japanese watched Jim hesitate in the deep grass, and stirred their boiled rice, in which floated a few pieces of fish. They made no attempt to pick up their rifles, but Jim knew that he should not try to run from them. He strolled through the grass to the edge of the pool and sat on the leaf-strewn tiles. The soldiers began to eat their meal, talking in low voices. They were thickset men with shaven heads, wearing better webbing and equipment than the Japanese sentries in Shanghai, and Jim guessed that they were seasoned combat troops.

Jim watched them eat, his eyes fixed on every morsel that entered their mouths. When the oldest of the four soldiers had finished he scraped some burnt rice and fish scales from the side of the cooking pot. A first-class private of some forty years, with slow, careful hands, he beckoned Jim forward and handed him his mess tin. As they smoked their cigarettes the Japanese smiled to themselves, watching Jim devour the shreds of fatty rice. It was his first hot food since he had left the hospital, and the heat and greasy flavour stung his gums. Tears swam in his eyes. The Japanese soldier who had taken pity on Jim, recognizing that this small boy was starving, began to laugh good-naturedly, and pulled the rubber plug from his metal water-bottle. Jim drank the clear, chlorine-flavoured liquid, so unlike the stagnant water in the taps of the Columbia Road. He choked, carefully swallowed his vomit, and tittered into his hands, grinning at the Japanese. Soon they were all laughing together, sitting back in the deep grass beside the drained swimming-pool.

For the next week Jim followed the Japanese on their patrols of the deserted streets. Each morning the soldiers emerged from their bivouac at the Great Western Road checkpoint, and Jim would run from the steps of the house in which he had spent the night and attach himself to them. The soldiers rarely entered the foreign mansions, and were concerned only to keep out any Chinese beggars and thieves who might be tempted into this residential area. Sometimes they climbed the walls and explored the overgrown gardens, whose ornamental trees and shrubs seemed of more interest to them than the lavishly equipped houses. Jim ran errands for them, hunting for the bathing caps that they collected, chopping wood and lighting fires. He watched silently as they ate their midday meal. Almost always they left a little rice and fish for him, and once the first-class private gave him a piece of hard candy which he broke from a strip in his pocket, but otherwise none of them showed any interest in Jim. Did they know that he was a vagrant? They would stare at his scuffed but well-made shoes, at the woollen cloth of his school blazer, perhaps assuming that he lived with some rich but feckless European family that no longer bothered to feed its children.

Within a week Jim was dependent on this Japanese patrol for almost all his food. More of the houses in the Columbia Road were being occupied by Japanese military and civilians. Several times, as he approached a deserted house, Jim was chased away by Chinese bodyguards.

One morning the Japanese soldiers failed to appear. Jim waited patiently in the garden of the house behind the American Country Club. Trying to calm his hunger, he broke twigs from the rhododendron bushes, ready to light a fire beside the drained pool. He watched the aircraft flying through the cool February light, and counted the three liqueur chocolates in his blazer pocket which he had saved for the emergency he knew would soon come.

The verandah doors opened behind him. He stood up, as the Japanese soldiers stepped on to the terrace. They were waving to him, and Jim had the confused idea that they had brought his parents with them, and so were making a formal entry through the house rather than climb over the wall.

He ran towards the Japanese, who were shouting at him in a surprisingly brusque way. When he reached the terrace he saw that they were members of a new patrol. The corporal cuffed him and pushed him around the flower-beds, then made him clear away the sticks beside the pool. Shouting a few words of German, he threw Jim into the drive and slammed the wrought-iron gate on his heels.

The houses stood around him in the sun, sealed worlds where he had briefly returned to his childhood. As he set out on the long journey to the Bund he thought of the Japanese soldiers who had fed him from their cooking pot, but he knew now that kindness, which his parents and teachers had always urged upon him, counted for nothing.

10
The Stranded Freighter

Cold sunlight shivered on the river, turning its surface into chopped glass, and transforming the distant banks and hotels of the Bund into a row of wedding cakes. To Jim, as he sat on the catwalk of the funeral pier below the deserted Nantao shipyards, the funnels and masts of the *Idzumo* seemed carved from icing sugar. He cupped his hands into a pair of make-believe binoculars and studied the white-suited sailors, as busy as lice, who moved around the decks and bridge. The cruiser's gun turrets reminded him of the candied decoration on the Christmas cakes whose overripe flavour he had always hated.

All the same, Jim would have liked to eat the ship. He imagined himself nibbling the masts, sucking the cream from the Edwardian funnels, sinking his teeth into the marzipan bows and devouring the entire forward section of the hull. After that he would gobble down the Palace Hotel, the Shell Building, the whole of Shanghai . . .

Steam throbbed from the *Idzumo*'s funnels, calmed itself and drifted across the water in a delicate veil. The cruiser had drawn its stern anchors and was swinging on the tide, bows pointing downstream. Having helped to impose Japanese rule upon Shanghai, it was about to sail for another theatre of war. As if celebrating, a regatta of corpses turned on the tide. The bodies of scores of Chinese, each on a raft of paper flowers, surrounded the *Idzumo*, ready to escort the cruiser to the mouth of the Yangtze.

Jim kept watch for the Japanese naval patrols. Across the river, on the Pootung shore, were the galvanized roofs and modern chimneys of his father's cotton mill. Jim vaguely remembered his visits there, embarrassing occasions when the Chinese managers paraded him under the expressionless gaze of thousands of mill girls. Now it was silent, and what concerned him was the boom of the sunken freighters. The nearest of the wrecks, a single-funnel coaster, sat in the deep-water channel only a hundred yards from the end of the funeral pier. Its rusting bridge, like a crumbling brown loaf, still held all its mystery for him. War, which had changed everything in Jim's world so radically, had long since left this forgotten wreck, but he was determined to go out to the ship. Rejoining his parents, giving himself up to the Japanese, even finding food to eat, meant nothing now that the freighter was at last within his reach.

For two days Jim had wandered along the Shanghai waterfront. After being discovered by the Japanese patrol he set off for the Bund. His only hope of seeing his parents again was to find one of their Swiss or Swedish friends. Although the European neutrals drove through the streets of Shanghai, Jim had not seen a single British or American face. Had they all been sent to prison camps in Japan?

Then, as he cycled along the Nanking Road, he was overtaken by a military truck. A group of fair-haired men in British uniforms sat behind the guards.

'Speed up, lad! Let's see you look lively!'

'Faster than that, lad! We won't wait for you!'

Jim crouched over the handlebars, feet whirling on the pedals. They were cheering and waving to him, clapping their hands as the Japanese guards frowned at this absurd British game. Jim shouted at the disappearing truck, and there was laughter, and a last thumbs-up when his front wheel locked itself in a tramline and pitched him under the feet of the pedicab drivers.

Soon after, he lost his bicycle. He was trying to straighten the front forks when a Chinese shopkeeper and his coolie came up to him. The shopkeeper held the handlebars, but Jim knew that he was not trying to help. He stared into the matter-of-fact eyes of the two Chinese. He was tired and had been slapped enough.

Jim watched them wheel the cycle through the crowd and vanish into one of the hundreds of alleyways. An hour later he reached the Szechwan Road on foot, but the entire financial sector of Shanghai was sealed by hundreds of Japanese soldiers and their armoured cars.

So Jim went down to the Bund to look at the *Idzumo*. All afternoon he wandered along the waterfront, past the mud-flats where the injured sailors of the *Petrel* had come ashore and he had last seen his father, past the sampan jetties and the fish market with its pallid mullet laid out between the tramlines, to the quays of the French Concession where the Bund ran out in the funeral piers and shipyards of Nantao. No one molested Jim there. This area of creeks and waste tips was covered with the timbers of opium hulks, the carcasses of dogs, and the coffins that had drifted ashore again on to the beaches of black mud. In the afternoon he watched the Japanese seaplanes moored to their buoys at the Naval Air Base. He waited for the pilots to come out in their flying goggles and stroll down the slipway. But no one except Jim seemed interested in the seaplanes, and they sat on their long pontoons, propellers irritated by the wind.

At night Jim slept in the back seat of one of the dozens of old taxis dumped on to the mud-flats. The klaxons of the Japanese armoured cars wailed along the Bund, and the searchlights of the patrol boats flared across the river, but Jim fell asleep quickly in the cold air. His thin body seemed to float on the night, hovering above the dark water as he clung to the faint human odours that rose from the taxi's seats.

★ ★ ★

It was high water, and the seaplanes had begun to circle their buoys. The river no longer pressed against the boom of freighters. For a few moments the surface congealed into an oily mirror, through which the rusting steamers emerged as if from their own reflections. Beside the funeral piers the sampans swayed forward, loosened from the mud-flats even as they filled with water.

Jim squatted on the metal catwalk, watching the water slap at the grille between his feet. From his blazer pocket he took one of his last two liqueur chocolates. He studied the cryptic scrolls, like the signs of the zodiac, and carefully weighed them. Saving the larger, he placed the smaller in his mouth. The fiery alcohol stung his tongue, but he sucked on the dark sweet chocolate. The brown water swelled glassily around the pier, and he remembered that his father had told him how sunlight killed bacteria. Fifty yards away the corpse of a young Chinese woman floated among the sampans, heels rotating around her head as if unsure in what direction to point her that day. Cautiously, Jim decanted a little water from one palm to the other, then drank quickly so that the germs would have no time to infect him.

The liqueur chocolate, and the swilling rhythm of the waves, made him feel giddy again, and he steadied himself against a waterlogged sampan that bumped against the pier. Looking up at the decaying freighter, Jim stepped without thinking into the sampan and pushed out into the jelly-like stream.

The rotting craft was half-filled with water that soaked Jim's shoes and trousers. He tore away part of the freeboard, and used the pulpy plank to paddle towards the freighter. When he reached the ship the sampan had almost submerged. He seized the starboard rail below the bridge and climbed on to the deck, as the waterlogged hulk drifted on its way to the next freighter in the boom.

Jim watched it go, then walked through the ankle-deep water that covered the metal deck. The river had begun to shift slightly, and the waxy surface was unbroken as it entered the open stateroom below the bridge and ran out through the port rail. Jim stepped into the stateroom, a rusting grotto that seemed even older than the German forts at Tsingtao. He was standing on the surface of the river, which had rushed from all the creeks and paddies and canals of China in order to carry this small boy on its back. If he stepped on to the waves by the port rail he could walk all the way to the *Idzumo* . . .

Towers of smoke shuddered from the cruiser's funnels as it prepared to raise anchor. Were his parents on board? Aware that he might now be alone in Shanghai, on this steamer he had always dreamed of visiting, Jim gazed from the bridge towards the shore. The tide was beginning to run, and the flower-decked corpses were following their heels to the open sea. The freighter leaned in the stream, and its rusty hull creaked and sang. The plates sawed against each other, and the trailing hawsers swung across the foredeck, the halyards of invisible sails still hoping to propel this ancient hulk to the safety of some warm sea a world away from Shanghai.

Happily, Jim felt the bridge shudder under his feet. As he laughed to himself at the rail he noticed that someone was watching him from the shipyard beyond the funeral piers. A man wearing the coat and cap of an American seaman stood in the wheelhouse of one of three partly constructed colliers. Shyly, but captain to captain, Jim waved to him. The man ignored him, and smoked the cigarette concealed in his hand. He was watching, not only Jim, but a young sailor in a metal dinghy which had cast loose from the next steamer in the boom.

Eager to welcome his first passenger and crewman, Jim left the bridge and made his way down to the deck. The sailor drew nearer, rowing in strong, short movements, careful not to disturb the water. Every few strokes he looked over his shoulder at Jim, and peered through the portholes as if he suspected that this rusty freighter was infested with small boys. The dinghy sat low in the water, weighted down by the sailor's broad back. He pulled alongside, and Jim saw a crowbar, spanners and hacksaw between his boots. On the bench seat were the brass rings of porthole mounts prised from the ships' hulls.

'Hello, kid – going for a run up the coast? Who else is with you?'

'Nobody.' For all the hope of safety that this young American offered, Jim was not eager to leave the ship. 'I'm waiting for my mother and father. They've been . . . delayed.'

'Delayed? Well, maybe they'll come later. You look like you need some help.'

He reached out to climb aboard, but as Jim took his hand the sailor pulled him roughly into the dinghy, jarring his knees against the brass portholes. He sat Jim upright and fingered his blazer lapels and badge. His loose blond hair framed an open American face, but he scanned the river in a furtive way, as if expecting a Japanese naval diver in full gear to break surface alongside the dinghy.

'Now, why are you trying to bother us? Who brought you out here?'

'I came by myself.' Jim straightened his blazer. 'This is my ship now.'

'Some kind of crazy British kid. You've been sitting on that pier for two days. Who are you?'

'Jamie . . .' Jim tried to think of something that would impress the American; already he realized that he should stay with this young sailor. 'I'm building a man-flying kite . . . and I've written a book on contract bridge.'

'Wait till Basie sees this.'

As they drifted from the freighter the American drew on his oars. With a few powerful strokes he pulled the dinghy towards the mud-flats. They entered a shallow creek between the funeral piers, a black and oil-stained channel that wound past the shipyards. The American stared morosely at an empty coffin that had jettisoned its occupant. He spat into it for good luck, and fended it off with an oar. Expertly he steered the dinghy behind the white hull of a mastless yacht lashed to a beached lighter. Hidden below the swan-like overhang of the yacht's stern, they tied up at a wooden stage. The American looped the porthole mounts on to his arm, gathered his tools together and beckoned Jim from the dinghy.

They crossed the floor of the shipyard, past stacks of steel plate, coils of chains and rusting wire, towards the shabby hulls of the three colliers. Jim scurried along, imitating the American's aggressive gait. At last he had met someone who could help him find his parents. Perhaps the American and his companion in the wheelhouse had also been trying to surrender? The three of them together would be too many for the Japanese to ignore.

An antique Chevrolet truck was parked under the propeller of the largest collier. They stepped through a missing plate into the hull. The American lifted Jim on to a bamboo platform laid along its keel. They climbed a companionway to the next deck, walked across the wheelhouse and ducked through a narrow hatch into a metal cabin behind the bridge.

Faint with hunger, Jim swayed against the door frame. A familiar scent hung in the air, reminding him of his mother's bedroom in Amherst Avenue, the odours of face-powder, cologne and Craven A cigarettes, and for a moment he was sure that she would emerge from this dark cubby-hole like the Christmas fairy and tell him that the war was over.

11
Frank and Basie

A charcoal stove burned softly in the centre of the cabin, its sweet fumes lifting through an open skylight. The floor was covered with oily rags and engine parts, brass portholes and stair-rails. On either side of the stove were a deck-chair with 'Imperial Airways' stitched into its fading canvas, and a camp-bed covered with a Chinese quilt.

The American flung his tools into the heap of metal parts. His large head and shoulders almost filled the cabin, and he slumped restlessly in the canvas chair. He peered into the saucepan on the stove and then gazed gloomily at Jim.

'He's getting on my nerves already, Basie. I don't know whether he's hungrier or crazier . . .'

'Come in, boy. You look like you need to lie down.'

A small, older man emerged from beneath the quilt and motioned to Jim with the cigarette he was holding in his white hand. He had a bland, unmarked face from which all the copious experiences of his life had been cleverly erased, and soft hands that were busy powdering each other under the quilt. His eyes took in every detail of Jim's mud-stained clothes, the tic that jumped across his mouth, his pinched cheeks and unsteady legs.

He dusted the talc from the bed and counted the pieces of salvaged brass. 'Is that all, Frank? That's not a lot to take to market. Those Hongkew merchants are charging ten dollars for a bag of rice.'

'Basie!' The young sailor drove a heavy boot into the heap of metal, exasperated more with himself than with the older man. 'The boy's been sitting on the pier for two days! Do you want the Japs in here?'

'Frank, the Japs aren't looking for us. Nantao Creek is full of the cholera – that's why we came here.'

'You practically put up a sign. Maybe you want them to look for us? Is that it, Basie?' Frank dipped a rag in a can of cleaning fluid. He began to rub vigorously at the grime that covered a porthole mount. 'If you want to work so hard try going out there – with that kid watching you all the time.'

'Frank, we've got my lungs, you agreed that.' Basie inhaled a little smoke from his Craven A, soothing these delicate organs. 'Besides, the boy didn't even notice you. He had other things on his mind, boy's things that you've forgotten, Frank, but I can still remember.' He made a warm place for Jim on the bed. 'Come over here, son. What did they call you, before the war started?'

'Jamie . . .'

Frank threw down his rag. 'All this scrap isn't going to buy us a sampan to Chungking! We'd need the *Queen Mary* out there.' He treated Jim to a dark glare. 'And we don't have enough rice for you, kid. Who are you? Jamie – ?'

'Jim . . .' Basie explained. 'A new name for a new life.' As Jim sat beside him he reached out a powdered hand and gently pressed his thumb against the hunger tic that jumped across the left corner of Jim's mouth. Jim sat passively as Basie exposed his gums and glanced shrewdly at his teeth.

'That's a well-kept set of teeth. Someone paid a lot of bills for that sweet little mouth. Frank, you'd be surprised how some people neglect their kids' teeth.' Basie patted Jim's shoulder, feeling the blue wool of his blazer. He scraped the mud from the school badge. 'That looks like a good school, Jim. The Cathedral School?'

Frank glowered over his heap of portholes. He seemed wary of Jim, as if this small boy might take Basie from him. 'Cathedral? Is he some kind of priest?'

'Frank, the Cathedral School.' Basie gazed with growing interest at Jim. 'That's a school for taipans. Jim, you must know some important people.'

'Well . . .' Jim was doubtful about this. He could think of nothing but the rice simmering on the charcoal stove, but then remembered a garden party at the British Embassy. 'Once I was introduced to Madame Sun Yat-Sen.'

'Madame Sun? You were . . . introduced?'

'I was only three and a half.' Jim sat still as Basie's white hands explored his pockets. The watch slipped from his wrist and vanished into the haze of cologne and face powder below the quilt. Yet Basie's attentive manner, like that of the servants who had once dressed and undressed him, was curiously reassuring. The sailor was feeling every bone in his body, as if searching for something precious. Through the open hatch Jim could see a flying boat about to take off from the Naval Air Base. A Japanese patrol boat had closed the channel, giving a wide berth to the currents that formed huge whirlpools around the boom of freighters. Jim returned to the cooking pot and its intoxicating smell of burnt fat. Suddenly it occurred to him that these two American sailors might want to eat him.

But Basie had removed the lid from the saucepan. A flavoursome steam rose from a thick stew of rice and fish. Basie produced a pair of tin plates and spoons from a leather bag under the bed. Still smoking his Craven A, he served portions for himself and Jim with the deftness of a waiter at the Palace Hotel. As Jim wolfed the hot fish Basie watched with the same wry approval that the Japanese soldier had shown.

Basie tucked into the stew. 'We eat later, Frank.'

Frank rubbed at a porthole, his eyes on the saucepan. 'Basie, I always eat after you.'

'I need to think for us both, Frank. Besides, we have to look after our young friend.' He wiped a grain of rice from

Jim's chin. 'Tell me, Jim, have you met any other Chinese big noises? Chiang Kai-Shek, maybe . . . ?'

'No . . . but his name isn't really Chinese, you know.' The hot food made Jim's brain swim. He remembered a word his mother had used, which he had always tried to work into his conversations with adults. 'It's a corruption of Shanghai Czech.'

'A corruption . . . ?' Basie was sitting up now. Having ended his meal, he began to powder his hands. Are you interested in words, Jim?'

'A bit. And contract bridge. I've written a book about it.'

Basie looked doubtful. 'Words are more important, Jim. Put aside a new word every day. You never know when a word might be useful.'

Jim finished his stew and sat back contentedly against the metal wall. He could remember none of his meals before the war and every one of them since. It annoyed him to think of all the food in his life that he had turned away, and the elaborate stratagems which Vera and his mother had devised to persuade him to finish his pudding. He noticed that Frank was staring at a few grains he had left in the spoon, and quickly licked it clean. Jim glanced into the saucepan, glad to see that there was enough rice for Frank. He was sure now that these two merchant seamen were not going to eat him, but the fear had been sensible – there had been rumours at the Country Club that British sailors torpedoed in the Atlantic had taken to cannibalism.

Basie served himself a small spoonful of rice. He made no attempt to eat this second helping, but played with the plate under Frank's burning gaze. Already Jim could see that Basie liked to control the young sailor and was using Jim to unsettle him. Jim's entire upbringing could have been designed to prevent him from meeting people like Basie, but the war had changed everything.

'What about your Daddy, Jim?' Basie asked. 'Why aren't you at home with your mother? Are they here in Shanghai?'

'Yes . . .' Jim hesitated. All his experience of the previous weeks told him not to trust anyone, except perhaps the Japanese. 'They're in Shanghai – but they're sailing on the *Idzumo*.'

'The *Idzumo*?' Frank jumped from his deck-chair. He seized a mess-tin from his haversack and helped himself vigorously to the saucepan of rice. Between mouthfuls, he shook his spoon at Jim. 'Kid, who are you? Basie . . . !'

'Not the *Idzumo*, Jim.' With his white hands Basie selected a piece of charcoal from a bag under the bed. 'The *Idzumo*'s heading for Foochow and Manila Bay. Jim's having you on, Frank.'

'Well, I think they're on the *Idzumo*.' Jim decided to fan the small doubt still in Basie's eyes. 'My father often goes to Manila.'

'Not on a Japanese cruiser, Jim.'

'Basie . . . !'

'Frank . . .' Basie mimicked the sailor's voice. 'Some day you'll want to trust me. I imagine Jim's folks had themselves picked up with all the other Britishers, and now Jim's looking for them. Jim . . . ?'

Jim nodded, taking the last liqueur chocolate from his blazer pocket. He unwrapped the silver foil and bit into the miniature chocolate bottle. Then, remembering what Vera had drummed into him about the need to be polite, he handed half the chocolate to Basie.

'Curaçao . . . Well, things have been looking up, Jim, since you arrived. All these new words, and now this fancy candy, we're getting a little of that Palace Hotel style.' As Basie sucked at the chocolate cup with his sharp teeth he resembled a white-faced rat teasing the brains from a mouse. 'So you've been living at home, Jim, all by yourself. Down there in the French Concession?'

'Amherst Avenue.'

'Frank . . . Before we leave Shanghai we ought to take a ride out there. There must be a lot of empty houses, Jim?'

Jim closed his eyes. He was very tired but awake, thinking of the rice he had just eaten, retasting every fishy grain. Basie talked, his devious voice circling the fume-filled air with its scent of cologne and Craven A. He thought of his mother smoking in the drawing-room at Amherst Avenue. Now that he had met these two American sailors he would be seeing her again. He would stay with Basie and Frank; together they could go out to the boom of freighters; sooner or later the Japanese patrol boats would notice them.

A hot, fishy breath filled his face. Jim woke with a gasp. Frank's huge body leaned across him, heavy arms on his thighs, hands feeling in his blazer pockets. Jim pushed him away, and Frank calmly returned to his deck-chair and continued to polish the portholes.

They were alone together in the cabin. Jim could hear Basie on the bamboo catwalk below. The door of the truck slammed, and the elderly engine began to throb, then stopped abruptly. There was a distant blast from the *Idzumo*'s siren. With a meaningful glance at Jim, Frank buffed the faded brass.

'You know, kid, you have a talent for getting on people's nerves. How is it the Japs haven't picked you up? You must be quick on your feet.'

'I tried to surrender,' Jim explained. 'But it isn't easy. Do you and Basie want to surrender?'

'Like hell – though I don't know about him. I'm trying to get Basie to buy a sampan so we can sail upriver to Chungking. But Basie keeps changing his mind. He wants to stay in Shanghai now the Japs are here. He thinks we can make a pile of money once we get to the camps.'

'Do you sell a lot of portholes, Frank?'

Frank peered at Jim, still unsure about this small boy. 'Kid, we haven't sold a single one. It's Basie's game, like a drug, he needs to keep people working for him. Down in the yard somewhere he has a bag of gold teeth that he sells in Hongkew.' With a knowing smile, Frank raised an oil-stained spanner, and touched Jim's chin. 'It's a good thing you don't have any gold teeth, or – ' He snapped his wrist.

Jim sat up, remembering how Basie had searched his gums. The sound of the truck's motor vibrated through the metal cabin. He was wary of these two merchant seamen, who had somehow escaped the Japanese net around Shanghai, and realized that he might have as much to fear from them as from anyone else in the city. He thought of Basie's secret bag of gold teeth. The creeks and canals of Nantao were full of corpses, and the mouths of those corpses were full of teeth. Every Chinese tried to have at least one gold tooth out of self-respect, and now that the war had begun their relatives might be too tired to pull them out before the funeral. Jim visualized the two American seamen searching the mud-flats at night with their spanners, Frank rowing the dinghy along the black creeks. Basie in the bows with a lantern, prodding the corpses that drifted past and exposing their gums . . .

12

Dance Music

This fearful image dominated the three days that Jim was to spend with the American sailors. At night, as Basie and Frank slept together under the quilt, he lay awake on his pile of rice sacking beside the charcoal stove. Reflected from the portholes and brass handrails, the embers gleamed like gold teeth. When he awoke in the mornings Jim would feel his jaw, to make sure that Frank had not removed one of his molars out of cussedness.

During the day Jim sat on the funeral pier and acted as lookout while Frank rowed to the scuttled freighters. When he began to shiver Jim returned to the cabin and lay under the quilt as Basie sat in the Imperial Airways deck-chair and made wire toys from old pipe cleaners. Basie had served as a cabin steward on the Cathay-American Line, and he treated Jim to the same patter and parlour tricks with which he had amused the young children of his passengers. He made the same effort to ensure that Jim ate his morning and evening meals, while endlessly questioning him about his mother and father. To a large extent Basie had modelled himself on the women passengers he had served, forever powdering themselves in the heat as they lit their cigarettes.

Every afternoon they set off together in the truck and toured the Chinese markets in Hongkew. Here Basie would haggle for a sack of rice and a few pieces of fish, trading packets of French cigarettes from the store of cartons under his bed. At times he would tell Frank to bring Jim over to the vendor's stall, where the Chinese trader would soberly inspect Jim before shaking his head.

It soon became clear to Jim that Basie was trying to sell him to the traders. Too tired to resist, he sat in the truck between the two Americans, like one of the chickens which the Chinese women carried beside them on the seats of the trams. Already he felt unwell most of the time, but his potential value at least assured him of the meals of boiled fish. Eventually the Chinese traders would realize that a few yen could be made by reporting them to the Japanese.

Meanwhile he avoided Frank's heavy hands, ransacked his mind for the unusual words which Basie liked to hear him use, and regaled the cabin steward with tales of the grand houses in Amherst Avenue. Jim invented lives of wholly imaginary glamour which he claimed his parents had led. Basie never ceased to be fascinated by these accounts of Shanghai high life.

'Tell me about their swimming-pool parties,' Basie asked as they waited for Frank to start the engine before their last visit to Hongkew market. 'I imagine there was a lot of . . . gaiety.'

'Basie, there certainly was gaiety.' Jim remembered the hours he had spent alone trying to retrieve the half-crown, gleaming at the bottom of the pool like one of Basie's teeth. 'They had liqueur chocolates, a white piano, whisky and soda. And conjurors.'

'Conjurors, Jim?'

'I think they were conjurors . . .'

'You're tired, Jim.' As they sat in the truck Basie put an arm around Jim's shoulders. 'You've been thinking too much, all those new words.'

'I've used up all my new words, Basie. Is the war going to end soon?'

'Don't worry, Jim. I give the Japs three months at the outside.'

'As soon as that, Basie?'

'Maybe a little more. It takes a long time to start a war,

people have a big investment to protect. Like Frank and me and this truck.'

It had never occurred to Jim that anyone might want the war to continue, and he puzzled over the bizarre logic as they set out for Hongkew. They bumped along the dirt road behind the shipyards, through a desolate area of empty godowns, garbage tips and burial mounds. Beggars lived beside the canals in hovels constructed from truck tyres and packing cases. An old woman squatted by the foetid water, scrubbing out a wooden toilet. Gazing down from the safety of the truck, Jim felt sorry for these destitute people, though only a few days earlier his plight had been even more desperate than theirs. A strange doubling of reality had taken place, as if everything that had happened to him since the war was occurring within a mirror. It was his mirror self who felt faint and hungry, and who thought about food all the time. He no longer felt sorry for this other self. Jim guessed that this was how the Chinese managed to survive. Yet one day the Chinese might emerge from the mirror.

When they crossed Nantao Creek into the French Concession they saw the first Japanese patrol, guarding the checkpoint on the northern end of the steel bridge. But Basie and Frank seemed unafraid of the armed soldiers – Americans, Jim had noticed, were not easily impressed by anyone. Frank even sounded his horn at a Japanese soldier who strolled into the road. Jim crouched below the dashboard, expecting them to be shot, but the Japanese waved them on with a surly stare, perhaps assuming that Frank and Basie were White Russian workmen.

For the next hour they toured the Hongkew markets, past the hundreds of barking dogs in their bamboo cages, not only the Chinese table-mongrels but spaniels and dachshunds, red setters and airedales released into the hungry streets of Shanghai by their allied owners. Several times they stopped for Basie to get out and approach a Chinese stall-holder, talking in his fluent dockside Cantonese. But no portholes or gold teeth changed hands.

'Frank, what's Basie trying to buy?'

'It looks like he's more interested in selling.'

'Why can't Basie sell me?'

'Nobody wants you.' Frank flicked the half-crown he had stolen from Jim's pocket, and snapped it in his heavy hand. 'You're worth nothing. What do you think you're worth?'

'I'm worth nothing, Frank.'

'You're skin and bone. Soon you're going to be sick all the time.'

'If they did buy me, what would they do with me? They couldn't eat me, I'm skin and bone.'

But Frank declined to answer. Basie climbed into the truck, shaking his head. They left Hongkew and crossed the Soochow Creek into the International Settlement. They drove along the main streets, losing themselves in the traffic on the Avenue Foch, following the slow, clanking trams through the wheel-to-wheel tide of pedicabs and rickshaws.

Jim tried to guide them towards the residential suburbs in the west of Shanghai, telling them about the fine houses filled with billiard tables, whisky and liqueur chocolates. But he guessed that Basie and Frank were killing time before dusk. Soon after six o'clock the light withdrew from the façades of the apartment houses in the French Concession. The two sailors wound up their windows. Frank left the Bubbling Well Road and set off into the unlit Chinese districts of north Shanghai.

'Frank, you're going the wrong way – ' Jim tried to point out. But Basie pressed the back of his powdered hand against Jim's mouth.

'Quiet, Jim. Silence is a good friend to a boy.'

Jim rested his swaying head against Basie's shoulder. They embarked on a rambling journey through the narrow streets. Hundreds of Chinese faces pressed against the windows as they edged between the rickshaw and buffalo carts. Jim felt hungry again, and the endless bumping of the wheels over the disused tramlines made him giddy. He wished that they would return to Nantao, to the charcoal-stove with its pot of rice.

An hour later, Jim woke to find that they had reached the western suburbs of Shanghai. The last of the sun touched the rooftops of the Columbia Road. As they cruised past the parked Opels and Buicks of the German compound Basie pointed to the unoccupied houses.

Jim revived, and blew into his hands to warm them. They had completed a pointless circuit of the city, but he realized that he had tempted these devious men with his chatter about the grand life. Like a courier with a party of gullible tourists, he began a commentary on the houses in which he had camped during the past two months.

'That has whisky and gin, Basie. That has whisky and gin and a white piano – no, just whisky.'

'Never mind the alcohol. Frank and I aren't planning to open a bar. Were you a choirboy, Jim? We'll stand you on the white piano, you can sing "Yankee Doodle Dandy".'

'That has a cinema,' Jim continued. 'And that one is full of teeth.'

'Teeth, Jim?'

'It belonged to a dentist. Maybe there are gold teeth, Basie.'

They turned into Amherst Avenue and drove past the deserted mansions. The electricity supply to the street was still disconnected, and the houses in their overgrown gardens seemed even more sombre in the early evening, stranded here like the scuttled freighters in the boom. But Basie stared at them with obvious respect, as if his years as a cabin steward on the Cathay-American Line had taught him the true worth of these beached hulks. Clearly he was glad to be associated with Jim.

'You had good sense, Jim, being born here. I admire a boy who appreciates a good home. Anyone can pick his own parents, but to have the sense to see beyond that . . .'

'Basie . . .' Frank interrupted this reverie. They had stopped under the trees two hundred yards from the entrance to Jim's drive.

'Right, Frank.' Basie opened his door and stepped into the road. There were no Japanese patrols, and the Chinese bodyguards had retreated behind their walls for the evening. Basie pointed to a narrow cul-de-sac that ran between uncut privet hedges towards one of the houses.

'Jim, time to stretch our legs. Take a stroll up there and see if anyone's playing that white piano.'

Jim listened to the low but stressed sound of the truck's engine. Frank sat back in a casual way, but his huge foot was poised above the accelerator. Basie's pallid face hung like a lantern below the trees. Jim knew that they planned to leave him there. Having failed to sell him to the Chinese traders, they would abandon him to the avenues of the Shanghai night.

'Basie, I . . .' Frank had placed a hand on his shoulder, ready to hurl him into the road. 'Could we go to my house? It's even more luxuriant.'

'Luxuriant?' Basie savoured the word in the grey air. He gazed at the houses around them, at the Tudor gables and white modern façades, at the replica chateaux and the haciendas with green tiled roofs.

He climbed aboard, and held the door to the frame without engaging the lock. 'All right, Frank, we'll look at Jim's house.'

They moved forward under the trees, and turned into the unguarded drive. As they approached the silent house Jim could see that Basie was disappointed. He eased open the door, ready to seize Jim and throw him out on to his own steps.

Jim clung to the dashboard, and at that moment two figures stepped from the entrance porch. They wore white gowns, with deep sleeves that floated from their arms. Jim was sure that his mother had come home and was greeting one of her guests.

'Basie! They're Japs . . .'

Jim heard Frank shouting, and saw that the two figures were off-duty Japanese soldiers in their military kimonos. The soldiers had seen them, and were bellowing at the open door. A uniformed sergeant emerged from the kerosene light that filled the hall. He stood on the top step, a Mauser holster against his stocky thigh. Frank was trying to reverse the truck when the soldiers in the kimonos jumped on to the running boards and struck with their fists at the glass. Two more soldiers carrying bamboo staves ran down the steps of the porch.

As the engine stalled, Jim felt himself pulled from the truck and hurled to the ground. Japanese in kimonos were running from the house, like a party of outraged women fresh from their baths. Jim sat on the sharp gravel between the polished boots of the Japanese sergeant, whose angry thighs rapped against his holster. The soldiers had trapped Frank within the cabin of the truck. His legs kicked out as they lunged at him with their bamboo staves, striking his bloody face and chest. Two soldiers watched from the steps of the house, taking turns to punch Basie who knelt at their feet in the drive.

Jim was glad to see the Japanese. Through the open doorway he could hear, between the heavy blows and Frank's cries, the scratchy sounds of a Japanese dance band playing on his mother's picnic gramophone.

13

The Open-Air Cinema

His arms warmed by the spring sun, Jim rested comfortably
in the front row of the open-air cinema. Smiling to himself,
he gazed at the blank screen twenty feet away. For the past
hour the blurred shadow of the Park Hotel had been moving
across the white canvas. After a long journey through the
godowns and tenement blocks of Chapei, the shadow of the
neon sign above the hotel had at last reached the screen.
The immense letters, each twice the height of the young
Japanese soldier patrolling the stage, moved from left to
right at a brisk pace, incorporating the silhouette of this
slim sentry and his rifle in a spectacular solar film.

Delighted with the display, Jim laughed behind his grimy
knees, feet up on the slatted teak bench. The afternoon
diorama staged in collaboration by the sun and the Park
Hotel had been Jim's chief entertainment during the three
weeks he had spent at the open-air cinema. Here, before the
outbreak of war, cartoons and adventure serials made by the
Shanghai film industry were projected at night to audiences
of Chinese mill-girls and dockyard workers. It often occurred to Jim that Yang, the family chauffeur, might have
appeared on this very screen. He had already carried out a
full reconnaissance of the detention centre, and in a disused
office above the projection room were reels of dusty film.
Perhaps the Japanese corporal from the signals corps who
was now trying to dismantle the projector would show one
of Yang's films?

His giggles brought a sour glance from the soldier on the
stage. He clearly mistrusted Jim, who kept out of his way.
Shielding his eyes, the soldier scanned the wooden benches,

where a few detainees sat in the afternoon sun. Three rows behind Jim was the grey-haired husband of the dying missionary woman who lay on her mat in the concrete dormitory under the seats. She had not moved from the former store-room since her arrival, but Mr Partridge looked after her patiently, bringing water from the tap in the latrine and feeding her the thin rice gruel which two Eurasian women cooked once a day in the yard behind the ticket office.

Jim felt concerned for the old Englishman with his patchy hair and deathly skin. At times he seemed unable to recognize his wife. Jim helped him to erect a screen around Mrs Partridge, who never spoke and had an unpleasant smell. They used Mr Partridge's English overcoat and his wife's yellowing nightdress, suspending them from a length of electric flex that Jim pulled from the wall. If he was bored Jim went down to the women's store-room and chased away the Eurasian children who ran in to play.

There were some thirty people in the detention centre, to which Jim had been sent after a week at the Shanghai Central Prison. Compared with the damp dormitory cell which he shared with a hundred Eurasian and British prisoners, the open-air cinema seemed as sunny as the resort beaches at Tsingtao. Jim had seen nothing of Basie since their capture by the Japanese, and was glad to be free of the cabin steward. None of the prisoners in the Central Prison, most of whom were contract foremen and merchant seamen from China coasters, had heard of Jim's parents, but the transfer to the detention centre was a move towards them.

Soon after his capture Jim had fallen ill with an aching fever, during which he vomited blood. He guessed that he had been sent to the detention centre in order to recover. Apart from several elderly English couples there were an old Dutchman and his adult daughter, and a quiet Belgian woman whose injured husband slept next to Jim in the men's store-room. The rest were Eurasian women who had been abandoned in Shanghai by British husbands in the armed services.

None of them was much fun to be with – they were all either very old or sick with malaria and dysentery, and few of the Eurasian children spoke any English. So Jim spent his time in the open-air cinema, roving around the wooden seats. Despite his headaches, he tried unsuccessfully to make friends with the Japanese soldiers. And every afternoon there was the shadow film of the Shanghai skyline.

Jim watched the letters of the Park Hotel's neon sign blur and fade. Although he was hungry all the time, he was happy in the detention centre. After the months of roving the streets of Shanghai he had at last managed to give himself up to the Japanese forces. Jim had pondered deeply on the question of surrender, which took courage and even a certain amount of guile. How did entire armies manage it?

He was aware that the Japanese had seized him only because he had been with Basie and Frank. He felt frightened when he thought of the soldiers in kimonos attacking Frank with their staves, but at least he would soon see his parents again. Prisoners were constantly coming and going at the detention centre. Two British people had died the previous day, a heavily bandaged woman whom Jim had not been allowed to see, and an old man with malaria who was a retired Shanghai police inspector.

If only he could discover to which of the dozen camps around Shanghai his mother and father had been sent. He left his place and tried to speak to Mr Partridge, but the old missionary was sunk inside his head. Jim approached the two Eurasian women sitting a few benches behind him. But as always they shook their heads and brusquely waved him away.

'Disgusting . . . !'
'Dirty boy . . . !'

110

'Go away . . . !'

Invariably they snapped at Jim, and tried to keep their children from him. Sometimes they mimicked his voice during his fevers. Jim smiled at them and returned to his seat. He felt tired, as he often did, and thought of going down to the store-room and sleeping for an hour on his mat. But a meal of boiled rice was served in the afternoon, and the previous day, when he had felt feverish, he had missed his ration. It surprised him how these old and sick people could manage to rouse themselves at meal times. No one had thought of waking Jim, and nothing was left in the brass cong. When he protested the Korean soldier had cuffed his head. Already Jim was certain that the Eurasian women who guarded the bags of rice in the ticket kiosk were giving him less than his fair share. He distrusted them all, and their strange children, who looked almost English but could speak only Chinese.

Jim was determined to have his share of rice. He knew that he was thinner than he had been before the war, and that his parents might fail to recognize him. At meal times, when he looked at himself in the cracked glass panes of the ticket kiosk, he barely remembered the long face with its deep eye-sockets and bony forehead. Jim avoided mirrors – the Eurasian women were always watching him through their compacts.

Deciding to think of something useful, Jim lay back on the teak bench. He watched a Kawanishi flying boat cross the river. The drone of its engines was comforting, and reminded him of all his dreams of flying. When he was hungry or missed his parents he often dreamed of aircraft. During one of his fevers he had even seen a flight of American bombers in the sky above the detention centre.

A whistle shrilled from the courtyard by the ticket kiosk. The Japanese sergeant in charge of the detention centre was holding another of his roll-calls. Jim had noticed that he

111

seemed unable to remember the prisoners' names for more than half an hour. Jim took Mr Partridge's hand, and together they followed the two Eurasian women. A military truck had stopped outside the entrance to the cinema, whose high brick walls had concealed its films from the Chinese in the nearby tenement blocks. In the intervals between the sergeant's whistles, Jim heard the crying of a British child.

A new group of prisoners had arrived. Invariably this meant that others would leave. Jim was sure that he would be on his way within minutes, probably to the new camps at Hungjao or Lunghua. In the store-room he and the old men still able to stand waited by their mats, mess-tins in hand. He listened to the new arrivals being herded from the truck. Annoyingly, there were several small children, who would cry continuously and distract the Japanese from the serious task of deciding where Jim should be sent.

Followed by two armed soldiers, the Japanese sergeant stood in the doorway. All three men wore cotton masks over their faces – there was a foul smell from the young Belgian asleep on the floor – but the sergeant's eyes inspected each of them in turn and counted the exact number of mess-tins. The daily ration of rice or sweet potatoes was allocated to the mess-tin and not to the person attached to it. Often, when Mr Partridge was tired after feeding his wife, Jim would collect the old man's ration for him. Once, without realizing it, he had found himself eating the watery gruel. Jim had felt uneasy, and stared at his guilty hands. Parts of his mind and body frequently separated themselves from each other.

Masking the tic in his cheek, he smiled brightly at the Japanese sergeant, and tried to look strong and healthy. Only the healthier people tended to leave the detention centre. But as usual the sergeant seemed depressed by Jim's cheerful gaze. He stepped aside as the new arrivals reached the store-room. Two Chinese prison orderlies bore a stretcher carrying an unconscious Englishwoman in a stained cotton dress. She lay with her damp hair in her mouth, while her two sons, boys of Jim's age, held the sides of the stretcher. A trio of elderly women hobbled past, unsure of the smell and the grey light. Behind them came a tall soldier wearing lumpy boots and British army shorts. He was bare-chested, and his emaciated ribs were like a birdcage in which Jim could almost see his heart fluttering.

'Well done, lad . . .' He gave Jim a rictus of a smile and patted his head. Quickly he sat down against the wall, his cadaverous face turned to the damp cement. A second team of orderlies lowered a stretcher on to the floor beside him. From the cradle of roped straw they lifted a small, middle-aged man in a bloodstained sailor's jacket. Strips of Japanese rice-paper bandages were stuck to the wounds on his swollen hands, face and forehead.

Jim stared at this derelict figure, and raised his forearm to his mouth to shut out the unpleasant smell. Several of the Eurasian women were leaving the detention centre with their children. Looking round at the sick and dying men in the store-room, and at the orderlies and Japanese soldiers with their cotton face-masks, Jim began for the first time to grasp the real purpose of the detention centre.

Mr Partridge and the old men stood by their mats, shaking their mess-tins at the guards, rattling for their evening meal. The wounded sailor beckoned to Jim with his bandaged hands, beating his empty tin with the same rhythm that the dying beggar had used outside the gates of Amherst Avenue. Even the emaciated soldier had found the lid of a mess-tin. With his face pressed to the wall, he banged the lid on the stone floor.

Jim began to rattle at the Japanese watching behind their white masks. Yet, at that moment when he was about to despair of ever finding his parents, he felt a surge of hope.

He knelt on the floor and took the mess-tin from the injured sailor, aware of a faint scent of cologne and certain now that together they could leave the detention centre and make their way to the safety of the prison camps.

'Basie!' he cried. 'Everything's all right!'

14

American Aircraft

'The war's going to be over soon, Basie. I've seen American planes, Curtiss bombers and Boeings . . .'

'Boeings . . .? Jim you're – '

'Don't talk, Basie. I'm working for you now, just like Frank.'

Jim squatted by the American sailor, trying to remember the amahs of his early childhood. He had never looked after anything before, except for an angora rabbit that had died tragically within a few days. He tilted the mess-tin and tried to pour a little water into Basie's mouth, then dipped his fingers in the murky fluid and let Basie suck them.

For three weeks Jim had devoted himself to the cabin steward, bringing his ration of boiled rice and sweet potatoes, fetching water from the tap in the corridor. He sat for hours beside Basie, fanning the sailor as he lay on his mat below the transom window. The stream of fresh air soon revived him, and one by one he pulled away the paper bandages fluttering on his face and wrists. Helped by Jim, he moved his mat from the English soldier dying against the wall. Within a week he had recovered enough of his strength to keep an eye on the Japanese guards and the comings and goings of the Eurasian woman who cooked for the prisoners.

As he cleaned Basie's mess-tin Jim wondered if the sailor really recognized him. Did he know that Jim had managed to trick him? Perhaps he would report Jim to the other prisoners, but there was little that they could do. Relieved that at last he had an ally in his struggle with the Eurasian women, he rested his head on his knees.

He felt Basie nudge him with the mess-tins.

'Chow time, Jim. Get in line.' As Jim sat up, hoping that he had not talked in his sleep, Basie wiped some of the dirt from his cheek. The steward's canny eyes took in every detail of Jim's shabby state. 'Make yourself useful to Mrs Blackburn, Jim. Ingratiate yourself a little. A woman always needs help with her fire.'

Somehow, during his visits to the latrine, Basie had learned the Eurasian woman's name. Jim ran from the store-room with the two mess-tins. The other prisoners followed, the old men stirring from their mats. Mr Partridge took the mess-tin from the hand of the English soldier who sat in a pool of urine by the wall.

Smoke rose from the courtyard behind the ticket kiosk. The Eurasian woman fanned the briquettes in her stove, but the rice and sweet potatoes in the congs had gone off the boil. A Japanese soldier stared gloomily at the tepid swill, and shook his head at the hungry prisoners. They shuffled among the teak benches of the cinema, sat down and stared at the smoke drifting across the empty screen.

Holding the mess-tins, Jim hovered around Mrs Blackburn and treated her to his keenest smile. She disliked Jim, but allowed him to chop the basket of firewood. He pushed the spills into the stove and blew hard to ignite them. He fanned the embers until the briquettes caught light again. Half an hour later, with the Japanese soldier's approval, Jim was rewarded with his first fair ration.

Basie was satisfied but unimpressed. After finishing his meal he propped himself on his elbows. He gazed at his fellow prisoners, some too exhausted to eat their rations, and tore the last of the paper bandages from the cuts over his eyes. Whatever had befallen him in Shanghai Central Prison – and Jim never dared to ask about Frank – he had once again become the ex-steward of the Cathay-American Line, ready to assemble a small part of a ramshackle world around himself. He surveyed Jim again, taking in his ragged clothes and scarecrow appearance, his deepset and yellowing eyes. Without comment, he gave Jim a piece of potato skin.

'Say, thanks, Basie.'

'I'm looking after you, Jim.'

Jim devoured the shred of potato. 'You're looking after me, Basie.'

'You helped Mrs Blackburn?'

'I ingratiated myself. I made myself very useful to Mrs Blackburn.'

'That's it. If you can find a way of helping people you'll live off the interest.'

'Like this piece of potato . . . Basie, when you were in Shanghai Central did anyone talk about my mother and father?'

'I think I did hear something, Jim.' Basie cupped his hand conspiratorially. 'Good news, they're in one of the camps and looking forward to seeing you. I'll find out which one for you.'

'Thanks, Basie!'

From then on Jim regularly helped Mrs Blackburn. Every morning he was up at dawn to rake the ash from the stove, chop firewood and lay the briquettes. Long before the water in the congs began to boil Jim had already earmarked sweet potatoes for Basie and himself, selecting those with the least blight and fungus. He saw to it that Mrs Blackburn served them the thicker rice, into which, at Basie's suggestion, he had been careful to stir the minimum of water. After their meal, when the other prisoners rinsed their tins at the latrine tap, Basie always sent Jim to fill their mess-tins with the tepid water in the potato cong. Basie insisted that he and Jim drank only this grey, pithy liquid.

Although, like everyone else, Basie was never keen for Jim to come too close to him, he clearly approved of Jim's

117

efforts. At the end of his second week at the detention centre Basie allowed him to move his sleeping mat beside his own. Lying at Basie's feet, Jim could intercept Mrs Blackburn on her way to the kiosk.

'Always look light on your toes, Jim.' Basie lay back as Jim fanned him. 'Whatever happens, keep moving around the court. Your dad would agree with me.'

'Actually, he would agree with you. After the war you can play tennis together. He's really good.'

'Well . . . What I meant, Jim, is that I'm trying to keep up your education. Your dad would appreciate that.'

'I think he'll give you a reward, Basie.' Jim assumed that the notion of a reward would spur Basie in his search for his father. 'Once he gave five dollars to a taxi-driver who brought me home from Hongkew.'

'Did he, Jim?' At times Basie seemed unsure whether Jim was having him on. 'Tell me, did you see any planes today?'

'A Nakajima Shoki and a Zero-Sen.'

'And American planes?'

'I haven't seen those again. Not since you came, Basie. I saw them for three days and then they went away.'

'I thought they had. They must have been a special kind of reconnaissance flight.'

'To see how we all are? Where did they come from, Basie? Wake Island?'

'A long way, Jim. It must have been just about the end of their range.' Basie took the fan from Jim's hand. An elderly Australian had arrived to talk to Basie about the war. 'Go and help Mrs Blackburn. And remember to bow to Sergeant Uchida.'

'I always bow, Basie.'

Jim hovered around the conversation, hoping to catch the latest news, but the two men waved him away. Basie was surprisingly well informed about the progress of the war, the fall of Hong Kong, Manila and the Dutch East Indies, the surrender of Singapore and the unbroken advance of Japan across the Pacific. The only good news in all this were the flights of American planes that Jim had seen over Shanghai, but for some reason Basie never mentioned them. He liked to talk out of the side of his mouth, telling the old Britishers about the other inmates at Shanghai Central Prison, who had died and who had been handed over to the Swiss Red Cross. Basie even sold information for small scraps of food. Mr Partridge gave him his potato for news of his brother-in-law in Nanking. Inspired by this, Jim tried to tell Mrs Blackburn about the American aircraft, but she merely sent him back to the briquettes.

Now that he felt stronger, Jim realized how important it was to be obsessed by food. Shared equally among the prisoners, their daily rations were not enough to keep them alive. Many of the prisoners had died, and anyone who sacrificed himself for the others soon died too. The only way to leave the detention centre was to stay alive. As long as he ran errands for Basie, worked hard for Mrs Blackburn and bowed to Sergeant Uchida all would be well.

Nonetheless, some of Basie's ruses unsettled Jim. On the morning Mrs Partridge died Basie learned some encouraging news about the brother-in-law in Nanking, and soon after was able to sell the old woman's hair-brushes to Mrs Blackburn. Whenever anyone died Basie would be on hand with news and comfort, though death was an elastic term for the cabin steward, open to all manner of interpretation. Jim collected Private Blake's rations for two days after he lay without moving on the store-room floor, the skin stretched across his ribs like rice-paper around a lantern. He knew that the private had died of the same fever that he and many of the prisoners had caught. But already Jim was looking at the elderly missionaries with an expectant eye, waiting for fever to recruit the old men. Once he and Basie had admitted their part in this supplementary ration scheme all guilt had gone.

Jim noticed how different Basie was from his father in this respect. At home, if he did anything wrong, the consequences seemed to overlay everything for days. With Basie they vanished instantly. For the first time in his life Jim felt free to do what he wanted. All sorts of wayward ideas moved through his mind, fuelled by hunger and the excitement of stealing from the old prisoners. As he rested between his errands in front of the empty cinema screen he thought of the American aircraft he had seen in the clouds above Shanghai. He could almost summon them into his vision, a silver fleet on the far side of the sky. Jim saw them most when he was hungry, and he hoped that Private Blake, who must always have been hungry, had also seen them.

15

On their Way to the Camps

On the day of the Englishwoman's death a fresh consignment of prisoners arrived at the detention centre. Jim was
hovering in the doorway of the women's store-room, as Mrs
Blackburn and the daughter of the old Dutchman tried to
comfort the two sons. The mother lay on the stone floor in
her drenched frock, like a drowned corpse raised from the
river. The brothers kept turning towards her, as if expecting her to give them some last instruction. Jim felt sad for
the boys, Paul and David, though he hardly knew them.
They seemed much younger than Jim, but in fact both were
more than a year older.

Jim had his eyes on the mother's mess-tin and tennis
shoes. Most of the Allied prisoners had far better shoes than
the Japanese soldiers, and he had noticed that the bodies
leaving the detention centre had bare feet. But as he sidled
into the room there was a shrill whistle from the courtyard,
and a series of barked shouts. Sergeant Uchida was working
himself up to the pitch of anger that he needed to attain in
order to issue the simplest instructions. Masks over their
faces, the Japanese soldiers began to herd from the store-
rooms everyone who could walk. A truck had stopped
outside the cinema, and its prisoners stood unsteadily in the
road.

All designs on the dead woman's tennis shoes vanished
from Jim's head. At last he would be leaving for the camps
in the countryside around Shanghai. Pushing past the two
boys, Jim dived between the guards and raced up the steps.
He lined up beside his fellow prisoners – Mr Partridge with
his wife's suitcase, as if about to take his memories of her on

a long journey, Paul and David, the Dutch woman and her father, and several of the old missionaries. Basie stood behind them, his white cheeks hidden behind the collar of his seaman's jacket, so self-effacing as to be almost invisible. He had erased himself from the small world of the detention centre, which he had manipulated for a few weeks, and would re-emerge like some marine parasite from its shell once he reached the more succulent terrain of the prison camps.

The new arrivals appeared, two Annamese women and a group of older Britishers and Belgians, the sick and elderly carried on stretchers by the Chinese orderlies. Counting their yellow eyes, Jim knew that there would soon be extra mess-tins.

His cotton mask over his face, Sergeant Uchida began to select prisoners for transport to the camps. He shook his head at Mr Partridge and kicked the suitcase in an exasperated way. He pointed to the Dutch woman and her father, Paul and David, and two elderly missionary couples.

Jim licked his fingers and wiped the soot from his cheeks. The sergeant motioned Basie towards the truck. Without a glance at Jim, the cabin steward stepped between the guards, his arms around the shoulders of the two boys.

Sergeant Uchida pressed his fingers against Jim's grimy forehead. With his constant bowing and smiling, his eagerness to run errands, Jim had been a perpetual nuisance to the sergeant, who was clearly glad to be rid of him. Then he glanced at the party of new arrivals, who stared listlessly at the cold stove, at the scum of boiled rice around the rim of the cong.

The sergeant cupped his hand around Jim's neck. With a shout muffled by his cotton mask he propelled him towards the stove. As Jim picked himself from his knees the sergeant kicked the coal-sacks, scattering briquettes across the stone floor.

Jim riddled the clinkers from the fire-box. The new arrivals wandered among the benches and took their seats facing the empty cinema screen, as if expecting a film show to begin. Basie and the Dutch couple, Paul and David, the old missionaries stood in the street behind the open army truck, watched at a distance by a crowd of rickshaw coolies and peasant women.

'Basie . . . !' Jim called. 'I'll still work for you . . . !' But the steward had lost interest in him. Already he had befriended Paul and David, inducting them into his entourage. They helped Basie as he clambered on his bruised knees over the tail-gate of the truck.

'Basie . . .' Jim riddled fiercely. He glared at the cinema screen, crossed by the first shadows of the Shanghai hotels. A Japanese soldier in a face-mask counted out a stack of mess-tins. As the injured prisoners were carried past on their stretchers Jim knew that most of the inmates of the detention centre had been sent there because they were very old or were expected to die, either of dysentery and typhoid, or whatever fever he and Private Blake had caught from the foul water. He was certain that many of the prisoners would soon die, and that if he stayed at the detention centre he would die with them. Already the Annamese women had collected the mess-tins from the soldier. They were pointing to the stove and the sacks of briquettes. When they took over the cooking of the rice and sweet potatoes they would not give Jim his fair ration. He would see the American aircraft again, and he would die.

'Basie . . . ?' Jim threw down the riddle. The last of the departing prisoners had taken their seats in the truck. The Japanese soldier by the tail-gate lowered the Dutch woman on to the wooden floor. Basie sat between the two English boys, making a toy from a piece of wire in his hand. The truck started up, moved forward a few feet and stopped. The Japanese driver shouted from his window. He waved a canvas map-wallet and slapped the metal door with his fist. The guards on the pavement shouted back, eager to close the gates of the detention centre and put their feet up in the orderly room. Then the engine stalled, and there was an instant clamour of angry voices, the soldiers and driver arguing over the destination of the truck.

'Woosung . . .' Sergeant Uchida lowered his cotton mask. His face was reddening, and drops of spittle formed on his lips, like pus forced from a wound. Already in a fury with the driver, he strode through the open gates. The driver had stepped from his cabin, unaware of the tornado about to engulf him. He dusted the map and spread it against the fender of the truck, shrugging hopelessly at the maze of nearby streets.

Jim followed Sergeant Uchida to the gates. He could see that neither the sergeant nor the Japanese driver had any idea of the whereabouts of Woosung, an agricultural district at the mouth of the Yangtze that lay beyond the northern suburbs of Shanghai. The driver gestured towards the Bund and Nantao, and climbed into his cabin. He sat passively when Sergeant Uchida pushed through the bored guards and began to scream abuse at him.

Standing beside the guards, Jim waited for Sergeant Uchida to reach the climax of his tirade, when he would be forced to make a decision. Sure enough, the sergeant searched the crowded skyline of tenement buildings and godowns, then pointed at random to a cobbled street with a disused tramline. Unimpressed, the driver cleared his throat. Wearily he started his engine and spat a ball of phlegm into the road, where it lay at Jim's feet.

'Straight on . . . !' Jim called up to him. 'Woosung – it's over there : . . !' He pointed to the street with the rusty tramlines.

Sergeant Uchida cuffed Jim on the head, bruising both his ears. He cuffed him again, bringing blood from his mouth. At that moment a cloud of smoke billowed through the gates. The Annamese women had lit the stove with the rain-soaked firewood, and the smoke filled the open-air cinema, drifting across the benches as if the screen were ablaze.

Glad to be rid of Jim, Sergeant Uchida seized him in his strong hands. He swung him over the tail-gate of the truck, shouting to the Japanese guard who sat with the prisoners. The soldier dragged Jim across the laps of the Dutch woman and her father. As the truck pulled away from the detention centre, its wheels already locked in the tramlines, Jim clambered forward to the camouflaged driving cabin. He steadied himself against the pitching roof, and ignored the stream of oaths hurled at him by the driver. He raised his bloody mouth to the wind, letting the foul odours of Shanghai flush his lungs, happy to be on the way to his parents again.

16
The Water Ration

Were they lost? For an hour, as they trundled through the industrial suburbs of northern Shanghai, Jim gripped the wooden bar behind the driving cabin, his head filled with a dozen compass bearings. He grinned to himself, forgetting his illness and the desperate weeks in the open-air cinema. His knees ached from the constant swaying, and at times he had to hold on to the leather belt of the Japanese soldier beside him. But at last he was moving towards the open countryside, and the welcoming world of the prison camps.

The endless streets of Chapei ran past, an area of tenements and derelict cotton mills, police barracks and shanty towns built on the banks of black canals. They drove below the overhead conveyors of a steel works decorated with dragon-festival hoardings, dreams of fire conjured from its silent furnaces. Shuttered pawnshops stood outside the abandoned radio and cigarette factories, and platoons of Chinese puppet troops patrolled the Del Monte brewery and the Dodge truck depot. Jim had never been to Chapei. Before the war a small English boy would have been killed for his shoes within minutes. Now he was safe, guarded by the Japanese soldiers – he laughed over this so much that the Dutch woman reached out a hand to calm him.

But Jim relished the foetid air, the smell of human fertilizer from the open sewage congs that signalled the approach of the countryside. Even the driver's hostility failed to worry him. Whenever they stopped at a military checkpoint the driver would put his head out of the cabin and wave a warning finger at Jim, as if this eleven-year-old prisoner was responsible for the absurd expedition.

Watching the sun's angle, as he had done for hours in the detention centre, Jim made certain that they were moving north. They passed the ruins of the Chapei ceramic works, its kilns shaped like the German forts at Tsingtao. Its trademark stood beside the gates, a Chinese teapot three storeys high built entirely from green bricks. During the Sino-Japanese War of 1937 it had been holed by shell-fire, and now resembled a punctured globe of the earth. Thousands of the bricks had migrated across the surrounding fields to the villages beside the works canal, incorporated in the huts and dwellings, a vision of a magical rural China.

These strange dislocations appealed to Jim. For the first time he felt able to enjoy the war. He gazed happily at the burnt-out trams and tenement blocks, at the thousands of doors open to the clouds, a deserted city invaded by the sky. It only disappointed him that his fellow prisoners failed to share his excitement. They sat glumly on the benches, staring at their feet. One of the missionary women lay on the floor, tended by another prisoner, a sandy-haired Britisher with a bruised cheek who held her wrist with one hand and pressed her diaphragm with the other. The two English boys, still barely aware of their mother's death, sat between Basie and the Dutch couple.

Jim waited until Basie looked up, but the cabin steward seemed hardly to recognize him. His attention had turned to the two boys, and he had moved deftly into the vacuum in their lives. From the page of a Chinese newspaper he folded a series of paper animals, chuckling when the boys gave a weak laugh. Like a depraved conjuror, he slid his hands into the pockets of their school trousers and cardigans, searching for anything of use.

Jim watched him without resentment. He and Basie had collaborated at the detention centre in order to stay alive, but Basie, rightly, had dispensed with Jim as soon as he could leave for the camps.

The truck struck a deep gully in the cobbles, slewed across the road and came to a halt by the grass bank. They had left the northern outskirts of Shanghai and were entering an area of untilled fields and rice-paddies. Beyond a line of burial mounds two hundred yards away a canal ran towards a deserted village. The Japanese driver jumped from his cabin and bent over the front wheels of the truck. He began to talk to the steaming engine, now and then including Jim in his mutterings. He was only twenty years old, but had clearly suffered a lifetime of exasperation. Jim kept his head down, but the driver stepped on to the running board, levelled a finger at him and delivered a long harangue that sounded like a declaration of war.

The driver returned to his cabin, grumbling over his map, and Basie commented: 'Add that up any way you like and we're still lost.' Already his attention had moved from the boys to whatever advantage could be gained from their situation. 'Jim, do you know where you're taking us?'

'Woosung. I've been to the country club there, Basie.'

Basie played with his paper animals. 'We're going to the country club,' he told the boys. 'If Jim can find it for us.'

'As long as we reach the river, Basie. Then it's either east or west.'

'That's a big help. East or west . . .'

The sandy-haired Briton beside the missionary woman rose from his knees. There was a large, leaking bruise on his forehead and left cheekbone, as if he had recently been struck in the face by a rifle stock. In some pain, he settled himself on the bench. Long freckled legs emerged from his khaki shorts and ended in a pair of thonged sandals. In his late twenties, he carried no luggage or possessions, but he had the self-assured manner of the Royal Navy officers who cut such a dash at the Shanghai garden parties, thrilling the mothers of Jim's friends. He ignored the Japanese guard, talking across him as if he were a mess-boy who would soon

128

be dismissed to his quarters. Jim assumed that he was one of those tiresome Englishmen who refused to grasp that they had been defeated.

The man touched the bruise on his face and turned to Jim, whose ragged figure he appraised without comment. 'The Japanese have captured so much ground they've run out of maps,' he remarked amiably. 'Jim, does that mean they're lost?'

Jim thought about this. 'Not really. They just haven't captured any maps.'

'Good – never confuse the map with the territory. You'll get us to Woosung.'

'Can't we go back to the detention centre, Dr Ransome?' one of the missionaries asked. 'We're very tired.'

The physician stared at the abandoned paddy fields, and at the prostrate old woman at his feet. 'It might be for the best. This poor soul can't take much more.'

The truck moved forward again, trundling at a half-hearted pace down the empty road. Jim returned to his post by the driving cabin, and scanned the fields for anything that might remotely resemble Woosung. The doctor's words unsettled him. Even if they were lost, how could he want to return to the detention centre?

Jim knew that the fury of Sergeant Uchida made it unlikely that the driver would dare to turn back. But he kept a careful watch on Dr Ransome, trying to guess whether he spoke enough Japanese to demoralize the driver. He seemed to have difficulty with his sight, especially when looking at Jim, at whom he squinted in a curious way. Jim decided that he had entered the war at a later stage than Basie and himself. He had probably come from one of the missionary settlements in the interior, and had no idea of what went on at the detention centre.

But were they lost, or on course? The direction of the shadows cast by the wayside telegraph poles had barely changed – Jim had always been interested in shadows, ever since his father had shown him how to calculate the height of even the highest building by pacing out its shadow on the ground. They were still heading north-west, and would soon reach the Shanghai-Woosung railway line. Steam hissed from the truck's radiator. The spray cooled Jim's face, but the driver's fist drummed warningly against the door, and Jim knew that he was deciding when to stop and turn back for Shanghai.

Resigning himself to the wasted journey, and to their return to the detention centre, Jim studied the guard's bolt-action rifle and its imperial chrysanthemum crest. The Dutch woman pulled at his soot-stained blazer.

'Over there, James. Is that . . . ?'

A burnt-out aircraft lay on the banks of a disused canal. Wild grass and nettles grew through its wings, almost invading the cockpit, but the squadron insignia were still legible.

'It's a Nakajima,' he told Mrs Hug, pleased by this shared interest in plane-spotting. 'It only has two machine-guns.'

'Only two? But that's very many . . .'

The Dutch woman seemed impressed, but Jim had turned his attention from the aircraft. On the far side of the paddy field, hidden by the nettles, was the embankment of a railway line. A squad of Japanese soldiers rested on the concrete platform of a wayside station, cooking a meal on a fire of sticks. A camouflaged staff car was parked beside the tracks. It was loaded with coils of wire which these signals engineers were re-stringing between the telegraph poles.

'Mrs Hug . . . that's the railway to Woosung!'

As steam bathed the driving cabin, the truck had stopped. It began to reverse. Beside Jim the Japanese guard was lighting a cigarette for the return journey. Jim pulled at his belt and pointed across the paddy field. The soldier followed his outstretched arm and then pushed him on to the floor. He shouted to the driver, who tossed his map-wallet on to the seat beside him. Engine steaming, the truck strained at the camber, made a half circle and set off along the dirt track to the railway station.

Dr Ransome steadied the English boys as they slipped from Basie's grasp and swayed against the missionary woman. He helped Jim from the floor.

'Good work, Jim. They'll have water for us – you must be thirsty.'

'A bit. I had a drink at the detention centre.'

'That was sensible. How long were you there?'

Jim had forgotten. 'Quite a long time.'

'So I imagine.' Dr Ransome brushed the dirt from Jim's blazer. 'It used to be a cinema?'

'But they didn't show films.'

'I can see that.'

Jim sat back, patting his knees and beaming at Mrs Hug. The prisoners sat weakly on the facing benches, jerked to and fro like life-size puppets that had lost their stuffing. Far from reviving them, the drive from Shanghai had made them look sallow and nervous. But Jim smiled at the rusting aircraft on the canal bank. There was now no danger that they would return to the detention centre. The Japanese soldier had thrown away his cigarette and held his rifle in a military way. A signals corporal jumped from the railway platform and crossed the track.

'Mrs Hug, I don't think we'll be going back to Shanghai.'

'No, James – you must have very sharp eyes. When you grow up you should be a pilot.'

'I probably will. I have been in a plane, Mrs Hug. At Hungjao Aerodrome.'

'Did it fly?'

'Well, in a way.' Confidences given to adults often led further than Jim intended. He was aware that Dr Ransome was watching him. The doctor sat beside Mrs Hug's father,

131

whose painful breathing he was trying to help. But his eyes were fixed on Jim, taking in his stick-like legs and ragged clothes, his small, excited face. As they reached the railway line he gave Jim an encouraging smile, which Jim decided not to return. He knew that for some reason Dr Ransome disapproved of him. But Dr Ransome had not been to the detention centre.

They stopped by the railway tracks. The driver saluted the corporal and followed him to the station, where he spread his map across the cabinet of the field telephone. The prisoners sat in the warm sunlight as the corporal pointed to the drained paddies. A haze of dust rose from the untilled earth, a white veil that screened the distant skyscrapers of Shanghai. A convoy of Japanese trucks drove along the road, a brief blare of noise that merged with the distant drone of a cargo aircraft.

Jim changed benches and sat beside Mrs Hug, who supported her aged father against her breast. Two of the missionary women lay on the floor of the truck, as the other prisoners dozed and fretted. Basie had lost interest in the English boys, and was watching Jim over the bloodstained collar of his coat.

Thousands of flies gathered around the truck, attracted by the sweat and the urine running across the wooden boards. Jim waited for the driver to return with his map, but he sat on a bale of telephone wire, talking to two soldiers who cooked the midday meal. Their voices and the clicks of the burning wood carried across the steel tracks, magnified by the dome of light that enclosed them.

Jim fidgeted in his seat as the sun pricked his skin. He could see the smallest detail of everything around him, the flakes of rust on the railway lines, the saw-teeth of the nettles beside the truck, the white soil bearing the imprint of its worn tyres. Jim counted the blue bristles around the lips of the Japanese soldier guarding them, and the globes of mucus which this bored sentry sucked in and out of his nostrils. He watched the damp stain spreading around the buttocks of one of the missionary women on the floor, and the flames that fingered the cooking pot on the station platform, reflected in the polished breeches of the stacked rifles.

Only once before had Jim seen the world as vividly as this. Were the American planes about to come again? With an exaggerated squint, intended to annoy Dr Ransome, he searched the sky. He wanted to see everything, every cobblestone in the streets of Chapei, the overgrown gardens in Amherst Avenue, his mother and father, together in the silver light of the American aircraft.

Without thinking, Jim stood up and shouted. But the Japanese guard pushed him roughly against the bench. The soldiers on the railway platform sat amid the clutter of signals equipment, cramming their mouths with rice and fish. The corporal called to the truck, and the guard stepped over the missionary women and jumped from the tail-gate. He rested his rifle on the railway line and moved with his bayonet through the dried stubble of the wild sugar-cane. As soon as he had gathered sufficient kindling for the fire he joined the soldiers on the platform.

For an hour the smoke rose into the sunlight. Jim sat on the bench and brushed the flies from his face, eager to explore the railway station and the crashed aircraft near the canal. Whenever anyone moved, the Japanese shouted from the platform and pointed their cigarettes in a warning way. The prisoners had taken no rations or water with them, but there were two jerry-cans in the staff car from which the soldiers filled their canteens.

When Mrs Hug's father was forced to lie on the floor Dr Ransome protested to the Japanese. He stood unsteadily by the tail-gate, ignoring their abuse and pointing to the exhausted passengers at his feet. The bruise on his cheek had been inflamed by the sun and the flies, and had almost closed his eye. Standing there stoically, he reminded Jim of the beggars parading their wounds on the streets of Shanghai. The Japanese corporal was unimpressed, but after a leisurely stroll around the truck he allowed the prisoners to dismount. Helped by the husbands, Basie and Dr Ransome eased the old women on to the ground, where they lay in the shade between the rear wheels.

Jim squatted on the white earth, tracing the tyre patterns with a stick. How many times would each tyre have to rotate before it wore itself through to the canvas? The problem, one of a host that perpetually bothered him, was in fact fairly easy to solve. Jim smoothed the white dust and made a start at the arithmetic. He gave a cheer when the first fraction cancelled itself, and then noticed that he was alone in the open sunlight between the truck and the railway embankment.

Tended by a weary Dr Ransome, the prisoners huddled in the scanty shade below the tail-gate. Basie sat slumped inside his seaman's jacket, and he and the old men looked as dead as the discarded mannequins Jim had often seen in the alley behind the Sincere Company's department store.

They needed water, or one of them would die and they would all have to return to Shanghai. Jim watched the Japanese on the platform. The meal had ended, and two of the soldiers uncoiled a bale of telephone wire. Kicking a stone in front of him, Jim wandered towards the railway embankment. He stepped across the rails, and without a pause climbed on to the concrete platform.

Still savouring their meal, the Japanese sat around the cinders of their fire. They watched Jim as he bowed and stood to attention in his ragged clothes. None of them waved him away, but Jim knew that this was not the time to treat them to his brightest smile. He realized that Dr Ransome could not approach the Japanese so soon after their meal without being knocked down or even killed.

He waited as the driver spoke to the signals corporal. Pointing repeatedly to Jim, he delivered what seemed to be a long lecture on the enormous nuisance to the Japanese Army caused by this one small boy. The corporal laughed at this, in a good humour after his fish. He took a Coca Cola bottle from his knapsack and half-filled it with water from his canteen. Holding it in the air, he beckoned Jim towards him.

Jim took the bottle, bowed steeply and stepped back three paces. Masking their smiles, the Japanese watched him silently. Beside the truck, Basie and Dr Ransome leaned from the shadows, their eyes fixed on the sun-bright fluid in the bottle. Clearly they assumed that he would carry the water to them and share out this unexpected ration.

Carefully, Jim wiped the bottle on the sleeve of his blazer. He lifted it to his lips, drank slowly, trying not to choke, paused and finished the last drops.

The Japanese burst into laughter, chortling to each other with great amusement. Jim laughed with them, well aware that only he, among the British prisoners, appreciated the joke. Basie ventured a wary smile, but Dr Ransome seemed baffled. The corporal took the Coca Cola bottle from Jim and filled it to the neck. Still chuckling to themselves, the soldiers climbed to their feet and returned to the task of stringing the telephone wire.

Followed by the driver and the armed guard, Jim carried the bottle across the tracks. He handed it to Dr Ransome, who stared at him without comment. He drank briefly, and passed the tepid liquid to the others, helping the driver to refill the bottle from the canteen. One of the missionary women was sick, and vomited the water into the dust at his feet.

Jim took up his position behind the driving cabin. He knew that he had been right to drink the first water himself. The others, including Basie and Dr Ransome, had been thirsty, but only he had been prepared to risk everything for the few drops of water. The Japanese might have thrown him on to the track and broken his legs across the railway lines, as they did to the Chinese soldiers whom they killed at Siccawei Station. Already Jim felt himself apart from the others, who had behaved as passively as the Chinese peasants. Jim realized that he was closer to the Japanese, who had seized Shanghai and sunk the American fleet at Pearl Harbor. He listened to the sound of a transport plane hidden beyond the haze of white dust, and thought again of carrier decks out on the Pacific, of small men in baggy flying suits standing by their unarmoured aircraft, ready to chance everything on little more than their own will.

17

A Landscape of Airfields

As the driver filled the truck's radiator with water, Dr Ransome settled Mrs Hug on the seat beside the English boys. To Jim it seemed that the two missionary women on the floor were now barely alive, with blanched lips and eyes like those of poisoned mice. Flies swarmed over their faces, darting in and out of their nostrils. After lifting them into the truck, Dr Ransome was too exhausted to help them, and rested his arms on his heavy knees. Their husbands sat side by side and stared at them in a resigned way, as if a taste for lying on the floor was a minor eccentricity shared by their wives.

Jim leaned against the roof of the driving cabin. Aware of the gap that now separated Jim from his fellow prisoners, Dr Ransome moved forward and sat on the bench next to him. The dusty sunlight and the long journey from Shanghai had leached the pigment from his freckles. Despite his strong chest and legs he was far more tired than Jim had realized. Blood had broken through the inflamed bruise on his face, and the first pus gathered around his eye.

He bowed and made way for the Japanese soldier who stationed himself next to Jim.

'Well, we all feel better for the water. That was brave of you, Jim. Where do you come from?'

'Shanghai!'

'You're proud of it?'

'Of course . . .' Jim scoffed at the question, shaking his head as if Dr Ransome was a provincial country healer. 'Shanghai is the biggest city in the world. My father says it's even larger than London.'

'Let's hope it can stay larger – there may be one or two hungry winters. Where are your parents, Jim?'

'They went away.' Jim thought about his answer, deciding whether to invent some spoof for Dr Ransome. There was a self-confident air about this young physician that he distrusted, the same attitude shown by people newly arrived from England – Jim wondered how the British newsreels were explaining away the surrender of Singapore. He could easily imagine Dr Ransome getting into a brawl with the Japanese guards, and causing everyone trouble. Yet for all his display of public spirit, Dr Ransome had drunk more than his fair share of the water. Jim had also noticed that Dr Ransome was less interested in the dying old people than he pretended. 'They're at Woosung Camp,' he said. 'They are alive, you know.'

'I'm very glad. Woosung Camp? So you might be seeing them soon?'

'Very soon . . .' Jim gazed across the silent paddy fields. The thought of seeing his mother made him smile, an act which strained the muscles of his face. She would have no idea of all his adventures during the past four months. Even if he told her everything it would seem like one of those secret afternoons before the war when he had cycled all over Shanghai and come back with hair-raising stories he could never tell. 'Yes, I'll be seeing them soon. I want them to meet Basie.'

Basie's sallow face withdrew behind the collar of his jacket. He peered warily at the Japanese beside the railway tracks, as if suspicious of what was in store for them in these naked fields. 'I'll meet your folks, Jim.' To Dr Ransome he added, without any enthusiasm: 'I've been keeping an eye on the boy.'

'You kept an eye on me. Basie tried to sell me in Shanghai.'

'Did he? That sounds like a good idea.'

138

'To the Hongkew merchants. But I wasn't worth anything. He looked after me as well.'

'He's done a good job.' Dr Ransome patted Jim's shoulder. He slipped a hand around Jim's waist and felt his swollen liver, then raised his upper lip and glanced at his teeth.

'It's all right, Jim. I was trying to guess what you've been eating. We'll all have to take up gardening at Woosung. Perhaps the Japanese will sell us a goat.'

'A goat?' Jim had never seen a goat, an exotic beast of great moodiness and independence, qualities he admired.

'Are you interested in animals, Jim?'

'Yes . . . not much. What I'm really interested in is aviation.'

'Aviation? Aeroplanes, you mean?'

'Not exactly.' Casually, Jim added: 'I sat in the cockpit of a Japanese fighter.'

'You admire Japanese pilots?'

'They're brave . . .'

'And that's important?'

'It's a good idea if you want to win a war.' Jim listened to the drone of a distant aircraft. He was suspicious of the physician, of his long legs and his English manner and his interest in teeth. Perhaps he and Basie would team up as corpse-robbers? Jim thought about the goat which Dr Ransome wanted to buy from the Japanese. Everything he had read about goats confirmed that they were difficult and wayward creatures, and this suggested that there was something impractical about Dr Ransome. Few Europeans had gold teeth, and the only dead people the doctor was likely to see for a long time would be Europeans.

Jim decided to ignore Dr Ransome. He stood next to the Japanese guard, his hands warmed by the camouflaged roof of the driving cabin. As they set off towards the highway the

139

soldiers were walking along the railway tracks, unwinding lengths of telephone wire. Were they about to launch a man-carrying kite? The furthest soldier was already lost in the haze of white dust, and his blurred figure seemed to rise from the ground. Jim laughed to himself, thinking that the soldier might suddenly soar into the sky over their heads. Helped by his father, Jim had flown dozens of kites from the garden at Amherst Avenue. He was fascinated by the dragon kites that floated behind the Chinese wedding and funeral parties, and by the fighting kites flown from the quays at Pootung, diving across each other with razor-sharp lines coated in powdered glass. But best of all were the man-flying kites which his father had seen in northern China, with a dozen lines held by hundreds of men. One day Jim would fly in a man-flying kite, and stand on the shoulder of the wind . . .

The air rushed into his watering eyes as the truck sped along the open road. Confident of his bearings, the driver was eager to deliver his prisoners to Woosung and return to Shanghai before nightfall. Jim held tight to the cabin roof, while the prisoners huddled on the seats behind him. The two missionary husbands were already sitting on the floor, and Dr Ransome helped Mrs Hug to lie under the bench.

But Jim had lost interest in them. They were now entering an area of military airfields. These former Chinese bases, which once guarded the Yangtze estuary, were being occupied by the Japanese Army and Navy Air Forces. They passed a bomb-damaged fighter base where Japanese engineers were welding a new roof on to the steel shell of a hangar. A line of Zero pursuit planes stood on the grass field, and a pilot in full flying gear strode between the wings. Without thinking, Jim waved to him, but the pilot was lost among the propellers.

Two miles ahead, beyond an empty village and its burnt-out pagoda, they were delayed by a convoy of trucks carrying the wings and fuselages of two-engined bombers. A squadron of the machines faced the afternoon sun, ready to take off and attack the Chinese armies to the west. All this activity excited Jim. When they stopped at the military checkpoint on the Soochow Road he was impatient to move on. He sat next to Basie, kicking his heels as a sergeant in the kempetai checked the list of prisoners and Dr Ransome protested about the condition of the missionary women.

Soon after, they left the highway and joined an unpaved secondary road that ran beside an industrial canal. Japanese tanks moved past, lashed to the decks of motorized lighters, while their gun crews slept on the canvas hatches. Usually Jim's imagination would have feasted on these battle vehicles, but by now he was only interested in aircraft. He wished he had flown with the Japanese pilots as they attacked Pearl Harbor and destroyed the US Pacific Fleet, or ridden in the torpedo bombers that had sunk the *Repulse* and the *Prince of Wales*. Perhaps, when the war ended, he would join the Japanese Air Force and wear the Rising Sun stitched to his shoulders, like the American pilots who had flown with the Flying Tigers and worn the flag of Nationalist China on their leather jackets.

Although his legs were exhausted, Jim was still standing behind the driver's cabin as they sped towards the gates of the internment camp at Woosung. In his mind, he had identified the Japanese aircraft of the Yangtze plain with his confidence that he would soon see his parents again. A single-engined fighter overtook them and climbed into the late afternoon sky, lifted by the golden glaze on the undersurface of its wings. Jim raised his arms and let the sun fall on the camouflage paint that stained his hands and wrists, imagining that he too was an aircraft. Behind him the Dutch woman had collapsed on the floor of the truck. She lay at the feet of her elderly father as Dr Ransome and the Japanese soldier tried to lift her on to the seat.

They crossed a wooden bridge over the arm of an artificial lake, and passed the burnt-out shell of the country club whose mock-Tudor timbers of painted cement had alone failed to catch fire. The hull of a pleasure launch lay in the shallows, its decks penetrated by reeds that advanced up the beach to the embers of the hotel.

Ahead of them a military truck was turning through the gates of a disused stockyard, through which an even greater fire had recently swept. Bored Japanese soldiers lounged outside the guardhouse, and watched a gang of Chinese labourers nailing lengths of barbed wire to a line of pine posts. Behind the guardhouse was the building contractor's store, surrounded by piles of planks and fencing timber, and a bamboo shelter where a second group of coolies dozed on their mats beside a charcoal brazier.

The truck stopped by the guardhouse, where the driver and his prisoners together gazed at this desolate site. The former stockyard was being converted into a civilian camp, but no prisoners would be interned here for months. Jim sat between Basie and Dr Ransome, annoyed with himself for assuming that his mother and father would be at the first camp they visited.

A prolonged argument began between the Japanese driver and the sergeant in charge of the camp's construction. It was clear that the sergeant had already decided that this truck and its consignment of Allied prisoners did not exist. He ignored the driver's protests and waved his cigarette in a thoughtful manner as he paced across the wooden porch of the guardhouse. At last he pointed to a patch of nettle-covered ground inside the gates, which he had apparently deemed to be a no man's land between the camp and the outside world.

Dr Ransome peered at the acres of fire-gutted stalls, a burnt-out maze through which cattle had once been steered. 'This can't be the camp. Unless they want us to build it.'

Basie's pale ears emerged from his seaman's collar. He was barely strong enough to sit upright, but could still catch the faintest scent of an opportunity. 'Woosung? There might be advantages, doctor . . . being the first people here . . .'

Dr Ransome began to help Mrs Hug from the floor, but the Japanese soldier raised the stock of his rifle and waved him back to his seat. The sergeant stood in the nettles, gazing over the tail-gate at the exhausted prisoners. The old women lay in the pools of urine at their husbands' feet. The English brothers huddled against Basie while Mrs Hug leaned on her father's knees.

Deliberately, Jim thought of his mother, and of the happy hours he had spent playing bridge in her bedroom. When the tears ran into his nose he sucked them into his parched throat. Could Dr Ransome teach himself how to cry? He looked at the glowing end of the sergeant's cigarette, and at the warm hearth of the charcoal stove in the twilight. The gang of labourers by the barbed-wire fence were walking back to their bamboo shelter.

'You're tiring everyone, Jim,' Dr Ransome warned him. 'Sit still or I'll ask Basie to sell you to the Japanese.'

'They wouldn't want me.' Jim slipped from the doctor's grasp. He knelt on the bench beside the driver's cabin. Rocking to and fro, he watched the sergeant lead the two Japanese to the guardhouse, where the soldiers were eating their evening meal. There were bottles of beer and rice wine on the wooden table, lit by a kerosene lamp. A Chinese coolie squatted by the brazier, fanning the charcoal to a white blaze, and the smell of warm fat drifted across the air.

Somehow Jim had to catch the eyes of the soldiers in the guardhouse. He knew that far from being concerned for their unwanted prisoners, the Japanese would leave them there all night. In the morning they would be too ill to move on to the next camp and would have to return to the detention centre in Shanghai.

The evening air settled over the burnt-out stockyards. The Chinese coolies finished their meal and sat under the bamboo shelter, drinking rice wine and playing cards. The Japanese drank beer in the guardhouse. Hundreds of stars were coming out over the Yangtze, and with them the navigation lights of the military aircraft. Two miles to the north, beyond the lines of burial mounds, Jim saw the rigging lights of a Japanese freighter heading for the open sea, its white superstructure sailing like a castle across the ghostly fields.

A foul smell rose from one of the missionary women. Her husband sat beside her on the floor, leaning against Dr Ransome's legs. Eager to catch sight of the freighter, Jim lifted himself on to the roof of the driving cabin. Sitting there, he watched the freighter slip away into the night, and then turned to the stars over his head. Since the previous summer, he had been teaching himself the main constellations.

'Basie . . .' Jim felt giddy; the night sky was sliding towards him. Losing his balance, he rolled across the cabin roof, then sat up to see the driver and the Japanese soldier stride from the guardhouse. They carried wooden staves in their hands, and Jim assumed that they were coming to beat him for sitting on the cabin. Quickly he slipped on to the floor and lay beside the Dutch woman.

The driver unshackled the tail-gate. As it fell with a clatter he rattled his stave against the swinging chains. He shouted at the prisoners and waved them from the truck. Helped by Dr Ransome, Mrs Hug and the old men lowered themselves into the nettles. Joined by Basie and the English boys, they followed the soldier towards the timber yard. The two missionary women lay on the soiled floor. They were still alive, but the driver waved his stave at Dr Ransome and beckoned him away from them.

Jim stepped across the damp floor and jumped on to the

144

ground. He was about to run after Dr Ransome when the driver held his shoulder and pointed to the sergeant in the guardhouse porch. He stood in the kerosene light, a small sack like a weighted cosh in his hand.

Cautiously, Jim walked up to the sergeant, who threw the sack on to the ground at his feet. Jim knelt in the deep ruts left by the truck's tyres, and treated the sergeant to his keenest smile. Inside the sack were nine sweet potatoes.

For the next hour Jim moved busily around the yard. While the prisoners rested in the timber store he relit the charcoal stove. Under the bored eyes of the Chinese coolies he fanned the embers into a flame, then fed the blaze with shavings of waste timber. Dr Ransome and the English boys brought him a bucket of water from the butt behind the guardhouse. Although Mrs Hug had been drinking from the bucket, Jim decided to wait until the potato water had cooled. Dr Ransome tried to help him with the iron cong, but Jim pushed him aside. The Eurasian women at the detention centre had taught him that potatoes cooked most quickly in shallow water under the tightest lid.

Later, before he carried the boiled potatoes to the timber store, Jim kept the largest one for himself. He sat next to Dr Ransome on the pine planks, while the missionary husbands lay in the sawdust, unable to eat. Jim regretted that they had been given even the smallest potato. At the same time, he needed these old people to survive, if they were to move on to the next camp. The Dutch woman seemed well, even if she had given her potato to the English boys. But Basie was already scanning the timber store, making an inventory of its possibilities inside his head, and if they stayed at Woosung camp Jim would never find his mother and father.

'Here you are, Jim.' Dr Ransome handed Jim his potato. He had taken a small bite, but most of the sweet pith was intact. 'It's a good one, you'll enjoy it.'

'Say, thanks . . .' He swiftly devoured the second potato.

Dr Ransome's gesture puzzled him. The Japanese were kind to children, and the two American sailors had befriended him in a fashion, but Jim knew that the English were not really interested in children.

He brought the pail of warm potato water for Basie and himself, and offered the pithy liquid to the others. He knelt beside the old missionary men, clicking his teeth and hoping that the sight of the Cathedral School badge would strike some religious spark in their minds and revive them.

'They don't look very well,' he confided to Dr Ransome. 'But they'll probably eat their potatoes in the morning.'

'They probably will. Rest, Jim – you'll wear yourself out looking after everyone. We'll be on our way tomorrow.'

'Well . . . there might be a long way to go.' The second potato had comforted Jim, and for the first time he felt sorry for the infected wounds on Dr Ransome's face. Returning the favour, he confided: 'If you ever go to the funeral piers at Nantao, don't drink the water.'

Jim lay on the soft sawdust, with its soothing scent of pine. Through the open doors of the timber store he watched the navigation lights of the Japanese aircraft crossing the night. After a few minutes he was forced to admit that he could recognize none of the constellations. Like everything else since the war, the sky was in a state of change. For all their movement, the Japanese aircraft were its only fixed points, a second zodiac above the broken land.

18
Vagrants

'Right . . . right . . . no . . . I mean left!'

Jim leaned through the passenger window of the cabin and shouted to the driver as the truck laboured on to the wooden deck of the pontoon bridge. The Japanese field engineers had built this temporary crossing over the Soochow Creek in the weeks following the Pearl Harbor attack, but already the bridge was coming apart under the heavy traffic. As the truck moved towards the first steel pontoon the wet planking began to splay in its worn ropes.

Posted as look-out by the Japanese driver, Jim watched the front tyre forcing the planks into the water. He had always enjoyed the sight of water rising through grilles or climbing the steps of a jetty. The brown steam washed the dust from the worn tyre, and revealed the manufacturer's name embossed on its side – befitting Jim's quest for his parents, a British company, Dunlop. The truck tilted sideways, leaning on its weak springs. Somewhere behind him a body rolled across the floor of the truck, but Jim was fascinated by the water sluicing across the dented hubcap, streaming through the wheel like the jets of a secret fountain.

'Left . . . left . . . !' Jim shouted, but the soldier at the tail-gate was already bellowing in alarm. With a weary sigh, the Japanese driver pulled on the handbrake, ordered Jim from the cabin and stepped on to the river-washed planks.

Jim crawled through the rear window on to the deck of the truck. He crossed Dr Ransome's outstretched legs and knelt on the bench, ready to take a close interest in the mounting argument between the driver and the Japanese guard.

Two hundred yards downstream the unit of field engineers

was raising the central span of the old railway bridge. Jim was happy to watch them at work. Most of the morning he had felt lightheaded, and the steady flow of water through the pontoons soothed his eyes. He counted his pulse, wondering if he had caught beri beri or malaria or any other of the diseases that he had heard Dr Ransome discussing with Mrs Hug. He was curious to try out some new disease, but then remembered the detention centre and the American planes he had seen over Shanghai. The previous night, when they had camped next to a pig farm run by the Japanese gendarmerie, Jim suspected that even Dr Ransome had seen the planes.

Certainly Dr Ransome did not look too well. Since leaving Woosung the wound in his face had infected the whole of his jaw and nose. He now lay on the floor of the truck, his freckled legs ominously white in the bright sun. He was asleep, but seemed to be thinking very hard about something with one half of his head. He had last spoken to Jim before their evening meal, when he made sure that Jim received the prisoners' full ration from the Japanese guard. By an enormous effort of will he had told Jim to strip and had washed his clothes in the pigs' water trough, using a piece of scented soap he borrowed from Mrs Hug.

Basie sat on the floor beside him, the two English boys asleep with their heads in his lap. The cabin steward was still conscious but had withdrawn into himself, his soft face like the flesh of a fading fruit. Often he was sick, and the floor of the truck was covered with vomit and urine which he nagged at Jim to clear away.

Mrs Hug and her father also lay on the floor, rarely speaking to each other, and concentrating on every bump in the road. Fortunately the two missionary couples had stayed behind at Woosung. Their places were taken by a middle-aged Englishman and his prim wife from the British Consulate at Nanking. They sat next to the Japanese guard

148

at the rear of the truck, their faces drained of expression by some tragedy that had overtaken them. Between them was a wicker suitcase filled with clothing, which the driver and the guard searched every evening, helping themselves to the shoes and slippers. The couple stared without ever speaking at the landscape of paddy fields and canals, and Jim assumed that they had lost interest in the war.

Twice a day, when the Japanese stopped to make themselves a wayside meal, the guard ordered Jim to pass an earthenware water jar around the prisoners. For the rest of the time he was left to himself, free to concentrate on the task of guiding this antiquated truck towards the internment camp that held his mother and father.

For days now they had been on the road, making an erratic circuit of the countryside ten miles to the north-west of Shanghai. Jim had lost count of the exact number of days, but at least they were moving forward, and luckily the Japanese were not in any way discouraged by the worsening condition of their prisoners.

On the first day, after setting out from Woosung, a three-hour drive through the open country took them to the former St Francis Xavier seminary on the Soochow Road, one of the first prison camps established by the Japanese in the weeks after Pearl Harbor. The seminary was already filled with military personnel. All afternoon they waited behind a queue of commandeered Shanghai Transit Company buses, which together carried several hundred Dutch and Belgian civilians. Jim peered keenly through the double wire fence. Gangs of British soldiers lounged by their huts, or sat out on the assembly ground in the polished pews taken from the seminary chapel, like the congregation of an open-air cathedral. But there were no male civilians, women or children. The Japanese guards were busy taking an endless series of roll-calls, and had no time for the new arrivals hoping to be admitted. Jim stood on the seat, waving over the wire so that everyone in the camp could see him.

However, the hundreds of bored soldiers were not interested in these civilians and their Shanghai buses. Jim was relieved when they were turned away. As they set off towards Soochow the driver allowed him to sit in the front cabin. In some way this restless English boy, who had so aggravated him, now offered a small measure of security. Jim was unable to read the map, printed in Japanese characters, or understand a word of the long monologues addressed to the insect-smeared windshield. But he knelt on the front seat, clicking his teeth and leaning out of the window to watch any passing aircraft. The entire Japanese air force seemed to be on its way to attack the Chinese armies in the west.

The flat countryside by the Shanghai-Soochow road had been a war ground, and the miles of rotting trenches and rust-stained blockhouses reminded Jim of encyclopaedia illustrations of Ypres and the Somme, an immense museum of battle that no one had visited for years. The debris of war, and the flights of bombers and fighter planes, revived him. He wanted to soar like a fighting kite over the winding parapets and land on one of the massive forts built out of thousands of sandbags among the burial mounds. It disappointed Jim that none of his fellow prisoners was interested in the war. It would have helped to keep up their spirits, a task which Jim was finding more and more difficult.

In many ways, Jim liked to imagine, he was the real leader of this troupe of travelling prisoners. At times, as he carried the heavy water jar and lit the stove in the evening, he knew that he was little more than their Number Two Coolie. But without Jim to gather the firewood and boil the sweet potatoes even Dr Ransome and Basie would have gone the way of the missionary women. He noticed that after leaving the gendarmerie station at the pig farm they all allowed themselves to become ill. During the night the Japanese had been beating a Chinese thief; the man's voice screamed across the water-filled paddies, shaking the dark surface. The next day everyone lay on the floor of the truck, Basie with his lungs and Dr Ransome unable to see through his infected eye.

Jim felt feverish, but he watched the Japanese planes overhead. The sound of their engines cleared his mind. Whenever his spirits flagged or he felt sorry for himself he thought of the silver aircraft he had seen at the detention centre.

The truck was moving across the pontoon bridge, man-handled by a squad of Japanese field engineers. Unable to steady himself, Jim slipped from the bench. Dr Ransome reached out weakly to hold him.

'Hang on, Jim. Stay up front with the driver – make sure he keeps going . . .'

Dozens of flies festered on Dr Ransome's face, feeding on the wound around his eye. Beside him Basie lay with Paul and David, Mrs Hug and her father. Only the English couple with the wicker suitcase full of shoes sat beside the soldier at the rear of the truck.

Jim straightened his blazer as a Japanese corporal climbed over the tail-gate. An angry man with wet boots, he shouted commands to the soldiers pushing the truck across the bridge. When they reached the opposite bank the soldiers walked along the water's edge to their work on the railway bridge. The corporal began to abuse the driver, clearly disgusted by the condition of the prisoners. He drew his Mauser pistol and gestured to an anti-tank ditch on the bank they had left behind.

Jim was relieved when the corporal strode back to his bridge. However ill they were, he did not want them to rest in the tank ditch. It was an effort to sit on the bench, and he was tempted to lie on the floor next to Dr Ransome, so that

151

he could stare straight at the sky. The landscape of paddy fields, creeks and deserted villages moved past, emerging from a white haze like the milled bones of all the dead of China. The dust cloaked the cabin and bonnet of the truck, camouflaging it for the realm it was about to enter. How long had they been on the road? The lines of burial mounds were trying to trick Jim's eyes, they moved in waves towards the lumbering vehicle, a sea of the dead. The open coffins lay empty, ready to catch the American pilots who would soon fall from the air. There were thousands of coffins, enough to take Dr Ransome and Basie, his mother and father and Vera, Number Two Coolie and himself . . .

The truck had stopped, the cabin striking Jim's head. A group of huts with tar-paper roofs stood beside the road, set back from a barbed-wire fence that separated them from the embankment of a canal. Idly, Jim gazed at this small internment camp built in the compound of a ceramics factory. A pair of metal lighters had capsized at their moorings, and miniature railcars still loaded with ceramic tiles stood in the yard beside the kilns. Two of the brick warehouses had been incorporated into the camp by the barbed-wire fence that divided the factory site. Men and women sunned themselves on the steps of the wooden huts, lines of washing fluttered between the windows, a cheerful spring semaphore.

Jim rested his chin on the side panel of the truck. Below him Dr Ransome was trying to sit up. The guard jumped from the tail-gate and walked towards the entrance, where a Shanghai University bus was surrounded by Japanese soldiers. The passengers stared through the dust-stained windows. There were two nuns in black wimples, several children of Jim's age, and some twenty British men and women. Already a crowd of prisoners had gathered at the wire. Hands in the pockets of their ragged shorts, they stared silently as a Japanese sergeant boarded the bus to inspect the prisoners.

Dr Ransome was kneeling at the rear of the truck, the wound on his face hidden behind his hand. Jim stared at an Englishwoman in a frayed cotton dress who stood by the fence, her hands clasping the wire. She looked at him with the same expression that he had seen on the face of the German mother in the Columbia Road.

The bus was moving into the camp through the open gates. The Japanese sergeant stood in the passenger door, pistol in hand, waving back the crowd of prisoners. From their sullen faces it was clear that they greeted these new arrivals with little enthusiasm, more mouths to be fed from their meagre rations. Jim sat up as the truck lumbered forward to the gates. Dr Ransome fell to the floor, and was helped on to a seat by the English couple with the wicker suitcase.

Jim smiled at the woman walking along the wire. When she stretched a hand to him he wondered if she were a friend of his mother. The camp was filled with families, and somewhere among the strolling couples might be his parents. He peered at the English faces, at the gangs of boys laughing behind the Japanese sentries. To his surprise he felt a moment of regret, of sadness that his quest for his mother and father would soon be over. As long as he searched for them he was prepared to be hungry and ill, but now that the search had ended he felt saddened by the memory of all he had been through, and of how much he had changed. He was closer now to the ruined battlefields and this fly-infested truck, to the nine sweet potatoes in the sack below the driver's seat, even in a sense to the detention centre, than he would ever be again to his house in Amherst Avenue.

The truck stopped by the gates. The Japanese sergeant peered over the tail-gate at the prisoners lying on the floor.

He pushed Dr Ransome back with his Mauser, but the injured physician lowered himself to the ground, where he knelt at the sergeant's feet, catching his breath. Already the crowd of internees had begun to disperse. Hands in their pockets, the men strolled back to the huts and sat with the women on the steps.

Flies swarmed over the truck and settled on the damp pools that covered the floor. They hovered around Jim's mouth, feeding at the sores on his gums. For ten minutes the Japanese soldiers argued with each other, while the driver waited with Dr Ransome. Two senior British prisoners stepped through the gates and joined the discussion.

'Woosung Camp?'

'No, no, no . . .'

'Who sent them? In this condition?'

Avoiding Dr Ransome, they approached the truck and stared at the prisoners through the cloud of flies. As Jim kicked his heels and whistled to himself they watched him without expression. The Japanese sentries opened the barbed-wire gates, but the British prisoners immediately closed them and began to shout at the Japanese sergeant. When Dr Ransome stepped forward to remonstrate with them the British waved him away.

'Get back, man . . .'

'We can't take you, doctor. There are children here.'

Dr Ransome climbed into the truck and sat on the floor beside Jim. The effort of standing had exhausted him, and he lay back with his hand over his wound as the flies fought between his fingers.

Mrs Hug and the English couple with the wicker suitcase had waited silently through the arguments. As the Japanese soldiers returned to the camp and locked the gates Mrs Hug said: 'They won't take us. The British camp leaders . . .'

Jim gazed at the prisoners wandering across the compound. Groups of boys played football in the brick yard of the ceramics works. Were his mother and father hiding among the kilns? Perhaps, like the British camp leaders, they wanted Jim to go away, frightened of the flies and the sickness that he had brought with him from Shanghai.

Jim helped Basie and Dr Ransome to drink, and then sat on the opposite bench. He turned his back on the camp, on the British prisoners and their children. All his hopes rested in the landscape around him, in its past and future wars. He felt a strange lightness in his head, not because his parents had rejected him, but because he expected them to do so, and no longer cared.

19
The Runway

In the hour before dusk they entered an area of abandoned
battlefields nine miles to the south of Shanghai. The
afternoon light rose into the air, as if returning to the sun a
small part of the strength it had cast to the indifferent fields.
The terrain of trenches and blockhouses seemed to have
sprung fully armed from Jim's head. A tank sat like a
wheeled shack at the junction of the Shanghai and Hangchow roads, the sun's spotlights shining through its open
hatches. The trenches hunted among the burial mounds, a
maze lost within itself.

Beyond the crossroads a wooden bridge spanned a canal.
Its white piles, from which the rain had leached all trace of
resin, were as soft as pumice. The driver folded his map,
and fanned himself with the canvas wallet, reluctant to risk
his wheels on the worn timbers. Mrs Hug and the English
couple sat at the back of the truck, their shadows reaching
across the white beds of the drained paddy fields. Jim
brushed the flies from Dr Ransome's face and patted his
head. He imagined that he was one of the shadows, a black
carpet lying across the tired land. A mile to the south,
between the burial mounds, he could see the tailplanes of a
row of parked aircraft, feathers of bone against the darken-
ing air. Jim studied the aircraft, recognizing the plump
fuselages and radial engines. They were Brewster Buffaloes,
a type of American fighter that had been no match for the
Japanese.

Was it here, among the burial mounds, that the American
aircraft waited before taking off into his mind? However,
the Japanese driver had also seen the tailplanes. He threw

down his cigarette and shouted to the guard, who had jumped from the truck and was testing the rotting planks of the bridge.

'Lunghua . . . Lunghua . . . !'

The engine started, and the driver turned east at the crossroads, setting course for this distant airfield.

'We're going to Lunghua Airfield, Dr Ransome,' Jim called between his knees. The physician lay on the floor beside Basie and the Dutch woman's father, watching Jim with his single eye. 'There are Brewster Buffaloes – the Americans must have won the war.'

Jim let the warm air rush into his face. They approached the military airfield, the largest grass aerodrome that he had seen near Shanghai. There were three metal hangars, and a wooden engineering workshop built in the former car-park of Lunghua Pagoda. Dozens of aircraft were drawn up on the tarmac beside the hangars, high-performance fighters of advanced design. The three Brewster Buffaloes, their American markings painted out, sat by the edge of the field. A team of engineers with a powerful crane lifted an anti-aircraft gun to the upper decks of the stone pagoda.

The driver stopped at a checkpoint, where Japanese soldiers manned a fortified emplacement. As the sentries paced about in the dusk their corporal spoke into a field telephone. They were waved through to the perimeter road. The rutted surface had been stiffened with straw matting, churned to a pith by a convoy of vehicles loaded with building stone. A truck swayed past them with a cargo of roofing tiles torn from the tenements of the Old City.

Pairs of armed guards patrolled the perimeter road, their bayonets cutting the sombre air. Two single-engined transport aircraft were parked on the edge of the field. Accompanied by his ground crew, a Japanese pilot spoke to two fellow officers in uniform. The pilot pointed to the truck as it rattled past, and it occurred to Jim that perhaps he and

157

Basie and Dr Ransome were about to be flown from Shanghai, and that he would soon join his parents in Hong Kong or Japan.

Jim waited for the truck to stop beside the planes, but the driver pressed on to the southern perimeter of the airfield. The smooth grass fell away into a broken terrain of wild sugar cane and unlevelled earth. They crossed the dried bed of an irrigation ditch, and followed the truck loaded with roofing tiles into a narrow valley hidden between walls of nettles. Clouds of ashy white dust rose into the evening air, as the military vehicles in front of them tipped their loads of stone and rubble on to the ground. Armed soldiers and air force police guarded the valley, rifles in hand, their uniforms blanched by the dust.

Watched by the Japanese sentries, hundreds of captured Chinese soldiers in ragged tunics were carrying the tiles and cobblestones from the tip and laying the bed of a concrete runway. Even in the dusk light, and despite all the privations of the past months, Jim could see the meagre condition of these Chinese prisoners. Many were emaciated to the point of death. They sat naked in the trampled nettles, a single roof tile held in their hands like the fragment of a begging bowl. Others climbed the shallow slope to the edge of the airfield, wicker baskets laden with stones clasped to their chests.

The truck stopped by the tip. With a rattle of chains, the tail-gate fell. Led by the Japanese soldier, Mrs Hug and the English couple lowered themselves to the ground. Dr Ransome knelt by the seats, barely able to control his clumsy body.

'Right, Jim – let's get everyone to their quarters. Help Mrs Hug. Basie, boys . . .'

He stood unsteadily, but managed to lift Basie to his feet. The cabin steward's face was already covered by a layer of talc, the delicate woman's skin that Jim had first seen near the funeral piers at Nantao. Holding Jim's shoulder, he shuffled along the damp floor of the truck.

They dismounted and stood together in the cloud of white dust beside the tip. Mrs Hug sat with her father on a heap of cobbles, holding the English boys by the hands. The Chinese soldiers filled their baskets and spat on the stones. As they climbed the broken earth to the runway their chalky figures seemed to illuminate the evening air.

Around them the Japanese sentries watched without moving. Fifty feet away, on the southern slope of the valley, two sergeants sat on bamboo chairs by the edge of a pit that had been freshly dug among the nettles. Their boots and the ground at their feet were covered with lime.

Jim picked up a grey ceramic tile. None of the Japanese guards appeared to care whether they worked on the runway, but Basie already held a cobblestone in his hands. Jim followed a naked Chinese soldier towards the runway. He climbed the slope and walked across the furrowed soil. The Chinese threw down their baskets and returned to the tip. Jim laid his tile on the shallow trench filled with stones and broken bricks that ran across the airfield into the night. Basie pushed past him and dropped the cobble at his feet. He swayed in the dust, trying to brush the chalky powder from his hands.

Behind them Dr Ransome stood at the tip with Mrs Hug and the English couple. He was arguing with a Japanese soldier, who waved him towards the runway. Holding his rifle in one hand, the soldier picked a roof tile from the tip and handed it to Dr Ransome.

Jim waited by the broken stones. He stared into the dusk along the white surface of the runway. He remembered the swirling grass at Hungjao Aerodrome, and tried to imagine the slipstreams of the Brewster Buffaloes. He turned to the transport aircraft parked by the perimeter road. The Japanese pilot and the uniformed officers were walking through the grass towards the runway. They stopped on the muddy verge, laughing to each other as they inspected the work. Their buckles and polished badges shone like the jewellery of the Europeans who had visited the battlefields near Hungjao before the war.

Jim stepped into the grass, leaving the dust clouds and the lines of Chinese soldiers. He wanted to see the parked aircraft for the last time, to stand under the dark span of their wings. He knew that the Chinese soldiers were being worked to death, that these starving men were laying their own bones in a carpet for the Japanese bombers who would land upon them. Then they would go to the pit, where the lime-booted sergeants waited with their Mausers. And after laying their stones, he and Basie and Dr Ransome would also go to the pit.

The last light had faded from the fuselages of the aircraft, but Jim could smell their engines on the night air. He inhaled the odour of oil and engine coolant. Already he had begun to shut out the voices around him, the white bodies of the Chinese soldiers and the runway of bones. He shut out the young Japanese pilot in his flying suit, who was pointing at him and shouting to the sergeants beside the pit. Jim hoped that his parents were safe and dead. Brushing the dust from his blazer, he ran towards the shelter of the aircraft, eager to enfold himself in their wings.

Part II

20
Lunghua Camp

Voices fretted along the murmuring wire, carried like stressed notes on the strings of a harp. Fifty feet from the perimeter fence, Jim lay in the deep grass beside the pheasant trap. He listened to the guards arguing with each other as they conducted their hourly patrol of the camp. Now that the American air attacks had become a daily event, the Japanese soldiers no longer slung their rifles over their shoulders. They clasped the long-barrelled weapons in both hands, and were so nervous that if they saw Jim outside the camp perimeter they would shoot at him without thinking.

Jim watched them through the netting of the pheasant trap. Only the previous day they had shot a Chinese coolie trying to steal into the camp. He recognized one of the guards as Private Kimura, a large-boned farmer's son who had grown almost as much as Jim in his years at the camp. The private's strong back had burst through his faded tunic, and only his ammunition webbing held the tattered garment together.

Before the war finally turned against the Japanese, Private Kimura often invited Jim to the bungalow he shared with three other guards and allowed him to wear his kendo armour. Jim could remember the elaborate ceremony as the Japanese soldiers dressed him in the metal and leather armour, and the ripe smell of Private Kimura's body that filled the helmet and shoulder guards. He remembered the burst of violence as Private Kimura attacked him with the two-handed sword, the whirlwind of blows that struck his helmet before he could fight back. His head had rung for days. Giving him his orders, Basie had been forced to shout until he woke the men's dormitory in E Block, and Dr Ransome had called Jim into the camp hospital and examined his ears.

Remembering those powerful arms, and the quickness of Private Kimura's eyes, Jim lay flat in the long grass behind the trap. For once he was glad that the trap had failed to net a bird. The two Japanese had stopped by the wire fence and were scanning the group of abandoned buildings that lay outside the north-west perimeter of Lunghua Camp. Beside them, just within the camp, was the derelict hulk of the assembly hall, the curved balcony of its upper circle open to the sky. The camp occupied the site of a teacher training college that had been bombed and overrun during the fighting around Lunghua Aerodrome in 1937. The damaged buildings nearest to the airfield had been excluded from the camp, and it was here, in the long grass quadrangles between the gutted residence halls, that Jim set his pheasant traps. After roll-call that morning he had slipped through the fence where it emerged from a bank of nettles surrounding a forgotten blockhouse on the airfield perimeter. Leaving his shoes on the blockhouse steps, he waded along a shallow canal, and then crawled through the deep grass between the ruined buildings.

The first of the traps was only a few feet from the perimeter fence, a distance that had seemed enormous to Jim when he first crept through the barbed wire. He had looked back at the secure world of the camp, at the barrack huts and water tower, at the guardhouse and dormitory blocks, almost afraid that he had been banished from them forever. Dr Ransome often called Jim a 'free spirit', as he roved across the camp, hunting down some new idea in his head. But here, in the deep grass between the ruined buildings, he felt weighed by an unfamiliar gravity.

For once making the most of this inertia, Jim lay behind the trap. An aircraft was taking off from Lunghua Airfield, clearly silhouetted against the yellow façades of the apartment houses in the French Concession, but he ignored the plane. The soldier beside Private Kimura shouted to the children playing in the balcony of the assembly hall. Kimura was walking back to the wire. He scanned the surface of the canal and the clumps of wild sugar cane. The poor rations of the past year – the Japanese guards were almost as badly fed as their British and American prisoners – had drawn the last of the adolescent fat from Kimura's arms. After a recent attack of tuberculosis his strong face was puffy and coolie-like. Dr Ransome had repeatedly warned Jim never to wear Private Kimura's kendo armour. A fight between them would be less one-sided now, even though Jim was only fourteen. But for the rifle, he would have liked to challenge Kimura . . .

As if aware of the threat within the grass, Private Kimura called to his companion. He leaned his rifle against the pine fencing-post, stepped through the wire and stood in the deep nettles. Flies rose from the shallow canal and settled on his lips, but Kimura ignored them and stared at the strip of water that separated him from Jim and the pheasant traps.

Could he see Jim's footprints in the soft mud? Jim crawled away from the trap but the clear outline of his body lay in the crushed grass. Kimura was rolling his tattered sleeves, ready to wrestle with his quarry. Jim watched him stride through the nettles. He was certain that he could outrun Kimura, but not the bullet in the second soldier's rifle. How could he explain to Kimura that the pheasant traps had been Basie's idea? It was Basie who had insisted on the elaborate camouflage of leaves and twigs, and who made him climb through the wire twice a day, even though they had never seen a bird, let alone caught one. It was important to keep in with Basie, who had small but reliable sources of food. He could tell Kimura that Basie knew about the secret camp radio, but then the extra food would cease.

165

What most worried Jim was the thought that, if Kimura struck him, he would fight back. Few boys of his own age dared to touch Jim, and in the last year, since the rations had failed, few men. However, if he fought back against Kimura he would be dead.

He calmed himself, calculating the best moment to stand up and surrender. He would bow to Kimura, show no emotion and hope that the hundreds of hours he had spent hanging around the guardhouse – albeit at Basie's instigation – would count in his favour. He had once given English lessons to Kimura, but although they were clearly losing the war the Japanese had not been interested in learning English.

Jim waited for Kimura to climb the bank towards him. The soldier stood in the centre of the canal, a bright black object gleaming in his hand. The creeks, ponds and disused wells within Lunghua Camp held an armoury of rusting weapons and unstable ammunition abandoned during the 1937 hostilities. Jim peered through the grass at the pointed cylinder, assuming that the tidal water in the canal had uncovered an old artillery shell or mortar bomb.

Kimura shouted to the second soldier waiting by the barbed wire. He brushed the flies from his face and spoke to the object, as if murmuring to a baby. He raised it behind his head, in the position taken by the Japanese soldiers throwing a grenade. Jim waited for the explosion, and then realized that Private Kimura was holding a large fresh-water turtle. The creature's head emerged from its carapace, and Kimura began to laugh excitedly. His tubercular face resembled a small boy's, reminding Jim that Private Kimura had once been a child, as he himself had been before the war.

After crossing the parade ground, the Japanese soldiers disappeared among the lines of ragged washing between the barrack huts. Jim emerged from the damp cavern of the blockhouse. Wearing the leather golfing shoes given to him by Dr Ransome, he climbed through the wire. In his hand he carried Kimura's turtle. The ancient creature contained at least a pound of meat, and Basie, almost certainly, would know a special recipe for turtle. Jim could imagine Basie tempting it out of its shell with a live caterpillar, then skewering its head with his jack-knife . . .

In front of Jim was Lunghua Camp, his home and universe for the past three years, and the suffocating prison of nearly two thousand Allied nationals. The shabby barrack huts, the cement dormitory blocks, the worn parade ground and the guardhouse with its leaning watch-tower lay together under the June sun, a rendezvous for every fly and mosquito in the Yangtze basin. But once he stepped through the wire fence Jim felt the air steady around him. He ran along the cinder path, his tattered shirt flying from his bony shoulders like the tags of washing between the huts.

In his ceaseless journeys around the camp Jim had learned to recognize every stone and weed. A sun-bleached sign, crudely painted with the words 'Regent Street', was nailed to a bamboo pole beside the pathway. Jim ignored it, as he did the similar signs enscribed 'Piccadilly', 'Knightsbridge' and 'Petticoat Lane' which marked the main pathways within the camp. These relics of an imaginary London – which many of the Shanghai-born British prisoners had never seen – intrigued Jim but in some way annoyed him. With their constant talk about pre-war London, the older British families in the camp claimed a special exclusiveness. He remembered a line from one of the poems that Dr Ransome had made him memorize – 'a foreign field that is for ever England . . .' But this was Lunghua, not England. Naming the sewage-stained paths between the rotting huts after a vaguely remembered London allowed too many of the British prisoners to shut out the reality of the camp, another excuse to sit back when they should have been

167

helping Dr Ransome to clear the septic tanks. To their credit, in Jim's eyes, neither the Americans nor the Dutch and Belgians in the camp wasted their time on nostalgia. The years in Lunghua had not given Jim a high opinion of the British.

And yet the London street signs fascinated him, part of the magic of names that he had discovered in the camp. What, conceivably, were Lord's, the Serpentine, and the Trocadero? There were so few books or magazines that an unfamiliar brand-name had all the mystery of a message from the stars. According to Basie, who was always right, the American fighters with the ventral radiators that strafed Lunghua Airfield were called 'Mustangs', the name of a wild pony. Jim relished the name; to know that the planes were Mustangs was more important to him than the confirmation that Basie had his ear to the camp's secret radio. He hungered for names.

Jim stumbled on the worn path, unable to control the golf shoes. Too often these days he became light-headed. Dr Ransome had warned him not to run, but the American air attacks and the imminent prospect of the war's end made him too impatient to walk. Trying to protect the turtle, he grazed his left knee. He limped across the cinder track and sat on the steps of the derelict drinking-water station. Here brackish water taken from the ponds in the camp had once been boiled by the prisoners. There was still a small supply of coal in the camp store-rooms, but the work gang of six Britons who stoked the fires had lost interest. Although Dr Ransome remonstrated with them, they preferred to suffer from chronic dysentery rather than make the effort of boiling the water.

While Jim nursed his knee the members of the gang sat outside the nearby barrack hut, watching the sky as if they expected the war to end within the next ten minutes. Jim recognized Mr Mulvaney, an accountant with the Shanghai Power Company who had often swum in the pool at

Amherst Avenue. Beside him was the Reverend Pearce, a Methodist missionary whose Japanese-speaking wife openly collaborated with the guards, reporting to them each day on the prisoners' activites.

No one criticized Mrs Pearce for this, and in fact most of the prisoners in Lunghua were only too keen to collaborate. Jim vaguely disapproved, but agreed that it was probably sensible to do anything to survive. After three years in the camp the notion of patriotism meant nothing. The bravest prisoners – and collaboration was a risky matter – were those who bought their way into the favour of the Japanese and thereby helped their fellows with small supplies of food and bandages. Besides, there were few illicit activities to betray. No one in Lunghua would dream of trying to escape, and everyone rightly ratted on any fool about to step through the wire, for fear of the reprisals to come.

The water-workers scraped their clogs on the steps and stared into the sun, moving only to pick the ticks from between their ribs. Although emaciated, the process of starvation had somehow stopped a skin's depth from the skeleton below. Jim envied Mr Mulvaney and the Reverend Pearce – he himself was still growing. The arithmetic that Dr Ransome had taught him made it all too clear that the food supplied to the camp was shrinking at a faster rate than that at which the prisoners were dying.

In the centre of the parade ground a group of twelve-year-old boys were playing marbles on the baked earth. Seeing the turtle, they ran towards Jim. Each of them controlled a dragonfly tied to a length of cotton. The blue flames flicked to and fro above their heads.

'Jim! Can we touch it?'

'What is it?'

'Did Private Kimura give it to you?'

Jim smiled benignly. 'It's a bomb.' He held out the turtle and generously allowed everyone to inspect it. Despite the gap in years, several of the boys had been close friends in the days after his arrival in Lunghua, when he had needed every ally he could find. But he had outgrown them and made other friends – Dr Ransome, Basie and the American seamen in E Block, with their ancient pre-war copies of the *Reader's Digest* and *Popular Mechanics* that he devoured. Now and then, as if recapturing his lost childhood, Jim re-entered the world of boyish games and would play tops and marbles and hopscotch.

'Is it dead? It's moving!'

'It's bleeding!'

A smear of blood from Jim's knee gave the turtle's head a piratical flourish.

'Jim, you killed it!'

The largest of the boys, Richard Pearce, reached out to touch the reptile, but Jim tucked it under his arm. He disliked and slightly feared Richard Pearce, who was almost as big as himself. He envied Richard the extra Japanese rations which his mother fed to him. As well as the food, the Pearces had a small library of confiscated books which they guarded jealously.

'It's a blood bond,' Jim explained grandly. By rights turtles belonged to the sea, to the open river visible a mile to the west of the camp, that broad tributary of the Yangtze down which he had once dreamed of sailing with his parents to the safety of a world without war.

'Watch out . . .' He waved Richard aside. 'I've trained it to attack!'

The boys backed away from him. There were times when Jim's humour made them uneasy. Although he tried to stop himself, Jim resented their clothes – hand-me-downs stitched together by their mothers, but far superior to his own rags. More than this, he resented that they had mothers and fathers at all. During the past year Jim had gradually realized that he could no longer remember what his parents looked like. Their veiled figures still entered his dreams, but he had forgotten their faces.

21
The Cubicle

'Young Jim . . . !'

An almost naked man wearing clogs and ragged shorts shouted to him from the steps of G Block. In his hands he held the shafts of a wooden cart with iron wheels. Although the cart carried no load, its handles had almost wrenched the man's arms from their sockets. He spoke to the English women sitting on the concrete steps in their faded cotton frocks. As he gestured to them his shoulder blades seemed to be working themselves loose from his back, about to fly across the barbed wire.

'I'm here, Mr Maxted!' Jim pushed Richard Pearce aside and ran along the cinder path to the dormitory block. Seeing the empty food cart, it occurred to him that he might have missed the daily meal. The fear of being without food for even a single day was so intense that he was ready to attack Mr Maxted.

'Come on, Jim. Without you it won't taste the same.' Mr Maxted glanced at Jim's golf shoes, these nailed brogues that had a life of their own and propelled his scarecrow figure on his ceaseless rounds of the camp. To the women he remarked: 'Our Jim's spending all his time at the 19th hole.'

'I promised, Mr Maxted. I'm always ready . . .' Jim had to stop as he reached the entrance to G Block. He worked his lungs until the dizziness left his head, and ran forward again. Turtle in hand, he raced up the steps into the foyer and swerved between two old men stranded like ghosts in the middle of a conversation they had forgotten.

On either side of the corridor was a series of small rooms, each furnished with four wooden bunks. After the first winter in the camp, when many of the children in the uninsulated barracks had died, families with children were moved into the residence halls of the former training college. Although unheated, the rooms with their cement walls remained above freezing point.

Jim shared his room with a young English couple, Mr and Mrs Vincent, and their six-year-old son. He had lived within inches of the Vincents for two and a half years, but their existences could not have been more separate. On the day of Jim's arrival Mrs Vincent had hung an old bedspread around his nominal quarter of the room. She and her husband – a broker on the Shanghai Stock Exchange – never ceased to resent Jim's presence, and over the years they had strengthened his cubicle, stringing together a worn shawl, a petticoat and the lid of a cardboard box, so that it resembled one of the miniature shanties that seemed to erect themselves spontaneously around the beggars of Shanghai.

Not content with walling Jim into his small world, the Vincents had repeatedly tried to encroach upon it, moving the nails and string from which the bedspread hung. Jim had defended himself, first by bending the nails until, to the Vincents' horror, the entire structure collapsed one night as they were undressing, and then by calibrating the wall with a ruler and pencil. The Vincents promptly retaliated by superimposing their own system of marks.

All this Jim took in his stride. For some reason he still liked Mrs Vincent, a handsome if frayed blonde, although her nerves were always stretched and she had never made the slightest attempt to care for him. He knew that if he starved to death in his bunk she would find some polite reason for doing nothing to help him. During the first year in Lunghua the few single children were neglected, unless they were prepared to let themselves be used as servants. Jim alone had refused, and had never fetched and carried for Mr Vincent.

Mrs Vincent was sitting on her straw mattress when he

burst into the room, her pale hands folded on her lap like a forgotten pair of gloves. She stared at the whitewashed wall above her son's bunk, as if watching an invisible film projected on to a screen. Jim worried that Mrs Vincent spent too much of her time watching these films. As he peered at her through the cracks in his cubicle he tried to guess what she saw – a home-made cine film, perhaps, of herself in England before she was married, sitting on one of those sunlit lawns that seemed to cover the entire country. Jim assumed that it was those lawns that had provided the emergency airfields for the Battle of Britain. As he was aware from his observations in Shanghai, the Germans were not too keen on sunlit lawns. Was this why they had lost the Battle of Britain? Many of his ideas were hopelessly confused in a way that even Dr Ransome was too tired to disentangle.

'You're late, Jim,' Mrs Vincent told him disapprovingly, her eyes on his golf shoes. Like everyone else, she was unable to cope with their intimidating presence. Already Jim felt that the shoes gave him a special authority. 'The whole of G Block has been waiting for you.'

'I've been with Basie, hearing the latest war news. Mrs Vincent, what's the 19th hole?'

'You shouldn't work for Basie. The things those Americans ask you to do . . . I've told you that we come first.'

'G Block comes first, Mrs Vincent.' Jim meant it. He ducked under the flap into his cubicle. Catching his breath, he lay on the bunk with the turtle inside his shirt. The reptile preferred its own company, and Jim turned his attention to his new shoes. With their polished toecaps and bright studs, they were an intact piece of the pre-war world that he could stare at for hours, like Mrs Vincent and her films. Laughing to himself, Jim lay back as the hot sunlight shone through the wall of the cubicle, outlining the curious stains on the old bedspread. Looking at them, he visualized the scenes of air-battles and armadas, the sinking of the *Petrel*, and even the garden at Amherst Avenue.

'Jim, kitchen time . . . !' he heard someone call from the steps below the window. But Jim rested on his bunk. It was a long haul to the kitchens, and there was no point in being early. The Japanese had celebrated VE Day in their own way, by cutting the already meagre rations in half. The first arrivals often received less than the later ones, when the cooks realized how many of the prisoners had died or were too ill to collect their rations.

Besides, there was no obligation on Jim to help with the food cart – nor, for that matter, on Mr Maxted. But as Jim had noticed, those who were prepared to help their fellow prisoners tended to do so, and this did nothing to stop those too lazy to work from endlessly complaining. The British were especially good at complaining, something the Dutch and Americans never did. Soon, Jim reflected with a certain grim pleasure, they would be too sick even to complain.

He gazed at his shoes, consciously imitating the childlike smile on Private Kimura's lips. The wooden bunk filled the cubicle, but Jim was at his happiest in this miniature universe. On the walls he had pinned several pages from an old *Life* magazine that Basie had given to him. There were photographs of Battle of Britain pilots sitting in armchairs beside their Spitfires, of a crashed Heinkel bomber, of St Paul's floating like a battleship on a sea of fire. Next to them was a full-page colour advertisement for a Packard motor-car, as beautiful in Jim's eyes as the Mustang fighters which strafed Lunghua Airfield. Did the Americans bring out a new-model Mustang every year or every month? Perhaps there would be an air raid that afternoon, when he could check the latest design modifications to the Mustangs and Superfortresses. Jim looked forward to the air raids.

Beside the Packard was a small section that Jim had cut from a larger photograph of a crowd outside the gates of

Buckingham Palace in 1940. The blurred images of a man and a woman standing arm-in-arm reminded Jim of his parents. This unknown English couple, perhaps dead in an air raid, had almost become his mother and father. Jim knew that they were complete strangers, but he kept the pretence alive, so that in turn he could keep alive the lost memory of his parents. The world before the war, his childhood in Amherst Avenue, his class at the Cathedral School, belonged to that invisible film which Mrs Vincent watched from her bunk.

Jim allowed the turtle to crawl across his straw mat. If he carried it around with him Private Kimura or one of the guards might guess that he had left the camp. Now that the war was ending the Japanese guards were convinced that the British and American prisoners were constantly trying to escape – the last notion, in fact, to cross their minds. In 1943 a few Britishers had escaped, hoping to be sheltered by neutral friends in Shanghai, but had soon been discovered by the army of informers. Several groups of Americans had set out in the summer of 1944 for Chungking, the National-ist Chinese capital nine hundred miles to the west. All had been betrayed by Chinese villagers terrified of reprisals, handed over to the Japanese and executed. From then on escape attempts ceased altogether. By June 1945, the landscape around Lunghua was so hostile, roamed by bandits, starving villagers and deserters from the puppet armies, that the camp and its Japanese guards offered the only security.

With his finger Jim stroked the turtle's ancient head. It seemed a pity to cook it – Jim envied the reptile its massive shell, a private fortress against the world. From below his bunk he pulled out a wooden box, which Dr Ransome had helped him to nail together. Inside were his possessions – a Japanese cap badge given to him by Private Kimura; three steel-bossed fighting tops; a chess set and a copy of Kennedy's *Latin Primer* on indefinite loan from Dr Ransome; his Cathedral School blazer, a carefully folded memory of his younger self; and the pair of clogs he had worn for the past three years.

Jim placed the turtle in the box and covered it with the blazer. As he raised the flap of his cubicle Mrs Vincent watched his every move. She treated him like her Number Two Coolie, and he was well aware that he tolerated this for reasons he barely understood. Like all the men and older boys in G Block, Jim was attracted to Mrs Vincent, but her real appeal for Jim lay elsewhere. Her long hours staring at the whitewash, and her detachment even from her own son – she fed the dysentery-ridden boy and changed his clothes without looking at him for minutes at a time – suggested to Jim that she remained forever above the camp, beyond the world of guards and hunger and American air attacks to which he himself was passionately committed. He wanted to touch her, less out of adolescent lust than simple curiosity.

'You can use my bunk, Mrs Vincent, if you want to sleep.'

As Jim reached to her shoulder she pushed his hand away. Her distracted eyes could come to a remarkably sharp focus.

'Mr Maxted is still waiting, Jim. Perhaps it's time you went back to the huts . . .'

'Not the huts, Mrs Vincent,' he pretended to groan. Not the huts, he repeated fiercely to himself as he left the room. The huts were cold, and if the war lasted beyond the winter of 1945 many more people would die in those freezing barracks. However, for Mrs Vincent perhaps he would go back to the huts . . .

22
The University of Life

All over the camp there sounded the scraping of iron wheels. In the windows of the barrack huts, on the steps of the dormitory blocks, the prisoners were sitting up, roused for a few minutes by the memory of food.

Jim left the foyer of G Block, and found Mr Maxted still holding the wooden handles of the food cart. Having made the effort twenty minutes earlier to lift the handles, he had exhausted his powers of decision. The former architect and entrepreneur, who had represented so much that Jim most admired about Shanghai, had been sadly drained by his years in Lunghua. After arriving at the camp Jim had been glad to find him there, but by now he realized how much Mr Maxted had changed. His eyes forever watched the cigarette butts thrown down by the Japanese guards, but only Jim was quick enough to retrieve them. Jim chafed at this, but he supported Mr Maxted out of nostalgia for his childhood dream of growing up one day to be like him.

The Studebaker and the afternoon girls in the gambling casinos had prepared Mr Maxted poorly for the world of the camp. As Jim took the wooden handles he wondered how long the architect would have stood on the sewage-stained path. Perhaps all day, watched until he dropped by the same group of British prisoners who sat on the steps without once offering to help. Half-naked in their ragged clothes, they stared at the parade ground, uninterested even in a Japanese fighter that flew overhead. Several of the married couples held their mess-plates, already forming a queue, a reflex response to Jim's arrival.

'At last . . .'

'. . . that boy . . .'

'. . . running wild.'

These mutters drew an amiable smile from Mr Maxted. 'Jim, you're going to be blackballed by the country club. Never mind.'

'I don't mind.' When Mr Maxted stumbled Jim held his arm. 'Are you all right, Mr Maxted?'

Jim waved to the men sitting on the step, but no one moved. Mr Maxted steadied himself. 'Let's go, Jim. Some work and some watch, and that's all there is to it.'

For the past year there had been a third member of the team, Mr Carey, the owner of the Buick agency in Nanking Road. But six weeks earlier he had died of malaria, and by then the Japanese had cut the food ration to a point where only two of them were needed to push the cart.

Propelled by his new shoes, Jim sped along the cinder path. The iron wheels struck sparks from the flinty stones. Mr Maxted held his shoulder, panting to keep up.

'Slow down, Jim. You'll get there before the war ends.'

'When will the war end, Mr Maxted?'

'Jim . . . is it going to end? Another year, 1946. You tell me, you listen to Basie's radio.'

'I haven't heard the radio, Mr Maxted,' Jim answered truthfully. Basie was far too canny to admit a Britisher into the secret circle of listeners. 'I know the Japanese surrendered at Okinawa. I hope the war ends soon.'

'Not too soon, Jim. Our problems might begin then. Are you still giving English lessons to Private Kimura?'

'He isn't interested in learning English,' Jim had to admit. 'I think the war's really ended for Private Kimura.'

'Will the war really end for you, Jim? You'll see your mother and father again.'

'Well . . .' Jim preferred not to talk about his parents, even with Mr Maxted. The two of them had formed a long-standing partnership, though Mr Maxted did little to help

178

Jim and rarely referred to his son Patrick or to their visits to the Shanghai clubs and bars. Mr Maxted was no longer the dapper figure who fell into swimming-pools. What worried Jim was that his mother and father might also have changed. Soon after arriving in Lunghua he heard that his parents were interned in a camp near Soochow, but the Japanese refused to consider the notion of a transfer.

They crossed the parade ground and approached the camp kitchens behind the guardhouse. Some twenty food carts and their teams were drawn up beside the serving hatch, jostling together like a crowd of rickshaws and their coolies. As Jim had estimated, he and Mr Maxted would take their place halfway down the queue. Late-comers clattered along the cinder paths, watched by hundreds of emaciated prisoners. One day during the previous week there had been no food, as a reprisal for a Superfortress raid that had devastated Tokyo, and the prisoners had continued to stare at the kitchens until late afternoon. The silence had unsettled Jim, reminding him of the beggars outside the houses in Amherst Avenue. Without thinking, he had removed his shoes and hidden them among the graves in the hospital cemetery.

Jim and Mr Maxted took their places in the queue. Outside the guardhouse a work party of British and Belgian prisoners were strengthening the fence. Two of the prisoners unwound a coil of barbed wire, which the others cut and nailed to the fencing posts. Several of the Japanese soldiers were working shoulder to shoulder with their prisoners, ragged uniforms barely distinguishable from the faded khaki of the inmates.

The object of this activity was a group of thirty Chinese camped outside the gates. Destitute peasants and villagers, soldiers from the puppet armies and abandoned children, they sat in the open road, staring at the barbed-wire gates being strengthened against them. The first of these impoverished people had appeared three months earlier. At night some of the more desperate would climb through the wire, only to be caught by the internees' patrols. Those who survived in the guardhouse till dawn were taken down to the river by the Japanese and clubbed to death on the bank.

As they moved forward to the serving hatch Jim watched the Chinese. Although it was summer the peasants still wore their quilted winter clothes. Needless to say, none of the Chinese was ever admitted to Lunghua Camp, let alone fed. Yet still they came, attracted to this one place in the desolate land where there was food. Worryingly for Jim, they stayed until they died. Mr Maxted was right when he said that with the conclusion of the war the prisoners' real problems would not end, but begin.

Jim worried about Dr Ransome and Mrs Vincent, and the rest of his fellow-prisoners. How would they survive, without the Japanese to look after them? He worried especially for Mr Maxted, whose tired repertory of jokes about the country club meant nothing in the real world. But at least Mr Maxted was trying to keep the camp going, and it was the integrity of the camp on which they depended.

During 1943, when the war was still moving in Japan's favour, the prisoners had worked together. The entertainments committee, of which Mr Maxted had been chairman, organized a nightly programme of lectures and concert parties. This was the happiest year of Jim's life. Tired of his cramped cubicle and Mrs Vincent's nail-tapping aloofness, he spent every evening listening to lectures on an endless variety of topics: the construction of the pyramids, the history of the world land-speed record, the life of a district commissioner in Uganda (the lecturer, a retired Indian Army officer, claimed to have named after himself a lake the size of Wales, which amazed Jim), the infantry weapons of the Great War, the management of the Shanghai Tramways Company, and a score of others.

Sitting in the front row of the assembly hall, Jim devoured these lectures, many of which he attended two or three times. He helped to copy the parts for the Lunghua Players' productions of *Macbeth* and *Twelfth Night*, he moved scenery for *The Pirates of Penzance* and *Trial by Jury*. For most of 1944 there was a camp school run by the missionaries, which Jim found tedious by comparison with the evening lectures. But he deferred to Basie and Dr Ransome. Both agreed that he should never miss a class, if only, Jim suspected, to give themselves a break from his restless energy.

But by the winter of 1944 all this had ended. After the American fighter attacks on Lunghua Airfield, and the first bombing raids on the Shanghai dockyards, the Japanese enforced an evening curfew. The supply of electric current to the camp was switched off for good, and the prisoners retreated to their bunks. The already modest food ration was cut to a single meal each day. American submarines blockaded the Yangtze estuary, and the huge Japanese armies in China began to fall back to the coast, barely able to feed themselves.

The prospect of their defeat, and the imminent assault on the Japanese home islands, made Jim more and more nervous. He ate every scrap of food he could find, aware of the rising numbers of deaths from beri beri and malaria. Jim admired the Mustangs and Superfortresses, but sometimes he wished that the Americans would return to Hawaii and content themselves with raising their battleships at Pearl Harbor. Then Lunghua Camp would once again be the happy place that he had known in 1943.

When Jim and Mr Maxted returned with the rations to G Block the prisoners were waiting silently with their plates and mess-tins. They stood on the steps, the bare-chested men with knobbed shoulders and birdcage ribs, their faded wives in shabby frocks, watching without expression as if about to be presented with a corpse. At the head of the queue were Mrs Pearce and her son, followed by the missionary couples who spent all day hunting for food.

Hundreds of flies hovered in the steam that rose from the metal pails of cracked wheat and sweet potatoes. As he heaved on the wooden handles Jim winced with pain, not from the strain of pulling the cart, but from the heat of the stolen sweet potato inside his shirt. As long as he remained doubled up no one would see the potato, and he put on a pantomime of grimaces and groans.

'Oh, oh . . . oh, my God . . .'

'Worthy of the Lunghua Players, Jim.' Mr Maxted had watched him remove the potato from the pail as they left the kitchens, but he never objected. Crouching forward, Jim abandoned the cart to the missionaries. He ran up the steps, past the Vincents, who stood plates in hand – it never occurred to them, nor to Jim, that they should bring his plate with them. He dived through the curtain into his cubicle and dropped the steaming potato under his mat, hoping that the damp straw would smother the vapour. He seized his plate, and darted back to the foyer to take his place at the head of the queue. Mr Maxted had already served the Reverend and Mrs Pearce, but Jim shouldered aside their son. He held out his plate and received a ladle of boiled wheat and a second sweet potato which he had pointed out to Mr Maxted within moments of leaving the kitchens.

Returning to his bunk, Jim relaxed for the first time. He drew the curtain and lay back, the warm plate like a piece of the sun against his chest. He felt drowsy, but at the same time light-headed with hunger. He rallied himself with the thought that there might be an American air raid that afternoon – who did he want to win? The question was important.

Jim cupped his hands over the sweet potato. He was almost too hungry to enjoy the grey pith, but he gazed at the photograph of the man and woman outside Buckingham Palace, hoping that his parents, wherever they were, also had an extra potato.

When the Vincents returned with their rations Jim sat up and folded back the curtain so that he could examine their plates. He liked to watch Mrs Vincent eating her meals. Keeping a close eye on her, Jim studied the cracked wheat. The starchy grains were white and swollen, indistinguishable from the weevils that infested these warehouse sweepings. In the early years of the camp everyone pushed the weevils to one side, or flicked them through the nearest window, but now Jim carefully husbanded them. Often there was more than a hundred insects in three rows around the rim of Jim's plate, though recently even their number was in decline. 'Eat the weevils,' Dr Ransome had told him, and he did so, although everyone else washed them away. But there was protein in them, a fact that Mr Maxted seemed to find depressing when Jim informed him of it.

After counting the eighty-seven weevils – their numbers, Jim calculated, were falling less steeply than the ration – he stirred them into the cracked wheat, an animal feed grown in northern China, and swallowed the six spoonfuls. Giving himself a breather, he waited for Mrs Vincent to begin her sweet potato.

'Must you, Jim?' Mr Vincent asked. No taller than Jim, the stockbroker and former amateur jockey sat on his bunk beside his ailing son. With his black hair and lined yellow face like a squeezed lemon, he reminded Jim of Basie, but Mr Vincent had never come to terms with Lunghua. 'You'll miss this camp when the war's over. I wonder how you'll take to school in England.'

'It might be a bit strange,' Jim admitted, finishing the last of the weevils. He felt sensitive about his ragged clothes and his determined efforts to stay alive. He wiped his plate clean with his finger, and remembered a favourite phrase of Basie's. 'All the same, Mr Vincent, the best teacher is the university of life.'

Mrs Vincent lowered her spoon. 'Jim, could we finish our meal? We've heard your views on the university of life.'

'Right. But we should eat the weevils, Mrs Vincent.'

'I know, Jim. Dr Ransome told you so.'

'He said we need the protein.'

'Dr Ransome is right. We should all eat the weevils.'

Hoping to brighten the conversation, Jim asked: 'Mrs Vincent, do you believe in vitamins?'

Mrs Vincent stared at her plate. She spoke with true despair. 'Strange child . . .'

The rebuff failed to bother Jim. Everything about this distant woman with her thinning blond hair intrigued him, although in many ways he distrusted her. Six months earlier, when Dr Ransome thought that Jim had contracted pneumonia, she had done nothing to look after him, and Dr Ransome was forced to come in every day and wash Jim himself. Yet the previous evening she had helped him with his Latin homework, matter-of-factly pointing out the distinction between gerunds and gerundives.

Jim waited until she began her sweet potato. After confirming that his own potato was the largest of the four in the room, and deciding not to save any for the turtle under his bunk, he broke the skin and swiftly devoured the warm pulp. When the last morsel had gone he lay back and lowered the curtain. Alone now – the Vincents, although only a few feet away from him, might as well have been on another planet – Jim pondered the jobs ahead of him that day. First, there was the second potato to be smuggled from the room. There were his Latin homework for Dr Ransome, errands to be run for Basie and Private Kimura, and then the afternoon air raid – all in all, a full programme until the evening curfew, when he would probably roam the G Block corridors with his chess set, ready to take on all comers.

The Kennedy *Primer* in hand, Jim stepped from his cubicle. The second potato bulged in his trouser pocket, but for several months the presence of Mrs Vincent had sometimes given him an unexpected erection, and he relied on the confusion to make his escape.

His spoon halfway to his mouth, Mr Vincent stared at the bulge with an expression of deep gloom. His wife gazed in her level fashion at Jim, who side-stepped quickly from the room. Glad as always to be free of the Vincents, he skipped down the corridor to the external door below the fire-escape, and vaulted over the children squatting on one step. As the warm air ruffled the ragged strips of his shirt he ran off into the familiar and reassuring world of the camp.

23
The Air Raid

On his way to the hospital, Jim paused to do his homework at the ruined assembly hall. From the balcony of the upper circle he could not only keep an eye on the pheasant traps across the wire, but also bring himself up to date on any fresh activity at Lunghua Airfield. The stairway to the circle was partly blocked by pieces of masonry that had fallen from the roof, but Jim squeezed himself through a narrow crevice worn smooth by the camp's children. He climbed the stairway, and took his seat on the cement step that formed the first row of the balcony.

The Kennedy propped on his knees, Jim made a leisurely meal of the second potato. Below him, the proscenium arch of the assembly hall had been bombed into a heap of rubble and steel girders, but the landscape now exposed in many ways resembled a panorama displayed on a cinema screen. To the north were the apartment houses of the French Concession, their façades reflected in the flooded paddy fields. To Jim's right, the Whangpoo River emerged from the Nantao district of Shanghai and bent its immense way across the abandoned land.

In front of him was Lunghua Airfield. The concrete runway moved diagonally across its grassy table to the foot of the pagoda. Jim could see the barrels of the anti-aircraft guns mounted on its ancient stone decks, and the powerful landing lights and radio antennae fixed to the tiled roof. Below the pagoda were the hangars and engineering shops, each guarded by sandbag emplacements. A few elderly reconnaissance planes and converted bombers sat on the concrete apron, all that was left of the once invincible air wing that had flown from Lunghua.

Around the edges of the field, in the deep grass by the perimeter road, lay the wreckage of what seemed to Jim to be the entire Japanese Air Force. Scores of rusting aircraft sat on their flattened undercarriages among the trees, or lay in the banks of nettles where they had swerved after crashlanding with their injured crews. For months crippled Japanese aircraft had fallen from the sky on to the graveyard of Lunghua Airfield, as if a titanic aerial battle was taking place far above the clouds.

Already gangs of Chinese scrap-dealers were at work among the derelict planes. With the tireless ability of the Chinese to transform one set of refuse into another, they stripped the metal skins from the wings and retrieved the tyres and fuel tanks. Within days they would be on sale in Shanghai as roofing panels, cisterns and rubber-soled sandals. Whether this scavenging took place with the permission of the Japanese base commander Jim could never decide. Every few hours a party of soldiers would ride out in a truck and drive some of the Chinese away. Jim watched them running across the flooded paddies to the west of the airfield as the Japanese hurled the tyres and metal plates from the salvage carts. But the Chinese always returned to their work, ignored by the anti-aircraft gun-crews in the sandbag emplacements along the perimeter road.

Jim sucked his fingers, drawing the last taste of the sweet potato from his scuffed nails. The warmth of the potato eased the nagging pain in his teeth. He watched the Chinese scavengers at work, tempted to slip through the wire and join them. There were so many new marques of Japanese aircraft. Only four hundred yards from the pheasant traps was the crashed hulk of a Hayate, one of the powerful high-altitude fighters that the Japanese were sending up to destroy the Superfortress bombers on fire-raids over Tokyo.

187

The long grass between the camp and the southern edge of the airfield was rarely patrolled. Jim's practised eye searched the dips and gullies in the banks of nettles and wild sugar-cane, following the course of a forgotten canal.

A second gang of Chinese coolies was at work in the centre of the airfield, repairing the concrete runway. The men carried baskets of stones from the trucks parked among the bomb craters. A steamroller moved to and fro, manned by a Japanese soldier.

The sharp whistle of its valve-gear held Jim to his seat. The gang of coolies reminded him that he too had once worked on the runway. During the past three years, whenever he watched the Japanese aircraft take off from Lunghua, Jim felt an uneasy pride as their wheels left the concrete surface. He and Basie and Dr Ransome, along with those Chinese prisoners being worked to death, had helped to lay the runway that carried the Zeros and Hayates into the air war against the Americans. Jim was well aware that his commitment to the Japanese Air Force stemmed from the still fearful knowledge that he had nearly given his life to build the runway, like the Chinese soldiers buried in their untraceable lime pit beneath the waving sugar-cane. If he had died, his bones and those of Basie and Dr Ransome would have borne the Japanese pilots taking off from Lunghua to hurl themselves at the American picket ships around Iwo Jima and Okinawa. If the Japanese triumphed, that small part of his mind that lay forever within the runway would be appeased. But if they were defeated, all his fears would have been worth nothing.

Jim remembered those pilots of the dusk who had ordered him from the work gang. Whenever he watched the Japanese moving around their aircraft he thought of the three young pilots with their ground crew who had walked through the evening light to inspect the runway.

But for the English boy wandering towards the parked aircraft the Japanese would not even have noticed the work gang.

The fliers fascinated Jim, far more than Private Kimura and his kendo armour. Every day, as he sat on the balcony of the assembly hall or helped Dr Ransome in the vegetable garden of the hospital, he watched the pilots in their baggy flying suits carrying out the external checks before climbing into the cockpits. Above all, Jim admired the kamikaze pilots. In the past month more than a dozen special attack units had arrived at Lunghua Airfield, which they used as their base for suicide missions against the American carriers in the East China Sea. Neither Private Kimura nor the other guards in the camp paid the least attention to the suicide pilots, and Basie and the American seamen in E Block referred to them as 'hashi-crashies' or 'screwy-siders'.

But Jim identified himself with these kamikaze pilots, and was always moved by the threadbare ceremonies that took place beside the runway. The previous morning, as he worked in the hospital garden, he left his sewage pail and ran to the barbed-wire fence in order to see them leave. The three pilots in their white headbands were little older than Jim, with childlike cheeks and boneless noses. They stood by their planes in the hot sunlight, nervously brushing the flies from their mouths, faces pinched as the squad leader saluted. Even when they cheered the Emperor, shouting hoarsely at the audience of flies, none of the anti-aircraft gunners noticed them, and Private Kimura, striding across the tomato plots to call Jim from the wire, seemed baffled by his concern.

Jim opened his Latin primer and began the homework which Dr Ransome had set him: the entire passive tenses of the verb *amo*. He enjoyed Latin; in many ways its strict formality and its families of nouns and verbs resembled the science of chemistry, his father's favourite subject. The Japanese had closed the camp school as a cunning reprisal against the parents, who were trapped all day with their offspring, but Dr Ransome still set Jim a wide range of tasks. There were poems to memorize, simultaneous equations to be solved, general science (where, thanks to his father, Jim often had a surprise for Dr Ransome), and French, which he loathed. There seemed a remarkable amount of schoolwork, Jim reflected, bearing in mind that the war was about to end. But perhaps this was Dr Ransome's way of keeping him quiet for an hour each day. In a sense, too, the homework helped the physician to sustain the illusion that even in Lunghua Camp the values of a vanished England still survived. Misguided though this was, Jim was keen to help Dr Ransome in any way.

'*Amatus sum, amatus es, amatus est* . . .' As he recited the perfect tense, Jim noticed that the Chinese scavengers were running from the derelict aircraft. The work gang of coolies had scattered, throwing their baskets of stones to the ground. The Japanese soldier leapt from the steamroller and ran bare-chested towards the anti-aircraft emplacements, whose guns were searching the sky. Already a flicker of light came from Lunghua Pagoda, as if the Japanese were setting off a devotional firecracker. The sound of this lone machine-gun crossed the airfield, soon drowned by the complaining drone of an air-raid siren. The klaxon above the guardhouse in Lunghua Camp took up the call, a harsh rattle that drilled through Jim's head.

Excited by the prospect of an air raid, Jim peered at the sky through the open roof of the assembly hall. All over the camp the internees were running along the cinder paths. The men and women dozing like asylum inmates on the steps of the huts scrambled through the doors, mothers leaned from ground-floor windows and lifted their children to safety. Within a minute the camp was deserted, leaving

Jim to conduct the air raid alone from the balcony of the assembly hall.

He listened keenly, already suspecting a false alarm. The air raids came earlier each day, as the Americans moved their bases forward across the Pacific and the Chinese mainland. The Japanese were now so nervous that they jumped at every cloud in the sky. A twin-engined transport plane flew across the paddy fields, its pilots unaware of the panic below.

Jim returned to his Latin primer. At that moment an immense shadow crossed the assembly hall and raced along the ground towards the perimeter fence. A tornado of noise filled the air, from which emerged a single-engined fighter with silver fuselage and the Stars-and-Bars insignia of the US Air Force. Only thirty feet above Jim's head, the Mustang's wings were broader than the assembly hall. The fuselage was stained with rust and oil, but its powerful engine had the smooth drive of his father's Packard. The Mustang crossed the perimeter fence and hurtled along the concrete runway of the airfield, the height of a man's head above the deck. In its wake a whirlwind of leaves and dust boiled from the ground.

Around the airfield the anti-aircraft guns turned towards the camp. The tiers of Lunghua Pagoda crackled with light like the Christmas tree display outside the Sincere Company department store in Shanghai. Undeterred, the Mustang flew straight towards the flak tower, the noise of its guns drowned in the blare of another Mustang that swept across the paddy fields to the west of the camp. A third plane came in behind it, so low that Jim was looking down at the cockpit. He could see the pilots, and the insignia on their fuselages blackened by oil spraying from the engine exhausts. Two more Mustangs overflew the camp, and the wash from their engines tore the corrugated iron sheets from the roof of the barrack hut beside G Block. Half a mile to the east, between Lunghua Camp and the river, a second wing of American fighters swept in from the sea, so close to their own shadows on the empty paddy fields that they were hidden behind the lines of grave mounds. They rose as they crossed the perimeter of the airfield, then dived again to fire at the Japanese aircraft parked beside the hangars.

Anti-aircraft shells burst above the camp, their shadows pulsing like heartbeats on the white earth. A shell exploded in a searing flash above the assembly hall, stunning the air. Dust cascaded from the concrete roof and poured on to Jim's shoulders. Waving his Latin primer, Jim counted the dozens of shellbursts. Did the Mustang pilots realize that Basie and the American merchant seamen were imprisoned at Lunghua Camp? Whenever they attacked the airfield the fighter pilots hid until the last moment behind the three-storey dormitory blocks, even though this drew Japanese fire on to the camp and had killed several of the prisoners.

But Jim was glad that the Mustangs were so close. His eyes feasted on every rivet in their fuselages, on the gun ports in their wings, on the huge ventral radiators that Jim was sure had been put there for reasons of style alone. Jim admired the Hayates and Zeros of the Japanese, but the Mustang fighters were the Cadillacs of air combat. He was too breathless to shout to the pilots, but he waved his primer at them as they soared past under the canopy of anti-aircraft shells.

The first flights of attacking planes had swept across the airfield. Clearly visible against the apartment houses of the French Concession, they flew towards Shanghai, ready to strafe the dockyards and the Nantao seaplane base. But the anti-aircraft batteries around the runway were still firing into the air. Cat's cradles of tracer stitched the sky, threads of phosphorus knit and reknit themselves. At their centre was the great pagoda of Lunghua, rising through the smoke that lifted from the burning hangars, its guns throwing out an unbroken flak ceiling.

Jim had never before seen an air attack of such scale. A second wave of Mustangs crossed the paddy fields between Lunghua Camp and the river, followed by a squadron of two-engined fighter-bombers. Three hundred yards to the west of the camp one of the Mustangs dipped its starboard wing towards the ground. Out of control, it slid across the air, and its wing-tip sheared the embankment of a disused canal. The plane cartwheeled across the paddy fields and fell apart in the air. It exploded in a curtain wall of flaming gasoline through which Jim could see the burning figure of the American pilot still strapped to his seat. Riding the incandescent debris of his aircraft, he tore through the trees beyond the perimeter of the camp, a fragment of the sun whose light continued to flare across the surrounding fields.

A second crippled Mustang pulled away from the others in its flight. Trailing a plume of oily smoke, it rose through the anti-aircraft bursts and climbed into the sky. The pilot was trying to escape from the airfield, but as his Mustang began to lose height he rolled the craft on to its back and fell safely from the cockpit. His parachute opened and he dropped steeply to the ground. His burning plane righted itself, towed its black plume in a wavering arc above the empty fields, and then plunged into the river.

The pilot hung alone in the silent sky. His companions sped on towards Shanghai, their silver fuselages lost in the sun-filled windows of the French Concession. The hammering noise of their engines had gone, and the anti-aircraft fire had ceased. A second parachutist was coming down among the canals to the west of the airfield. A stench of burnt oil and engine coolant filled the disturbed air. All over the camp, miniature tornadoes of leaves and dead insects subsided and then whirled along the pathways again as they hunted for the slipstreams of the vanished Mustangs.

The two parachutes fell towards the burial mounds. Already a squad of Japanese soldiers in a truck with a steaming radiator sped along the perimeter road, on their way to kill the pilots. Jim wiped the dust from his Latin primer and waited for the rifle shots. The halo of light which had emerged from the burning Mustang still lay over the creeks and paddies. For a few minutes the sun had drawn nearer to the earth, as if to scorch the death from its fields.

Jim grieved for these American pilots, who died in a tangle of their harnesses, within sight of a Japanese corporal with a Mauser and a single English boy hidden on the balcony of this ruined building. Yet their end reminded Jim of his own, about which he had thought in a clandestine way ever since his arrival at Lunghua. He welcomed the air raids, the noise of the Mustangs as they swept over the camp, the smell of oil and cordite, the deaths of the pilots, and even the likelihood of his own death. Despite everything, he knew he was worth nothing. He twisted his Latin primer, trembling with a secret hunger that the war would so eagerly satisfy.

24

The Hospital

'Jim . . . ! Are you up there . . . ? Have you been hurt . . . ?'

Dr Ransome stood in the rubble on the floor of the assembly hall, shouting at the balcony. He had been exhausted by the effort of running from D Block, and his lungs rattled inside his chest. The years in Lunghua had made him seem taller, but his large bones were held together by little more than a rigging of tendons. Above the rusty beard his one sound eye had seen the top of Jim's head, white with dust as if aged by the air raid.

'Jim, I need you at the hospital. Sergeant Nagata says you can stay with me for the roll-call.'

Jim roused himself from his reverie. Uncannily, the halo cast by the burning body of the American pilot still lay over the empty fields, but he decided not to mention this optical illusion to Dr Ransome. The all-clear siren wailed from the pagoda, a signal repeated by the guard-house klaxon. Jim left the balcony and squeezed his way down the staircase.

'I'm here, Dr Ransome. I think I was nearly killed. Is anyone else dead?'

'Let's hope not.' Dr Ransome leaned against the balustrade, and fanned the dust from his beard with his straw coolie hat. Although unsettled by the air raid, he watched Jim in a weary but patient way. After the raids, when the Japanese guards began to abuse the prisoners, he was often short-tempered with Jim, as if he held him responsible. He ran his hand through Jim's hair, brushing away the powdered cement, and examined his scalp for any signs of blood. 'Jim, we agreed that you wouldn't go up there during the raids. The Japanese have enough to contend with – they may think you're trying to signal to the American pilots.'

'I was, but they didn't see me. The Mustangs are so fast.' Jim liked Dr Ransome, and wanted to reassure him that all was well. 'I've done my Latin prep, doctor.'

Surprisingly, Dr Ransome was not interested in whether Jim had memorized his verbs. He strode towards the hospital, a cluster of bamboo shacks which the prisoners, in a realistic estimate of the camp's medical resources, had built next to the cemetery. The roll-call had already begun, and the pathways were deserted. Japanese guards barged through the barrack huts, breaking the last panes of window glass with their rifle butts. This precaution had been insisted on by Mr Sekura, the camp commandant, to protect the prisoners from bomb blast. In fact, it was a reprisal for the air raid, as the prisoners would know to their cost that dusk when thousands of anopheles mosquitoes rose at feeding time from the stagnant ponds around the camp.

On the steps of E Block, one of the all-male dormitories, Sergeant Nagata screamed into the face of the block leader, Mr Ralston, the organist at the Metropole Cinema in Shanghai. Behind the sergeant three guards stood with fixed bayonets, as if they expected a platoon of American marines to burst from the building. The hundreds of ragged prisoners waited patiently. As the war moved through its closing year the Japanese had become unsettled and dangerous.

'Dr Ransome, what will happen if the Americans land at Woosung?' This port at the mouth of the Yangtze controlled the river approach to Shanghai. Everyone in the camp talked about Woosung.

'The Americans probably will land at Woosung, Jim. I've always thought you should be at MacArthur's headquarters.' Dr Ransome stopped to catch his breath. He forced the air into his bony chest, staring at his reflection in the toecaps of Jim's shoes. 'Try not to think about it – you've so many other things swimming about in your head. The Americans may not land there.'

'If they do, the Japanese will fight.'

'Jim, they'll fight. As you've loyally maintained, the Japanese are the bravest soldiers in the world.'

'Well . . .' Talk of bravery embarrassed Jim. War had nothing to do with bravery. Two years earlier, when he was younger, it had seemed important to work out who were the bravest soldiers, part of his attempt to digest the disruptions of his life. Certainly the Japanese came top, the Chinese bottom, with the British wavering in between. But Jim thought of the American aircraft that had swept the sky. However brave, there was nothing the Japanese could do to stop those beautiful and effortless machines.

'The Japanese are brave,' Jim conceded. 'But bravery isn't important now.'

'I'm not so sure. Are you brave, Jim?'

'No . . . of course not. But I could be,' Jim asserted.

'I think you are.'

Although offhand, Dr Ransome's comment had an unpleasant edge. Clearly he was annoyed with Jim, as if he blamed him for the raiding Mustangs. Was it because he had learned to enjoy the war? Jim debated this as they reached the hospital. On the ground beside the worn bamboo steps was the intact cone of an anti-aircraft shell. He picked it up, curious to see if it would still be warm, but Dr Ransome took it from him and hurled it over the barbed-wire fence.

Jim stood on the rotting steps, flexing his shoes against the bamboo rods. He had been tempted to snatch the shell back from Dr Ransome. He was now almost as tall as the physician and in many ways stronger – during the past three years, as Jim grew, Dr Ransome's large body had shrunk and wasted. Jim could scarcely believe his memories of the burly, red-haired man with heavy thighs and arms, twice the size of the Japanese soldiers. But during their first two years in the camp Dr Ransome had given too much of his own food to Jim.

They entered the hospital, and Jim took his place outside the dispensary with Dr Bowen – an ear, nose and throat specialist at Shanghai General Hospital – and the four missionary widows who formed the nursing staff. While they waited for Sergeant Nagata to conduct the roll-call he peered into the adjacent wards, where the thirty patients lay on their bunks. After every air raid there were a few deaths, from shock or exhaustion. The reminder that the war was nearly over seemed to encourage some people to give up the ghost. However, for those still keen to stay alive, a death was good news. For Jim it meant an old belt or a pair of braces, a fountain pen, and once, miraculously, a wrist-watch that he had worn for three days before handing it over with everything else to Basie. The Japanese had confiscated all watches and clocks – as Dr Ransome said, they wanted their prisoners to be without time. During the three days, Jim had measured the time it took to do everything.

Most of the patients were suffering from malaria, dysentery and heart infections brought on by malnutrition. The beri beri patients particularly unsettled Jim, with their swollen legs and waterlogged lungs, minds so confused that they thought they were dying in England. In their last hours they were given a special privilege, the hospital's one mosquito net, and lay in this makeshift sepulchre before being consigned to the cemetery beside the kitchen garden.

As Sergeant Nagata approached the hospital, accompanied by two soldiers, Jim glanced into the men's ward. For days Mr Barraclough, the secretary of the Shanghai Country Club, had been about to die, and Jim noticed his gold signet ring. It might not be gold – nothing he offered to Basie ever was – but it would be worth something. Jim had no compunction about stealing from the dead. The only patients foolish enough to come to the hospital were those without relatives or friends willing to look after them in the huts or dormitory blocks. Apart from the fact that it contained no medicines – the small supply allocated by the Japanese had been used in the first year – the hospital rarely cured anyone. The Japanese, correctly assuming that all those who entered the hospital would soon be dead, immediately halved their food ration. Even so, Jim thought, it could take a remarkable time before Dr Ransome and Dr Bowen pronounced them officially dead. Jim knew that a large number of the extra potatoes he had eaten were dead men's rations. Dr Ransome worked hard for the sick, and Jim was sorry that recently he had seemed to lose hope.

'They're here,' Dr Ransome called out. 'Jim, stand to attention. Don't argue with Sergeant Nagata today. And don't tell him about the air raid.'

Noticing that Jim's eyes were fixed on the signet ring, he turned his head to face Sergeant Nagata as he clattered up the bamboo steps. Dr Ransome disapproved of the grave-robbery, though he was aware that Jim traded the belt-buckles and braces for food. However, as Jim quietly reflected, Dr Ransome had his own sources of supply. Unlike most of the prisoners in Lunghua, who had been allowed to pack a suitcase before being interned, Dr Ransome had entered the camp with nothing but his shirt, shorts and leather sandals. Yet his cubicle in D Block housed an impressive inventory of possessions – a complete change of clothes, a portable gramophone and several records, a tennis racquet, a rugby football, and the shelf of textbooks that had provided Jim with his education. These, like all the clothes that Jim had worn in the camp and like the magnificent golf shoes that instantly caught Sergeant Nagata's eye, Dr Ransome had obtained from the stream of

patients who visited his D Block cubicle each evening.
Many had nothing to give, but the younger wives always
brought a modest cumshaw for whatever mysterious service
Dr Ransome provided. Richard Pearce had even recognized
that Jim was wearing one of his old shirts, but too late.

Sergeant Nagata stopped in front of the prisoners. The
scale of the American air raid had clearly shaken him. His
jaws clenched as he expressed a few drops of spittle on to his
lips. The bristles around his mouth trembled like miniature
antennae picking up an advance warning of the rage to
come. He needed to work himself up into a fury, but the
gleaming toecaps of Jim's shoes distracted him. Like all
Japanese soldiers, the sergeant wore rotting boots through
which his big toes protruded like immense thumbs.

'Boy . . .' He paused in front of Jim and tapped his head
with the roll-sheet, releasing a cloud of white dust. He knew
from Private Kimura that Jim was involved in every illicit
activity in the camp, but had never been able to catch him.
He waved away the dust, and with an effort uttered the only
two consecutive words of English which the years in
Lunghua had taught him: 'Difficult boy . . .'

Jim waited for him to go on, fascinated by the spittle on
his lips. Perhaps Sergeant Nagata would appreciate a
first-hand account of the air raid?

But the sergeant strode into the men's ward, shouting in
Japanese to the two doctors. He stared down at the dying
men, in whom he had never shown the slightest interest,
and Jim had the sudden exhilarating notion that Dr Ransome was hiding a wounded American pilot. He wanted to
touch the pilot before the Japanese killed him, feel his
helmet and flight suit, run his fingers over the dust and oil
on his goggles.

'Jim . . . ! Stop thinking . . . !' Mrs Philips, one of the
missionary widows, caught him as he swayed forward,
almost swooning before the image of this archangelic figure

fallen among the paddies. Jim stood to attention, pretending to be weak with hunger, and trying to avoid the suspicious stare of the Japanese sentry at the dispensary door. He waited for the roll-call to end, reflecting on the likely booty attached to a dead American pilot. Soon enough, one of the Americans would be shot down into Lunghua Camp. Jim tried to decide which of the ruined buildings would best conceal his body. Carefully eked out, the kit and equipment could be bartered with Basie for extra sweet potatoes for months to come, and even perhaps a warm coat for the winter. There would be sweet potatoes for Dr Ransome, whom Jim was determined to keep alive.

He rocked on his heels and listened to an old woman crying in the nearby ward. Through the window was the pagoda at Lunghua Airfield. Already the flak tower appeared in a new light.

For another hour Jim stood in line with the missionary widows, watched by the sentry. Dr Ransome and Dr Bowen had set off with Sergeant Nagata to the commandant's office, perhaps to be interrogated. The guards moved around the silent camp with their roster boards, carrying out repeated roll-calls. The war was about to end, and yet the Japanese were obsessed with knowing exactly how many prisoners they held.

Jim closed his eyes to calm his mind, but the sentry barked at him, suspecting that Jim was about to play some private game of which Sergeant Nagata would disapprove. The memory of the air raid excited Jim. The Mustangs still streaked across the camp on their way to attack the flak tower. He imagined himself at the controls of one of the fighters, falling to earth when his plane exploded, rising again as one of the childlike kamikaze pilots who cheered the Emperor before hurling their Zeros into the American carriers at Okinawa. One day Jim would become a wounded pilot, fallen among the burial mounds and armoured pagodas. Pieces of his flying suit and parachute, even perhaps his own body, would spread across the paddy fields, feeding the prisoners behind their wire and the Chinese starving at the gate . . .

'Jim . . . !' Mrs Philips hissed. 'Practise your Latin . . .'

Forcing himself not to blink, to the irritation of the Japanese sentry, Jim stared into the sunlight outside the dispensary window. The silent landscape seemed to seethe with flames, the halo born from the burning body of the American pilot. The light touched the rusting wire of the perimeter fence and the dusty fronds of the wild sugar-cane, bleached the wings of the derelict aircraft and the bones of the peasants in the burial mounds. Jim longed for the next air raid, dreaming of the violent light, barely able to breathe for the hunger that Dr Ransome had recognized but could never feed.

25
The Cemetery Garden

When the roll-call ended Jim rested on the hospital steps. Dr Ransome and Dr Bowen returned from the commandant's office and immediately shut themselves in the dispensary with the four missionary widows. Dr Ransome seemed as nervous as the Japanese. The old scar below his eye was flushed with blood. Had Sergeant Nagata slapped him for protesting at a further cut in the food ration?

Hands in pockets, Jim sauntered down the cinder track behind the hospital. He surveyed the rows of tomatoes, beans and melons in the kitchen garden. The modest crop was meant to supplement the patients' meagre diet, though many of the vegetables found their way to the American seamen in E Block. Jim enjoyed his work with the plants. He knew each of them personally, and could tell at a glance if the children had stolen a single tomato. Fortunately the long lines of graves in the adjacent cemetery kept them away. Apart from its nutritional benefits, botany was an intriguing subject. In the dispensary Dr Ransome sliced and stained the slivers of plant stems and roots, mounted them under Dr Bowen's microscope and made Jim draw the hundreds of cells and nutrient vessels. Plant classification was an entire universe of words; every weed in the camp had a name. Names surrounded everything; invisible encyclopaedias lay in every hedge and ditch.

The previous afternoon Jim had dug two fertilizer trenches for a new crop of tomato plants. Between the garden and the cemetery was a row of fifty-gallon drums which he and Dr Ransome had buried in the ground, then filled with sewage from the overflowing septic tank in G Block. A party of prisoners in the block had decanted most of the sewage into one of the drained ponds, but Jim and Dr Ransome made their own trips with bucket, rope and cart. As Dr Ransome said, there was no point in wasting anything that could keep them alive for even a few days longer. The glowing tomatoes and puffed-up melons proved him right.

Jim moved the wooden hatch from one of the drums. He waited for the thousands of flies to have the first share, then picked up the bamboo ladle with its wooden cup and began to pour the manure into the shallow trenches. He worked with the slow but measured rhythm of the Chinese peasants he had watched as they fertilized their crops before the war.

An hour later, when he had covered the manure with a layer of soil, Jim rested on one of the graves in the nearby cemetery. Various people were visiting the hospital, the block leaders and their deputies, a party of Americans from E Block, the senior Dutch and Belgians. But Jim was too tired to pester them for news. It was peaceful in the kitchen garden with its green walls of beans and tomato plants. Often he visualized staying there forever, even after the war ended.

He pushed this rustic fantasy to the back of his mind and listened to the drone of a Zero fighter warming up at the end of the runway. A single kamikaze plane was about to take off, all that the Japanese could muster as a reprisal for the American air raid. The young pilot, barely older than Jim, wore his ceremonial sashes, but the honour guard consisted only of a corporal and a junior private. Both turned away before the pilot had climbed into his cockpit, and walked back to their repair work on the damaged hangars.

Jim watched the plane rise shakily from the runway. It climbed over the camp, engine labouring under the weight of the bomb, banked towards the river and set course for the open China Sea. He cupped his hands over his eyes and followed the plane until it vanished among the clouds. None of the Japanese at Lunghua Airfield had given the aircraft the briefest glance. Fires were still burning in the hangars by the pagoda, and a cloud of steam rose from the bombed engineering sheds. Already, though, the craters were being filled by the work gang of Chinese coolies, and the scrap-dealers were scavenging the hulks of the derelict planes.

'Are you still interested in aeroplanes, Jim?' Mrs Philips asked, as she and Mrs Gilmour emerged from the hospital courtyard. 'You'll have to join the RAF.'

'I'm going to join the Japanese Air Force.'

'Oh? The Japanese . . . ?' The missionary widows tittered, still unsure of Jim's sense of humour, and pushed their wooden cart. The iron wheels rang on the stony track, shaking the body which the two women were about to bury.

Jim polished the three tomatoes he had picked from the plants. None was larger than a marble, but Basie would appreciate them. He slipped them into his shirt pocket and watched Mrs Philips and Mrs Gilmour digging the grave. Soon exhausted, the two women sat on the cart and rested beside the corpse.

He walked over to them and took the spade from Mrs Philips' worn hands. The body was that of Mr Radik, the former head chef at the Cathay Hotel. Jim had enjoyed his scholarly lectures on the Atlantic liner *Berengaria*, and was glad to repay his debt. He dug the soft soil. In one of their few acts of foresight, when they were still strong enough to do so, the prisoners had part-excavated the narrow graves. But the effort of removing a further spade's depth of damp soil was now too much for the missionary widows. The dead were buried above ground, the loose soil heaped around them. The heavy rains of the monsoon months softened the mounds, so that they formed outlines of the bodies within them, as if this small cemetery beside the military airfield were doing its best to resurrect a few of the millions who had died in the war. Here and there an arm or a foot protruded from the graves, the limbs of restless sleepers struggling beneath their brown quilts. Rats had burrowed deep into the grave of Mrs Hug, the Dutchwoman who had arrived at Lunghua with Basie and Dr Ransome, and the tunnels reminded Jim of the Maginot Line he had constructed behind the rockery at Amherst Avenue for his army of lead soldiers.

He dug away, deciding to sink Mr Radik well below the ground so that the chef would not become an instant meal for the rats. Mrs Gilmour and Mrs Philips sat on the cart beside the corpse and watched without comment. Whenever he paused to rest they treated him to two identical smiles, as blanched as the flowers in the patterns of their tattered cotton dresses.

'Jim! Leave that and come over! I need you here!' Dr Ransome was shouting from the dispensary window. He had always disliked Jim digging the graves.

Hundreds of flies buzzed around the cart and settled on Mr Radik's face. With the *Berengaria* in mind, Jim continued to spade the soil.

'Jim, doctor's calling . . .'

'All right – it's ready.'

The women pulled Mr Radik from the cart. Although wearied by the effort, they handled him with the same care they had shown when he was alive. Was he still alive for these two Christian widows? Jim had always been impressed by strong religious beliefs. His mother and father were agnostics, and he respected devout Christians in the same way that he respected people who were members of the Graf Zeppelin Club or shopped at the Chinese department stores, for their mastery of an exotic foreign ritual. Besides, those who worked hardest for others, like Mrs Philips and Mrs Gilmour and Dr Ransome, often held beliefs that turned out to be correct.

'Mrs Philips,' he asked as they settled Mr Radik into his

grave, 'when does the soul leave the body? Before it's buried?'

'Yes, Jim.' Mrs Philips knelt on the ground and began to scoop the earth over Mr Radik's face. 'Mr Radik's soul has already left. Doctor's calling again. I hope you've done your Latin prep.'

'Of course.' Jim reflected on all this as he walked to the hospital. He often watched the eyes of the patients as they died, trying to detect a flash of light when the soul left. Once he had helped Dr Ransome as he massaged the naked chest of a young Belgian woman wasted by dysentery. Dr Bowen had said that she was dead, but Dr Ransome squeezed her heart under her ribs and suddenly her eyes swivelled and looked at Jim. At first Jim thought that her soul had returned to her, but she was still dead. Mrs Philips and Mrs Gilmour took her away and buried her an hour later. Dr Ransome explained that for a few seconds he had pumped the blood back into her brain.

Jim entered the dispensary and sat at the metal table facing Dr Ransome. He would have liked to take up the matter of Mr Radik's soul, but the doctor was curiously reluctant to discuss religious topics with Jim, although he himself went to the church services on Sunday morning. The scar on his face was still flushed with blood, and he was ominously busy with his tray of melted wax. Whenever he was tired, or annoyed with Jim, Dr Ransome would melt a few candles and immerse squares of old cloth in the hot liquid, then hang them up to cool. The previous winter he had made hundreds of these wax panels, which the prisoners had used to replace the broken window panes. Although the hours of work had helped to keep out the freezing winds that swept down from northern China, few of the prisoners were grateful to Dr Ransome. Still, as Jim had observed, Dr Ransome was not interested in their gratitude.

Jim dipped a finger in the hot wax, but Dr Ransome brusquely waved him away. Clearly his conversation with the camp commandant had upset him – he was preparing for the winter as if trying to convince himself that they would all be there when it arrived.

Taking off his shoes, Jim began to buff the toecaps. After three years in clogs and cast-offs, he enjoyed impressing everyone with these expensive leather brogues.

'Jim, it's admirable of you to look so smart, but try not to polish them *all* the time.' Dr Ransome stared heavily at the wax square. 'They unsettle Sergeant Nagata.'

'I like them to look bright.'

'They're very bright. Even the American pilots must have seen them. They probably think we have a golf course here and set their compasses to your toecaps.'

'That means I'm helping the war effort?'

'In a way . . .' Before Jim could put on his shoes Dr Ransome held his ankle. Most of the sores on Jim's legs were infected, and given the poor diet would never properly heal, but above the right ankle was an ulcer the size of a penny, engorged with pus. Dr Ransome moved the tray of melted wax from the candle-lamp. He boiled a spoonful of water in a metal pail, then drained and cleaned the ulcer with a cotton swab.

Jim submitted without protest. He had formed his only close bond in Lunghua with Dr Ransome, though he knew that in many ways the physician disapproved of him. He resented Jim for revealing an obvious truth about the war, that people were only too able to adapt to it. At times he even suspected that Jim enjoyed Latin for the wrong reasons. The brother of a games master at an English boarding school (one of those repressive institutions, so like Lunghua, for which Jim was apparently destined), he had been working up-country with Protestant missionaries. Dr Ransome was rather like a school prefect and head of rugby, though Jim was unsure how far this manner was calculated. He had noticed that the doctor could be remarkably devious when it suited him.

'Now, Jim, I'm sure you've done your prep . . .' Dr Ransome opened the Latin primer. Although distracted by the prisoners who gathered outside the huts and dormitory blocks, he stared hard at the text. Hundreds of men and their wives, many with their children, were crossing the parade ground. He began to question Jim, who continued to polish his shoes under the table.

'"They were being loved" . . . ?'

'*Amabantur.*'

'"I shall be loved" . . . ?'

'*Amabor.*'

'"You will have been loved" . . . ?'

'*Amatus eris.*'

'Right – I'll set you an unseen. Mrs Vincent will help you with the vocabulary. She doesn't mind your asking?'

'Not now.' Jim reported her change of heart matter-of-factly. He guessed that Dr Ransome had been useful with some special woman's problem.

'Good. People need to be encouraged. She may not be much use with the trig.'

'I don't need her to help me.' Jim enjoyed trigonometry. Unlike Latin or algebra, this branch of geometry was directly involved in a subject close to his heart – aerial warfare. 'Dr Ransome, the American bombers that flew with the Mustangs were going at 320 miles an hour – I timed their shadows across the camp with my heart-beat. If they want to hit Lunghua Airfield they have to drop their bombs about a thousand yards away.'

'Jim, you're a war-child. I imagine the Japanese gunners know that too.'

Jim sat back thinking this over. 'They might not.'

'Well, we can't tell them – or can we? That would be

unfair to the American pilots. As it is, the Japanese are shooting too many of them down.'

'But they're shooting them down over the airfield,' Jim explained. 'Then they've already dropped their bombs. If they want to stop them hitting the runway they should shoot them down more than a thousand yards away.' The prospect excited Jim – applied to the Japanese bases all over the Pacific area this new tactic might turn the war against the Americans and so save Lunghua Camp. He drummed his fingers on the table, imitating the way in which he had played the white piano in the empty house in Amherst Avenue.

'Yes . . .' Dr Ransome reached out and gently pressed Jim's hands to the table, trying to calm him. He submerged another cotton square in the wax tray. 'Perhaps we'll leave the trig, and I'll mark up some algebra. We want the war to end, Jim.'

'Of course, Dr Ransome.'

'*Do* you want the war to end, Jim?' Dr Ransome often seemed doubtful about this. 'A lot of the people here won't last much longer. You're keen to see your mother and father again?'

'Yes, I am. I think about them every day.'

'Good. Do you remember what they look like?'

'I do remember . . .' Jim hated lying to Dr Ransome, but in a sense he was thinking of the photograph of the unknown man and woman he had pinned to the wall of his cubicle. He had never divulged to the physician that these were his surrogate parents. Jim knew that it was important to keep alive the memory of his mother and father, in order to sustain his confidence in the future, but their faces had become hazy. Dr Ransome might not approve of the way in which he was tricking himself.

'I'm glad you remember them, Jim. They may have changed.'

'I know – they'll be hungry.'

210

'More than hungry, Jim. When the war does end everything is going to be very uncertain.'

'So we should stay in the camp?' Jim liked the sound of this. Too many of the prisoners talked about leaving the camp without any real idea of what would happen to them. 'As long as we stay in Lunghua the Japanese will look after us.'

'I'm not sure that they will. We've become an embarrassment to them. They can't feed us any longer, Jim . . .'

So this was what Dr Ransome had been leading towards. Jim felt a quiet tiredness come over him. His long hours spent hauling the buckets of sewage, planting and watering the crops in the hospital garden, pulling the ration cart with Mr Maxted, had been part of his attempt to keep the camp going. Yet, as he had known all along, the supply of food depended on the whim of the Japanese. His own feelings, his determination to survive, counted for nothing in the end. The activity meant no more than the movement in the eyes of the Belgian woman who had seemed to come back from the dead.

'Is there going to be any more food, Dr Ransome?'

'We hope some will come through. The Japanese can no longer feed themselves. The American submarines . . .'

Jim stared at the polished toecaps of his shoes. He wanted his mother and father to see them before they died. He rallied himself, trying to summon his old will to survive. Deliberately he thought of the curious pleasure the corpses in the hospital cemetery gave him, the guilty excitement of being alive at all. He knew why Dr Ransome disliked him digging the graves.

Dr Ransome marked the exercises in the algebra textbook, and gave him two strips of rice-paper bandage on which to solve the simultaneous equations. As he stood up Dr Ransome removed the three tomatoes from Jim's pocket. He laid them on the table by the wax tray.

'Did they come from the hospital garden?'

'Yes.' Jim gazed frankly at Dr Ransome. Recently he had begun to see him with a more adult eye. The long years of imprisonment, the constant disputes with the Japanese, had made this young physician seem middle-aged. Dr Ransome was often unsure of himself, as he was of Jim's theft.

'I have to give Basie something whenever I see him.'

'I know. It's a good thing that you're friends with Basie. He's a survivor, though survivors can be dangerous. Wars exist for people like Basie.' Dr Ransome placed the tomatoes in Jim's hand. 'I want you to eat them, Jim. I'll get you something for Basie.'

'Dr Ransome . . .' Jim searched for some way of reassuring him. 'If we told Sergeant Nagata about the thousand-yard range . . . the Japanese wouldn't shoot down any more planes, but they might give us some food . . . ?'

Dr Ransome smiled for the first time. He unlocked the medicine cabinet and from a steel cash box he removed two rubber condoms.

'Jim, you're a pragmatist. Give these to Basie, he'll have something for you. Now eat your tomatoes and go.'

26
The Lunghua Sophomores

'We're the Lunghua Sophomores,
We're the girls every boy adores,
C.A.C. don't mean a thing to me,
For every Tuesday evening we go on a spree . . .'

As he crossed the parade ground towards E Block, Jim paused to watch the Lunghua Players rehearsing their next concert party on the steps of Hut 6. The leader of the troupe was Mr Wentworth, the manager of the Cathay Bank, whose exaggerated and theatrical manner fascinated Jim. He enjoyed the amateur dramatics, when everyone involved was at the centre of public attention. Jim had played a page in *Henry V*, a role he relished. The costume which Mrs Wentworth had run up for him out of purple velvet was the only decent garment he had worn for three years. He had offered to wear it in the Lunghua Players' next production, *The Importance of Being Earnest*, but Mr Wentworth had declined to cast him.

'. . . We've debates and lectures too,
And concerts just for you . . .'

The rehearsal was not a success. The four chorus girls in their pierrot costumes stood on the makeshift stage of packing cases, trying to remember the song. Upset by the air raid, the women ignored Mr Wentworth and listened to the sky. Despite the hot sunlight, they rubbed their arms to keep warm.

The audience of bored internees wandered away, and Jim decided to leave the actors to it. The Lunghua Players recruited their members from the snootiest of the English

213

families, and there was something absurd about their high-pitched voices – as affected as the rugby match which Dr Ransome, in a rare lapse from common sense, had arranged the previous winter. The teams of starving prisoners (husbands of the Lunghua Sophomores) had tottered around the parade ground in a grotesque parody of a rugby game, too exhausted to pass the ball and jeered at by a crowd of fellow-prisoners excluded from the game because they had never learned the rules.

Jim passed the guardhouse, carrying out a quick survey of the camp. A group of prisoners had gathered by the gates, waiting for the military truck which brought the daily rations from Shanghai. No official announcement had been made that the ration was to be cut, but the news had already spread through the camp.

Significantly, there were fewer Chinese beggars outside the gates. A dead peasant woman lay on the grass verge, but the disbanded puppet soldiers and out-of-work rickshaw coolies had gone, leaving behind a circle of squatting old men and a few wan-faced children.

Jim entered E Block, the men's dormitory building, and climbed the stairway to the third floor. Regardless of the weather, the British prisoners in E Block spent almost all their time in their bunks. A few were too ill with malaria to move, and lay stretched out on straw mats soaked with sweat and urine. But others still strong enough to walk lounged beside them, examining their hands for hours or staring at the walls.

The sight of so many adult men unwilling to cope with the reality of the camp always puzzled Jim, but he recovered as soon as he reached the American dormitory. He liked the Americans and approved of them in every way. Whenever he entered this enclave of irony and good humour his spirits rose.

Two of the former classrooms were occupied by the

214

American merchant seamen. The partition doors had been removed, and the high-ceilinged chamber was filled by some sixty men. Jim surveyed the maze of cubicles. The Britons in E Block lived in open dormitories, but each of the American seamen had constructed a small cubicle from whatever materials he could scavenge – threadbare sheets, wooden planks, straw mats and woven bamboo. Now and then a party of Americans would emerge from E Block and play a relaxed game of softball, but usually they remained in their cubicles. There they lay on their bunks and entertained a steady stream of adolescent girls, single British women and even a few wives drawn to them for reasons not very different from Jim's.

By some mechanism that Jim had never understood, the sexual activity seemed to generate an endless supply of those items that most fascinated him. This treasure had been brought into the camp by the American sailors and now circulated like a second currency – comic books and copies of *Life, Reader's Digest* and *Saturday Evening Post*, novelty pens, lipsticks and powder compacts, gaudy tie-pins, cigarette lighters and celluloid belts, fairground cufflinks and wild west buckles – a collection of gewgaws that in Jim's eyes had the style and magic of the Mustang fighters.

'Say, it's Shanghai Jim . . .'

'Kid, Basie's mad at you . . .'

'You want to play chess, son?'

'Jim, I need hot water and a shave.'

'Jim, bring me a left-handed screwdriver and a bucket of steam . . .'

'Why's Basie mad at Jim?'

Jim exchanged greetings with the Americans – Cohen, the softball wizard and chess fanatic; Tiptree, the large, kindly stoker who was the comic-book king; Hinton, yet another cabin steward and philosopher: Dainty, the telegraphist and premier cocksman of Lunghua – amiable men whose rôles they played for Jim's benefit and constantly guyed. When they noticed him, most of them liked Jim, who in return, and out of respect for America, ran endless errands for them. Several of the cubicles were closed as the merchant seamen entertained their visitors, but the others had their curtains raised so that the sailors could lie on their bunks and observe the passing world. Two of the older seamen were racked by malaria, but they made little fuss about being ill. All in all, Jim felt, the Americans were the best company, not as strange and challenging as the Japanese, but far superior to the morose and complicated British.

Why was Basie angry with him? Jim stepped down the narrow corridor between the suspended sheets. He could hear an English woman from Hut 5 complaining about her husband, and two Belgian girls who lived with their widowed father in G Block giggled over some object they were being shown.

Basie's cubicle was in the north-east corner of the room, with two windows that gave him a clear view of the entire camp. As always he was sitting on his bunk, keeping an eye on the Japanese soldiers outside the guardhouse as he received the latest report from Demarest, his cubicle neighbour and chief henchman. His long-sleeved cotton shirt was faded but neatly creased – after Jim had washed and dried the shirts Basie would fold them in a complex, origami-like package and slide them under his sleeping mat, from which they emerged with a department-store sharpness. Since Basie rarely moved from his bunk he seemed even cooler and crisper in Jim's eyes than Mr Sekura, and in most respects the years in Lunghua had been less of a strain for Basie than for the Japanese commandant. His hands and cheeks were still soft and unworn, though with a pallor like that of an unhealthy woman. Moving around his cubicle, as if in his pantry on the SS *Aurora*, he regarded Lunghua

216

Camp in the same way he had viewed the world beyond it, a suite of cabins to be kept ready for a succession of unwary passengers.

'Come in, kid. Stop breathing so much, you're making Basie all hot.' Demarest, a former bar steward, spoke without moving his lips – either, as Jim believed, he had spent an earlier career as a ventriloquist or, as Mr Maxted maintained, he had passed long terms in prison.

'The boy's all right . . .' Basie beckoned Jim to sit down, as Demarest returned to his cubicle. 'There just isn't enough air for him in the whole of Lunghua. Isn't that it, Jim?'

Jim tried to control his panting – not enough red cells, according to Dr Ransome, but often he and Basie meant the same thing.

'You're right, Basie. The Mustangs took it all with them. Did you see the air raid?'

'I heard it, Jim . . .' Basie glanced darkly at Jim, as if holding him responsible for the noise. 'Those Filipino pilots must have gone to flight school at Coney Island.'

'Filipino?' Jim at last mastered his lungs. 'Were they really Filipino pilots?'

'Some of them, Jim. There are a couple of wings operating with MacArthur's outfit. The rest are old Flying Tigers based at Chungking.' Basie nodded sagely, watching Jim to make sure he appreciated his superior savvy.

'Chungking . . .' Jim was agog. This was the kind of information on which his mind feasted, even though he knew that Basie embroidered the reports for his benefit. Somewhere in the camp was a concealed radio, which had never been discovered, not because it was well hidden, but because the Japanese were confused by the false tips given by prisoners eager to collaborate. Despite all his efforts, Jim had been unable to track down the radio, which was inactive for long periods. Then Basie would supply him with news bulletins of his own describing a parallel war. Jim always pretended to be impressed, though he could rarely separate rumour from outright fiction. It was an important way of keeping them close together.

Also, there was Basie's interest in Jim's expanding vocabulary.

'You did your schoolwork today, Jim? You learned all your words?'

'I did, Basie. A lot of Latin words.' Basie was intrigued by Jim's command of Latin, but easily bored, so he decided not to recite the whole passive tense of *Amo*. 'And some new English words. "Pragmatist",' he suggested, which Basie greeted with gloom, 'and "survivor".'

'"Survivor"?' Basie chuckled at this. 'That's a useful word. Are you a survivor, Jim?'

'Well . . .' Dr Ransome had not meant the term as a compliment. Jim tried to remember another word of interest. Basie never used the words, but seemed to store them away, keeping them in reserve for a better day, as if preparing himself for a life of elaborate formality.

'Is there any more news, Basie? When are the Americans going to land at Woosung?'

But Basie was preoccupied. He rested his head against the pillow and stared at the contents of the cubicle, as if burdened by all his possessions. At first sight the cubicle seemed to be filled with old rags and wicker baskets, but it actually contained a complete general store. There were aluminium pots and pans, an assortment of women's slacks and blouses, a mah-jong set, several tennis racquets, half a dozen unmatched shoes and a king's ransom of old copies of the *Reader's Digest* and *Popular Mechanics*. All these had been obtained by barter, though Jim had never understood what Basie gave in return – like Dr Ransome, he had come into the camp with nothing.

On the other hand, it had occurred to Jim that much of

this equipment was useless. No one was strong enough to play tennis, the shoes were full of holes and there was nothing to cook in the saucepans. The cabin steward, for all his guile, was the same limited man whom Jim had first met at the Nantao shipyards, with the same clear but small view of the world. Basie's talents expanded to fill only the most modest possibilities of petty thievery around him. Jim worried about what would happen to Basie when the war was over.

'Jobs, Jim,' Basie announced. 'You set out the traps? How far did you go? Across the creek?'

'Right across the creek, Basie. I went as far as the old drill hall.'

'Good . . .'

'I didn't see any pheasants, Basie. I don't think there are any pheasants. It's too close to the airfield.'

'There are pheasants, Jim. But we need to move the traps to the Shanghai road.' He peered shrewdly at Jim. 'Then we'll have to set up a decoy.'

'We could set up a decoy, Basie.' Jim guessed that there already was a decoy – himself. The whole enterprise of setting the traps had nothing to do with catching pheasants. Perhaps one of the Americans was planning to visit Shanghai, and Jim was being used to test the escape route. Alternatively, these bored sailors might be playing a game, betting amongst each other on how far he could push the traps before being shot by the Japanese sentry in the watch-tower. Although they liked Jim, they were quite capable of gambling with his life. That was American humour of a most special kind.

He swayed with fatigue, wishing he could lie across the foot of the bunk. Basie was watching him in an expectant way. From his window he would have seen Jim at work in the hospital garden, and he was waiting for a few beans or tomatoes. Basie always demanded these tidbits, though he was generous in his own way. When Jim was younger Basie spent hours making toys for him out of copper wire and cotton reels, sewing exquisite fish flies that hung from free-floating buoys. On his birthdays it was only Basie who gave him a present.

'Basie, I brought something for you . . .' Jim took the two condoms from his pocket. Basie pulled a rusty biscuit tin from below his bunk. As he removed the lid Jim saw that the tin was packed with hundreds of the prophylactics, as the Americans called them. Once the original stock of cigarettes was exhausted, these grubby rubbers formed Lunghua Camp's main unit of currency. The number in circulation had barely fallen in three years, not because there was little sexual intercourse at Lunghua, but for the reason that the contraceptives were too valuable as units of exchange to be used for idle purposes. Playing poker, the American sailors used stacks of the condoms as chips. It was doubly ironic, as Jim had heard Dr Ransome remark, that their value continued to rise even though almost all the prisoners in the camp were either impotent or infertile.

Basie inspected the condoms, suspicious of their pristine condition.

'Where did you get these, Jim?'

'They're good ones, Basie. That's the best type.'

'Is that so?' Basie often accepted Jim's expertise in unlikely areas. 'Perhaps you were looking inside Dr Ransome's medical cabinet?'

'There weren't any tomatoes, Basie. The air raid spoiled them.'

'Those Filipino pilots . . . Never mind. Tell me about Dr Ransome's cabinet. There were medicines there, I imagine.'

'Basie, there were a lot of medicines. Iodine, mercurichrome . . .' In fact the cupboard was bare. Jim tried to remember the medicine chest in his father's bathroom, and

220

the strange names that summed up the mysterious world of the adult body. '. . . pessaries, linctus, suppositories . . .'

'Suppositories? Lie down, Jim. You're getting tired.' Basie put an arm around Jim's shoulders. Together they gazed through the window at the crowd of prisoners waiting for the overdue ration truck from Shanghai. 'Don't worry, Jim, there'll be plenty to eat soon. Forget all this talk about the Japs cutting our rations.'

'They might do it, Basie. We're an embarrassment to them.'

'An embarrassment? Dr Ransome is worrying you with all these words. Believe me, Jim, it's going to take more than us to embarrass the Japs.' He reached under his pillow and brought out a small sweet potato. 'You eat this while I work out our jobs. When you've finished I'll give you a *Reader's Digest* you can take back to G Block.'

'Say, thanks, Basie!' Jim devoured the potato. He liked Basie's cubicle. The abundance of objects, even if they were useless, was reassuring, like the abundance of words around Dr Ransome. The Latin vocabulary and the algebraic terms were useless too, but they helped to make up a world. Basie's confidence in the future encouraged him.

Sure enough, as he licked the last pith from his fingers, saving the skin for the evening, the military truck arrived from Shanghai with the prisoners' food ration.

27

The Execution

Two Japanese soldiers with fixed bayonets stood behind the driving cabin of the truck, their thighs lost among the sacks of potatoes and cracked wheat. However, as he leaned from Basie's window, Jim could see that the ration had been halved. He was glad that some food had come, but at the same time he felt almost disappointed. A crowd of several hundred prisoners followed the truck towards the kitchens, hands in the pockets of their ragged shorts, their clogs clattering. How would they have behaved if the truck had been empty? None of the prisoners, not even Dr Ransome, seemed able to rally themselves for the last stages of the war. Jim almost welcomed the hunger, when he would see again the curious light the Mustangs had brought with them . . .

Around him the Americans were leaving their cubicles and pressing against the windows. Demarest pointed to the columns of smoke that rose from the dockyard districts of northern Shanghai. Although they were more than ten miles away, Jim could hear a hard rumble across the deserted paddy fields, a forgotten thunder that reverberated over the land long after the bombs had exploded. The sounds drummed at the windows, a vague ultimatum to the listless prisoners of Lunghua.

Jim searched the smoke clouds for any signs of American aircraft. None of the dozen serviceable Zeros at Lunghua Airfield had taken off to intercept them.

'B-29s, Basie?'

'That's it, Jim. Superfortress bombers, what we call a hemisphere defence weapon. All the way from Guam.'

'From Guam, Basie . . . .' Jim was impressed by the

thought of these four-engined bombers making the long journey across the Pacific, in order to attack the Shanghai dockyards where he had spent so many happy hours playing hide and seek. The B-29s awed Jim. The huge, streamlined bombers summed up all the power and grace of America. Usually the B-29s flew above the Japanese anti-aircraft fire, but two days earlier Jim had seen a single Superfortress cross the paddy fields to the west of the camp, only five hundred feet above the ground. Two of its engines were on fire, but the sight of this immense bomber with its high, curving tail convinced Jim that the Japanese had lost the war. He had seen captured American aircrews who were held for a few hours in the Lunghua guardhouse. What impressed him so much was that these complex machines were flown by men such as Cohen and Tiptree and Dainty. That was America.

Jim thought intently about the B-29s. He wanted to embrace their silver fuselages, caress the nacelles of their engines. The Mustang was a beautiful plane, but the Superfortress belonged to a different order of beauty . . .

'Take it easy, kid . . .' Basie put an arm around his shaking chest. 'They're a long way from Lunghua. You're going to mess yourself.'

'I'm all right, Basie. The war's nearly over, isn't it?'

'That's it. Not too soon for you, Jim. Tell me, did you ever see the Hell Drivers in Shanghai?'

'Sure I did, Basie! I saw them crash right through a burning wall!'

'Okay, then. Let's calm down and get on with our jobs.'

For the next hour Jim was busy with the tasks that Basie had assigned him. First, there was water to be collected from the pond behind the guardhouse. When he had carried the bucket back to E Block, Jim set about gathering fuel for the stove. Basie still insisted on boiling his drinking water, but the shortage of fuel made this difficult. After rounding up a few sticks and shreds of straw mats, Jim searched the pathways around E Block, hunting for fragments of coke embedded in the cinder track. Even the cinders gave off a surprising heat.

Having lit his stove, Jim blew on the lazy flames. He placed the pieces of coke at the neck of the clay venturi, where, as Dr Ransome had explained, the air moved most swiftly. As soon as the drinking water had boiled he decanted some grey fluid into the mess tin, which he carried upstairs and left to cool on Basie's window ledge. He collected Basie's clothes and washed the dirty shirts in the remaining water. These could be left for an hour, while he queued for Basie's rations. The male prisoners in E Block were the last to be fed each day, and the men queued at the kitchens. Jim always enjoyed the long wait for Basie's ration of cracked wheat and sweet potato, and felt himself a growing man in the company of men. The lines of sweating prisoners covered with ulcers and mosquito bites, gave off a heady odour of aggression, and Jim could understand the Japanese guards being wary of them. Much of their foul language was above his head, their brutally crude talk of women's bodies and private parts, as if these emaciated males were trying to provoke themselves by describing what they could no longer perform. But there were always phrases to be catalogued away and savoured as he lay in his cubicle.

By the time Jim returned to E Block with Basie's shirts and food ration he felt entitled to push past Demarest and sit at the foot of the bunk. He watched Basie eat the cracked wheat, flicking the weevils to and fro like a Chinese shopkeeper with his abacus.

'We worked hard today, Jim. Your dad would be proud of us. Which camp did you say he was in?'

'Soochow Central. And my mother. You can meet them soon.' Jim wanted Basie to be present at their reunion, so that the cabin steward could identify him if his parents failed to recognize him.

'I'd like to meet with them, Jim. If they're not moved up-country . . .'

Jim noticed the odd inflexion in Basie's voice. 'Up-country?'

'Well, it's possible, Jim. Maybe the Japs will move people from the camps near Shanghai.'

'We'll be out of the war, then?'

'Yes, you'll be out of the war, all right . . .' Basie hid the sweet potato among the saucepans under his bunk. He rummaged among the shoes and tennis racquets and then produced a copy of the *Reader's Digest*. He flipped through the grimy pages, which had been read a dozen times by every resident of E Block. Layers of greasy tape, stained with dried blood and pus, held the cover to the threadbare spine.

'Jim, are you still reading the *Digest*? August '41, it has some good things in it . . .'

Basie relished every moment of Jim's excitement. This elaborate teasing was part of the ritual. Jim waited patiently, well aware that Basie exploited him, setting him to work each day in return for the old magazines. These bored merchant seamen could see that he was obsessed by everything American, and in their good-natured way they kept him dangling, rationing the ancient copies of *Life* and *Collier's* that Jim needed as much as the extra sweet potatoes. The magazines fed a desperate imagination.

This unequal exchange, jobs for magazines, was also part of Jim's conscious attempt to keep the camp going, whatever the cost. The activity screened his mind from certain fears that he had tried to repress, that the years in Lunghua would come to an end, and he would find himself building the runway again. The light that emerged from the burning body of the Mustang pilot had been a warning to him. As long as he ran his errands for Basie and Demarest and Cohen, to and from the kitchens, carrying water and playing chess, Jim could sustain the illusion that the war would last forever.

Reader's Digest in hand, Jim sat on the steps outside E Block. He squinted at the sunlight, forcing himself not to glance through the pages. Groups of prisoners lounged on the balconies after their meal. The shade between the pillars was reserved for the sick internees, who squatted together like the families of beggars in the entrances to the office blocks behind the Shanghai Bund.

Next to Jim was a young man who had been a floor manager in the Sincere Company department store, and was now suffering from the last stages of malaria. His body rattling with fever, he sat naked on the cement steps and watched the Lunghua Players rehearsing their concert party. His white lips, from which all iron had long been leached, repeated an inaudible phrase.

Jim wondered how to help this skeletal figure. He offered him the *Reader's Digest*, a gesture he instantly regretted. The man clasped the magazine in his hands and crushed the pages, as if the printed words inflamed his memories. He began to sing, in a harsh but barely audible voice.

> '. . . we're the girls every boy adores,
> C.A.C. don't mean a thing to me . . .'

A stream of colourless urine ran between his legs and trickled down the steps. He dropped the magazine, which Jim quickly retrieved, before the pages could be soaked. As Jim straightened the spine he heard the air raid siren sound from the guardhouse. After a few seconds, before the prisoners could run for shelter, it stopped abruptly. Everyone stared at the empty sky, expecting the Mustangs to roar in from the paddy fields.

However, the siren blast signalled an altogether different display. Four Japanese soldiers, among them Private Kimura, emerged from the guardhouse. They surrounded a Chinese coolie who pulled a rickshaw which had brought one of their officers from Shanghai. Still exhausted by the long run, the coolie plodded in his straw sandals across the bare earth of the parade ground. His head was lowered as he pulled the shafts, and he tittered in the strained way of frightened Chinese.

The Japanese soldiers strode briskly on either side of him. None of them was armed but they carried wooden staves with which they struck at the wheels of the rickshaw and at the shoulders of the coolie. Private Kimura walked behind the rickshaw and kicked the wooden seat, hurling the vehicle against the coolie's legs. At the centre of the parade ground Kimura and another soldier seized the rickshaw and propelled it forward, pitching the coolie on to the ground.

The soldiers began to saunter around the upended rickshaw. Private Kimura kicked its wheels, shattering the spokes. The others stamped on the wooden handles and snapped the shafts. Together they threw the vehicle on to its back, scattering the cushions.

The coolie knelt on the ground, laughing to himself. In the silence Jim could hear the strange sing-song that the Chinese made when they knew they were about to be killed. Around the parade ground the hundreds of prisoners watched without moving. Men and women sat in makeshift deck-chairs outside the barrack huts, or stood on the steps of the dormitory blocks. The Lunghua Players paused in their rehearsal. None of them spoke as the Japanese soldiers strolled around the rickshaw, kicking its seats and framework into matchwood. From the locker below the seat fell a bundle of rags, a tin pail, a cotton bag filled with rice, and a Chinese newspaper, the entire worldly possessions of

227

this illiterate coolie. He sat among the grains of rice scattered on the ground, and began to sing at a higher note, raising his face to the sky.

Jim smoothed the pages of the *Reader's Digest*, wondering whether to read an article about Winston Churchill. He would have liked to leave, but all around him the prisoners were motionless as they watched the parade ground. The Japanese turned their attention to the coolie. Raising their staves, they each struck him a blow on the head, then strolled away as if deep in thought. Breathlessly now, the coolie sang to himself as the blood ran from his back and formed a pool around his knees.

The Japanese soldiers, Jim knew, would take ten minutes to kill the coolie. Although they had been confused by the bombing, and the prospect of the imminent end of the war, they were now calm. The whole display, like their lack of weapons, was intended to show the British prisoners that the Japanese despised them, first for being prisoners, and then for not daring to move an inch to save this Chinese coolie.

Jim realized that the Japanese were right. None of the British internees would raise a finger, even if every coolie in China was beaten to death in front of them. Jim listened to the blows from the staves, and to the muffled cries as the coolie choked on his blood. Dr Ransome would probably have tried to stop the Japanese. But the physician was careful never to go near the parade ground.

Jim thought about his algebra prep, part of which he had already done inside his head. Ten minutes later, when the Japanese returned to the guardhouse, the hundreds of prisoners moved away from the parade ground. The Lunghua Players continued their rehearsal. Slipping the *Reader's Digest* inside his shirt, Jim returned to G Block by another route.

Later that evening, when he had finished Basie's potato

skin, Jim lay on his bunk and at last opened the magazine. There were no advertisements in the *Reader's Digest*, which was a shame, but Jim looked at the reassuring picture of the Packard limousine pinned to the wall of his cubicle. He listened to the Vincents talking in their low voices, and to the faint whoops of their son's cough. On Jim's return from E Block he had found the boy playing on the floor with the turtle. There had been a brief confrontation between Jim and Mr Vincent, who had tried to stop him replacing the turtle in the wooden case under his bunk. But Jim had stood his ground, confident that Mr Vincent would not try to wrestle with him. Mrs Vincent watched without expression as her husband sat on his bed, staring in his desperate way at Jim's raised fists.

28

An Escape

'Is the war over again, Mr Maxted?'

All around Jim, as he waited by the kitchen doors, the prisoners were pushing aside the food carts, shouting and pointing to the gates. The all-clear siren sounded across the camp, the wail of a broken bird trying to hide from the American bombing. Arms on each other's shoulders, the prisoners watched the Japanese soldiers leaving the guard-house. Each of the thirty men carried his rifle with fixed bayonet, and a canvas pannier holding his personal kit. Among the straw mats and kendo armour there were two baseball bats, pairs of sneakers hung by their laces, and a portable gramophone, all obtained from the prisoners in return for cigarettes, food and news of relations in other camps.

'It looks as if your little friends are leaving, Jim.' Mr Maxted ran his grimy fingers between his ribs, hunting for loose shreds of skin. He squinted at them in the August sun, as if concerned that he was mislaying pieces of himself around the camp. 'I'll keep your place for you, if you want to wave to Private Kimura.'

'He knows my address, Mr Maxted. I don't like saying goodbye. They'll probably come back this afternoon when they find there isn't anywhere to go.'

Unwilling to risk his place at the head of the kitchen queue, where he and Mr Maxted had waited since dawn, Jim climbed on to the food cart. Over the heads of men in front of him he watched the Japanese file through the gates of the camp. They lined up along the road, their backs to the fire-gutted fuselage of a Japanese aircraft that lay in the paddy field a hundred yards away. The twin-engined aircraft had been shot down two days earlier as it took off from Lunghua Airfield, torn apart by the machine-guns of the Lightning fighters that rose without warning from the deserted countryside.

As he balanced on the metal cart, Jim could see Private Kimura peering uneasily at the eastern horizon, from which the fearsome American planes emerged like pieces of the sun. Even in the warm August light Kimura's face had the toneless texture of cold wax. He licked his fingers and wiped his cheeks with the spittle, nervous of leaving the secure world of Lunghua Camp. In front of him the group of Chinese peasants sat on the grass verge. They stared at the gates, which had rejected them for so many months and were now unguarded. Jim was sure that these starving Chinese, in their universe of death, were unable to grasp the meaning of an open gate.

Jim gazed at the untended space between the posts. He too found it difficult to accept that he would soon be able to walk through the gates to freedom. The soldier in the watch-tower made his way down the ladder to the guardhouse roof, his light machine-gun clipped to the webbing across his shoulders. Sergeant Nagata emerged from the guardhouse and joined his men outside the camp. Since the disappearance of the commandant in the confusion of the previous week, the sergeant had been the senior Japanese officer in the camp.

'Mr Maxted, Sergeant Nagata is going – the war *has* ended!'

'Ended again, Jim? I don't think we can stand it . . .'

During the past week, when rumours of the war's end had swept the camp every hour, Mr Maxted had found Jim's high spirits more and more tiresome. As he ran on his errands down the pathways, Jim shouted at any passers-by, waved to the prisoners resting outside the barrack huts,

231

excitedly jumped among the graves in the hospital cemetery when the American aircraft flew overhead, all part of his attempt to cover the insecurities of the coming world beyond the camp. Dr Ransome had twice slapped him.

Yet now that the war was over he felt surprisingly calm. Soon he would be seeing his mother and father, returning to the house in Amherst Avenue, to that forgotten realm of servants and Packards and polished parquet. At the same time, Jim reflected that the prisoners *ought* to celebrate, throw their clogs in the air, seize the air raid siren and play it back at the incoming American planes. But too many of them were like Mr Maxted, staring silently at the Japanese. They seemed glum and wary, the men almost naked in their ragged shorts, the women in faded sunsuits and patched cotton frocks, their malarial eyes unable to face the glare of freedom. Exposed to the light that seemed to flood into the camp through the open gates, their bodies were even darker and more wasted, and for the first time they looked as if they were guilty of a crime.

Rumour and confusion had exhausted everyone in Lunghua. During July the American air attacks had become almost continuous. Waves of Mustangs and Lightnings flew in from the air bases on Okinawa, strafing the airfields around Shanghai, attacking the Japanese forces concentrated at the mouth of the Yangtze. From the balcony of the ruined assembly hall Jim witnessed the destruction of the Japanese military machine as if he were watching an epic war film from the circle of the Cathay Theatre. The apartment houses of the French Concession were hidden by hundreds of smoke columns that rose from burning trucks and ammunition wagons. Fearful of the Mustangs, the Japanese convoys moved only after dusk, and the sound of their engines kept everyone awake for night after night. Sergeant Nagata and his guards had given up any attempt to patrol the camp's perimeter for fear of being shot by the military police supervising the convoys.

By the end of July almost all Japanese resistance to the American bombers had ceased. A single anti-aircraft gun mounted on the upper deck of Lunghua Pagoda continued to fire at the incoming aircraft, but the batteries around the runway had been withdrawn to defend the Shanghai dockyards. In these last days of the war Jim spent hours at the assembly hall, waiting for the high-flying Superfortresses in whose silver wings and fuselages he had invested so much of his imagination. Unlike the Mustangs and Lightnings, which skimmed like racing cars across the paddy fields, the B-29s would appear without warning in the sky above his head, as if summoned by Jim's starving brain. Their rolling thunder advanced across the land from the dockyards of Nantao. A Japanese troopship leaned against the mud-flats, bombed again and again until Jim could see daylight through its superstructure.

Throughout all this, the concrete runway at Lunghua Airfield remained intact. By an heroic effort, the Japanese engineers continued to fill in the craters after each raid, as if expecting a fleet of rescue aircraft to arrive from the Home Islands. The whiteness of the runway excited Jim, its sun-bleached surface mixed with the calcinated bones of the dead Chinese, and even perhaps with his own bones in a death that might have been. Impatiently he waited for the Japanese to make their last stand.

This confusion of loyalties, the fear of what would happen to them once the Japanese were defeated, affected everyone in the camp. Often there were cheers from the light-headed prisoners squatting outside the barrack huts as a stricken B-29 dropped out of its formation. Dr Ransome had been correct to predict that the food supply to Lunghua would soon end. Once a week a single truck arrived from Shanghai with a few bags of fermenting potatoes, and the godown sweepings of animal feed filled with weevils and rat droppings. Fights broke out among the prisoners queuing for their small ration. Irritated by the sight of Jim waiting all day by the kitchen doors, a group of Britons from E Block pushed him aside and overturned his iron cart. From then on, he recruited the help of Mr Maxted, nagging the architect until he clambered from his bunk.

Through the last week of July they watched the Shanghai road together, hoping that the ration truck had not been attacked by a low-flying Mustang. During these hungry days Jim discovered that most of the prisoners in G Block had been quietly stockpiling a small reserve of potatoes, and that he and Mr Maxted, who had volunteered to collect the daily ration, were among the few not to have planned ahead.

Jim sat on his bunk, empty plate in hand, and watched the Vincents share a rancid potato. They nibbled at the pith with their yellowing teeth. At last Mrs Vincent gave him a small piece of skin. Was she afraid that Jim would attack her husband? Fortunately, Jim was fed from the modest reserve that Dr Ransome had accumulated from his dying patients.

But by 1st August even these supplies had come to an end. Jim and Mr Maxted roamed the camp with their cart, as if hoping that a consignment of rice or cracked wheat might materialize under the legs of the water-tower, or among the graves in the cemetery. Once Mr Maxted caught Jim looking at the wrist-bones of Mrs Hug that had emerged from her grave, as white as the runway at Lunghua Airfield.

For Jim, a curious vacuum enclosed the camp. Time had ceased to exist at Lunghua, and many of the prisoners were convinced that the war was already over. On 2 August, after the rumour that the Russians had entered the war against Japan, Sergeant Nagata and his soldiers withdrew to the guardhouse and no longer patrolled the fence, abandoning the camp to its inmates. Parties of British prisoners stepped through the wire and wandered around the nearby paddy fields. Parents stood with their children on the burial mounds, pointing to the watch-tower and the dormitory blocks as if seeing the camp for the first time. One group of men led by Mr Tulloch, the senior mechanic at the Packard Agency in Shanghai, set off across the fields, intending to walk to the city. Others gathered around the guardhouse, jeering at the Japanese soldiers who watched from their windows.

Throughout the day Jim was confused by the apparent collapse of order within the camp. He was unwilling to believe that the war was over. He climbed through the fence and spent a few minutes with the pheasant traps, then returned to the camp and sat alone on the balcony of the assembly hall. At last rallying himself, he went in search of Basie. But the American sailors no longer received their lady callers, and had barricaded the doors of the dormitory. From his window Basie called to Jim, cautioning him not to leave the camp.

Sure enough, the war's end proved to be short-lived. At dusk a motorized column of Japanese troops passed the camp on its way to Hangchow. The military police returned to the guardhouse the six Britons who had tried to walk to Shanghai. Severely beaten, they lay unconscious for three hours on the guardhouse steps. When Sergeant Nagata allowed them to be carried to their bunks they described the confused terrain to the south and west of Shanghai, the thousands of desperate peasants driven back to the city with the retreating Japanese, the gangs of bandits and starving soldiers from the puppet armies left to fend for themselves.

Despite these dangers, the very next day Basie, Cohen and Demarest escaped from Lunghua.

* * *

235

The prisoners pressed forward to the empty guardhouse, their clogs clacking on the cinder path. Buffeted by the almost naked men, Jim held tight to the handles of the iron cart. The other prisoners had abandoned their carts, but Jim was determined not to be caught out if the ration truck arrived. He had not eaten since the previous afternoon. Although the inmates were about to seize control of the guardhouse, he could think of nothing except food.

A group of British and Belgian women stood by the gates, calling through the wire to the line of Japanese soldiers in the road. Weighed down by their rifles and bedding rolls, they fretted in the August sunlight. Private Kimura gazed uneagerly at the desolate paddy fields, as if wishing he was back in the secure world of the camp.

Flecks of spittle brightened the dust around the soldiers' ragged boots. Venting the anger of years on their former guards, the women spat through the wire, shouting and jeering. A Belgian woman began to scream in Japanese, tearing pieces of faded cloth from the sleeve of her cotton dress and hurling them at the feet of the soldiers.

Jim clung to his cart, jerking the handles when Mr Maxted wearily tried to sit on the wooden shaft. He felt detached from the spitting women and their excited husbands. Where was Basie? Why had he escaped? Despite the rumours that the war had ended, it surprised Jim that Basie should leave Lunghua and expose himself to all the hazards of the countryside. The cabin steward was too cautious, never the first to try anything new or gamble away his modest security. Jim guessed that he had heard some warning message on the secret radio. He had abandoned his cubicle filled with the hard-earned treasure of years, the shoes and tennis racquets and hundreds of condoms.

Jim remembered that Basie had talked about the inmates of the camps near Shanghai being moved up-country. Was he warning him that it was time to leave before the Japanese ran amok as they had done in Nanking in 1937? The Japanese always killed their prisoners before they made their last stands. But Basie had been wrong; at that moment he was probably lying dead in a ditch after being murdered by bandits.

Headlamps flared along the Shanghai road. Wiping their chins, the women stepped back from the wire. Necklaces of spit lay on their breasts. A Japanese staff car was approaching, followed by a convoy of military trucks, each packed with armed soldiers. One of the trucks had already stopped, and a platoon of soldiers jumped down into the road and then ran across the drained paddy field beside the western perimeter of the camp. Bayonets fixed, they took up their positions facing the wire.

Silent now, the hundreds of prisoners turned to watch them. A second platoon of air force police was wading across the canal that separated Lunghua Airfield from the camp. To the east, the long bend of the Whangpoo River completed the circle with its maze of creeks and irrigation ditches.

The convoy reached the camp, headlamps reflected in the dusty spit. Armed soldiers leapt to the ground, bayonets fixed to their rifles. From the fresh uniforms and equipment, Jim could see that these security troops were a special field unit of the Japanese gendarmerie. They moved swiftly through the gates, taking up their positions outside the guardhouse.

The prisoners drew back, bumping into each other like a flock of sheep. Caught by the retreat, Jim was knocked from his cart by the crush of bodies. A Japanese corporal, a short but strongly-built man whose holstered Mauser swung from his waist like a club, seized the handles of the cart and propelled it towards the gates. Jim was about to run forward and wrestle the handles from the Japanese, but Mr Maxted gripped his arms.

'Jim, for God's sake . . . Leave it!'

'But – it's G Block's cart! Are they going to kill us, Mr Maxted?'

'Jim . . . we'll find Dr Ransome.'

'Is the ration truck coming?' Jim pushed Mr Maxted away, tired of having to support this ailing figure.

'Later, Jim. Perhaps it will come later.'

'I don't think the ration truck will come.' As the line of Japanese soldiers forced the prisoners across the parade ground, Jim watched the guards patrolling the wire. Seeing the Japanese again had restored his confidence. The prospect of being killed excited him; after the uncertainties of the past week he welcomed any end. For a few last moments, like the rickshaw coolie who had sung to himself, they would be fully aware of their own minds. Whatever happened, he would survive. He thought of Mrs Philips and Mrs Gilmour and their discussion of the exact moment at which the soul left the body of the dying. Jim's soul had already left his body and no longer needed his thin bones and open sores in order to endure. He was dead, as were Mr Maxted and Dr Ransome. Everyone in Lunghua was dead. It was absurd that they had failed to grasp this.

They stood on the grass verge behind the throng of prisoners who now filled the parade ground. Jim began to titter, relieved that he understood the real meaning of the war.

'They don't need to kill us, Mr Maxted . . .'

'Of course they don't, Jim.'

'Mr Maxted, they don't need to, because . . .'

'Jim!' Mr Maxted cuffed Jim, then pressed the boy's head to his emaciated chest. 'Remember you're British.'

Circumspectly, Jim eased the smile from his face. He calmed himself, then wormed his shoulders from Mr Maxted's embrace. The moment of humour had passed, but the insight into their true situation, and his sense of being apart from himself, remained. Concerned for Mr Maxted, who was dribbling an oily phlegm on to the ground before his bare feet, Jim put an arm around his bony hips. He felt sorry for the former architect, remembering their Studebaker jaunts around the Shanghai nightclubs, and sad that he should have been so demoralized that all he could do to reassure Jim was to remind him that he was British.

Outside the guardhouse, where the commander of the gendarmerie unit had established himself, the block leaders were talking to a Japanese sergeant. A wan-faced Dr Ransome, coolie hat in hand, his shoulders stooped in his cotton shirt, stood beside them. Mrs Pearce entered the guardhouse, smoothing her hair and cheeks, already giving orders to a soldier in her rapid Japanese.

The prisoners at the front of the crowd turned and ran across the parade ground, shouting to the others.

'One suitcase! Everyone back here in an hour!'

'We're leaving for Nantao!'

'Everybody out! Line up by the gates!'

'They're holding our rations at Nantao!'

'One suitcase!'

Already the missionary couples were standing on the steps of G Block, bags in hand, as if they had somehow sensed the coming move. Watching them, Jim reassured himself that the camp was only being moved, not closed.

'Come on, Mr Maxted – we're going back to Shanghai!'

He helped the weakened man to his feet, and steered him through the hundreds of running prisoners. When Jim reached his room he found that Mrs Vincent was already packed. As her son slept in his bunk, she stood by the window, watching her husband return from the parade ground. Jim could see that she had begun to shed all memories of the camp.

'We're leaving, Mrs Vincent. We're going to Nantao.'

'Then you'll have to pack.' She was waiting for him to go, so that she could be alone in the room for a few last minutes.

'Right. I've been to Nantao, Mrs Vincent.'

'So have I. I can't imagine why the Japanese should want us to go again.'

'Our rations are in a godown there.' Jim was already debating whether to carry Mrs Vincent's suitcase. New alliances needed to be forged, and Mrs Vincent's slim but strong-hipped body might well have more stamina than Mr Maxted's. As for Dr Ransome, he would be busy with his patients, most of whom would soon start dying.

'I'll be seeing my parents soon, Mrs Vincent.'

'I'm glad.' With the mildest irony, she asked: 'Do you think they'll give me a reward?'

Embarrassed, Jim lowered his head. During his illness he had mistakenly tried to bribe Mrs Vincent with the promise of a reward, but it intrigued him that she could see the humour in her refusal to raise a finger to help him. Jim hesitated before leaving the room. He had spent nearly three years with Mrs Vincent, and still found himself liking her. She was one of the few people in Lunghua Camp who appreciated the humour of it all.

Trying to match her, he said: 'A reward? Mrs Vincent, remember you're British.'

29
The March to Nantao

Like the migration of a shabby country carnival, the march
from Lunghua Camp to the dockyards at Nantao began two
hours later. Exhausted even before they started by the long
wait, Jim watched the prisoners assemble from his place at
the head of the column. Under the bored gaze of the
Japanese gendarmerie, the internees stepped cautiously
through the gates, the men loaded with suitcases and bed-
rolls, the women with bundles of ragged clothes wrapped in
straw panniers. Fathers carried sick infants on their backs,
while mothers steered the smaller children by the hand. As
he stood behind the Japanese staff car that was to lead the
march, Jim was surprised by the sight of so many possessions, which had remained under the bunks throughout the
years at Lunghua.

Recreation had clearly come high on the prisoners' list of
priorities while they packed their suitcases before being
interned. Having spent the years of peace on the tennis
courts and cricket fields of the Far East, they confidently
expected to pass the years of war in the same way. Dozens of
tennis racquets hung from the suitcase handles; there were
cricket bats and fishing rods, and even a set of golf clubs
tied to the bundles of pierrot costumes carried by Mr and
Mrs Wentworth. Ragged and undernourished, the prisoners shuffled along the road on their wooden clogs and
formed themselves into a procession some three hundred
yards in length. Already the effort of carrying the baggage
had begun to tell, and one of the Chinese peasant women
seated outside the gates now clutched a white tennis racquet.

Lounging against their vehicles, the soldiers and NCOs of the gendarmerie watched without comment. Well-fed and well-equipped, these security troops so feared by the Chinese were the strongest men whom Jim had seen during the war. Yet for once they seemed curiously unhurried. They smoked their cigarettes in the hot sunlight, gazed at the few American reconnaissance planes and made no attempt to abuse the prisoners or urge them along. Two of the trucks drove through the gates and made a circuit of the camp, collecting the patients from the hospital and those prisoners in the dormitory blocks who were too sick to move.

Jim sat on his wooden case, trying to adjust his mind and eye to the open perspectives of the world outside the camp. The act of walking without challenge through the gates had been an eerie experience, and Jim had been unnerved enough to slip back into the camp on the pretext of tying his shoelaces. Reassuring himself, he patted the wooden case containing his possessions – Latin primer, his school blazer, the Packard advertisement and the small newspaper photograph. Now that he was about to see his real mother and father he had thought of tearing up the picture of the unknown couple outside Buckingham Palace, his surrogate parents for so many years. At the last moment, as a precautionary measure, he had slipped the photograph into his box.

He listened to the crying of the exhausted children. Already people were sitting down in the road, trying to shield their faces from the swarm of flies that had vacated the camp and moved towards the sweating bodies on the other side of the wire. Jim looked back at Lunghua. The terrain of paddy fields and canals around the camp, and the road of return to Shanghai, which had been so real when observed through the fence, now seemed lurid and overlit, part of a landscape of hallucination.

242

Jim clenched his aching teeth, deciding to turn his back on the camp. He reminded himself of their food supplies in the godown at Nantao. It was important to remain at the head of the procession, and if possible to ingratiate himself with the two Japanese soldiers beside the staff car. Jim was considering this when an almost naked figure in ragged shorts and a pair of wooden clogs shuffled up to him.

'Jim . . . I thought I'd find you here.' Mr Maxted raised his sallow face to the sun. A fine malarial sweat covered his cheeks and forehead. He rubbed the dirt from the open spaces between his ribs, as if to expose the waxy skin to the healing light. 'So this is what we've been waiting for . . .'

'You haven't brought your luggage, Mr Maxted.'

'No, Jim. I don't think I'll be needing any luggage. You must find it strange out here.'

'I don't any more.' Jim peered cautiously at the open fields, their endless perspectives broken only by the burial mounds, and at the secretive canals. It was as if these bored Japanese soldiers had switched off the clock. 'Mr Maxted, do you think Shanghai will have changed?'

A faded smile, lit by the memories of happier days, briefly eased Mr Maxted's face. 'Jim, Shanghai will never change. Don't worry, you'll remember your mother and father.'

'I was thinking of that,' Jim admitted. His other problem was Mr Maxted. Jim had come to the head of the column, partly to be first in the queue for their rations when they reached Nantao, but also to free himself from all the duties that the camp had imposed upon him. Because he was alone he had been forced to do too many jobs, in return for favours that had rarely materialized. Clearly Mr Maxted needed help, and was hoping that he could lean on Jim.

Doggedly refusing to co-operate, Jim sat on his wooden case thinking about Mr Maxted as the architect swayed beside him. His pale hands, almost worn through by the months of pushing the food cart, hung at his sides like white flags. His bones were held together by little more than his memories of the bars and swimming-pools of a younger self. Mr Maxted was starving, like many of the men and women joining the procession. But he reminded Jim of the dying British soldier in the open-air cinema.

In the ditch beside the grass verge lay the grey cylinder of a Mustang drop-tank. Looking for some way of leaving Mr Maxted, Jim was about to cross the road when a burst of hot smoke ripped from the exhaust of the staff car. The Japanese sergeant stood on the rear seat, waving everyone on. Armed soldiers were moving down the road on either side of the column, shouting at the prisoners.

There was a clatter of clogs, as if hundreds of packs of wooden cards were being shuffled and dealt. First off the mark Jim stepped forward, case in hand and shoes bright in the hot Yangtze sun. He waved to the Japanese sergeant and strode purposefully down the dirt road, his eyes fixed on the yellow façades of the apartment houses in the French Concession that rose like a mirage from the canals and paddy fields.

Guided by the swarm of flies that danced over their heads, the prisoners moved along the country road to Nantao. Across the burial mounds and ancient trench works came the sound of American planes bombing the dockyards and marshalling yards to the north of Shanghai. The thunder drummed at the surface of the flooded paddies. Anti-aircraft fire flickered against the windows of the office buildings along the Bund, and lit up the dead neon signs – Shell, Caltex, Socony Vacuum, Philco – the waking ghosts of the great international companies that had slept through the war. Half a mile to the west was the main Shanghai road, still busy with convoys of Japanese trucks and field artillery moving towards the city. The labouring noise of their engines droned like pain across the stoical land.

Jim walked at the head of the procession, trying to listen to the men and women behind him. All he could hear was the sound of their breathing, as if the experience of freedom had left them speechless. Jim ignored his own rackety breath. Despite the ceaseless activity in Lunghua, he had never undertaken a task like this shuffling walk burdened by his wooden case. For the first hour he was too concerned about Mr Maxted's exhaustion to notice his own. But soon after reaching the Shanghai-Hangchow railway line Mr Maxted was forced to stop, defeated by the shallow gradient that led up to the level crossing.

'We're climbing, Jim . . . feels like the Shanghai Hills.'

'We ought to keep going, Mr Maxted.'

'Yes, Jim . . . you're like your father.'

Jim stayed with Mr Maxted, annoyed with him but unable to help. Mr Maxted stood in the centre of the road, hands on the bowl-like crests of his pelvis, nodding at the people stepping past. He patted Jim on the shoulder and waved him forward.

'You go on, Jim. Get to the head of the queue.'

'I'll save your place, Mr Maxted.'

By then several hundred people had passed Jim, and it took him half an hour to return to the head of the column. Within minutes he had fallen back, lungs aching as he gasped at the humid air. Only the lengthy halt at a canal checkpoint saved him from having to join Mr Maxted.

They had reached an industrial canal that ran westwards from the river to Soochow. Two young Japanese soldiers forgotten by the war, guarded the sandbag emplacement beside the wooden bridge. Their faces were as pinched as those of the prisoners whose clogs dragged over the scored planks.

While the trucks edged across the rotting timbers, the eighteen hundred prisoners sat on the embankment, occupying the deep grass for a quarter of a mile. Around them they settled their baggage of suitcases, tennis racquets and cricket bats. Like drowsy spectators at a rowing regatta, they stared at the algae-filled water. The current drifted past the burnt-out hulk of an armoured junk beached against the opposite bank.

Jim was glad to lie down. He felt sleepy in a feverish way, his brain irritated by the hot sun and the hard light reflected from the yellow grass. He could see Dr Ransome standing in the last of the three trucks, swaying unsteadily among the patients on their stretchers. Jim thought of his Latin prep, now a week overdue, but Dr Ransome was a hundred yards away.

Watched by the Japanese soldiers on the road above them, many of the men walked down to the water's edge. They filled their mess-tins and stood drinking together in the shallows. Jim was wary of the water, remembering the black creeks at Nantao, and the thousands of gallons he had boiled for Basie. Was there a crew of corpses in the armoured junk? Inside the iron turret, now washed by the green waters of the canal, perhaps lay the captain of this puppet Chinese naval vessel, Jim could almost see the dead blood running out into the canal, slaking the thirst of these British prisoners, on its way to nourish the roots of the rice crops raised for another generation of Chinese turncoats.

Jim opened his wooden case and took out his mess-tin. He walked down the bank between the resting women and their exhausted children. Squatting on the narrow beach, he carefully filled his mess-tin with the surface water, hoping that the algae might sustain him. He drank the tepid fluid, watching the dissolving patterns of his golf shoes in the fine sand.

Filling the mess-tin, Jim climbed the bank to his case. On his right was the wife of a Shell engineer in D Block. She lay weakly in the long grass, whose blades had already sprung through the rents in her cotton frock. Her husband sat beside her, dipping his fingers into his mess-tin and moistening her large, carious teeth with the green water.

Lying on Jim's left was Mrs Philips. It irked Jim that she had seen him drinking on the bank and decided to rest beside him. No doubt she had some little chore in mind, and would nag him about his Latin prep. Although he had left Lunghua, Jim felt imprisoned by the camp. Everyone he had ever helped was still clinging to him. He almost expected to see Basie emerge from the turret of the armoured junk and call out: 'Jobs, Jim . . .'

But Mrs Philips did not look as if she was about to set him a task. The walk from Lunghua had exhausted her. She lay in the bright grass with her wicker suitcase, all that survived of the decades she had spent in the Chinese hinterland. Her face was now the palest mother-of-pearl, as if she had been drowned and then lifted from the water on to this quiet bank. Her eyes were fixed on a remote point in the sky. Jim touched her cheeks, wondering if she was dead.

'Mrs Philips – I've brought you some water.'

She smiled at him and sipped the water, her small fists clinging to the handles of her suitcase like a pair of white mice. 'Thank you, Jim. Are you very hungry?'

'I was this morning.' Jim tried to think of a joke that would cheer Mrs Philips. 'It's air I'm short of after all that walking, not food.'

'Yes, Jim . . .' Mrs Philips opened her case. She felt inside and produced a small potato. 'There you are. Remember to pray for us all.'

'Oh, I will!' Jim bit into the potato before she had a chance to change her mind. 'I'll pay you back when we get to Nantao. All our rations are there.'

'You've already paid me back, Jim. Many times.' Mrs Philips resumed her pinpoint scrutiny of the sky. 'Could you eat the potato?'

'It was really good.' As Jim finished the potato he noticed

the old woman's eyes move fractionally. 'Mrs Philips, are you looking for God?'

'Yes, Jim.'

'Say . . .' Jim was impressed. He was keen to repay Mrs Philips' generosity, if only with a modest discussion of theology. He followed the angle of the old woman's gaze. 'Do you mean God is right above us?'

'Of course, Jim.'

'Above the 31st Parallel? Mrs Philips, wouldn't God be above the magnetic pole? You ought to look at the ground, under Shanghai . . .' Intoxicated by the fermenting potato, Jim giggled at the thought of the deity trapped in the bowels of the earth below Shanghai, perhaps in the basement of the Sincere Company department store.

Mrs Philips held his hand, trying to comfort him. Still staring at the sky, she decided: 'Nantao – then they're taking us up-country . . .'

'No . . . our rations . . .' Jim turned towards the Japanese guards. The three trucks had crossed the bridge, and he could see Dr Ransome moving among his patients with a small child in his arms. Its cries sounded through the overbright sun. The hundreds of prisoners sat in the feverish light like figures in the lurid paintings that advertised the Chinese film spectacles. The Japanese squatted beside the trucks eating a boiled rice paste which they took from their haversacks. They made no attempt to share their food with the young soldiers defending the bridge.

Up-country . . . ? There were docks at Nantao, but why would the Japanese want to move them from Shanghai? Jim watched Mrs Vincent paddling at the water's edge fifty yards away. Finding a portion of the current that satisfied her, she filled a mess-tin for her husband and child. Dr Ransome had recruited a human chain from the men sitting on the embankment below the trucks, and they passed pails of water up to the patients.

Jim shook his head, puzzled by all this effort. Obviously they were being taken up-country so that the Japanese could kill them without being seen by the American pilots. He listened to the Shell man's wife crying in the yellow grass. The sunlight charged the air above the canal, an intense aura of hunger that stung his retinas, and reminded him of the halo formed by the exploding Mustang. The burning body of the American pilot had quickened the dead land. It would be for the best if they all died; it would bring their lives to an end that had been implicit ever since the *Idzumo* had sunk the *Petrel* and the British had surrendered at Singapore without a fight.

Perhaps they were already dead? Jim lay back and tried to count the motes of light. This simple truth was known to every Chinese from birth. Once the British internees had accepted it they would no longer fear their journey to the killing-ground . . .

'Mrs Philips . . . I've thought about the war.' Jim rolled over in the grass. He was about to explain to Mrs Philips that she was dead but the old missionary was asleep. Jim studied her blanched eyes, her mouth open to reveal a broken dental plate. 'Mrs Philips, we mustn't worry any more . . .'

Headlamps flared through the dust. The gendarmerie staff car trundled along the road. Japanese soldiers strode down the bank, waving their rifles and beckoning the prisoners to their feet. The trucks at the rear of the column had started their engines. Men and women were climbing the embankment, children and suitcases in hand. Others remained in the trampled grass, unwilling to leave this placid canal.

Jim lay on his side, making a pillow of his arm. He felt drowsy after Mrs Philips' potato, and the rumble of bombing and the voices of the British wives seemed far away. He stared at the blades of grass, trying to work out the speed at which the leaves grew – an eighth of an inch each day, a millionth of a mile per hour . . . ?

Then he noticed a Japanese soldier standing in the grass beside him. All but a hundred of the prisoners had climbed the slope and formed a procession behind the staff car. Around Jim a few people lay quietly. Mrs Philips clasped her wicker suitcase, and the woman from D Block whimpered as her husband pressed his hands to her shoulders.

Grains of rice clung to the stubble around the Japanese soldier's lips. They moved like lice as he assessed Jim's condition. His expression was one that Jim had seen before, at the detention centre in Shanghai, but for the first time Jim felt unconcerned. He would remain here beside the unhurried water and help Mrs Philips to look for God.

'Come on, Jim! We're waiting for you!'

An emaciated figure tottered down the bank. Mr Maxted bowed and smiled to the Japanese soldier, as if glad to recognize him. He collapsed in the grass and pulled Jim's shoulder.

'Good boy, Jim. We're moving on to Nantao.'

'They're taking us up-country, Mr Maxted. I might stay here with Mrs Philips.'

'I think Mrs Philips wants to rest. They're holding our rations in Nantao, Jim. We need you to lead the way.'

Hitching up his shorts, Mr Maxted bowed again to the Japanese soldier and helped Jim to his feet.

The column shuffled forward, following the staff car. Jim looked back at the hundred or so prisoners left behind on the embankment. As the soldier licked the rice grains from his chin, Mrs Philips lay at his feet in the yellow grass, beside the woman from D Block and her kneeling husband. Other soldiers moved along the bank, rifles slung while they stepped among the resting prisoners. Would they later help Mrs Philips and the others to Nantao?

Jim doubted it. Shutting Mrs Philips from his mind, he

gripped his wooden case and placed his feet in the dusty imprints left by the man limping in front of him. Already Mr Maxted had fallen behind. The brief rest on the embankment had fatigued everyone. Half a mile from the bridge, by a burnt-out shell of an ammunition truck, the Nantao road turned at right angles from the canal and ran along a causeway between two paddy fields. The procession came to a halt. Watched by the Japanese, who made no attempt to hurry them along, the prisoners waited limply in the sun. Jim listened to the tired breathing. Then there was a shuffle of clogs, and the procession moved forward again.

He looked back at the ammunition truck. He was startled to see that hundreds of suitcases lay on the empty road. Exhausted by the effort of carrying their possessions, the prisoners had abandoned them without a spoken word. The suitcases and wicker baskets, the tennis racquets, cricket bats and pierrot costumes lay in the sunlight, like the luggage of a party of holidaymakers who had vanished into the sky.

Holding tight to his case, Jim increased his stride. After so many years without any belongings, he did not intend to discard them now. He thought of Mrs Philips and their talk together by the sunny canal, a setting so much more pleasant than the camp cemetery where he had usually questioned her about matters of life and death. It had been kind of Mrs Philips to give him her last potato, and he remembered his dreamy thoughts of having died. But he had not died. Jim stamped his shoes in the dust, surprised by his own weakness. Death, with her mother-of-pearl skin, had almost seduced him with a sweet potato.

30

The Olympic Stadium

All afternoon they moved northwards across the plain of the Whangpoo River, through the maze of creeks and canals that separated the paddy fields. Lunghua Airfield fell behind them, and the apartment houses of the French Concession rose like advertisement hoardings in the August sunlight. The river was a few hundred yards to their right, its brown surface broken by the wrecks of patrol boats and motorized junks that sat in the shallows.

Here, in the approaches to the Nantao district, the devastation caused by the American bombing lay on all sides. Craters like circular swimming-pools covered the paddy fields, in which floated the carcasses of water buffaloes. They passed the remains of a convoy that had been attacked by the Mustang and Lightning fighters. A line of military trucks and staff cars sat under the trees, as if dismantled in an outdoor workshop. Wheels, doors and axles were scattered around the vehicles, whose fenders and body panels had been torn away by the cannon fire.

Swarms of flies rose from the bloodstained windshields as the prisoners stopped to relieve themselves. A few steps behind Jim, Mr Maxted left the procession and sat on the running board of an ammunition wagon. Still carrying his case, Jim went back for him.

'We're nearly there, Mr Maxted. I can smell the docks.'

'Don't worry, Jim. I'm keeping an eye on us.'

'Our rations . . .'

Mr Maxted reached out and held Jim's wrist. Gutted by malaria and malnutrition, his body was about to merge with the derelict vehicle behind him. The three trucks moved past, their tyres crushing the broken glass that covered the ground. The hospital patients lay across each other like rolls of carpet. Dr Ransome stood in the last truck, his back to the driver's cabin, feet hidden among the packed bodies. Seeing Jim, he gripped the side bar of the truck.

'Maxted . . . ! Come on, Jim! Leave your case!'

'The war's over, Dr Ransome!'

Jim watched the thirty Japanese soldiers who brought up the rear of the procession. Rifles slung over their shoulders, they strolled along at a thoughtful pace. They reminded Jim of his father's friends returning from a shooting party in Hungjao before the war. Clouds of white dust rose from the trucks, hiding Dr Ransome. The first of the soldiers passed Jim, large men whose eyes were fixed to the ground. Their nostrils flickered at the scent of the urine. As they strode through the dust a fine film covered their uniforms and webbing, and reminded him of the runway at Lunghua Airfield.

'Right, Jim . . .' Mr Maxted stood up, and Jim was aware of the odour of excrement that rose from his shorts. 'Let's get you to Nantao . . .'

Holding Jim's shoulder, he hobbled forward, clogs cracking the broken glass. Unable to overtake the trucks, they moved through the clouds of dust, joining the few stragglers at the tail of the column. A number of prisoners had given up, and sat with their children on the running boards of the bombed staff cars, gypsies about to make a new life among these partly dismantled vehicles. But Jim looked down at the powdery dust that covered his legs and shoes, like the undertaker's talc blown on to the bones of a Chinese skeleton before its re-burial, and knew that it was time to move on.

By late afternoon this layer of dust on Jim's legs and arms began to glow with light. The sun fell towards the Shanghai hills, and the flooded paddy fields became a liquid chess-

253

board of illuminated squares, a war-table on which were placed crashed aircraft and abandoned tanks. Lit by the sunset, the prisoners stood on the embankment of the railway line that ran to the warehouses at Nantao, like a party of film extras under the studio spotlights. Around them the creeks and lagoons were filled with saffron water, the conduits of a perfume factory blocked by dead mules and buffaloes drowned in its scents.

The trucks bumped forward over the wooden sleepers. Jim balanced on the steel rail, and gazed through the dusk at the brick godowns beside the jetty. A concrete mole ran across the river to a derelict lighthouse. Through their binoculars a party of Japanese soldiers examined the smoking hulk of a steel collier, which had been struck by the American bombers and beached on a sandbank in the centre of the stream. Scorched by the explosions, its bridge-house was now as black as its masts and coal-holds.

A mile downstream from the collier were the Nantao seaplane base and the funeral piers where Jim had found refuge with Basie. Wondering if the cabin steward had returned to his old hiding place, Jim steered Mr Maxted between the rails, as the prisoners followed the railway embankment to the riverside causeway. To the west of the docks, in the waters of a shallow lagoon, lay the burnt-out shell of a B-29, its tail rising into the dusk like a silver billboard advertising its squadron insignia.

Jim stared at this huge stricken plane, and sat beside Mr Maxted among the press of bodies in the dusk. Hunger numbed him. He sucked on his knuckles, glad even for the taste of his pus, then tore stems of grass from the bank and chewed the acid leaves. A Japanese corporal was escorting Dr Ransome and Mrs Pearce towards the dockyards. The wharves and godowns, which from the distance had seemed intact, had been bombed almost to rubble. The rising tide rocked the rusting hulls of two torpedo boats beached beside the mole, and stirred the corpses of the Japanese sailors lying among the reeds fifty yards from where Jim was crouching. Undeterred, several of the British prisoners walked down the bank and drank at the water's edge. An exhausted woman held her child like a Chinese mother, gripping it behind the knees as it relieved itself on the oil-stained mud, then squatted and followed suit. Others joined her, and when Jim went to drink at the water's edge the evening air was filled with the stench of defecating women.

Jim stood by the river, the wooden case at his feet. The tide swilled the white dust from his shoes. In his mess-tin the water gleamed with oil washed from the sunken freighters in Shanghai harbour. Overlapping slicks covered the surface of the Whangpoo, as if trying to smother all life from the river.

He drank carefully, then watched the water lap around his case. He had carried the wooden box all the way from Lunghua, holding tight to the few possessions that he had assembled with such effort. He had been trying to keep the war alive, and with it the security he had known in the camp. Now it was time to rid himself of Lunghua and face up squarely to the present, however uncertain, the one rule that had sustained him through the years of war.

He pushed his case on to the greasy surface. In the last moments of the dusk the dead water came alive with roses of iridescent colour. As the box floated away, like the coffin of a Chinese child, the circles of oil raced to embrace it and sent tremors of light across the river.

Jim climbed through the resting prisoners and sat down beside Mr Maxted. He handed him the mess-tin of water and then cleaned the sand from his shoes.

'All right, Jim?'

'The war must end, Mr Maxted.'

'It will, Jim.' Mr Maxted had revived briefly. 'We're going back to Shanghai tonight.'

'Shanghai – ?' Jim was unsure whether Mr Maxted was

255

delirious, dreaming of Shanghai in the way that the dying prisoners in the camp hospital had babbled of returning to England. 'Aren't they taking us up-country?'

'Not now . . .' Mr Maxted pointed through the darkness to the collier burning off the mole.

Jim watched the smoke rising from the collier's bridge and superstructure, everywhere but from its funnel. The fire in the engine-room had taken hold, and the stern of the vessel glowed like furnace coal. This was the ship that would have taken them up-country, to the killing-grounds beyond Soochow. For all his relief, Jim felt disappointed.

'What about our rations, Mr Maxted?'

'They're waiting for us in Shanghai. Just like the old days, Jim.'

Jim watched Mr Maxted sink back among the exhausted prisoners. He had made his last effort to sit upright, trying to convince Jim that all was well, that the good luck and the skill of some unknown American bomb-aimer, which had saved them from being shipped aboard the collier, would continue to watch over them.

'Mr Maxted, do you want the war to end? It must end soon.'

'It has almost ended. Think about your mother and father, Jim. The war has ended.'

'But, Mr Maxted, when will the next one begin . . . ?'

Japanese soldiers were walking along the railway line, followed by Dr Ransome and Mrs Pearce. The corporals shouted to each other, their voices drumming along the rails. A faint rain fell, and the guards waiting by the trucks put on their capes. Steam lifted from the warm rails, as the prisoners rose to their feet and clutched their small children. Voices murmured through the darkness, and wives grasped their husbands' hands.

'Digby . . . Digby . . .'

'Scotty . . .'

'Jake . . .'

'Bunty . . .'

A woman with a sleeping child on her shoulder seized Jim's arm, but he pushed her away and tried to steady Mr Maxted. The darkness and the tacky river water had made them both light-headed, and at any moment they would fall across the rails. Led by the three trucks, the prisoners left the embankment and gathered on the jetty beside the ruined godowns. A hundred of the prisoners had stayed behind on the causeway, too weary to carry on and resigned to whatever future the Japanese had prepared for them. They sat in the rain below the railway embankment, watched by the soldiers in their streaming capes.

As the column of prisoners set off, Jim realized that a quarter of those inmates who had left Lunghua that morning had fallen behind. Even before they reached the gates of the dockyard several prisoners turned back. An elderly Scotsman from E Block, a retired accountant at the Shanghai Power Company with whom Jim had often played chess, suddenly stepped from the column. As if he had forgotten where he had been for all the years of the war, he wandered across the stony yard, then walked through the rain towards the railway embankment.

An hour after nightfall they reached a football stadium on the western outskirts of Nantao. This concrete arena had been built on the orders of Madame Chiang Kai-Shek, in the hope that China might be host to the 1940 Olympic Games. Captured by the Japanese after their invasion in 1937, the stadium became the military headquarters for the war zone south of Shanghai.

The column of prisoners crossed the silent car park. Dozens of bomb craters had torn the tarmac surface, but the white marker lines still stretched through the darkness. Damaged army vehicles were parked in neat rows – shrapnel-torn trucks and fuel wagons, treadless tanks and armoured half-tracks each pulling two artillery guns. Jim stared at the pock-marked façade of the stadium. Bomb fragments had dislodged sections of the white plaster, and the original Chinese characters proclaiming the power of the Kuomintang had emerged once again, threatening slogans that hung over the darkness like the hoardings above the Chinese cinemas in pre-war Shanghai.

They entered a concrete tunnel that led into the darkened arena. With its curved stands it reminded Jim of the detention centre in Shanghai, all its dangers magnified a hundredfold by the war. The Japanese soldiers formed a cordon around the running track. The rain dripped from their capes, and lit the bayonets and breeches of their rifles. Already the first prisoners were sitting down on the wet grass. Mr Maxted dropped to the ground at Jim's feet, as if released from a harness. Jim squatted beside him, waving away the mosquitoes that had followed them into the stadium.

The three trucks emerged from the tunnel and stopped on the cinder track. Dr Ransome climbed across his patients and lowered himself from the tail-gate. Mrs Pearce stepped from the cabin of the second truck, leaving her husband and son beside the Japanese driver. Through the rain Jim could hear Dr Ransome arguing with the Japanese. Hidden under his cape, the senior sergeant of the gendarmerie watched him without expression, then lit a cigarette and strolled away to the stands, where he sat in the front row as if about to observe a display of midnight acrobatics.

Jim was glad when Mrs Pearce returned to the cabin of her truck. Dr Ransome's complaining voice, in the tones he had used so often when remonstrating with Jim over his games in the hospital cemetery, was out of place in Nantao stadium. Within a few minutes of their arrival a complete silence had come over the twelve hundred prisoners. They huddled together on the grass, watched by the guards in the stands. Dr Ransome moved through the women and children, still trying to carry out his Lunghua inspections. Jim waited until he stumbled in the dark, prompting a surly shout from a group of men.

The rain fell across the stadium, and Jim lay back and let it run across his face, warming his cold cheeks. Despite the rain, thousands of flies settled on the prisoners. Jim wiped the flies from Mr Maxted's mouth, and tried to wash his face with the rain, but they festered on his lips, picking at his gums.

Jim watched the faint breath from Mr Maxted's mouth. He wondered what he could do for him, and regretted throwing away his suitcase. Pushing the wooden box into the river had been a sentimental but pointless gesture, his first adult act. He might have bartered his possessions and obtained a little food for Mr Maxted. A few of the Japanese soldiers were Catholics, and used the Latin Mass. One of the guards in his rain-soaked cape might have valued the Kennedy *Primer*, and Jim could perhaps have arranged to give him Latin lessons . . .

But Mr Maxted slept peacefully. A grey breath emerged through the flies on his lips, and from the other prisoners nearby. An hour later, when the rain had stopped, the flashes of an American air raid lit up the stadium, like the sheet lightning of the monsoon season. As a child, safe in his bedroom at Amherst Avenue, Jim had watched the sudden glares that exposed the rats caught in the centre of the tennis court and on the verges of the swimming-pool. God, Vera agreed, was taking photographs of the wickedness of Shanghai. The noiseless glimmer of the night raids, somewhere among the Japanese naval bases at the mouth of the Yangtze, cast a damp sheen over Jim's arms and legs, another reminder of that fine dust he had first seen as he helped to build the runway at Lunghua Airfield. He knew that he was awake and asleep at the same time, dreaming of the war and yet dreamed of by the war.

Jim propped his head against Mr Maxted's chest. The rapid flashes of the air raids filled the stadium and dressed the sleeping prisoners in their shrouds. Perhaps they would all take part in the construction of a gigantic runway? In his mind the sound of the American planes set off powerful premonitions of death. Conjugating his Latin verbs, the nearest that he could move towards prayer, he fell asleep beside Mr Maxted and dreamed of runways.

31

The Empire of the Sun

A humid morning sun filled the stadium, reflected in the pools of water that covered the athletics track, and in the chromium radiators of the American cars parked behind the goal posts at the northern end of the football pitch. Supporting himself against Mr Maxted's shoulder, Jim surveyed the hundreds of men and women lying on the warm grass. A few prisoners squatted on the ground, their sunburnt but pallid faces like blanched leather from which the dye had run. They stared at the cars, suspicious of their bright grilles, with the wary eyes of the Hungjao peasants looking up from their rice-planting at his parents' Packard.

Jim brushed the flies from Mr Maxted's mouth and eyes. The architect lay without moving, his white ribs unclasped around his heart, but Jim could hear his faint breath.

'You're feeling better, Mr Maxted . . . I'll bring you some water.' Jim squinted at the lines of cars. Even the small effort of focusing his eyes exhausted him. Trying to hold his head steady, he felt the ground sway, as if he and the hundreds of prisoners were about to be tipped out of the stadium.

Mr Maxted turned to stare at Jim, who pointed to the cars. There were more than fifty of them – Buicks, Lincoln Zephyrs, two white Cadillacs side by side. Had they come to collect their British owners now that the war had ended? Jim stroked Mr Maxted's cheeks, then reached into the cavern below his ribs and tried to massage his heart. It would be a pity for Mr Maxted to die just as his Studebaker arrived to take him back to the Shanghai nightclubs.

However, the Japanese soldiers sat on the concrete

benches near the entrance tunnel, sipping tea beside a charcoal stove. Its smoke drifted between the hospital trucks. Two young soldiers were passing pails of water to a weary Dr Ransome, but the security troops seemed no more interested in the Lunghua prisoners who occupied the football field than they had been during the previous day's march.

His legs trembling, Jim stood up and scanned the parked cars for his parents' Packard. Where were the chauffeurs? They should have been waiting by their cars, as they always did outside the country club. Then a small raincloud dimmed the sun, and a drab light settled over the stadium. Looking at their rusting chrome, Jim realized that these American cars had been parked here for years. Their windshields were caked with winter grime, and they sat on flattened tyres, part of the booty looted by the Japanese from the Allied nationals.

Jim searched the stands on the north and west slopes of the stadium. The concrete tiers had been stripped of their seats, and sections of the stands were now used as an open-air warehouse. Dozens of black-wood cabinets and mahogany tables, their varnish still intact, and hundreds of dining-room chairs were packed together as if in the loft of a furniture depository. Bedsteads and wardrobes, refrigerators and air-conditioning units were stacked above each other, rising in a slope towards the sky. The immense presidential box, where Madame Chiang and the Generalissimo might once have saluted the world's athletes, was now crammed with roulette wheels, cocktail bars and a jumble of gilded plaster nymphs holding gaudy lamps above their heads. Rolls of Persian and Turkish carpets, hastily wrapped in tarpaulins, lay on the concrete steps, water dripping through them as if from a pile of rotting pipes.

To Jim, these shabby trophies seized from the houses and nightclubs of Shanghai seemed to gleam with a show-window freshness, like the floors filled with furniture through which he and his mother had once wandered in the Sincere Company department store. He stared at the stands, almost expecting his mother to appear in a silk dress and run a gloved hand over these terraces of black lacquer.

He sat down and shielded his eyes from the glare. He massaged Mr Maxted's cheeks with his thumb and forefinger, pinching his lips and hooking out the flies trapped in his mouth. Around them the inmates of Lunghua Camp lay on the damp grass, staring at this display of their former possessions, a mirage that grew more vivid in the steepening August sunlight.

Yet the mirage soon passed. Jim wiped his hands on Mr Maxted's shorts. The Japanese had frequently used the stadium as a transit camp, and the worn grass was covered with oily rags and the ash of small fires, strips of canvas tent and wooden crates. There were unmistakable human remains, bloodstains and pieces of excrement, on which feasted thousands of flies.

The engine of a hospital truck began to run noisily. The Japanese soldiers had come down from the stands and were forming themselves into a march party. Pairs of guards climbed the tail-gates, cotton masks over their faces. Helped by three English prisoners, Dr Ransome lifted down those patients either dead or too ill to continue the day's journey. They lay in the tyre-ruts that scored the grass, as if trying to fold the soft earth around themselves.

Jim squatted beside Mr Maxted, working his diaphragm like a bellows. He had seen Dr Ransome bring his patients back from the dead, and it was important for Mr Maxted to be well enough to join the march. Around them the prisoners were sitting upright, and a few men stood beside their huddled wives and children. Several of the older internees had died in the night – ten feet away Mrs Wentworth, who had played the part of Lady Bracknell, lay in her faded cotton dress, staring at the sky. Others were surrounded by shallow pools of water formed by the pressure of their bodies on the soft grass.

Jim's arms ached from the effort of pumping. He waited for Dr Ransome to jump down from the hospital truck and look after Mr Maxted. However, the three vehicles were already leaving the stadium. Dr Ransome's sandy head ducked as the truck lumbered through the tunnel. Jim was tempted to run after it, but he knew that he had decided to stay with Mr Maxted. He had learned that having someone to care for was the same as being cared for by someone else.

Jim listened to the trucks crossing the parking lot, their gearboxes gasping as they gathered speed. Lunghua Camp was at last being dismantled. A marching party formed itself beside the tunnel. Some three hundred British prisoners, the younger men with their wives and children, had lined up on the running track and were being inspected by a sergeant of the gendarmerie. Beside them, on the football pitch, were those prisoners too exhausted to sit or stand. They lay on the grass like battlefield casualties. The Japanese soldiers strolled among them, as if searching for a lost ball, uninterested in these British nationals who had strayed into a cul-de-sac of the war.

An hour later the column moved off, the prisoners plodding through the tunnel without a backward glance. Six Japanese soldiers followed them, and the rest continued their casual patrol of the blackwood cabinets and refrigerators. The senior NCOs waited by the tunnel and watched the American reconnaissance planes that flew overhead, making no attempt to mobilize the prisoners in the stadium. Within fifteen minutes, however, a second group had begun to assemble, and the Japanese came forward to inspect them.

Jim wiped his hands on the damp grass and put his fingers into Mr Maxted's mouth. The architect's lips trembled around his knuckles. But already the August sun was driving the moisture from the grass. Jim turned his attention to a pool of water lying on the cinder track. He waited for the sentry to pass, and then walked across the grass and drank from his cupped hands. The water ran down his throat like iced mercury, an electric current that almost stopped his heart. Before the Japanese could order him away, Jim quickly cupped his hands and carried the water to Mr Maxted.

As he decanted the water into Mr Maxted's mouth the flies scrambled from his gums. Beside him lay the elderly figure of Major Griffin, a retired Indian Army officer who had lectured in Lunghua on the infantry weapons of the Great War. Too weak to sit up, he pointed to Jim's hands.

Jim pinched Mr Maxted's lips, relieved when his tongue shot forward in a spasm. Trying to encourage him, Jim said: 'Mr Maxted, our rations should be coming soon.'

'Good lad, Jamie – you hang on.'

Major Griffin beckoned to him. 'Jim . . .'

'Coming, Major Griffin . . .' Jim crossed the cinder track and returned with a handful of water. As he squatted beside the major, patting his cheeks, he noticed that Mrs Vincent was sitting on the grass twenty feet away. She had left her son and husband with a group of prisoners in the centre of the football field. Too exhausted to move any further, she stared at Jim with the same desperate gaze to which she had treated him as he ate his weevils. The night's rain had washed the last of the dye from her cotton dress, giving her the ashen pallor of the Chinese labourers at Lunghua Airfield. Mrs Vincent would build a strange runway, Jim reflected.

'Jamie . . .'

She called him by his childhood name, which Mr Maxted, without thinking, had summoned from some pre-war memory. She wanted him to be a child again, to run the endless errands that had kept him alive in Lunghua.

As he scooped the cold water from the cinder track he remembered how Mrs Vincent had refused to help him when he was ill. Yet he had always been intrigued by the sight of her eating. He waited while she drank from his hands.

When she had finished he helped her to stand. 'Mrs Vincent, the war's over now.'

With a grimace, she pushed his hands away, but Jim no longer cared. He watched her walk unsteadily between the seated prisoners. Jim squatted beside Mr Maxted, brushing the flies from his face. He could still feel Mrs Vincent's tongue on his fingers.

'Jamie . . .'

Someone else was calling, as if he were a Chinese coolie running at the command of his European masters. Too light-headed even to sit, Jim lay beside Mr Maxted. It was time to stop running his errands. His hands were frozen from the water on the cinder track. The war had lasted too long. At the detention centre, and in Lunghua, he had done all he could to stay alive, but now a part of him wanted to die. It was the one way in which he could end the war.

Jim looked at the hundreds of prisoners on the grass. He wanted them all to die, surrounded by their rotting carpets and cocktail cabinets. Many of them, he was glad to see, had already obliged him, and Jim felt angry at those prisoners still able to walk who were now forming a second march party. He guessed that they were being walked to death around the countryside, but he wanted them to stay in the stadium and die within sight of the white Cadillacs.

Fiercely, Jim wiped the flies from Mr Maxted's cheeks. Laughing at Mrs Vincent, he began to rock on his knees, as he had done as a child, crooning to himself and monotonously beating the ground. 'Jamie . . . Jamie . . .'

A Japanese soldier patrolled the cinder track nearby. He walked across the grass and stared down at Jim. Irritated by the noise, he was about to kick him with his ragged boot.

But a flash of light filled the stadium, flaring over the stands in the south-west corner of the football field, as if an immense American bomb had exploded somewhere to the north-east of Shanghai. The sentry hesitated, looking over his shoulder as the light behind him grew more intense. It faded within a few seconds, but its pale sheen covered everything within the stadium, the looted furniture in the stands, the cars behind the goal posts, the prisoners on the grass. They were sitting on the floor of a furnace heated by a second sun.

Jim stared at his white hands and knees, and at the pinched face of the Japanese soldier, who seemed disconcerted by the light. Both of them were waiting for the rumble of sound that followed the bomb-flashes, but an unbroken silence lay over the stadium and the surrounding land, as if the sun had blinked, losing heart for a few seconds. Jim smiled at the Japanese, wishing that he could tell him that the light was a premonition of his death, the sight of his small soul joining the larger soul of the dying world.

These games and hallucinations continued until the late afternoon, when an air raid at Hongkew again lit up the stadium. Jim lay in his dream-wake, feeling the earth spring below his back like the ballroom floor at the Shanghai Country Club. The flares of light moved from one section of the stands to another, transforming the furniture into a series of spotlit tableaux illustrating the lives of the colonial British.

At dusk the last march party assembled by the tunnel. Jim sat by Mr Maxted, watching the fifty prisoners form themselves into a column. Where were they going? Many of the men and women could barely stand, and Jim doubted if they could get as far as the car park outside the stadium.

For the first time since leaving Lunghua, the Japanese had become impatient. Eager to be rid of the last prisoners still able to walk, the soldiers moved across the football field. They cuffed the prisoners and pulled their shoulders. A corporal with a cotton face mask shone his torch into the faces of the dead, then turned them on their backs.

A Eurasian civilian in a white shirt moved behind the Japanese, eager to help those ordered to join the march, like the courier of an efficient travel company. At the edges of the field the Japanese guards were already stripping the bodies of the dead, pulling off shoes and belts.

'Mr Maxted . . .' In a last moment of lucidity Jim sat up, knowing that he must leave the dying architect and join the march party into the night. 'I ought to go now, Mr Maxted. It's time for the war to be over . . .'

He was trying to stand when he felt Mr Maxted grasp his wrist. 'Don't go with them . . . Jim . . . stay here.'

Jim waited for Mr Maxted to die. But he pressed Jim's wrist to the grass, as if trying to bolt it to the earth. Jim watched the march party shuffle towards the tunnel. Unable to walk more than three paces, a man fell and was left on the cinder track. Jim listened to the voices of the Japanese draw nearer, muffled by the masks over their faces, and heard the sergeant gag and spit in the stench.

A soldier knelt beside him, his breath hoarse and exhausted behind his mask. Strong hands moved across Jim's chest and hips, feeling his pockets. Brusquely they pulled his shoes from his feet, then flung them on to the cinder track. Jim lay without moving, as the fires from the burning oil depots at Hongkew played across the stands, lighting the doors of the looted refrigerators, the radiator grilles of the white Cadillacs and the lamps of the plaster nymphs in the box of the Generalissimo.

Part III

32
The Eurasian

A restful sunlight warmed the stadium. From the cloudless sky fell a squall of hail, a flurry of frozen vapour dislodged from the wings of an American aircraft three miles above the Yangtze valley. Lit by the sun, the crystals fell on to the football field like a shower of Christmas decorations.

Jim sat up and touched the hailstones, nuggets of white gold scattered on the grass. Beside him, Mr Maxted's body was dressed in a suit of lights, his ashen face speckled with miniature rainbows. But within a few seconds the hail had melted into the ground. Jim listened for the aircraft, hoping that it might launch another cascade of hail, but the sky was empty from horizon to horizon. A few of the prisoners in the stadium knelt on the grass, eating the hail and talking to each other across the bodies of their dead companions.

The Japanese had gone. The NCOs and soldiers of the gendarmerie had taken their equipment and vanished during the night. Jim stood in his bare feet on the icy grass, staring at the exit tunnel. The shallow sunlight veered against the concrete walls from the deserted parking lot. Already one of the British prisoners hobbled through the tunnel on his worn clogs, followed by his wife in her ragged dress, hands pressed to her face.

Jim waited for a rifle shot to throw the man at his wife's feet, but the couple stepped into the parking lot and gazed at the lines of bomb-damaged vehicles. Jim left Mr Maxted and walked along the running track, intending to follow them, but then cautiously decided to climb one of the stands.

The concrete steps seemed to reach beyond the sky. Jim

271

paused to rest among the terraces of looted furniture. He sat on a straight-backed chair beside a dining-room table and drank the warm rain-water from the polished blackwood. Below him the thirty or so prisoners on the football field were rousing themselves as if from a dishevelled picnic. The women sat on the grass, quietly straightening their hair among the bodies of their former friends while a few of the husbands peered through the dusty windows at the instrument panels of the parked cars.

More than a hundred prisoners were dead, scattered on the football pitch as if they had fallen from the sky during the night. Turning his back on them, Jim climbed through the pools of water to the top tier of the stand. Now that he had left Mr Maxted he felt guilty that he had died, a guilt in some way connected with his missing shoes. He stared at his wet footprints, and told himself that he should have sold his shoes to the Japanese for a little rice or a sweet potato. As it was, by pretending to be dead he had lost both Mr Maxted and his shoes.

Yet the dead had protected Jim, and saved him from the night march. Lying with their bodies through the dark hours, both asleep and awake, he had felt closer to them than he felt to the living. Long after Mr Maxted had grown cold, Jim had continued to massage his cheeks, keeping away the flies until he was sure that his soul had left him. During the next days he had stayed close to Mr Maxted, despite the flies and the smell from the body of the dead architect. The prisoners resting in the centre of the field waved Jim away whenever he approached. Drinking the rain-water that dripped from the furniture in the stands, he had survived on a single potato he found in the trouser pocket of Mr Wentworth, and on the rancid rice scattered towards him by the Japanese soldiers.

Jim leaned against the metal rail and looked down at the parking lot. The British couple were staring at the lines of derelict vehicles, alone in a silent world. Jim laughed at them, a harsh cough that spat a ball of yellow pus from his mouth. He wanted to shout to them: The world has gone away! Last night everyone jumped into their graves and pulled the earth over themselves!

Good riddance . . . Jim stared at the moribund land, at the water-filled bomb craters in the paddy fields, at the silent anti-aircraft guns of Lunghua Pagoda, at the beached freighters on the banks of the river. Behind him, no more than three miles away, was the silent city. The apartment houses of the French Concession and the office blocks of the Bund were like a magnified image of that distant prospect that had sustained him for so many years.

Chilled by the river, a cool wind moved across the stadium, and for a moment that strange north-eastern light he had seen over the stands returned to dim the sun. Jim stared at his pallid hands. He knew that he was alive, but at the same time he felt as dead as Mr Maxted. Perhaps his soul, instead of leaving his body, had died inside his head?

Thirsty again, Jim walked down the concrete steps, scooping the water from the tables and cabinets. If the war had ended it was time to look for his mother and father. However, without the Japanese to protect them it would be dangerous for the British to set off on foot for Shanghai.

Beyond the goal posts, a British prisoner had managed to lift the hood of one of the white Cadillacs. Watched by his companions, he bent over the engine and touched the cylinders. Jim roused himself and raced down the steps, eager to be the driver's navigator. He could still remember every street and alleyway in Shanghai.

As he crossed the athletics track he noticed that three men had entered the stadium. Two were Chinese coolies, bare-chested with black cotton trousers tied at the ankles above their straw sandals. The third was the Eurasian in the white shirt whom Jim had seen with the Japanese security troops. They stood by the tunnel, while the Eurasian inspected the stadium. He glanced at the prisoners sitting on the grass, but his attention was clearly fixed on the looted furniture in the stands.

The Eurasian carried a heavy automatic pistol tucked into the waistband of his trousers, but he smiled at Jim in an ingratiating way, as if they were old friends separated by the misadventure of war.

'Say, kid . . . You're okay?' He surveyed Jim's ragged shirt and shorts, his legs and bare feet covered with dirt and sores. 'Lunghua CAC? I guess you've had to tough it out.'

Jim stared stolidly at the Eurasian. Despite the smile, there was no sympathy in the man's eyes. He spoke with a strong but recently acquired American accent, which Jim assumed he had learned while interrogating captured American aircrews. He wore a chromium wristwatch, and the Colt pistol in his waistband was like those that the Japanese guards at Lunghua had taken from the pilots of the downed Superfortresses. His baggy nostrils quivered in the stench rising from the football field, distracting him from his scrutiny of the stands. He stepped aside for two British prisoners who hobbled through the tunnel.

'It's some set-up,' he reflected. 'Your Ma and Pa here? Looks like you could use a couple of bags of rice. Ask around, kid, if they have any bracelets, wedding rings, charms. We can work together on it.'

'Is the war over?'

The Eurasian's eyes lowered, eclipsed by some passing shadow. He rallied himself and smiled keenly. 'That's for sure. Any time now the whole US Navy is going to tie up at the Bund.' When Jim looked unconvinced, the Eurasian explained: 'Kid, they dropped atomic bombs. Uncle Sam threw a piece of the sun at Nagasaki and Hiroshima, killed a million people. One great big flash . . .'

'I saw it.'

'Kid . . .? Did it light up the whole sky? Could be.' The Eurasian sounded doubtful, but turned his eyes from the booty in the stands and began to examine Jim. For all his easy manner he was unsure of himself, as if aware that the incoming US Navy might be less than convinced by his pro-American act. He glanced warily at the sky. 'Atomic bombs . . . too bad for all those Japs, but lucky for you, kid. And for your Ma and Pa.'

Jim weighed this as the Eurasian stepped to the concrete rubbish bin by the entrance tunnel and began to root around inside it. 'Is the war really over?'

'Yeah, it's over, finished, we're all friends. The Emperor just announced the surrender.'

'Where are the Americans?'

'They're coming, kid, they have to get here with their atom bombs.'

'A white light?'

'That's correct, kid. The atom bomb, US super-weapon. Maybe you saw the Nagasaki bomb.'

'Yes, I saw the atom bomb. What happened to Dr Ransome?' When the Eurasian seemed puzzled, Jim added: 'And the people who left on the march?'

'Too bad, kid.' The Eurasian shook his head, as if regretting a small oversight. 'The American bombing, some diseases. Maybe your friend will make it . . .'

Jim was about to walk away, when the Eurasian turned from the rubbish bin. In one hand he held a pair of worn clogs which he threw on to the track. In the other he carried Jim's leather golf shoes, tied together by their laces. He was about to speak to the waiting coolies, when Jim stepped forward.

'Those are mine – Dr Ransome gave them to me.' He spoke flatly and pulled the shoes from the Eurasian's hands. Jim waited for him to draw his gun, or order the coolies to knock him to the ground. Though exhausted by hunger, and by the effort of climbing the stand, Jim was aware that he was once again asserting the ascendancy of the European.

'That's okay, kid.' The Eurasian was genuinely concerned. 'I was keeping those shoes in case you turned up. Tell your Ma and Pa.'

Jim walked past the coolies and entered the light-filled tunnel. Groups of British men and women were wandering among the tanks and burnt-out trucks in the parking lot. They followed the faded marker lines, with no idea of where they were going, as if they had survived the entire war only to expire in this shabby maze. Outside the stadium the August sunlight was made even more intense by the complete silence that lay over the paddy fields and canals. A white glaze covered the derelict land. Had the fields been seared by the flash of the atomic bomb which the Eurasian had described? Jim remembered the burning body of the Mustang pilot, and the soundless light that had filled the stadium and seemed to dress the dead and the living in their shrouds.

33

The Kamikaze Pilot

Secure in his shoes, Jim stood by the concrete blockhouse that guarded the vehicles in the parking lot. The Shanghai road ran past the entrance, heading towards the southern suburbs of the city. Nothing moved in the surrounding fields, but three hundred yards away a platoon of Chinese puppet soldiers sat in an anti-tank ditch beside the road. Still wearing their faded orange-green uniforms, they squatted by a charcoal stove, holding their rifles between their knees. An NCO climbed from the ditch and waited, hands on hips, watching Jim as he stepped into the road.

If he approached them, they would kill him for his shoes. Jim knew that he was too weak to walk to Shanghai, let alone cope with all the dangers of the open road. Hidden behind the blockhouse, he set out towards the safety of Lunghua Airfield. Its western perimeter was little more than half a mile away, a terrain of nettles and wild sugar-cane covered with fuel drums and the fuselages of abandoned aircraft. Between the rusty tailplanes he could see the concrete runway, its white surface almost evaporating into the heat.

The stadium fell behind him. The road was an empty meridian circling a planet discarded by war. Jim followed the verge, stepping among the broken clogs and rags of clothing left by the British prisoners during the last yards of their march to the stadium. On either side of him were bombed-out trenchworks and blockhouses, a world of mud. On the slopes of a water-filled tank-trap, among the tyres and ammunition boxes, lay the body of a Chinese soldier, orange uniform split by his ballooning buttocks and shoulders, glistening with oily light like a burst paint-pot. A pack-horse rested beside the road, hide flayed from its ribs. Jim peered into this capacious cage, half-hoping to find a rat imprisoned within it.

He left the road when it turned eastwards to the Nantao docks. He crossed the flooded paddy fields, following the earth embankment of an irrigation ditch. Even here, a mile to the west of the river, fuel oil from the beached freighters leaked through the creeks and canals, covering the drowned paddies with a lurid sheen. Jim rested on the perimeter road of the airfield, then climbed through the wire fence and walked up to the nearest of the abandoned aircraft. Far across the airfield, below the massive flak tower of Lunghua Pagoda, were the bombed hangars and workshops. A few Japanese mechanics wandered among the wreckage, but the Chinese scrap-dealers had yet to arrive, clearly fearful of this zone of silence. Jim listened for the noise of hacksaws or cutting equipment, but the air was empty, as if the fury of the American bombardment had driven all sound from the region for years to come.

Jim stopped under the tailplane of a Zero fighter. Wild sugar-cane grew through its wings. Cannon fire had burned the metal skin from the fuselage spars, but the rusting shell still retained all the magic of those machines which he had watched from the balcony of the assembly hall, taking off from the runway he had helped to build. Jim touched the feathered vanes of the radial engine and ran his hand along the warped flank of the propeller. Glycol had leaked from the radiator of the oil cooler and covered the plane with a pink tracery. He stepped on to the wing root and peered into the cockpit, at the intact display of dials and trim wheels. An immense pathos surrounded the throttle and undercarriage levers, the rivets stamped into the metal fabric by some unknown Japanese woman on the Mitsubishi assembly line.

278

Jim wandered among the stricken planes, which seemed to float on their green banks of nettles, letting them fly once again inside his head. Dizzied by their derelict beauty, he sat down to rest on the tail of a Hayate fighter. He watched the sky over Shanghai, waiting for the Americans to arrive at Lunghua Airfield. Although he had eaten nothing for two days, his mind was clear.

'. . . aah . . . aah . . .'

The sound, a deep sigh of anger and resignation, came from the edge of the landing field. Before Jim could hide there was a scuffle in the nettles behind the Zero. A Japanese airman stood twenty feet from him. He wore a pilot's baggy flying overall, with the insignia of a special attack group stitched to the sleeves. He was unarmed, but carried a pine stake he had wrenched from the perimeter fence. He thrashed at the nettles around him and gazed irritably at the rusting aircraft, sucking in his breath as if trying to inspire them to flight.

Jim crouched over his knees, hoping that the faded camouflage of the Hayate would conceal him. He noticed that this Japanese pilot-officer was still in his late teens, with an unformed face, boneless nose and chin. His sallow skin and the prominent knuckles of his wrists told Jim that the schoolboy pilot was as starved as himself. Only his guttural sighs were driven by the breath of a mature man, as if on joining his kamikaze unit he had been assigned the throat and lungs of an older pilot.

'. . . ugh . . .' He noticed Jim sitting on the tailplane and for a few seconds watched him across the nettles. Then he turned away and continued his bad-tempered patrol of the airfield perimeter.

Jim watched him beating at the sugar-cane, perhaps trying to clear a space for a helicopter to land. Had the Japanese prepared a secret weapon in answer to the atomic bomb, a high-performance rocket fighter that would need a longer runway than Lunghua's? Jim waited for him to signal to the guards at the foot of the pagoda. But the Japanese was intent only on his search of the derelict aircraft. He stopped to shake his head, and Jim was reminded again of the pilot's youth. At the outbreak of war, and until a few months earlier, he would have been a schoolboy, recruited straight from the classroom to the flight training academy.

Jim stood up and walked through the nettles to the yellowing grass at the edge of the airfield. He began to follow the Japanese, fifty yards behind him, and stopped when the pilot paused to work the elevators of a damaged Zero. He waited until the Japanese moved on again, and then walked after him, making no effort to hide and carefully placing his feet in the pilot's footsteps.

For the next hour they moved around the southern edge of the airfield, the young pilot with the boy in tow. The barrack huts and dormitory blocks of Lunghua Camp rose through the heat. Far away, across the airfield, the Japanese ground-crews lounged in the sun beside the burnt-out hangars. Although aware that Jim was following him, the pilot made no attempt to summon them. Only when they came within eyeshot of two soldiers guarding a rifle pit did the Japanese stop and beckon Jim to him.

They stood together by a rusting plane that had been stripped of its wings by the scrap-dealers. The pilot sucked at the air, distracted by Jim's patient gaze like an older schoolboy forced to acknowledge an admiring junior. For all his youth, he seemed to be willing himself to the edge of an adult despair. Clouds of flies rose from the decomposing body of a Chinese coolie lying in the sugar-cane among the fuel tanks and engine blocks. The flies hovered around the pilot's mouth, tapping his lips like impatient guests at a banquet. They reminded Jim of the flies that had covered Mr Maxted's face. Did they know that this teenage pilot should have died in an attack on the American carriers at Okinawa?

For whatever reason, the Japanese made no move to brush them away. No doubt he knew that his own life was over, that the Kuomintang forces about to reoccupy Shanghai would be eager to deal with him.

The Japanese raised his wooden stake. Like a sleeper waking from a dream, he hurled it into the nettles. As Jim flinched, he reached into the waist-pocket of his flight overalls and drew out a small mango.

Jim took the yellow fruit from the pilot's calloused hand. The mango was still warm from his body. Trying to show the same self-discipline, Jim forced himself not to eat. He waited while the pilot stared at the concrete runway.

With a last cry of disgust, the pilot stepped forward and cuffed Jim on the head, waving him towards the perimeter fence as if warning him away from contaminated ground.

34
The Refrigerator in the Sky

The sweet mango slithered around Jim's mouth, like Mrs Vincent's tongue in his hands. Ten feet from the perimeter fence, Jim sat on a Mustang drop-tank that had fallen into the grass beside a flooded paddy field. He swallowed the soft pulp, and chewed at the stone, scraping away the last of the pith. Already he was thinking of the next mango. If he could attach himself to this young Japanese pilot, run errands for him and make himself useful, there might be more mangoes. Within a few days he would be strong enough to walk to Shanghai. By then the Americans would have arrived, and Jim could present the kamikaze pilot to them as his friend. Being generous people at heart, the Americans would overlook the small matter of the suicide attacks on their carriers at Okinawa. When peace came, the Japanese might teach him to fly . . .

Almost drunk on the mango's milky sap, Jim slid to the ground, his back against the drop-tank. He stared at the level surface of the flooded paddy, deciding to be serious with himself. First, could he be sure that the war was really over? The Eurasian in the white shirt had been suspiciously offhand, but he was only concerned to steal the furniture and cars stored at the stadium. As for learning to fly, a kamikaze pilot might not be the ideal instructor . . .

A familiar drone crossed the August sky, a threat of engines. Jim stood up, almost choking on the mango stone. Straight ahead, some eight hundred feet above the empty paddies, was an American bomber. A four-engined Super-fortress, it flew more slowly than any American plane that Jim had seen throughout the war. Was it about to land at

Lunghua Airfield? Jim began to wave to the pilot in the glass-domed cockpit. As the Superfortress swept overhead, its engines shook the ground with their noise, and the derelict aircraft at the edge of the landing field began to tremble together.

The doors of the bomb-bays opened, revealing the silver cylinders ready to fall from their racks. The Superfortress drummed past, the higher pitch of one of its starboard engines cracking the air. Too weak to move, Jim waited for the bombs to explode around him, but the sky was filled with coloured parachutes. Dozens of canopies floated gaily on the air, as if enjoying the August sun. The vivid parasols reminded Jim of the hot-air balloons that the Chinese conjurors sent soaring over the gardens of Amherst Avenue at the climax of the children's parties. Were the pilots of the B-29s trying to amuse him, to keep up his spirits until they could land?

The parachutes sailed past, falling towards Lunghua Camp. Unsteadily, Jim tried to focus his eyes on the coloured canopies. Two of the parachutes had collided, entangling their shrouds. A silver canister dragged its collapsed parachute and plummeted to the ground, striking a canal embankment two hundred yards away.

Making a final effort, before he had to lie down for the last time among the derelict aircraft, Jim stepped through the sugar-cane into the flooded paddy. He strode across the shallow water to a submerged bomb crater in the centre of the field, then followed its ridge towards the canal.

As he climbed the embankment the last of the parachutes had fallen into the fields to the west of Lunghua Camp. The murmur of the B-29s engines faded over the Yangtze. Jim approached the scarlet canopy, large enough to cover a house, which lay across the embankment. He gazed at the lustrous material, more luxurious than any fabric he had ever seen, at the immaculate stitching and seams, at the white cords that trailed into the culvert beside the canal.

The canister had burst on impact. Jim lowered himself down the slope of sun-baked earth, and squatted by the open mouth of the cylinder. Around him, on the floor of the culvert, was a ransom in canned food and cigarette packets. The canister was crammed with cardboard cartons, and one had broken loose from the nose cone and scattered its contents over the ground. Jim crawled among the cans, wiping his eyes so that he could read the labels. There were tins of Spam, Klim and Nescafé, bars of chocolate and cellophaned packs of Lucky Strike and Chesterfield cigarettes, bundles of *Reader's Digest* and *Life* magazines, *Time* and *Saturday Evening Post*.

The sight of so much food confused Jim, forcing on him a notion of choice that he had not known for years. The cans and packets were frozen, as if they had just emerged from an American refrigerator. He began to fill the broken box with canned meat, powdered milk, chocolate bars and a bundle of *Reader's Digest*s. Then, thinking ahead for the first time in several days, he added a carton of Chesterfield cigarettes.

When he climbed from the culvert the scarlet canopy of the parachute was billowing gently in the air that moved along the canal. Holding the cold treasure to his chest, Jim left the embankment and waded across the paddy field. He was following the ridge of the bomb crater towards the perimeter of the airfield when he heard the leisurely drumming of a B-29's engines. He stopped to search for the plane, already wondering how he could cope with all this treasure falling from the sky.

Almost at once, a rifle shot rang out. A hundred yards away, separated from Jim by the open paddy, a Japanese soldier was running along the embankment of the canal. Bare-footed in his ragged uniform, he raced past the parachute canopy, leapt down the weed-covered slope and sprinted across the paddy field. Lost in the spray kicked up by his frantic heels, he disappeared among the grave mounds and clumps of sugar-cane.

Jim crouched by the ridge of the bomb crater, hiding in the few blades of wild rice. A second Japanese soldier appeared. He was unarmed, but still wore his webbing and ammunition pouches. He sprinted along the canal embankment, and stopped to recover his breath beside the scarlet canopy of the parachute. He turned to look over his shoulder, and Jim recognized the puffy, tubercular face of Private Kimura.

A group of European men were following him along the embankment, clubs of weighted bamboo in their hands. One of the men carried a rifle, but Kimura ignored him and straightened his webbing around his tattered uniform. He kicked one of his rotting boots into the water, and then walked down the slope to the flooded paddy field. He had covered ten paces when there was a second rifle shot.

Private Kimura lay face down in the shallow water. Jim waited in the wild rice as the four Europeans approached the parachute canopy. He listened to their nervous quarrelling. All were former British prisoners, barefoot and in ragged shorts, though none had been inmates of Lunghua. Their leader was an agitated young Englishman whose fists were wrapped in a pair of grimy bandages. Jim guessed that he had been imprisoned for years in an underground cell. His white skin flinched in the sunlight like the exposed flesh of a snail teased from its shell. He waved his bandages in the air, bloody pennants that signalled some special kind of anger to himself.

The four men began to roll up the parachute canopy. Despite the starvation of the past months, they worked swiftly and had soon pulled the metal canister from the culvert. They repacked its contents, lashed the nose cone in place and dragged the heavy cylinder along the embankment.

Jim watched them make their way between the burial mounds towards Lunghua Camp. He was tempted to run over and join them, but all the caution learned in the past years warned him not to expose himself. Private Kimura lay in the water fifty feet away, a red cloud unfurling from his back like the canopy of a drowned parachute.

Fifteen minutes later, when he was certain that no one was watching from the nearby paddy fields, Jim emerged from the clump of wild rice and returned to his hiding-place among the derelict aircraft.

Quickly, without bothering to wash his hands in the flooded paddy, Jim tore the key from the Spam tin and rolled back the metal strip. A pungent odour rose from the pink mass of chopped meat, which gaped in the sunlight like a wound. He sank his fingers into the meat and pressed a piece between his lips. A strange but potent flavour filled his mouth, the taste of animal fat. After years of boiled rice and sweet potatoes, his mouth was an ocean of exotic spices. Chewing carefully, as Dr Ransome had taught him, drawing the last ounce of nutrition from every morsel, Jim finished the meat.

Thirsty after all the salts, he opened the can of Klim, only to find a white powder. He crammed the fatty grains into his mouth, reached through the grass to the edge of the paddy and scooped a handful of the warm water to his lips. A rich, creamy foam almost choked him, and he vomited the white torrent into the paddy. Jim stared with surprise at this snowy fountain, wondering if he would starve to death because he had forgotten how to eat. Sensibly he read the instructions and mixed a pint of milk so rich that its fat swam in the sun like the oil on the surrounding creeks and canals.

Dazed by the food, Jim lay back in the hot grass and sucked contentedly on the bar of hard, sweet chocolate. He had eaten the most satisfying meal of his life, and his stomach stood out below his ribs like a football. Beside him, on the surface of the paddy, swarms of flies festered over the cloud of white vomit. Jim wiped the mud from the second Spam tin and waited for the Japanese pilot to appear again, so that he could repay him for the mango.

Three miles to the west, near the camps of Hungjao and Siccawei, dozens of coloured parachutes were dropping from a B-29 that cruised across the August sky. Surrounded by this vision of all the abundance of America falling from the air, Jim laughed happily to himself. He began his second, and almost more important meal, devouring the six copies of the *Reader's Digest*. He turned the crisp, white pages of the magazines, so unlike the greasy copies he had read to death in Lunghua. They were filled with headlines and catchphrases from a world he had never known, and a host of unimaginable names – Patton, Eisenhower, Himmler, Belsen, jeep, GI, AWOL, Utah Beach, von Rundstedt, the Bulge, and a thousand other details of the European war. Together they described an heroic adventure on another planet, filled with scenes of sacrifice and stoicism, of countless acts of bravery, a universe away from the war that Jim had known at the estuary of the Yangtze, that vast river barely large enough to draw all the dead of China through its mouth. Feasting on the magazines, Jim drowsed among the flies and vomit. Trying not to be outdone by the *Reader's Digest*, he remembered the white light of the atomic bomb at Nagasaki, whose flash he had seen reflected across the China Sea. Its pale halo still lay over the silent fields, but seemed barely equal to D-Day and Bastogne. Unlike the war in China, everyone in Europe clearly knew which side he was on, a problem that Jim had never really solved. Despite all the new names that it had spawned, was the war recharging itself here by the great rivers of eastern Asia, to be fought forever in that far more ambiguous language that Jim had begun to learn?

35

Lieutenant Price

By the early afternoon Jim had rested sufficiently to turn his mind from this question and eat a second meal. The warm Spam, no longer chilled by its high-altitude flight in the bomb-bays of the B-29, slipped between his fingers on to the dusty ground. He retrieved the block of jellied meat, scraped away the flies and dirt, and washed it down with the last of the powdered milk.

Chewing on a chocolate bar, and thinking about the Ardennes offensive, Jim watched a B-29 soar across the open countryside two miles to the south-west. A Mustang fighter accompanied the bomber, drifting in wide circles a thousand feet above the Superfortress, as if its pilot was bored by the chore of guarding the relief plane. A flock of parachutes sailed towards the ground, perhaps aimed at an exhausted group of Lunghua prisoners abandoned by the Japanese during their march from Nantao stadium.

Jim turned to the Shanghai skyline. Was he strong enough to walk the few, dangerous miles to the western suburbs? Perhaps his parents had already returned to the house in Amherst Avenue? They might be hungry after the journey from Soochow, and would be glad of the last tin of Spam and the carton of Chesterfields. Smiling to himself, Jim thought of his mother – he could no longer remember her face but he could all too well imagine her response to the Spam. As an extra treat, she would have plenty to read . . .

He stood up, eager to begin the walk back to Shanghai. He patted his bloated stomach, wondering if there was a new American disease that came from eating too much food. At that moment, through the branches of the trees, he saw faces turn towards him. Six Chinese soldiers strode past the derelict aircraft, following the perimeter road. They were northern Chinese, tall and heavy-boned men wearing full packs and quilted blue uniforms. There were five-pointed red stars on their soft caps, and the leader carried a machine-gun of foreign design, with an air-cooled barrel and drum magazine. He wore spectacles and was younger and slighter than his men, with the fixed gaze of an accountant or student.

At a steady pace, as if they had already covered an immense distance, the six soldiers stepped between the aircraft. They passed within twenty feet of Jim, who concealed the Spam and the carton of Chesterfields behind his back. He assumed that these men were Chinese communists. By all accounts, they hated the Americans. Seeing the cigarettes, they might shoot him before he could explain that he too had once thought seriously of becoming a communist.

But the soldiers glanced at him without interest, their faces free of that unsettling blend of deference and contempt with which the Chinese had always regarded Europeans and Americans. They walked swiftly and soon vanished among the trees. Jim stepped over the perimeter wire, searching for the Japanese pilot. He wanted to warn him of these communist soldiers, who would kill him on sight.

Already he had decided not to walk alone to Shanghai. The Lunghua and Nantao districts were infested with armed men.

He would first return to the camp, and join the British internees who had shot Private Kimura. As soon as they recovered their strength they would want to set out for the bars and nightclubs of Shanghai. Jim, with all his expertise gained in Mr Maxted's Studebaker, would be their guide.

* * *

Although the gates of Lunghua Camp were little more than a mile from him, it took Jim two hours to cross the empty countryside. Avoiding Private Kimura, Jim waded through the flooded paddy field, and then followed the canal embankment to the Shanghai road. The verges were littered with the debris of the air attacks. Burnt-out trucks and supply wagons lay in the ditches, surrounded by the bodies of dead puppet soldiers, the carcasses of horses and water buffalo. A glimmer of golden light rose from the thousands of spent cartridge cases, as if these dead soldiers had been looting a treasury in the moments before their death.

Jim walked along the silent road, watching an American fighter cruise in from the west. Sitting in his open cockpit, the pilot circled Jim, engine throttled back so that the silver machine whispered through the air. Then Jim saw that its guns were cocked, their ejection ports open, and it occurred to him that the pilot might kill him for fun. He raised the carton of Chesterfields and the *Reader's Digest*s, displaying them to the pilot like a set of passports. The pilot waved to him and banked the aircraft, setting course for Shanghai.

The presence of this American aviator cheered Jim. He confidently strode the last hundred yards towards the camp. The sight of the familiar buildings, the watch-tower and barbed-wire fence, warmed and reassured him. He was going back to his real home. If Shanghai was too dangerous, perhaps his mother and father would leave Amherst Avenue and live with him in Lunghua. In a practical sense it was a pity that the Japanese soldiers would not be there to guard them . . .

As Jim reached the camp he was surprised to find that the Chinese peasants and army deserters had returned to their plot beside the gates. They squatted in the sun, staring patiently at the bare-chested Briton who stood inside the wire, a holstered pistol strapped to his bony hips. Jim recognized him as Mr Tulloch, the chief mechanic at the

291

Packard agency in Shanghai. He had spent the entire war playing cards in D Block, pausing once to have a brisk row with Dr Ransome for refusing to help with the sewage detail. Jim had last seen him lying outside the guardhouse after his abortive attempt to walk to Shanghai.

He now lounged against the gates, picking at an infected bruise on his lip and watching the activity on the parade ground. Two Britons were dragging a parachute canister and its canopy through the door of the guardhouse. A third man stood on the roof, scanning the countryside with a pair of Japanese binoculars.

'Mr Tulloch . . .' Jim pulled at the gates, rattling the heavy padlock and chain. 'Mr Tulloch, you've locked the gates.'

Tulloch stared distastefully at Jim, clearly not recognizing this ragged fourteen-year-old, and suspicious of the carton of cigarettes.

'Where the hell did you come from? Are you British, boy?'

'Mr Tulloch, I was in Lunghua. I lived here for three years.' When Tulloch began to wander away, Jim shouted: 'I worked at the hospital with Dr Ransome!'

'Dr Ransome?' Tulloch returned to the gates. He peered sceptically at Jim. 'Doctor shit-stirrer . . .?'

'That's it, Mr Tulloch. I stirred shit for Dr Ransome. I have to go to Shanghai and find my mother and father. We had a Packard, Mr Tulloch.'

'He's stirred his last shit . . .' Tulloch took Sergeant Nagata's key-ring from the ammunition pouch of his holster. He was still unsure whether to admit Jim to the camp. 'A Packard? Good car . . .'

He unlocked the gates and beckoned Jim inside. Hearing the clatter, the Englishman with the bandaged hands who had shot Private Kimura strode from the guardhouse. Although emaciated, he had a strong, nervous physique, and a pallor that was heightened by his bloodied knuckles. Jim had seen the same chalk-like skin and deranged eyes in those prisoners released after months in the underground cells of the Bridgehouse police headquarters. His chest and shoulders were covered with the scars of dozens of cigarette burns, as if his body had been riddled with a hot poker in an attempt to set it alight.

'Lock those gates!' He pointed a bloody hand at Jim. 'Throw him out!'

'Price, I know the lad. His people bought a Packard.'

'Get rid of him! We'll have everyone with a Packard in here . . .'

'Right, Lieutenant. Hop it, lad. Look sharpish.'

Jim tried to hold the gates open with his golf shoe, and Lieutenant Price punched him in the chest with a bandaged fist. Winded Jim sat down hard on the ground beside the watching Chinese. He held on to the Spam and the carton of Chesterfields, but the six *Reader's Digest*s inside his shirt spilled on to the grass and were instantly seized by the peasant woman. The small, starving women in their black trousers sat around him, each holding a magazine as if about to take part in a discussion group on the European war.

Price slammed the gates in their faces. Everything around him, the camp, the empty paddy fields, even the sun, seemed to anger him. He shook his head at Jim, and then caught sight of the Spam in his hand.

'Where did you get that? The Lunghua drops belong to us!' He screamed in Chinese at the peasant women, suspecting them of complicity in this theft. 'Tulloch . . .! They're stealing our Spam!'

He unlocked the gates, intending to wrest the can from Jim, when there was a shout from the watch-tower. The man with the binoculars stepped down the ladder, pointing to the fields beyond the Shanghai road.

Two B-29s appeared from the west, their engines droning

over the deserted land. Seeing the camp, they separated from each other. One flew towards Lunghua, its bomb doors opening to reveal their canisters. The other altered course for the Pootung district to the east of Shanghai.

As the Superfortress thundered over their heads, Jim crouched beside the Chinese peasants. Armed with the rifle and bamboo clubs, Price and three of the Britons ran through the gates and set off across the nearby field. Already the sky was filled with parachutes, the blue and scarlet canopies sailing down into the paddies half a mile from the camp.

The engine noise of the B-29 softened to a muffled rumble. Jim was tempted to follow Price and his men, and offer to help them. The parachutes had landed behind a system of old trenchworks. Losing their bearings, the Britons ran in all directions. Price climbed the parapet of an earth redoubt and waved his rifle in a fury. One of the men slipped into a shallow canal, and waded in circles through the water-weed, while the others ran along the mud walls between the paddies.

As Tulloch watched them despairingly, Jim stood up and stepped past him through the gates. The Packard mechanic loosened the heavy pistol in his holster. The sight of the falling parachutes had aroused him, and the string-like muscles of his arms and shoulders trembled in a cat's cradle of excitement.

'Mr Tulloch, is the war over?' Jim asked. 'Really over?'

'The war . . .?' Tulloch seemed to have forgotten that it had ever taken place. 'It better be over, lad – any time now the next one's going to begin.'

'I saw some communist soldiers, Mr Tulloch.'

'They're everywhere. You wait till Lieutenant Price gets to work on them. We'll park you in the guardhouse, lad. Keep out of his way . . .'

Jim followed Tulloch across the parade ground, and

together they entered the guardhouse. The once immaculate floor of the orderly room, polished by the Chinese prisoners between their beatings, was covered with dirt and refuse. Japanese calendars and documents lay among the empty Lucky Strike cartons, spent ammunition clips and the tatters of old infantry boots. Against the rear wall of the commandant's office were stacked dozens of ration boxes. A naked Britisher in his late fifties, a former barman at the Shanghai Country Club, sat on a bamboo stool, separating the canned meat from the coffee and cigarettes. He packed the bars of chocolate on the commandant's desk, and brusquely threw aside the bundles of *Reader's Digest*s and *Saturday Evening Post*s. The entire floor of the office was covered with discarded magazines.

Beside him, a young British soldier in the rags of a Seaforth Highlander's uniform was cutting the nylon cords from the parachutes. He tied the ropes into neat coils, then expertly folded the blue and scarlet canopies.

Tulloch gazed at this treasure house, clearly awed by the fortune that he and his companions had amassed. He pushed Jim from the door, concerned that the sight of so many bars of chocolate would derange the boy.

'Don't dwell on it, son. Eat your Spam in there.'

But Jim was staring at the magazines heaped on the floor at his feet. He wanted to tidy them up, and hoard them for the next war. 'Mr Tulloch, I ought to go back to Shanghai now.'

'Shanghai? There's nothing there except six million starving coolies. They'll cut off your foreskin before you can say Bubbling Well Road.'

'Mr Tulloch, my mother and father – '

'Lad! Nobody's mother and father are going to Shanghai. All those FRB dollars chasing a hundred bags of rice? Here it's falling out of the sky.'

A rifle shot rang out across the paddy fields, followed by

two more in quick succession. Leaving the naked barman to protect their treasure store, Tulloch and the Seaforth Highlander ran from the guardhouse and climbed the ladder of the watch-tower.

Jim began to straighten the magazines on the floor of the commandant's office, but the barman shouted at him and waved him away. Left to himself, Jim stepped into the cell-yard behind the orderly room. The warm Spam in his hand, he peered into the empty cells, at the dark blood and dried excrement that stained the concrete walls.

In the cell at the far end of the yard, shaded by a straw mat hung from the bars, was the body of a dead Japanese soldier. He lay on the cement bench that was the cell's only furniture, his shoulders lashed to the remains of a wooden chair. His head had been bludgeoned to a pulp that resembled a crushed water melon, filled with the black seeds of hundreds of flies.

Jim stared through the bars at the soldier, shocked that one of the Japanese who had guarded him for so many years should have been imprisoned and then beaten to death in one of his own cells. Jim had accepted Private Kimura's death, in the anonymity of the flooded paddy field, but this reversal of all the rules governing their life in the camp at last convinced Jim that the war might be over.

He left the cell-yard and returned to the orderly office. He sat behind Sergeant Nagata's desk, a luxury he had never once been allowed, and began to read the discarded copies of *Life* and the *Saturday Evening Post*. For once the lavish advertisements, the headlines and slogans – 'When Better Cars are built, Buick will build them!' – failed to touch him. Despite the food he had eaten, he felt numbed by the task of finding a way to Shanghai, and by all the confusions of the arbitrary peace imposed on the settled and secure landscape of the war. Peace had come, but it failed to fit properly.

Through the broken windows Jim watched a B-29 cross the river two miles away, searching the warehouses of Pootung for any groups of Allied prisoners. The peasants outside the gates of Lunghua ignored the bomber. Jim had noticed that the Chinese never looked up at the planes. Although they were nationals of one of the Allied powers at war with Japan, they would not share in these relief supplies.

He listened to the angry voices of the Britons returning from their foray across the paddy fields. Despite all their efforts, they had seized only two of the parachute canisters. While Lieutenant Price stood guard by the gates, rifle trembling in his hands, the others dragged the canisters into the camp. The sweat dripped from their bodies on to the scarlet silk. The remaining parachutes had vanished into the countryside, spirited from under Price's nose by the secret tenants of the burial mounds.

As large as bombs, the canisters lay on the floor in the commandant's office. The naked barman sat astride them, the sweat from his buttocks dulling the silver, while the Seaforth Highlander struck off the nose cones with the rifle butt. The men tore the cartons apart, loading their emaciated arms with cans of meat and coffee, chocolates and cigarettes. Lieutenant Price hovered among them, the bones in his shoulders shaking like castanets. He was excited and exhausted at the same time, eager to work up his irritation again and put to good use all the violence he had found within himself on beating the Japanese to death.

He noticed Jim quietly reading his magazines behind Sergeant Nagata's desk. 'Tulloch! He's here again! The boy with the Packard . . .'

'The lad was in the camp, Lieutenant. He skivvied for one of the doctors.'

'He's roaming around everywhere! Lock him up in one of the cells!'

'He isn't the talkative type, Lieutenant.' Tulloch held Jim's arm, reluctantly pulling him towards the cell-yard. 'He's walked all the way from Nantao Stadium.'

'Nantao . . .? The big stadium?' Price turned to Jim with interest, gazing at him with all the guilelessness of the fanatic. 'How long were you there, boy?'

'Three days,' Jim replied. 'Or I think it was six days. Until the war ended.'

'He can't count.'

'He must have had a good look, Lieutenant.'

'I bet he had a good look. Roaming around all the time. Boy, what did you see in the stadium?' Price treated Jim to a roguish grimace. 'Rifles? Stores?'

'Cars, mostly,' Jim explained. 'At least five Buicks, two Cadillacs, and a Lincoln Zephyr.'

'Forget about the cars! Were you born in a garage? What else did you see?'

'Just a lot of carpets and furniture.'

'Fur coats?' Tulloch interjected. 'There was no ordnance there, Lieutenant. What about Scotch whisky, son?'

Price pulled the copy of *Life* from Jim's hands. 'For God's sake, you'll ruin your eyes. Listen to Mr Tulloch. Did you see any Scotch whisky?'

Jim stepped back, keeping the silver canisters between himself and this unstable man. As if excited by the booty in Nantao Stadium, the lieutenant's hands were bleeding through their bandages. Jim knew that Lieutenant Price would have liked to get him alone and then beat him to death, not because he was cruel, but because only the sight of Jim's pain would clear away all the agony that he himself had endured.

'There might have been Scotch whisky,' he said tactfully. 'There were a lot of bars.'

'Bars . . .?' Price stepped across the cartons of Chesterfields, ready to slap Jim. 'I'll give you bars . . .'

'Cocktail bars – at least twenty of them. There might have been whisky there.'

'Sounds like a hotel. Tulloch, what sort of war did you people have here? Right, boy, what else did you see?'

'I saw the atom bomb drop at Nagasaki,' Jim said. He spoke in a clear voice. 'I saw the white flash! Is the war over now?'

The sweating men put down their cans and cartons. Lieutenant Price stared at Jim, surprised by this statement but prepared to believe it. He lit a cigarette as an American aircraft flew over the camp, a Mustang returning to its base on Okinawa.

Through the noise Jim shouted: 'I saw the *atom bomb* . . .!'

'Yes . . . you must have seen it.' Lieutenant Price fastened the bandages around his bleeding fists. He sucked fiercely on his cigarette. Gazing hungrily at Jim, he picked up the copy of *Life* and left the commandant's office. As the Mustang's engine faded across the paddy fields they could hear Price striding up and down the cell-yard, striking the doors of the cells with the rolled magazine.

36
The Flies

Did Lieutenant Price believe that he had been poisoned by the atom bomb? Jim walked across the parade ground, looking up at the empty barrack huts and dormitory blocks. The windows hung open in the sunlight, as if the tenants had fled at his approach. The mention of the Nagasaki raid, and its confusion with the booty waiting for Price in Nantao Stadium, had calmed this former officer in the Nanking Police. For an hour Jim had helped the men to unpack the parachute canisters, and Price had not objected when Tulloch gave their young recruit a bar of American chocolate. Images of hunger and violence fused in Price's mind, as they had done during the years of his imprisonment by the kempetai.

Holding his tin of Spam and a bundle of *Life* magazines, Jim climbed the steps into the foyer of D Block. He paused by the notice boards with their fading camp bulletins and commandant's orders. In the dormitories he strolled along the lines of bunks. The home-made lockers had been looted by the Japanese after the departure of the prisoners, as if there were still something of value to be found in this rubbish of urine-stained mats and packing-case furniture.

Yet despite the emptiness of the camp it seemed ready for instant occupation. Outside G Block he looked at the baked earth, at the worn ruts of years left by the iron wheels of the food cart, pointing their way to the camp kitchens. He stood in the doorway of his room, barely surprised to see the faded magazine cuttings pinned to the wall above his bunk. In the last minutes before joining the march Mrs Vincent had torn down the curtain of his cubicle, satisfying a long-held need to occupy the whole room. Neatly folded, the curtain lay under Jim's bunk, and he was tempted to pin it up again.

A marked smell hung in the room, one he had never noticed during all the years of the war, at once enticing and ambiguous. He realized that it was the odour of Mrs Vincent's body, and for a moment he imagined that she had returned to the camp. Jim stretched out on Mrs Vincent's bunk, and balanced the tin of Spam on his forehead. He surveyed the room from this unfamiliar angle, a privilege he had never been allowed during the war. Tucked behind the door, his cubicle must have resembled one of those ramshackle hutches which the beggars of Shanghai erected around themselves out of newspapers and straw mats. Often he must have seemed to Mrs Vincent like a beast in a kennel. It was no wonder Jim reflected as he perused a copy of *Life*, that Mrs Vincent had been intensely irritated by him, wishing him away even to the point of hoping he would die.

Jim lay on her straw mattress, smelling the scent of her body, fitting his hips and shoulders into the shallow mould she had left behind. Seen from Mrs Vincent's vantage-point, the past three years appeared subtly different; even a few steps across a small room generated a separate war, a separate ordeal for this woman with her weary husband and sick child.

Thinking with affection of Mrs Vincent, Jim wished that they were still together. He missed Dr Ransome and Mrs Pearce, and the group of men who sat all day on the steps outside the foyer. It occurred to Jim that they might also miss Lunghua. Perhaps one day they would all return to the camp.

He left the room and walked down the corridor to the rear door where the children had played. The marks of their games – hopscotch, marbles and fighting tops – still covered the ground. Jim kicked a small stone into the hopscotch

301

court and deftly flicked it around the squares, then set out on a circuit of the deserted camp. Already he could feel Lunghua gathering itself around him again.

As he approached the hospital he began to hope that Dr Ransome would be there. By the entrance to Hut 6 a rain-soaked pierrot costume of the Lunghua Sophomores lay in a muddy pool. Jim stopped to clean the Spam tin. He wiped the label with the ruff of the costume, remembering Dr Ransome's lectures on hygiene.

The bamboo shutters were lowered across the windows of the hospital, as if Dr Ransome wanted the patients to sleep through the afternoon. Jim climbed the steps, aware of a faint murmur within the building. When he pushed back the doors a cloud of flies enveloped him. Maddened by the light, they filled the narrow entrance hall, as if trying to shake off the foul odour that clung to their wings.

Brushing the flies from his mouth, Jim walked into the men's ward. The decaying air streamed down the plywood walls, bathing the flies that fed on the bodies piled across the bunks. Identifiable by their ragged shorts and flowered dresses, and by the clogs embedded in their swollen feet, dozens of Lunghua prisoners lay on the bunks like sides of meat in a condemned slaughterhouse. Their backs and shoulders glistened with mucilage, and the splayed mouths in their ballooning cheeks still gaped as if these bloated men and women, dragged from a banquet, were gripped by a ravenous hunger.

He walked through the darkened ward, the tin of Spam held tightly to his chest, breathing through the magazines cupped over his mouth. Despite their caricature faces, Jim recognized several of the prisoners. He searched for Dr Ransome and Mrs Vincent, assuming that the bodies were those of the Lunghua internees who had fallen behind during the march from the stadium. The flies festered over the bodies, in some way aware that the war had ended and determined to hoard every morsel of flesh for the coming famine of the peace.

Jim stood on the steps of the hospital, looking out at the deserted camp and the silent fields beyond the wire. The flies soon left him and returned to the ward. He set out for the kitchen garden. He walked among the fading plants, wondering whether to water them, and plucked the last two tomatoes. He raised the berries to his lips, but stopped before eating them. He remembered his fears that his soul had died in the stadium at Nantao, even though his body had survived. If his soul had been unable to escape, and had died within him, would feeding his body engorge it like the corpses in the hospital?

Thinking about his last night in Nantao Stadium, Jim sat on the balcony of the assembly hall. In the late afternoon a Chinese merchant arrived at the gates of the camp, accompanied by three coolies. They carried earthenware jars of rice wine suspended from bamboo yokes across their backs. Jim watched the barter of goods take place outside the guardhouse. Wisely, Lieutenant Price had closed the door of the treasure chest in the commandant's office. Cartons of Lucky Strikes and a single parachute canopy were exchanged for the jars of wine. When the merchant left, followed by his coolies with their bale of scarlet silk, the Britons were soon drunk. Jim decided not to return to the guardhouse that evening. Lieutenant Price's white body lurched through the dusk, the cigarette burns on his chest inflamed by the wine.

From the balcony Jim gazed across Lunghua Airfield. Carefully he opened his tin of Spam. It was a pity that Dr Ransome would not be sharing it with him. As he raised the warm meat to his mouth he thought of the bodies in the hospital. He had not been shocked by the sight of the dead prisoners. In fact, he had known all along that those who

303

fell behind during the march from Lunghua would be left to die or killed where they rested. Nonetheless, he associated the chopped ham with those fattened corpses. Each was enveloped in the same mucilage. The living who ate or drank too quickly, like Tulloch and the police lieutenant with his bloody hands, would soon join the overfed dead. Food fed death, the eager and waiting death of their own bodies.

Jim listened to the drunken shouts from the guardhouse, and the volley of rifle shots as Price fired over the heads of the Chinese at the gates. With his dungeon pallor and bandaged hands, this albino figure frightened Jim, the first of the dead to rise from the grave, eager to start the next world war.

He rested his eyes on the reassuring geometry of the airfield runway. Four hundred yards away, the young Japanese pilot walked among the derelict aircraft. Bamboo stick in hand, he searched the nettles. His baggy flying suit, lit by the evening air, reminded Jim of another pilot of the dusk who had saved him three years earlier and opened the doors of Lunghua.

37

A Reserved Room

Soon after dawn Jim was woken by the first reconnaissance flights of the American fighters. He had spent the night sleeping in Mrs Vincent's bunk, and from the windows of G Block he watched the pairs of Mustangs circle the pagoda at Lunghua Airfield. An hour later the air drops began to the prisoner-of-war camps near Shanghai. The squadrons of B-29s emerged from the hazy light over the Yangtze and cruised over the empty paddy fields with their open bomb-doors, an armada for hire of vacant limousines.

Now that the war was over, the American bombardiers seemed either unwilling, or too bored, to concentrate on their sights. Much to the annoyance of Tulloch and Lieutenant Price, they dropped their cargoes into the open fields around the camp, rolled their wings and set off in a leisurely way for home, the day's work done.

When were the American Army and Navy coming to Shanghai? From the roof of G Block Jim examined the calm surface of the river three miles to the north. No doubt the Americans were wary of sailing up the Yangtze, fearing that the Japanese submarine commanders might have decided not to surrender. But until they arrived it was too dangerous for Jim to set out in search of his mother and father. The whole of Shanghai and the surrounding countryside was locked into a zone where there was neither war nor peace, a vacuum that would soon be filled by every warlord and disaffected general in China.

After waiting for Price and his men to leave the camp in search of the parachute canisters, Jim went down to the guardhouse. The wash from the engines of the relief

Superfortress had driven the stench of rotting meat from the hospital, a pall that hung over the camp for hours. But Tulloch appeared not to notice. Once Lieutenant Price was out of the way, a spectre hunting other spectres among the burial mounds, Tulloch was prepared to admit Jim to the commandant's office. Jim helped himself to the cans stacked against the wall. He made a quick meal of Spam and powdered milk, then sat behind Sergeant Nagata's desk in the orderly room, chewing a chocolate bar and sorting out the copies of the American magazines.

Later, when Tulloch went off to abuse the growing crowd of starving Chinese outside the gates, Jim climbed the ladder of the watch-tower. He could see Price and his raiding party searching the creeks to the west of the camp. They had joined forces with a group of Allied prisoners from Hungjao, and the armed men were running along the embankments of the anti-tank ditches, firing across the flooded paddy fields.

Already it was clear that the former British internees were not the only scavengers roving the countryside. The Chinese peasants were returning to the villages they had abandoned in the weeks before the war's end. Gangs of coolies roamed the area, stripping the tyres and body panels from the burnt-out Japanese vehicles. Squads of renegade Kuomintang soldiers who had deserted to the Chinese puppet armies wandered the roads, well aware of their fate if they fell into the hands of their former Nationalist comrades but drawn towards Shanghai by the American air-drops. As Jim stood in the observation box of the watch-tower a company of these demoralized troops straggled past the gates of Lunghua. Still fully armed, in ragged uniforms from which they had torn their badges, they passed within a few feet of the solitary Packard mechanic guarding his treasure of chocolate bars and *Saturday Evening Posts*.

At noon, when Lieutenant Price appeared, dressed like a corpse in the scarlet canopy of the parachute canister dragged by his men, Jim gathered together his bundle of magazines and returned to G Block. He spent an hour sorting them into their correct order, and then set out on a tour of the camp. Avoiding the hospital, he climbed through the wire and explored the overgrown terrain between the camp and Lunghua Airfield, hoping to find the turtle which he had released in the last weeks of the war.

But the canal beside the fence contained only the body of a dead Japanese airman. Sections of Lunghua Airfield – the pagoda, barracks and control tower – were now occupied by an advance brigade of Nationalist troops. For reasons of their own, the Japanese aircraftsmen and ground crews made no attempt to escape, and lived on in the gutted hangars and workshops. Each day the Nationalist soldiers took a few of the Japanese and killed them in the waste ground to the south and west of the airfield.

The sight of this dead Japanese airman, floating face down in the canal among the Mustang drop-tanks, unsettled Jim as much as the bodies of the Britons in the camp hospital. From then on he decided to remain within the safety of the camp. He slept at night in Mrs Vincent's bed, and spent the days sampling the American canned food and chocolate, and sorting out his collection of magazines. By now he had assembled a substantial library, which he stacked neatly on the spare bunks in his room. The copies of *Time, Life* and the *Reader's Digest* covered every conceivable aspect of the war, a world at once familiar and yet totally removed from his own experiences in Shanghai and Lunghua. At moments, as he studied the dramatic accounts of tank battles and beach-heads, he wondered if he himself had been in the war at all.

But he continued to collect the magazines from the floor of the commandant's office, concealing within them a few extra cans of Spam and powdered milk, part of a long-term reserve that he had sensibly begun to stockpile. Already it was clear to Jim that the American air-drops were becoming less frequent, and sooner or later they would stop. Now that his strength had returned, Jim was able to scavenge busily around the camp and was never more pleased than when, under a bunk in D Block, he found a tennis racquet and a tin of balls.

On the third morning, as Price and his men stood with the binoculars on the roof of the guardhouse, waiting impatiently for the American relief planes, an ancient Opel truck arrived at the gates of the camp. Two bare-chested Britons, sometime Lunghua prisoners, sat in the driving cabin, while their Chinese wives and children rode in the back with their possessions. Jim had last seen the men, foremen at the Moller Line dockyards, in the stadium at Nantao, lifting the hoods of the white Cadillacs on the morning the war had ended. Somehow they had made their way to Shanghai and collected their families, who had not been interned by the Japanese. Finding themselves destitute in the hostile city, they had decided to return to Lunghua.

Already they had collected their first booty. A silver parachute canister lay like a bomb on the floor of the truck, dwarfing the dark-eyed children in their Chinese tunics. Jim watched from Basie's window in E Block, smiling contentedly as Tulloch and Lieutenant Price climbed down from the roof of the guardhouse. They strolled over to the gates but made no attempt to unlock them. A rambling argument ensued between Price and the former Lunghua prisoners, who pointed angrily at E Block, deserted now except for the fourteen-year-old boy laughing to himself at the top-floor window.

Jim drummed his fists on the concrete sill, and waved to the men and their glowering Chinese wives. After three years of trying to leave the camp they were now back at its gates, ready to take up their stations for World War III. At long last they were beginning to realize the simple truth that Jim had always known, that inside Lunghua they were free.

The gates were opening; a bargain had been struck. Lieutenant Price had taken a fancy to the Opel. Within a minute the two Britons and their families sped across the parade ground towards D Block, followed by the first Mustangs of the morning. As they soared over the camp the wash from their engines drove a foul wind through the empty buildings, a reek of offal borne on a plague of thousands of glutted flies.

The Chinese beggars sitting by the gates shielded their faces. But Jim inhaled the heady stench, shutting out his thoughts of the hospital and the dead Japanese airman in the canal beyond the wire. The time had come to forget the dead. In its way the camp was coming alive again. The days of powdered milk and chocolate bars had made him stronger, but not yet equal to the long walk back to Shanghai. Other people would be returning to the camp, and perhaps his mother and father would join him there. Even with the reduced American air-drops there would be a constant supply of food. Jim looked down at the silent kitchens behind the guardhouse, and the rusting collection of metal carts. Already he was thinking of a sweet potato . . .

His shoes rang through the empty corridors, and down the stone steps. As he raced from the foyer he heard the throbbing engine of the Opel. Tulloch and the Seaforth Highlander were loading parachute canopies and cartons of canned food over the tail-gate.

'Jim! Hold it!' Tulloch beckoned to him. 'Where do you think you're going?'

'G Block, Mr Tulloch . . .' Gasping for breath, Jim leaned against the Opel's shaking fender. In the doorway of the guardhouse Lieutenant Price was feeding cartridges into the ammunition clip of his rifle, the ritual of a man counting his secret gold. 'I want to reserve a room for my parents – they might be coming to Lunghua. I'll reserve a room for you, Mr Tulloch.'

'Jim . . . Jim . . .' Tulloch placed his hand on Jim's head, trying to steady the over-excited boy. 'It's time you found your father, lad. The war's over, Jim.'

'But the next war, Mr Tulloch. You said it's going to begin soon.'

The Packard mechanic helped Jim on to the floor of the truck. 'Jim, you need to get the last war over before you start the next. We'll give you a lift – you're going back to Shanghai!'

38
The Road to Shanghai

The truck careened from one side of the Shanghai road to the other, throwing Jim on to the agitated bundle of parachute silk. He clung to the cartons of K-rations stacked around him, and listened to Tulloch and Lieutenant Price shouting to each other above the bellows-like roar of the engine.

Through the fading camouflage on the rear window, Jim could see the policeman's bandaged hands, deliberately raised from the wheel as he allowed the speeding truck to wobble and drift from the centre of the road. The tyres reached the verge, ripping up a storm of dust and leaves. Tulloch sat in the passenger seat beside the jar of rice wine, holding the rifle through the open window. He pounded on the dented hood, as the apartment blocks of the French Concession appeared between the bomb-torn trees.

For all the dangers of Lieutenant Price's driving, Jim was glad that the two men were in such high spirits. For the first mile the lieutenant had been unable to find second gear, and they had laboured along the Shanghai road at a noisy walking pace that threatened to boil the water from the radiator. Then an air-drop at Hungjao brought back Price's driving skills. They hurtled along the farm tracks and canal embankments, following the parachutes towards the landing ground, cheered by the prospect of even more American merchandise to be sold in the black markets of Shanghai.

Others, however, had reached the treasure before them. For half an hour they trundled around the deserted paddy fields, unable to find a single parachute canister. Price waved his rifle, threatening an entire world of silent canals.

311

Fortunately, Price's anger soon abated. After returning to the Shanghai road the lieutenant steered the truck towards the body of a dead Japanese despatch rider lying beside a motorcycle. The dead man's head burst in a spray of bloodied maggots and brain tissue that drenched the roadside trees. This feat of steering put Price in an excellent mood, which Jim hoped would last long enough for him to reach Shanghai and jump from the truck at the first traffic lights.

Jim looked back at the distant rooftops of the camp. It was strange to be leaving Lunghua, but he realized that once again he had been imprisoned by the camp as he had been during the war. At a single word from Tulloch, the apparently secure world he had begun to rebuild for himself out of one small room and a few tins of Spam had collapsed at his feet.

They passed Lunghua Pagoda at the northern edge of the airfield, the barrels of its anti-aircraft guns still pointing to the sky. Jim searched the ruined hangars for any sight of the young kamikaze pilot, sorry that he had never been able to repay him for the mango. A mile to the east was the Olympic stadium at Nantao. The Chinese characters on the shell-pocked façade, celebrating the generosity of Generalissimo Chiang, rose ever more vividly above the parking lot, as if China's feudal past had returned to claim its time.

The truck swerved, skidding across the camber. On a whim, Lieutenant Price had turned on to a mud track that ran towards the stadium. Jim heard Tulloch protest, but then the wine jar was passed across the steering wheel. They sped between the first of the earth bunkers and rifle pits that guarded the former Japanese headquarters. Lines of crumbling tank ditches crossed the fields, their slopes strewn with webbing and ammunition boxes.

Jim lay back on the bale of parachute silk. He had known all along that the sight of the Olympic stadium would prove too large a temptation. Since his arrival at Lunghua Camp the group of Britons had never ceased to question him about the looted furniture in the stands. Jim had been forced to embroider his memories, in order to ensure his supplies of canned goods and magazines from the commandant's office. By now his make-believe had seized Price's imagination, and it was too late to turn back.

A hundred yards from the parking lot they left the road and stopped in a culvert between two tank-trap embankments. Price and Tulloch, both drunk on the rice wine, stepped from the driving cabin. They lit cigarettes, staring slyly at the stadium.

Price tapped the side of the truck with his rifle. In a mocking voice, he called out: 'Shanghai Jim . . .'

'Just a detour, Jim,' Tulloch assured him boozily. 'We'll pick out a case of Scotch, and a few fur coats for the girls in the Nanking Road.'

'I didn't see any fur coats, Mr Tulloch, or any Scotch. Lots of chairs and dining tables.'

Lieutenant Price pushed Tulloch aside. 'Dining tables? Do you think we came here to have lunch?' He stared at the façade of the stadium, as if its shabby chalk challenged his own pallid skin.

Jim avoided the rifle barrel aimed at his head. 'There were cupboards and wardrobes.'

'Wardrobes?' Tulloch swayed between them. 'That could be it, Lieutenant.'

'Right . . .' Price calmed himself. He touched the cigarette burns on his chest, tapping out a secret code of pain and memory. 'I told you the boy had his eyes open.'

The two men crossed the road and entered the parking lot. Price leaned against a trackless tank, and spat the prison phlegm from his lungs through an open hatch. Jim hung back among the lines of trucks, thinking of Mr Maxted. Was he still lying on the blood-stained grass? Having eaten so much, Jim felt guilty, and remembered that he might have sold his shoes. For all the looted cocktail bars it contained, the Olympic stadium seemed sombre and threatening, a place of omens. Here he had seen the afterglow of the atomic flash at Nagasaki. Its white glare still lay over the road of their death-march from Lunghua, the same pale light that he could see in the chalky façade of the stadium and in Lieutenant Price's lime-pit skin.

Fanning away the flies with a copy of *Life*, Jim sat on the running board of a truck. He studied a photograph of American marines raising the flag on the summit of Mount Suribachi after their battle for Iwo Jima. The Americans in these magazines had fought an heroic war, closer to the comic books than Jim had read as a child. Even the dead were glamourized, the living's idea of the dead . . .

Two Mustang fighters flew overhead, leading a Superfortress that lumbered in from the west, its bomb doors open, ready to scatter its Spam and *Reader's Digests* across the empty fields. The engines drummed at the ground below Jim's feet, shaking the lines of derelict vehicles.

Jim lowered the magazine, and noticed that armed men were running from the entrance tunnel of the stadium, their voices drowned in the noise of the aircraft. The Superfortress ambled through the sky, but the men scattered in panic from the tunnel, as if expecting the stadium to be bombed. A bearded European in the leather jacket of an American pilot raced across the parking lot, followed by two more men carrying shotguns. A bare-chested Chinese with a pistol belt around his black trousers scuttled along at a crouch, leading a group of coolies with bamboo staves.

Pursuing them through the tunnel was a platoon of Nationalist soldiers, rifles raised to the strong sunlight. They stopped to fire at the fleeing men, letting off a ragged volley of shots. Jim opened the door of the truck and climbed into the driving cabin. Fifty feet from the entrance tunnel Tulloch lay in the white dust that had fallen from the façade of the stadium. Lieutenant Price ran past him towards the line of trucks, his face like a lantern scanning the ground. Shaking off his bandages, he leapt the perimeter wall of the parking lot and plunged into the flooded paddy field beyond the road.

The Chinese officer fired a last pistol shot at Price's splashing figure, then knelt in the stadium entrance. Rifles raised, his men approached the rusting vehicles. They made a token show of flushing out any wounded members of the raiding party, turned and retreated to the safety of the stadium. Tulloch lay dead in the sun, his blood leaking into the chalky dust.

Blue and scarlet parachutes were falling over Hungjao. Jim slid across the seat, opened the door on the far side of the cabin and slipped on to the ground. Screened by the ammunition wagons and field guns, he ran towards the perimeter wall.

Lieutenant Price had abandoned the Opel and its cargo of silks and K-rations. When Jim reached the culvert he found the truck standing alone among the anti-tank embankments. On the ground beside the passenger door a faint smoke still rose from the butt of Tulloch's last Lucky Strike.

Jim stared through the window at the instrument panel. Could he drive the vehicle to Shanghai? It was too dangerous to give himself up to the Nationalist soldiers at the stadium – they would shoot him on sight, taking for granted that Jim was a member of the raiding party.

Thinking of Tulloch, who had died before seeing the white Cadillacs of Nantao, Jim decided to walk to Shanghai. He was climbing over the tail-gate of the Opel, about to select several cans of food and copies of the *Reader's Digest*, when he heard footsteps beside the truck. Before he could turn, someone seized him by the shoulders. Hard fists punched the back of his head, and hurled him to the floor.

Sitting among the cartons of cigarettes, Jim felt the blood run from his nose and mouth, dripping through his hands on to the parachute canopy. He looked up at the bare-chested Chinese with the pistol belt who had raced from the stadium. He stared at Jim with the expressionless gaze he had often seen on the cook's face at Amherst Avenue before he killed a chicken. Behind him, impatient to get his hands on the truck's cargo, was a Chinese coolie with a bamboo stave.

On both sides of the culvert armed men were walking down the embankment, led by the bearded European in the leather flying jacket. Half the members of this bandit group were Chinese, some of them coolies with staves, others in Nationalist and puppet uniforms, still with their rifles and webbing. The others were Europeans or Americans, wearing an assortment of clothes and ammunition belts, holsters and Shanghai Police pouches hung over Chinese tunics. From their starved bodies, Jim assumed that most were former internees.

When the coolie raised the bamboo stave, Jim sucked back the blood and swallowed the hot phlegm. 'I'm going to Lunghua Camp . . . I'm a British prisoner.' He pointed to the south-west. Through his swollen nose his voice sounded strangely bass, as if his body were ageing in the few moments of life left to it. 'Lunghua Camp . . .'

Ignoring him, the armed men sat on the embankment and smoked their cigarettes. The European in the flying jacket paced around the truck. A coolie picked up Tulloch's cigarette butt and inhaled the smoke. Everyone watched the sky and the deserted road past the stadium. They had brought with them the slow, empty time of the prison camp. Their faces were drawn and colourless, and they seemed to have emerged from a deep lair below the ground.

'Lunghua . . .' Jim repeated. The coolie with the stave still had his eyes on him. At the smallest signal, Jim knew, the coolie would step forward and crush his skull. The bare-chested Chinese who had struck him was examining the truck, peering at the rear tyres. Hoping somehow to catch the attention of the Europeans, Jim pointed to the stadium. 'Lincoln Zephyrs – in Nantao. Buicks, white Cadillacs . . .'

'What's this talk about Cadillacs?' A small man with silvery hair and an effeminate American voice walked towards the truck, rifle slung over his shoulder. No one listened to him, and he lit a cigarette to cover the lack of response. The flame trembled in his powdered cheeks, exposing a familiar pair of wary eyes, with their sharp but modest focus.

'Basie!' Jim wiped the blood from his nose. 'It's me, Basie – Jim! Shanghai Jim!'

The cabin steward stared at Jim. After a moment's thought he shook his head in an almost formal way, as if recognizing the fourteen-year-old but no longer interested in him. He scanned the cartons of K-rations and fingered the silk of the parachute. He stepped aside to give the coolie more room to swing his stave.

'Basie!' Jim picked up the scattered magazines and cleaned the blood from their covers with his fingers. He held them up before the angry gaze of the bare-chested Chinese with the pistol. '*Life* magazine, Basie, *Reader's Digest*! I kept the latest copies for you . . . Basie, I've learned hundreds of new words – Belsen, von Rundstedt, GI Joe . . .'

39
The Bandits

The car sped along the shore of an oil-filled lagoon, past the rusting hull of a beached torpedo boat. Squeezed between Basie and the bearded Frenchman in the rear seat, Jim watched the spray leap from the wheels of the Buick. The lurid rainbows opened like peacock tails, transforming the distant office blocks of Shanghai into the towers of a paint-box city. The same gaudy light veiled the torpedo boat and cloaked the bodies of the dead Japanese lying in the shallows.

Jim tried to look over his shoulder at the receding skyline of Shanghai, but the bruises on his neck made it difficult for him to turn his head.

'Hey, boy . . .' The Frenchman struck Jim's arm with the carbine held between his knees. 'Settle down. You want some more bloody nose . . .?'

'Jim, there's no room to wrestle in here. We'll just sit quiet and learn our words.' Basie put an arm around him. 'Keep an eye on that *Digest* so you stay awake.'

'Right, Basie. I'll stay awake.'

Staying awake was all-important, as Jim knew. He propped his feet against the ammunition boxes on the floor of the car, then pinched his lips until his eyes brightened. Next to the Frenchman, against the right-hand passenger door, sat the coolie with the bamboo stave who had been about to kill Jim before Basie intervened. In the front seat beside the Chinese driver, were two Australians from Siccawei Camp.

The seven of them were packed into the mud-spattered Buick. Its windows were still adorned with the insignia and rice-paper stickers of the puppet Chinese general whose staff car this had been throughout the war. Dried vomit, blood from Jim's nose and from the wounds of injured men stained the seats. Along with the staves and weapons, the car was crammed with ammunition boxes, cartons of American cigarettes, earthenware jars of rice wine, and beer bottles into which the men continually urinated as they sped along the country roads to the south-west of Shanghai.

They came to a halt, and the oily water of the lagoon swilled around the Buick's wheels. Ahead of them was the Japanese truck carrying a dozen members of this bandit gang. The top-heavy vehicle swayed up a narrow ramp of grey bricks that led from the beach to the embankment road. It was loaded with parachute canisters, Japanese stores seized that morning from the military godowns at Nantao, and a collection of mattress rolls, bicycles and sewing-machines looted from the villages in the open country south of Lunghua.

The Buick climbed the ramp of crumbling bricks, and followed the truck through the clouds of dust that swirled from its wheels. The road ran inland from the lagoon, soon losing itself in a maze of paddy fields and canals. Jim wondered if this bandit group had any idea where it was going, a poisonous shuttle that flicked to and fro across the quilted land. Yet eight hundred yards away, along a parallel road, a second truck sped through the deserted paddies. The antique Opel captured at the Olympic stadium carried the remaining five members of the gang. They had left the seaplane base at Nantao soon after dawn, but somehow had managed to rendezvous within a few minutes of their next objective.

As the roads converged, Jim could see the bare-chested figure of the Chinese gunman with the black trousers and revolver belt. He stood behind the driving cabin, shouting commands to the coolie at the wheel. Jim feared this former officer in the Chinese puppet army, whose iron knuckles he could still feel in the bruised bones at the back of his neck. Only Basie's presence had saved him, but the reprieve might be short-lived. Captain Soong paid little attention to Basie, or to the other European members of the bandit gang, and regarded Jim as no more than a dog to be worked to death if necessary. Within an hour of his capture by the bandits, Jim was crawling among the burial mounds that overlooked a village near Hungjao, sent on ahead like a beagle to sniff out the land and draw any surprise fire. Still half stunned, the blood from his nose dripping on to the *Reader's Digest* in his hand, he waited among the rotting coffins until the shooting subsided and the bandits returned from the village with their looted bicycles, bed-rolls and sacks of rice. Recognizing that Captain Soong was the real leader of this bandit group, he had tried to make himself useful to the Chinese. But Captain Soong did not want Jim to run any errands for him. The war had changed the Chinese people – the villagers, the wandering coolies and lost puppet soldiers looked at Europeans in a way Jim had never seen before the war, as if they no longer existed, even though the British had helped the Americans to defeat the Japanese.

The trucks stopped at a crossroads. Captain Soong jumped from the Opel and strode over to the Buick. Without thinking, Basie held Jim's arm. Basie had been prepared to see him die, and only Jim's lavish descriptions of the booty waiting for the bandits in the stadium at Nantao sustained Basie's interest in him.

A tornado of dust seethed around the three vehicles as they reversed and set off along a disused canal. Within half a mile they stopped on a stone bridge above a deserted village. Captain Soong and two of his men dismounted from their truck, joined by the Frenchman in the Buick and the coolie with the stave. The Australians sat in the front of the car, drinking from a wine jar and ignoring the shabby dwellings.

Usually Captain Soong would have called Jim and sent him to ferret through the buildings, but the village was clearly abandoned, looted many times over by the bandit groups in the area.

'Are we going back to Shanghai, Basie?' Jim asked.

'Soon, Jim. First we have to pick up some special equipment.'

'Equipment you stored in the villages? Equipment for the war effort?'

'That's it, Jim. Equipment the OSS left here for us while I was working undercover with the Kuomintang. You wouldn't want the communists to get it, would you, Jim?'

Both of them went along with this pretence. Jim stared at the empty village, its single mud street divided by an open sewer. 'There must be a lot of communists here. Is the war over, Basie?'

'It's over, Jim. Let's say it's effectively over.'

'Basie . . .' A familiar thought occurred to him. 'Has the next war effectively begun?'

'That's a way of putting it, Jim. I'm glad I helped you with your words.'

'There are still a lot of words I haven't learned, Basie. I'd like to go back to Shanghai. If I'm lucky I might see my mother and father today.'

'Shanghai? That's one dangerous city, Jim. You need more than luck in Shanghai. We'll wait till we see the US Navy tie up alongside the Bund.'

'Will Uncle Sam soon be here, Basie? Every Gob and GI Joe?'

'He'll be here. Every GI Joe in the Pacific area . . .' Basie sounded unenthusiastic at the prospect of being reunited with his fellow countrymen. Jim had questioned him about his escape from Lunghua, but Basie was sly and evasive. As always, whatever happened after the escape had long since ceased to interest him. He remained the same small, finicky man worrying about his hands, ignoring everything but the shortest-term advantage. His one strength was that he never allowed himself to dream, because he had never been able to take anything for granted, whereas Dr Ransome had taken everything for granted. However, Dr Ransome had probably died on the death-march from Lunghua, while Basie had survived. Yet now, for the first time, the prospect of the treasure-store in the Olympic stadium had sprung the safety catch of Basie's caution. Jim assiduously fed the cabin steward's vision of enough wealth to return him in luxury to the United States. He assumed that Basie had heard on the camp radio of the imminent march to the killing-grounds, and had bribed a night-watchman to conceal him in one of the Nantao godowns.

Sitting beside Basie as he polished his nails, Jim realized that the entire experience of the war had barely touched the American. All the deaths and starvation were part of a confused roadside drama seen through the passenger window of the Buick, a cruel spectacle like the public stranglings in Shanghai which the British and American sailors watched during their shore-leaves. He had learned nothing from the war because he expected nothing, like the Chinese peasants whom he now looted and shot. As Dr Ransome had said, people who expected nothing were dangerous. Somehow, five hundred million Chinese had to be taught to expect everything.

Jim nursed his bruised nose, as the armed men squatted on the bridge with their jars of rice wine. Despite the years of malnutrition in the camps, few of the former prisoners bothered to eat the canned food heaped on the back of the trucks. They drank alone in the hot sun, rarely speaking to each other. Jim knew almost none of their names. At dusk, when they returned to the seaplane base at Nantao, most of them dispersed with their share of the day's booty to their hide-outs in the tenements of the Old City, reassembling the next morning like factory workers. Jim slept in the Buick parked on the concrete slipway, surrounded by the hulks of the burnt seaplanes, while Basie and the bearded Frenchman drank through the night in the pilots' mess.

The Frenchman wandered back from the village and leaned against Basie's window. 'Nothing – not even one piece of shit.'

'They could have left us that,' Basie said in disgust. 'Why don't the Chinese come back to their villages?'

'Do they know the war's over?' Jim asked. 'You ought to tell them, Basie.'

'Maybe . . . We can't wait forever, Jim. There are big guns moving up to Shanghai, about six different Kuomintang armies.'

'So it might be difficult to collect your equipment?'

'That's it. We'll go now to this communist village. Then I'll take you back to your Dad. You can tell him how I looked after you through the war, taught you all your words.'

'You did look after me, Basie.'

'Right . . .' Basie gazed thoughtfully at Jim. 'You stay with us. It would be too bad if you got yourself kidnapped.'

'Are there a lot of kidnappers here, Basie?'

'Kidnappers *and* communists. People who don't want to know the war is over. Remember that, Jim.'

'Right . . .' Trying to distract the cabin steward with some more cheerful topic, Jim asked: 'Basie, did you see the atom bomb go off? I saw the flash over Nagasaki from Nantao stadium.'

'Say, kid . . .' Basie peered at Jim, puzzled by the calm voice of this bloody-nosed boy. He took a gun-rag from the rear window-sill and wiped Jim's nose. 'You saw the atom bomb . . .?'

'For a whole minute, Basie. A white light covered Shanghai, stronger than the sun. I suppose God wanted to see everything.'

'I guess he did. That white light, Jim. Maybe I can get your picture in *Life* magazine.'

'Say, could you, Basie?'

The thought of appearing in *Life* exhilarated Jim. He wiped the blood from his mouth and tried to straighten his ragged shirt, in case a photographer were to appear suddenly on the scene. At a signal from Captain Soong, the bandits returned to their vehicles. As they left the village and set out towards the river Jim imagined his photograph among the pictures of Tiger tanks and US Marines. He had now spent four days with Basie's bandit group, and it occurred to him that his parents might think that he had died in the death-march from Lunghua. Perhaps they would be sitting by the swimming-pool at Amherst Avenue, leafing through the latest issue of *Life*, when they would recognize their son's face among the admirals and generals . . .

They were passing the eastern perimeter of Lunghua Airfield. Jim leaned across Basie and hung from the window. He scanned the creeks and paddy fields for the bodies of Japanese aircrew. The Kuomintang units which had seized part of the airfield were still killing the Japanese in batches.

'You like those airplanes, Jim?'

'I'm going to be a pilot, Basie, one day. I'll take my mother and father down to Java. I've thought a lot about that.'

'A good dream to have . . .' Basie pushed Jim aside and pointed to the derelict aircraft among the trees. 'There's a Jap pilot over there – no one's got him yet.'

Basie cocked the bolt on his rifle. Jim craned through the window, searching the line of trees. Beside the tailplane of a Zero fighter he saw the pallid face of the young pilot, lost among the upended wings and fuselages.

'He's a hashi-crashi,' Jim said quickly. 'A screwy-sider. Basie, do you want me to tell you about the stadium? There might be fur coats, I think Mr Tulloch saw them before he was shot, and hundreds of crates of Scotch whisky . . .'

Fortunately, Basie was winding up the window. A pungent grit filled the Buick. It rose from the chalky surface of the road, joining the haze of dust that climbed from the bleached fields, the tank ditches and burial mounds, the same light that Jim had seen from the Olympic stadium, heralding the end of one war and the beginning of the next.

Shortly before dusk they reached the communist town on the river two miles to the south of Lunghua. The shabby, single-storey houses huddled against the walls of a ceramics factory, like the mediaeval dwellings Jim had seen in his childhood encyclopaedias, clustering around a gothic cathedral. The domed kilns and brick chimneys drew the last of the day's sunlight towards them, as if advertising the warmth and benefit which communist rule had brought to this collection of hovels.

'Right, Jim, never mind the word-power. You're going in.'

Before Jim could place his *Reader's Digest* on the window-sill Captain Soong had flung open the door. The bare-chested officer bundled Jim from the Buick. Handling the bloody-nosed boy like a drover with a truffling pig, he propelled Jim across the road with a series of whoops and grunts, prodding him sharply with his automatic pistol. The two trucks and the Buick had stopped beside the embankment carrying the Shanghai–Hangchow railway line. Three hundred yards ahead, a spur of the line ran in a wide arc towards the ceramics works, concealing them from the town. The armed men stepped down on to the drained paddy that followed the embankment. Some opened their ammunition pouches and cleaned the breeches of their rifles. Others smoked cigarettes and drank wine from the earthenware jars they placed on the hood of the Buick. Each man on his own, they stood silently in the fading light.

As the whoops and whistles of Captain Soong faded behind him, Jim trotted across the hard surface of the paddy. He pinched his nose, hoping to stop the bleeding, then let the blood smear his cheeks in the wind. With luck, any communist sentry stationed on the embankment would think that Jim was already wounded and turn his fire on the gunmen behind him.

He reached the foot of the embankment and crouched among the clumps of wild rice. He wiped the blood from their stems and licked his fingers. Already he had served his purpose. Fifty yards away, Captain Soong had crossed the paddy and was scuttling up the soft soil of the embankment. Armed with their staves, his coolies followed, accompanied by Basie and the Frenchman. Two groups of gunmen were moving across the next paddy field. The Australians and a Kuomintang deserter sat on the running board of the Buick, drinking their wine.

Jim climbed the talc-like slope. Rain had washed away parts of the embankment, and he crawled below the rusting rails and their rotting sleepers. Several sections of the line had recently been replaced, presumably by the communist troops who had made the town their base. The jetty of the ceramics factory, the railway line and the reserve of bricks in the fabric of the old kilns and chimneys, together with the proximity to Lunghua Airfield, had drawn the communist garrison to this modest backwater. According to Basie, however, they had left two days earlier, continuing their advance on Shanghai, and the town's few hundred inhabitants were undefended. Apart from their possessions, there might be stores of communist arms, and collaborators to be traded for the goodwill of the Kuomintang generals approaching Shanghai.

Concealed by the railway sleepers, Jim crouched on the

edge of the embankment. Below him lay a plain of unworked paddies, separated by a navigation canal from the patchwork of vegetable plots that encircled the town. The narrow streets were empty, but a weak smoke rose from several chimneys.

Across the river, a naval gun fired a single booming round. Two Nationalist Chinese gunboats were moored in midstream. The shell landed in the store-yard of the ceramics works, throwing up a cloud of red dust. The sound of small arms fire came from the beaches of the river to the south, where a company of Kuomintang soldiers disembarked from a wooden lighter.

Its diesels thudding, an armoured junk motored up the canal below the railway embankment. Chinese officers in smart American uniforms and steel helmets stood on the bridge, scanning the town and its vegetable plots through binoculars. The nearer of the two gunboats fired a second shell, which exploded among the grey-tiled rooftops, sending up a shower of debris. Immediately there was a flurry of movement. Like ants escaping from a broken flower-pot, hundreds of Chinese ran from the narrow alleys into the surrounding fields. Over their heads they carried bed-rolls and bundles of clothing. They raced down the pathways between the vegetable plots. An old woman in black trousers and jacket waded waist-deep in a creek beside the road, shouting to her relatives who clambered down the bank.

The motorized junk sailed along the canal, its engines drumming like fists against the wooden hull. Jim could see clearly the fresh pleats in the uniforms of the senior Chinese officers, and their elegant American combat boots. Even the platoons of private soldiers on the deck below the bridge were lavishly equipped with weapons and radios. Parked across the midships of the junk was a black Chrysler limousine, the pennant of a Kuomintang general flying from its chromium mast.

The metal barbette of an automatic cannon was mounted

in the bows of the junk. Without warning, the gunners opened fire at the town. The tracers soared over the heads of the fleeing villagers and burst against the roofs of the houses. At a signal from the bridge, the gunners swung the barrel, setting their sights on a small hamlet a few hundred yards to the west of the town. Already the first shells from the gunboats were landing on the dusty road beside the single-storey hovels. The company of Nationalist soldiers who had disembarked from the wooden lighter were now running across the paddies, hunting down the fleeing townspeople.

Then the first shell of the next salvo tripped off an immense explosion. The group of mud dwellings had vanished, sucked into the air by the boiling cloud of its own debris. The cache of detonating ammunition continued to erupt, throwing towers of smoke into the sky. On the road approaching the hamlet dozens of villagers lay among their bundles and bed-rolls, as if the inhabitants of this town had decided to spend the night sleeping in the fields.

Jim cupped his hands over his nose and mouth, trying to stop himself from shouting. He watched the plain of fire below him, the smoke-covered fields lit by the flashes of the naval guns and by the burning houses beside the ceramics factory. The kilns and chimneys glowed in the sunset as if the ancient ovens had been lit again, to be fuelled by the bodies of the villagers lying in their vegetable gardens. Jim listened to the engines of the motorized junk as it moved down the canal, an ugly heart bearing the beat of its death across China, while immaculate generals masked their eyes with binoculars, calculating their astronomy of guns.

'Basie . . .' The bandits were withdrawing from the railway line. Captain Soong and his coolies had climbed down the embankment and were returning to the trucks. 'Basie, can we go back to Lunghua?'

'Back to the camp?' The cabin steward squinted through

the dust falling from the air. He had been stunned by the concussion wave of the exploding ammunition store, and stared at the landscape below him as if waking from a dream. 'You want to go back to the camp, Jim . . .?'

'We ought to get ready, Basie. When are the Americans coming?'

For the first time Basie seemed lost for an answer. He lay back among the wooden sleepers, and then pointed to the north and gave a whistle of triumph. Ten miles away, across the sombre surface of the river, the sunlit masts and superstructure of an American cruiser had taken their place beside the office blocks and hotels of the Shanghai Bund.

40
The Fallen Airmen

All morning the sound of artillery fire had crossed the river
from Pootung. A column of incendiary smoke, broader than
the group of burning warehouses, leaned over the water and
darkened the Nantao shore. From the front seat of the
Buick parked on the mud-flat, Jim watched the flashes of
gunfire in the dusty windshield. The American artillery
pieces brought up by the Nationalists emitted a harsh and
wet noise, as if their barrels were filled with water. Hidden
from the sun, a gloomy air lay over the slack tide that
swilled against the beach. The glowing barrel of the
Kuomintang howitzer behind the Pootung mole flickered
against Jim's knuckles as he held the steering wheel of the
Buick, and lit up the conning tower of the beached submarine a hundred yards away.

Jim noticed a reconnaissance aircraft emerge from the
smoke-cloud, shaking off the wisps of black vapour that
streamed from its wings. A flight of three American bombers approached from the south-west. The gunfire ceased,
and a torpedo boat fortified with sandbags set out across the
river, ready to collect any stray canisters.

A dozen parachutes fell from the B-29s, and streaked
swiftly to the ground. The canisters were loaded, not with
Spam, Klim and the *Reader's Digest*, but with ammunition
and explosives for the Kuomintang troops. The battalion,
with its artillery support, was rooting out the last of the
communist units which still hung on among the ruins of the
Pootung warehouses. On the mole, the corpses of dead
communist soldiers were stacked like firewood.

In the silence after the bombers had passed Jim could

hear the aching rumble of artillery barrages from Hungjao and the open country to the west of Shanghai. At least three Nationalist armies were closing around the city, jockeying among themselves for control of the airfields, dockyards and railway lines, and above all for the stocks of weapons and munitions left behind by the Japanese. Collaborating with the Nationalists, though sometimes fighting against them, were the remnants of the puppet armies, groups of renegade Kuomintang driven back to the coast, and various militia forces recruited by the local warlords who had returned to Shanghai.

Swept in front of these rival armies, like dust before a set of colliding brooms, were tens of thousands of Chinese peasants. Columns of refugees wandered the countryside, trying to shelter in the fields and looted villages, turned away from the gates of Shanghai by advance units of the Nationalist armies.

It was these refugees, the bands of starving coolies armed with knives and hoes, whom Jim most feared. Avoiding them at all costs, Basie and his bandit group stayed close to any battle that was taking place. On the eastern fringes of Nantao, between the dockyards and the seaplane base, was a no man's land of wharves, warehouses and deserted barracks which the Kuomintang militias and the peasant refugees found too near to the fighting across the river at Pootung. Here Basie and the remaining six members of the gang camped out in the bunkers and concrete forts, with little left to them but the pre-war Buick and the vague hope of selling themselves to a Nationalist general.

Now even the car was proving too obvious a target for the Kuomintang gunners.

'You sit behind the wheel, Jim,' Basie had told him as the bandits left the Buick on the mud-flat. 'Pretend you're driving this fine car.'

'Say, can I, Basie . . .?' Jim held the steering-wheel as the men stood on the black beach beside the car and prepared their weapons. Their faces flinched at the sound of the explosions that crossed the water. 'Are you going to the stadium, Basie?'

'Right, Jim. Remember those years in Lunghua – we have an investment to protect. The Nats want to take over Shanghai and keep out any foreign business interests.'

'Is that us, Basie?'

'That's you, Jim. You're part of the foreign business community. When we get back you'll have a fur coat and a case of Scotch whisky for your Dad.'

Basie stared at the ruined warehouses and the corpses stacked on the mole, as if seeing them loaded with all the treasure of the east about to be freighted back to Frisco. Jim felt sorry for Basie, and was tempted to warn him that the stadium was probably empty, stripped by the Kuomintang troops of the few valuables that had survived the sun and rain. But Basie had taken the hook and was now running eagerly towards the gaff. With luck, if he survived the attack on the stadium, he would throw away his rifle and walk back to Shanghai. Within a few days he would be a wine-waiter at the Cathay Hotel, serving with a flourish all the American officers who stepped ashore from the cruiser moored by the Bund . . .

When Basie and the men had gone, vanishing among the ruined warehouses on the quay, Jim studied the magazines on the seat beside him. He was sure now that the Second World War had ended, but had World War III begun? Looking at the photographs of the D-Day landings, the crossing of the Rhine and the capture of Berlin, he felt that they were part of a smaller war, a rehearsal for the real conflict that had begun here in the Far East with the dropping of the Nagasaki and Hiroshima atomic bombs. Jim remembered the light that lay over the land, the shadow of another sun. Here, at the mouths of the great rivers of

332

Asia, would be fought the last war to decide the planet's future.

Jim wiped his blood from the steering-wheel, as the shelling began again from the Pootung shore. His nose had been bleeding on and off for four days. He swallowed the blood and watched the open road that ran from the wharves towards the distant stadium. A hundred yards from the Buick, two Chinese militiamen had climbed on to the bows of the beached submarine. Rifles slung over their shoulders, they ignored the battle across the river and walked along the deck to the conning tower.

Jim unlatched the driver's door. It was time to leave, before the militiamen noticed the Buick. From the heap of cans, cigarette cartons and ammunition clips on the floor of the car he selected a chocolate bar, a tin of Spam and a copy of *Life*. When the two Chinese were behind the conning tower he stepped on to the mud-flat. Crouching below the embankment wall, he ran towards the stone ramp of a Shanghai River Police jetty. Little more than two miles to the north were the tenements and godowns of the Old City, and beyond them the office blocks of downtown Shanghai, but Jim ignored them and set out again for Lunghua Airfield.

Smoke rose from the Olympic stadium, a thin white plume fed by a single flame, as if Basie and his gang had lit a bonfire of furniture in the stands. The artillery barrages from Pootung and Hungjao had fallen silent, and Jim could hear the brief bursts of rifle fire from the stadium.

Searching for shelter, Jim left the exposed country road. He walked through the wild sugar-cane that covered the waste ground beside the northern perimeter of Lunghua Airfield. A screen of trees and rusting fuel tanks separated him from the open plain of the landing field, the ruined hangars and pagoda. Cartridge cases lay on the narrow path

333

at his feet, chips laid in a brassy trail. He followed the straggling wire, avoiding the swarms of flies which clustered over the miniature bowers in the banks of nettles.

On either side of the pathway the bodies of dead Japanese lay where they had been shot or bayoneted. Jim stopped by a shallow irrigation ditch, in which an air force private lay with his hands tied behind him. Hundreds of flies devoured his face, enclosing it in a noisy mask. Unwrapping his chocolate bar, and fanning the flies from his face with the magazine, Jim walked through the sugar-cane. Dozens of dead Japanese lay in the nettles as if they had fallen from the sky, the members of a youthful armada shot down as they tried to fly to their home airfields in Japan.

Jim stepped over a collapsed section of the perimeter fence, and moved through the derelict aircraft that lay among the trees. Their fuselages had wept rivers of rust in the summer rain. The flies raged at the morning light, a vast anger about nothing. Leaving them, Jim set out across the grass expanse of the airfield. Inside one of the ruined hangars a group of Japanese waited in the shade, listening to the rifle fire from the stadium, but they ignored Jim as he walked across the field.

He stared at the concrete runway below his feet. To his surprise, he found that the surface was badly cracked and stained with patches of oil, scored by the marks of tyres and wheel struts. But now that World War III had begun, a new runway would soon be laid. Jim reached the end of the concrete strip, and strode through the grass towards the southern perimeter of the airfield. The ground rose to the overgrown hillocks left by the original earthworks, then shelved into the valley where the Japanese trucks had once delivered their loads of building rubble and roof tiles.

Despite the deep nettles and the hot September sunlight, the valley seemed filled with the same ashy dust. The banks of the canal were as pale as the conduit of a mortuary stream in which the dead were washed. The burst casing of an unexploded bomb lay in the shallow water, like a large turtle that had fallen asleep trying to bury its head in the mud.

Aware that the vibration of a low-flying Mustang might trip its detonator, Jim pressed on into the valley, parting the nettles with his magazine. He tossed the tin of Spam into the air, caught it with one hand, but on the second throw lost it among the reeds. Hunting about in the thick grass, he at last found it near the water's edge, and decided to eat the chopped ham before it slipped through his hands for good.

Sitting on the bank of the canal, he washed the dirt from the lid. A drop of blood fell from his nose into the water, and was instantly attacked by myriads of small fish no longer than a match-head. As a second drop struck the surface there was a violent struggle that seemed to involve entire nations of minute fish. They swerved through the water, unaware of the sunlit surface, ferociously attacking each other. Clearing his mouth, Jim leaned over and released a ball of pus from his infected gums. It fell like a depth charge among the fish, driving them into a frenzy of panic. Within a second the water was empty except for the dissolving pus.

Losing interest in the fish, Jim stretched out among the reeds and studied the advertisements in his magazine. He listened to the deeper sound of the artillery fire. The guns of Siccawei and Hungjao were louder, as the rival Nationalist armies closed their grip on Shanghai. He would eat his Spam, and then make a last effort to return to Shanghai. He was certain that Basie and the bandit gang never intended to return to the Buick, and had left him on the mud-flat to draw away any Chinese soldiers who might have followed them to the river.

In the grass nearby, a head nodded twice, approving this strategy. Jim lay rigidly, the last of the chocolate trapped in his throat, startled by this intimate apparition. Someone was lying in the reeds a few feet from him, his knees almost touching the water's edge. As if trying to reassure Jim, the head nodded again. He reached out one hand and parted the grass, carefully examining the figure's face. The round cheeks and soft nose, pinched by the privations of a wartime childhood, were those of a teenage Asiatic, some villager's son come here to fish. The boy lay on his back, surrounded by a wall of grass and reeds, as if sharing a four-poster bed with Jim and quietly listening to his thoughts.

Jim sat up, the rolled magazine raised above his head. Through the swarming flies he waited for the sound of footsteps in the long grass. But the valley was empty, its bright air devoured by the flies. The figure moved slightly, crushing the grass. Too idle to stop himself, the lazing youth was sliding down the bank into the water.

With all the caution learned during the long years of the war, Jim climbed to his knees, then stood up and stepped through the reeds. Calming himself, he looked down at this dozing figure.

In front of him, wearing a bloodstained flying overall with the insignia of a special attack group, was the body of the young Japanese pilot.

41

Rescue Mission

Jim despaired. Flattening the grass with his hands, he made a small place for himself beside the Japanese. The pilot lay in his overall, one arm under his back. He had been thrown down the slope towards the canal, and his legs were caught beneath him. His right knee touched the water, which had begun to soak the thigh of his overall. Above his head Jim could see the chute of bruised grass down which he had fallen, the stems straightening themselves in the sun.

He stared at the pilot, for once glad of the swarm of flies interceding between himself and this corpse. The face of the Japanese was more childlike than Jim remembered, as if in his death he had returned to his true age, to his early adolescence in a provincial Japanese village. His lips were parted around his uneven teeth, as if expecting a morsel of fish to be placed between them by his mother's chopsticks.

Numbed by the sight of this dead pilot, Jim watched the youth's knees slide into the water. He squatted on the sloping earth, turning the pages of *Life* and trying to concentrate on the photographs of Churchill and Eisenhower. For so long he had invested all his hopes in this young pilot, in that futile dream that they would fly away together, leaving Lunghua, Shanghai and the war forever behind them. He had needed the pilot to help him survive the war, this imaginary twin he had invented, a replica of himself whom he watched through the barbed wire. If the Japanese was dead, part of himself had died. He had failed to grasp the truth that millions of Chinese had known from birth, that they were all as good as dead anyway, and that it was self-deluding to believe otherwise.

Jim listened to the artillery barrages at Hungjao and Siccawei, and to the circling drone of a Nationalist spotter plane. The sound of small arms fire crossed the airfield, as Basie and the bandits tried to break into the stadium. The dead were playing their dangerous games.

Deciding to ignore them, Jim continued to read his magazine, but the flies had swarmed from the corpses further along the creek and soon discovered the body of the young pilot. Jim stood up and seized the Japanese by the shoulders. Holding him under the armpits, he pulled his legs from the water, then dragged him on to a narrow ledge of level ground.

Despite his plump face, the pilot weighed almost nothing. His starved body was as light as the children in Lunghua with whom Jim had wrestled when he was young. The waist and trousers of his flying overall were thick with blood. He had been bayoneted in the small of his back, and again through the thighs and buttocks, then thrown down the bank with the other aircrew.

Squatting beside the body, Jim snapped the key from the Spam tin, and began to wind off the lid. Once he had eaten he would use the can to dig a grave for the Japanese. When he had buried the pilot he would walk to Shanghai, regardless of the games the dead were playing. If he saw his parents he would tell them that World War III had begun, and that they should return to their camp at Soochow.

The hot jelly of chopped ham bulged within its mucilage of melted fat. Jim washed his hand in the canal, and used the lid to cut a modest slice. He raised the meat to his mouth, but spat the fragment into the water. The greasy flesh was still alive, as if carved from the body of a breathing animal. Its lungs and liver quivered in the can, still driven by a heart. Jim cut a second slice and placed it in his mouth. He could feel its pulse between his lips, and the fear of the creature in the moments before its slaughter.

He picked the slice from his lips and stared at the oily meat. Living flesh was not meant to feed the dead. This was food that would devour those who tried to eat it. Jim spat the last shred into the grass beside the Japanese. Leaning across the corpse, he patted the blanched lips with his forefinger, ready to slip the morsel of ham into its mouth.

The chipped teeth closed around his finger, cutting the cuticle. Jim dropped the can of meat, which rolled through the grass into the canal. He wrenched his hand away, aware that the corpse of this Japanese was about to sit up and consume him. Without thinking, Jim punched the pilot's face, then stood back and shouted at him through the swarm of flies.

The pilot's mouth opened in a noiseless grimace. His eyes were fixed in an unfocused way on the hot sky, but a lid quivered as a fly drank from his pupil. One of the bayonet wounds in his back had penetrated the front of his abdomen, and fresh blood leaked from the crutch of his overall. His narrow shoulders stirred against the crushed grass, trying to animate his useless arms.

Jim gazed at the young pilot, doing his best to grasp the miracle that had taken place. By touching the Japanese he had brought him to life; by prising his teeth apart he had made a small space in his death and allowed his soul to return.

He spread his feet on the damp slope and wiped his hands on his ragged trousers. The flies swarmed around him, stinging his lips, but Jim ignored them. He remembered how he had questioned Mrs Philips and Mrs Gilmour about the raising of Lazarus, and how they had insisted that far from being a marvel this was the most ordinary of events. Every day Dr Ransome had brought people back from the dead by massaging their hearts.

Jim looked at his hands, refusing to be overawed by them. He raised his palms to the light, letting the sun warm his skin. For the first time since the start of the war he felt a surge of hope. If he could raise this dead Japanese pilot he could raise himself, and the millions of Chinese who had died during the war and who were still dying in the fighting for Shanghai, for a booty as illusory as the treasure in the Olympic stadium. He would raise Basie when he had been killed by the Kuomintang guards defending the stadium, but not the other members of the bandit gang, and never Lieutenant Price or Captain Soong. He would raise his mother and father, Dr Ransome and Mrs Vincent, and the British prisoners in Lunghua hospital. He would raise the Japanese aircrew lying in the ditches around the airfield, and enough ground staff to rebuild a squadron of aircraft.

The Japanese pilot made a small gasp. His eyes tilted, as if trying to revolve like those of the patients whom Dr Ransome revived. He was barely clinging to life, but Jim knew that he would have to leave him beside the canal. His hands and shoulders were trembling, electrified by the discharge that had passed through them, the same energy that powered the sun and the Nagasaki bomb whose explosion he had witnessed. Already Jim could see Mrs Philips and Mrs Gilmour rising politely from the dead, listening in their concerned but puzzled way as he explained how he had saved them. He could imagine Dr Ransome shrugging the earth from his shoulders, and Mrs Vincent looking back disapprovingly at the grave . . .

Jim sucked the blood and pus from his teeth and quickly swallowed them. He slipped on the damp grass and slid into the shallow water of the canal. Steadying himself, he washed his face. He wanted to look his best when Mrs Vincent opened her eyes and saw him again. He wiped his wet hands on the cheeks of the young pilot. He would have to leave him, but like Dr Ransome he had only a few seconds to spare for each of the impatient dead.

* * *

As he ran through the valley towards the camp Jim noticed that the artillery guns at Pootung and Hungjao had fallen silent. Across the airfield a column of trucks had stopped by the hangars and armed men in American helmets were climbing the staircase of the control tower. Flights of Mustangs circled Lunghua in close formation, their engines roaring at the exhausted grass. Waving to them, Jim ran to the perimeter fence of the camp. He knew that the American planes were coming in to land, ready to take away the people he had raised. By the burial mounds to the west of the camp three Chinese stood with their hoes among the eroded coffins, the first of those aggrieved by the war now coming to greet him. He shouted to two Europeans in camp fatigues who climbed from a flooded creek with a home-made fishing net. They stared at Jim and called to him, as if surprised to find themselves alive again with this modest implement in their hands.

Jim climbed through the fence and ran down the cinder track to the camp hospital. Men with spades stood in the cemetery, shielding their eyes from the unfamiliar daylight. Had they dug themselves free from their own graves? As he neared the steps of the hospital Jim tried to control his trembling. The bamboo doors opened and a swarm of flies fled through the air, their feast-days done. Brushing them from his face, over which he wore a green surgical mask, was a red-haired man in a new American uniform. In his hand he carried an insecticide bomb.

'Dr Ransome . . .!' Jim spat the blood from his mouth and ran up the rotting steps. 'You came back, Dr Ransome! It's all right, everyone's coming back! I'm going to get Mrs Vincent . . .!'

He stepped past Dr Ransome into the dark, but the physician's hands gripped his shoulders.

'Hold on, Jim . . . I thought you might be here.' He removed his mask and pressed Jim's head to his chest, inspecting the boy's gums and ignoring the blood that stained the crisp fabric of his US Army shirt. 'Your parents are waiting for you, Jim. Poor fellow, you'll never believe the war is over.'

Part IV

42
The Terrible City

Two months later, on the eve of his departure for England, Jim remembered Dr Ransome's words as he walked down the gangway of the SS *Arrawa* and stepped on to Chinese soil for the last time. Dressed in a silk shirt and tie, and a grey flannel suit from the Sincere Company's department store, Jim waited politely for an elderly English couple to make their way down the wooden ramp. Below them was the Shanghai Bund, and all the clamour of the gaudy night. Thousands of Chinese filled the concourse, jostling among the trams and limousines, the jeeps and trucks of the US military, and a horde of rickshaws and pedicabs. Together they watched the British and American servicemen moving in and out of the hotels along the Bund. At the jetties beside the *Arrawa*, hidden below its stern and bows, American sailors came ashore from the cruiser moored in mid-river. As they stepped from their landing craft the Chinese surged forward, gangs of pickpockets and pedicab drivers, prostitutes and bar-touts, vendors hawking bottles of home-brew Johnny Walker, gold dealers and opium traders, the evening citizenry of Shanghai in all its black silk, fox fur and flash.

The young American sailors pushed past the sampan men and shouting military police. They tried to stay together and fight off the crowd so eager to welcome them to China. But before they reached the first set of tram-tracks down the centre of the Bund they were swept away in a convoy of pedicabs, their arms around the bar-girls screaming obscenities at the sleek Chinese pimps in their pre-war Packards, down from the blocks in the back-alley garages of the Nanking Road.

Dominating this panorama of the Shanghai night were three cinema screens which had been set up on scaffolding along the Bund. In collaboration with the US Navy, the Nationalist general who was the military governor of the city had arranged this continuous screening of newsreels from the European and Pacific theatres, in order to give the population of Shanghai a glimpse of the world war that had recently ended.

Jim cleared the last step of the swaying gangway, and looking up at the trembling images, which were barely strong enough to hold their own against the neon signs and strip lighting on the hotel and nightclub façades. Fragments of their amplified sound-tracks boomed like guns over the roar of the traffic. He had begun the war watching the newsreels in the crypt of Shanghai Cathedral, and was now ending it below the same repetitive images – Russian machine-gunners advanced through the ruins of Stalingrad, US marines turned their flame-throwers on the Japanese defenders of a Pacific island, RAF fighters strafed an ammunition train in a German railyard. Promptly at ten-minute intervals, Chinese characters filled the screens, and vast Kuomintang armies saluted the victorious Generalissimo Chiang on his reviewing podium in Nanking. The only forces not to be celebrated were the Chinese communists, but they had been cleared out of Shanghai and the coastal cities. Whatever contribution their troops had made to the Allied victory had long been discounted, lost under the layers of newsreels that had imposed their own truth upon the war.

During the two months since his return to Amherst Avenue, Jim often visited the reopened cinemas in Shanghai. His parents recovered only slowly from their years of imprisonment in the camp at Soochow, and Jim had ample time to tour Shanghai. After calling at the White Russian dentist in the French Concession, he would order Yang to drive him in the Lincoln Zephyr to the Grand or the Cathay, those vast and cool palaces where he sat in the front row of the circle and watched yet another screening of *Bataan* and *The Fighting Lady*.

Yang was puzzled why Jim should want to see these films so many times. In turn Jim wondered how Yang himself had spent the years of the war – as a valet to a Chinese puppet general, as an interpreter for the Japanese, or as a Kuomintang agent working on the side for the communists? On the day of his parents' arrival Yang had appeared with the limousine, promptly sold the car to Jim's father and re-enrolled himself as its chauffeur. Yang was already performing in small roles in two productions of the renascent Shanghai film studios. Jim suspected that while he sat through another double feature at the Cathay Theatre the car was being rented out as a film prop.

These Hollywood movies, like the newsreels projected above the crowds on the Bund, endlessly fascinated Jim. After the dental work to his jaw, and the healing of the wound in his palate, he soon began to put on weight. Alone at the dining-room table, he ate large meals by day, and at night slept peacefully in his bedroom on the top floor of the unreal house in Amherst Avenue, which had once been his home but now seemed as much an illusion as the sets of the Shanghai film studios.

During his days at Amherst Avenue he often thought of his cubicle in the Vincent's room at the camp. At the end of October he ordered the unenthusiastic Yang to drive him to Lunghua. They set off through the western suburbs of Shanghai, and soon reached the first of the fortified check-points that guarded the entrances to the city. The Nationalist soldiers in their American tanks were turning back hundreds of destitute peasants, without rice or land to crop, trying to find refuge in Shanghai. Shanty towns of mud dwellings, walls reinforced with truck tyres and kerosene drums, covered the fields near the burnt-out Olympic stadium at Nantao. Smoke still rose from the stands, a beacon used by the American pilots flying across the China Sea from their bases in Japan and Okinawa.

As they drove along the perimeter road, Jim stared at Lunghua Airfield, now a dream of flight. Dozens of US Navy and Air Force planes sat on the grass, factory-new fighters and chromium-sheathed transport aircraft that seemed to be waiting delivery to a show-room window in the Nanking Road.

Jim expected to see Lunghua Camp deserted, but far from being abandoned the former prison was busy again, fresh barbed wire strung along its fences. Although the war had been over for nearly three months, more than a hundred British nationals were still living in the closely guarded compound. Entire families had taken over the former dormitories in E Block, in which they had built suites of rooms within walls of American ration cartons, parachute canisters and bales of unread *Reader's Digests*. When Jim, searching for Basie's cubicle, tried to pull one of the magazines from its makeshift wall he was brusquely warned away.

Leaving the inmates to their treasure, he signalled Yang to drive on to G Block. The Vincents' room was now the quarters of a Chinese amah working for the British couple across the corridor. She refused to admit Jim, or open the door more than a crack, and he returned to the Lincoln and ordered Yang on a last circuit of the camp.

The hospital and the camp cemetery had vanished, and the site was an open tract of ash and cinders, from which a few charred joists protruded. The graves had been carefully levelled, as if a series of tennis courts was about to be laid. Jim walked through the empty drums of kerosene which had fuelled the fire. He gazed through the wire at the airfield, and at the concrete runway pointing to Lunghua

Pagoda. Dense vegetation covered the wrecks of the Japanese aircraft. As he stood by the wire, tracing the course of the canal through the narrow valley, an American bomber swept across the camp. For a moment, reflected from the underside of its silver wings, a pale light raced like a wraith between the nettles and stunted willows.

While Yang drove uneasily back to Amherst Avenue, annoyed in some way by the visit to Lunghua, Jim thought of the last weeks of the war. Towards the end everything had become a little muddled. He had been starving and perhaps had gone slightly mad. Yet he knew that he had seen the flash of the atomic bomb at Nagasaki even across the four hundred miles of the China Sea. More important, he had seen the start of World War III, and realized that it was taking place around him. The crowds watching the newsreels on the Bund had failed to grasp that these were the trailers for a war that had already started. One day there would be no more newsreels.

In the weeks before he and his mother sailed to England in the *Arrawa*, Jim often thought of the young Japanese pilot he had seemed to raise from the dead. He was not sure now that this was the same pilot who had fed him the mango. Probably the youth had been dying, and Jim's movements in the grass had woken him. All the same, certain events had taken place, and with more time perhaps others would have returned to life. Mrs Vincent and her husband had died on the march from the stadium, far from Shanghai in a small village to the south-west. But Jim might have helped the prisoners in the camp hospital. As for Basie, had he died during his attack on the stadium, within sight of the gilded nymphs in the Presidential stand? Or were he and Lieutenant Price still roving the landscape of the Yangtze in the puppet general's Buick, waiting for a third war to bring them into their own?

Jim had told his parents nothing of all this. Nor had he

349

confided in Dr Ransome, who clearly suspected that Jim had chosen to stay on at Lunghua after the armistice, playing his games of war and death. Jim remembered his return to the house in Amherst Avenue, and his mother and father smiling weakly from their deck-chairs in the garden. Beside the drained swimming-pool the untended grass grew around their shoulders, and reminded him of the bowers of nettles in which the dead Japanese airmen had lain. As Dr Ransome stood formally on the terrace in his American uniform, Jim had wanted to explain to his parents everything that he and the doctor had done together, but his mother and father had been through their own war. For all their affection for him, they seemed older and far away.

Jim walked across the quay from the *Arrawa*, looking up at the newsreels projected above the evening crowd. The second of the screens, in front of the Palace Hotel, was now blank, its images of tank battles and saluting armies re-replaced by a rectangle of silver light that hung in the night air, a window into another universe.

As the army technicians on their tower of scaffolding repaired the projector, Jim walked across the tramlines towards the screen. Noticing it for the first time, the Chinese stopped to look up at the white rectangle. Jim brushed the sleeve of his jacket as a rickshaw coolie blundered into him, pulling two bar-girls in fur coats. Their powdered faces were lit like masks by the weird glimmer.

However, the heads of the Chinese were already turning to another spectacle. A crowd had gathered below the steps of the Shanghai Club. A group of American and British sailors had emerged through the revolving doors and stood on the top step, arguing with each other and waving drunkenly at the cruiser moored by the Bund. The Chinese watched as they formed a chorus line. Provoked by their curious but silent audience, the sailors began to jeer at the

Chinese. At a signal from an older sailor, the men unbuttoned their bell-bottomed trousers and urinated down the steps.

Fifty feet below them, the Chinese watched without comment as the arcs of urine formed a foaming stream that ran down to the street. When it reached the pavement the Chinese stepped back, their faces expressionless. Jim glanced at the people around him, the clerks and coolies and peasant women, well aware of what they were thinking. One day China would punish the rest of the world, and take a frightening revenge.

The army projectionists had rewound their film, and an air battle started again over the heads of the crowds. As the sailors were carried away in a convoy of rickshaws, Jim walked back to the *Arrawa*. His parents were resting in the passenger saloon on the upper deck, and Jim wanted to spend a last evening with his father before he and his mother sailed for England the next day.

He stepped on to the gangway, conscious that he was probably leaving Shanghai for the last time, setting out for a small, strange country on the other side of the world which he had never visited, but which was nominally 'home'. Yet only part of his mind would leave Shanghai. The rest would remain there forever, returning on the tide like the coffins launched from the funeral piers at Nantao.

Below the bows of the *Arrawa* a child's coffin moved on to the night stream. Its paper flowers were shaken loose by the wash of a landing-craft carrying sailors from the American cruiser. The flowers formed a wavering garland around the coffin as it began its long journey to the estuary of the Yangtze, only to be swept back by the incoming tide among the quays and mud-flats, driven once again to the shores of this terrible city.

P.S.

Ideas,
interviews
& features ...

An Investigative Spirit

Travis Elborough talks to J.G. Ballard

In several of your novels you have used a small community, the residents of a luxury housing development or a high-rise block for example, as a microcosm with which to explore the fragility of civil society. Do you think that your preoccupation with social regression, de-evolution even, stems from your childhood experiences in the internment camp when you saw, first hand, how easily the veneer of civilization could slip away?

Yes, I think it does; although anyone who has experienced a war first hand knows that it completely overturns every conventional idea of what makes up day-to-day reality. You never feel quite the same again. It's like walking away from a plane crash; the world changes for you forever. The experience of spending nearly three years in a camp, especially as an early teenage boy, taking a keen interest in the behaviour of adults around him, including his own parents, and seeing them stripped of all the garments of authority that protect adults generally in their dealings with children, to see them stripped of any kind of defence, often losing heart a bit, being humiliated and frightened – and we all felt the war was going to go on forever and heaven knows what might happen in the final stages – all of that was a remarkable education. It was unique, and it gave me a tremendous insight into what makes up human behaviour.

You've written that the landscape of even your first novel, *The Drowned World,* **a futuristic portrait of a flooded twenty-first-century London, was clearly informed by your memories of Shanghai. I wondered if you could say a little about how, after having possibly explored it obliquely in your works of science fiction, you came to write so directly about your childhood experiences in** *Empire of the Sun***?**

I had always planned to write about my experiences of the Second World War, Shanghai under the Japanese and the camp. I knew that it was such an important event, and not just for me. But when I came to England in 1946 I had to face the huge problem of adjusting to life here. England in those days was a very, very strange place. There was an elaborate class system that I'd never come across in Shanghai. England . . . it was a terribly shabby place, you know, locked into the past and absolutely exhausted by the war. It was only on a technicality that we could be said to have won the war; in many ways we'd lost it. Financially we were desperate. I had to cope with all this. By 1949 the Communists had taken over China and I knew I would never go back. So there seemed no point in keeping those memories alive, I felt I had to come to terms with life in England. This is, after all, where I was educated. I got married and began my career as a writer.

England interested me. It seemed to be a sort of disaster area. It was a subject and a ▶

6 Anyone who has experienced a war first hand knows that it completely overturns every conventional idea of what makes up day-to-day reality. It's like walking away from a plane crash. 9

3

◄ disaster in its own right. I was interested in change, which I could see was coming in a big way, everything from supermarkets to jet travel, television and the consumer society. I remember thinking, my God, these things will bring change to England and reveal the strange psychology of these tormented people.

So I began writing science fiction, although most readers of science fiction did not consider me to be a science fiction writer. They saw me as an interloper, a sort of virus that had got into the cell of science fiction, entered its nucleus and destroyed it. But all this while I could see bits of my China past floating up and I knew I was going to write it up at some point.

You have to remember that an enormous period of time had elapsed between the publication of *Empire of the Sun* in 1984 and my time in the camp, some forty-odd years. And I think partly this was because I had children of my own. I didn't want to expose them to the kind of experiences that I had had. Once my children had grown up, I thought, well, if I don't write this book now I am going to forget it. So in about 1982 or something, I thought, now is the time. Of course the act of writing it brought back a huge flood of memories. I don't want to over glamorize my wartime experience. It was pretty awful. My parents had much harsher memories of it than I did. Teenage children, especially if they are with their parents or other adults, tend to be unaware of the dangers they are in. They get by on

6 An enormous period of time had elapsed between the publication of *Empire of the Sun* in 1984 and my time in the camp, some forty-odd years. And I think partly this was because I had children of my own. I didn't want to expose them to the kind of experiences that I had had. 9

very little food, they live for the excitement of the camp, and to some extent I'd suppressed all that.

Can I ask you what you made of Steven Spielberg's film of *Empire of the Sun*?
I liked the film. I think it is a very impressive piece of work. I see it once every couple of years. It was made, oh, getting on for twenty years ago now, in 1987, and it seems to have got richer and more interesting as the years pass. I see it not as the film of my book but as a film in its own right. Seeing a novel that you've written filmed is always an enormously peculiar experience because you are conscious of a thousand and one discrepancies. You can't help thinking: 'It wasn't like that in my book.' There's no reason why it should be exactly alike, after all, but it was a very impressive film.

You studied medicine and have stated that you believe that the contemporary novelist should be like a scientist. Do you ever regret not qualifying as a doctor?
I was very interested in medicine. The experience of dissecting cadavers for two years was a very important one for me, for all sorts of reasons. I do think that novelists should be like scientists, dissecting the cadaver . . . I would like to have become a doctor, but the urge to write was too great. I knew from friends of mine who were a year or two ahead of me that once you actually joined a London hospital or became a junior doctor the pressures of ▶

6 One of the things I took from my wartime experiences was that reality was a stage set . . . Nothing is as secure as we like to think it is. 9

Author photograph by Jerry Bauer

LIFE
at a Glance

BORN
Shanghai, China, 1930

EDUCATED
Cathedral School,
Shanghai

The Leys School,
Cambridge

King's College,
Cambridge

FAMILY
Married Helen Mathews,
1956. One son, two
daughters

LIVES
Shepperton, Middlesex

An Investigative Spirit *(continued)*

◄ work were too great. I'd never have any
time to write, and the urge to write was
just too strong.

**Do you think there is a moral purpose to
your fiction?**
I am not sure about that. I see myself more
as a kind of investigator, a scout who is sent
on ahead to see if the water is drinkable or
not.

**As a scout or investigator you've been
uncannily prescient, famously predicting
Reagan's presidency in *The Atrocity
Exhibition*, and I noticed that one
commentator made reference to *The
Drowned World* in the aftermath of the
New Orleans disaster. Have you
ever worried that you might be *too*
prescient?**
An investigator and a sort of early warning
system, let's put it like that. I suppose one of
the things I took from my wartime
experiences was that reality was a stage set.
The reality that you took for granted – the
comfortable day-to-day life, school, the
home where one lives, the familiar street
and all the rest of it, the trips to the
swimming pool and the cinema – was just a
stage set. They could be dismantled
overnight, which they literally were when
the Japanese occupied Shanghai and turned
our lives upside down. I think that
experience left me with a very sceptical eye,
which I've turned onto something even as
settled as English suburbia where I now live.
Nothing is as secure as we like to think it is.

One doesn't just have to think of Hurricane Katrina and New Orleans – this applies to everything. A large part of my fiction tries to analyse what is going on around us, and whether we are much different people from the civilized human beings we imagine ourselves to be. I think it's true of all my fiction. I think that investigative spirit forms all my novels really. ■

The End of My War
by J.G. Ballard

HAD THE WAR ENDED? For days, in that
second week of August 1945, rumours had
swept Lunghua camp. Shanghai lay eight
miles to the north, beyond the abandoned
villages and paddy fields, and I remember
staring for hours at the apartment buildings
of the French Concession along the horizon.
The Swiss and Swedish neutrals who had
lived there throughout the war would be
tuning their short-wave radios to the latest
news of the American bombing raids on
Japan and the reported peace negotiations.

But in Lunghua camp we knew nothing.
Their work-tasks forgotten, the British
internees gathered in groups below the
balcony of the Japanese commandant's
offices in F block, watching the edgy guards
for the smallest clue. The rest of us stood
outside the huts and dormitory buildings,
gazing at the strangely silent sky. Every day
the Mustangs and B-29s had attacked the
nearby Japanese airfield and the Shanghai
dockyards, but now they had failed to
appear. Our food supplies had broken down
weeks ago, and we were kept alive only by
the emergency rations of the Swiss Red
Cross.

I waited for my father to announce that
the war had ended, but he knew as little as I
did. He and my mother sat in our little room
in G block as Margaret, my seven-year-old
sister, played outside with the other children.
Two-and-a-half years of imprisonment,
sharing their rice conjee and sweet potatoes
with me, had desperately drained them. I

sensed that they knew something they had decided to keep from me, fearing that our years of internment might end in some sudden and brutal way.

Then, on August 8, we woke to find that the Japanese guards had disappeared during the night. At last we were sure that the war had ended! People gathered silently at the open gates, peering at the dusty road to Shanghai. A few of the bolder men stepped through the barbed-wire fence, testing the empty air. I joined them, and cautiously walked to a grave-mound two hundred yards away. I looked back at the camp, at the intense, crowded world that for so long had been my home. Freedom and the war's end seemed fraught with danger, like the silent sky. I ran back to the wire, glad to be within the safety of the camp again.

Others had already decided to leave Lunghua for good. Half a dozen British men from E block stepped through the wire and set off across the fields for Shanghai, confidently waving goodbye to the camp. They returned the next day, lying unconscious in the trucks that brought another squad of Japanese soldiers to guard the camp. After carousing in the bars of downtown Shanghai the six Britons had been arrested by the Kempetai, the Japanese Gestapo, and severely beaten.

Enraged by their treatment, a crowd of English and Belgian women gathered below the commandant's balcony. Standing in their tattered cotton frocks, they screamed ▶

6 Shanghai in the 1930s was the Paris of the Pacific, one of the gaudiest cities in the world . . . It was a place of bizarre contrasts, of foetid back alleys and graceful boulevards . . . art deco apartment blocks and half-timbered Tudor mansions. 9

The End of My War *(continued)*

◄ abuse at the impassive Japanese soldiers, necklaces of spittle shining on their breasts.

Then at last it was all over. The day after Hirohito's broadcast, we heard from the Swiss Red Cross that the war had ended. The Japanese armies had agreed to lay down their arms. We were told of the atomic bombs dropped on Hiroshima and Nagasaki, which had vaporized both cities and brought the war to a sudden halt.

'Is the war over?' I asked my father. 'Really, really over?'

'Yes, it's really over.' My father stared at me sombrely. 'Jamie, you'll miss Lunghua.'

Much as I might miss Lunghua, I was keen to see Shanghai again and visit our house in Amherst Avenue. Most of the 2000 internees remained in the camp, too tired to make their way on foot to the city, and without money or jobs to support them. Chiang Kai-shek's Chinese armies were far inland, and the nearest American forces were on the island of Okinawa. Meanwhile the countryside around Lunghua was a zone of danger, roamed by undisciplined Japanese troops, destitute peasants and gangs of leaderless soldiers of the Chinese puppet forces. It would be days before the Allied advance guard arrived and took control.

The B-29s had returned and flew slowly over the camp at little more than five hundred feet, bomb doors open. This time they were dropping food supplies, cartons of C rations filled with unimaginable treasures – tins of Spam and Klim, packs of Lucky Strikes and Chesterfields, and bars of hard, gritty chocolate that flooded my mouth with an overpowering sweetness. The parachutes sailed over the camp, landing in the nearby fields and canals, and parties of internees ran out to seize them from the Chinese peasants, forgetting that they too were Allied civilians.

Unsettled by all this, I decided to walk to Shanghai. Three days after Hirohito's broadcast, and without telling my parents, I made my way to the northern perimeter of the camp, beyond the old shower house, and climbed through the barbed wire.

In front of me was a terrain of derelict canals and deserted villages. To my right the Japanese military airfield lay between the camp and the broad arm of the Whangpoo River. Lunghua pagoda, converted by the Japanese into a flak tower, rose into the humid August air. During the American raids the pagoda had lit up like a Christmas tree, tracers streaming towards the low-flying Mustangs, but now its guns were silent and unmanned.

Avoiding the airfield, with its restless Japanese sentries, I climbed the embankment of the Hangchow–Shanghai railway line, and set off between the humming rails. Half an hour later I approached a small wayside station, where a platoon of Japanese soldiers squatted among their rifles and ammunition boxes, waiting for a train that would never come.

When I was twenty yards away I saw that they had taken a prisoner, a young Chinese in black trousers and white shirt. They had tied him to a post with telephone wire cut from the poles beside the tracks, and one ▶

6 Although protected by chauffeurs and White Russian nannies, I was soon aware of a darker Shanghai, of kidnappings, gangster killings, and political bombings. 9

11

◀ of the soldiers was now slowly strangling him. The Chinese rolled his head as the wire tightened, singing to himself in a high voice.

The other soldiers had lost interest in the dying man and watched me walk up to them without comment, curiously eyeing my ragged khaki shorts and shirt. I wanted to tell them that the war was over, but I scarcely believed it myself, and I knew that the war's end carried little meaning for these Japanese soldiers. Caring nothing for their own lives, they cared nothing for the lives of others.

Leaving the station, I walked away along the railway line. The choking sing-song of the dying Chinese floated on the air as he sang himself towards his death. I have never forgotten that sound, but at the time, regrettably, I accepted this casual murder as no more than one of the minor realities of war.

Two hours later, thirsty and exhausted, I reached the western suburbs of Shanghai. At the end of Amherst Avenue I stopped at the house of my closest friends, the Kendal-Wards, who were interned in another of the camps near Shanghai. Hoping to see them, I walked up the steps to the open front door, and gazed through it at the sky above. The house was a brick shell. Everything had been stripped by the passing Chinese. Joists and floorboards, roof timbers and door-frames, pipes and electric cables had gone, leaving only the ghosts of the games we had played as children.

A few hundred yards away was the Ballard house at 31 Amherst Avenue. The roof and windows were still intact, and when I rang the bell the door was opened by a young Chinese soldier in a puppet army uniform.

'This is my house,' I told him. He tried to bar my way with his rifle, but when I pushed past him he gave up, aware that for him too the war was over. I stared at the silent rooms, which seemed strangely grand and formal after the shabby clutter of Lunghua. Everything was in place – the carpets, furniture and bookshelves, the cooker and large refrigerator in the American-style kitchen. The house had been occupied by a general in the puppet army, and the war had ended too abruptly for him to steal its entire contents.

I wandered through the airless house, trying to put a hundred memories of my childhood into their right places. But I had forgotten too much, and felt like a stranger visiting myself. I climbed to my room on the top floor and lay on the bed, looking at the empty shelves where I had kept my *Chums* annuals and American comics, and at the rusty hooks in the ceiling from which I had hung my model planes. Most of my mind was still in Lunghua, but a small part of it had come home.

My parents had arrived in Shanghai in 1929, aboard a P&O liner that took five weeks to make the long voyage from Southampton. I was born in the Shanghai General Hospital the following year. My father ran a textile firm, the China Printing and Finishing Company, a subsidiary of the Manchester-based Calico Printers Association. Shanghai in the 1930s was the Paris of the Pacific, ▶

‘ In my school classroom there were empty desks, as families left Shanghai for the safety of Hong Kong and Singapore. The steamers leaving the Bund were crowded with Europeans turning their backs on the city. ’

The End of My War *(continued)*

◀ one of the gaudiest cities in the world, a stronghold of unlimited venture capitalism. With a Chinese population of five million, and a hundred thousand Europeans and Americans, it was a place of bizarre contrasts, of foetid back alleys and graceful boulevards, of skyscrapers and Provençal villas, art deco apartment blocks and half-timbered Tudor mansions.

Driven to the Cathedral School by the family chauffeur, I looked out at a lurid realm of gambling dens and opium parlours, beggar kings, rickshaw coolies and mink-coated prostitutes. Each morning the trucks of the British-dominated administration toured the International Settlement and removed the bodies of the Chinese who had died during the night of disease and starvation. If Shanghai's neon lights were the world's brightest, its pavements were the hardest.

Although protected by chauffeurs and White Russian nannies, I was soon aware of a darker Shanghai, of kidnappings, gangster killings, and political bombings as the Chinese communists kept up their underground struggle against Chiang Kai-shek's Kuomintang. The first sign that the lights would really dim came in 1937, when Japanese forces invaded China and seized its coastal cities. They respected the International Settlement, the central district of Shanghai, but bitter fighting took place in the outlying suburbs. The combined land, naval and air assault was a preview of the battlegrounds of the Second World War.

Huge areas of the city were razed to the

ground, and a stray bomb in the Avenue Edward VII killed more than a thousand people. Amherst Avenue lay outside the International Settlement, and when artillery shells from rival Chinese and Japanese batteries began to fly over our roof we moved to a rented house in the comparative safety of the French Concession. Neglected by its owner, the swimming pool had begun to drain. Looking down at its sinking surface, I felt that more than water was ebbing away.

When the fighting ended, Chiang's defeated armies withdrew into the vast interior of China, and we returned to Amherst Avenue. Life in the International Settlement resumed its glittery whirl. A week after the ceasefire my parents and their friends set out on a tour of the silent battlefields to the south of Shanghai. A motorcade of chauffeur-driven Packards and Buicks, filled with children, smartly dressed mothers and their straw-hatted husbands, moved past the shattered trenches and earth bunkers, like the landscapes of the Somme I had seen in the sepia photographs of the *Illustrated London News*.

Skirts in their hands, my mother and her fellow wives stepped through the hundreds of cartridge cases. The skeleton of a horse lay on the bank of a creek, and the canals were filled with dead Chinese soldiers, arms and legs stirred by the water. Belts of machine-gun bullets snaked through the grass, and live ammunition was scattered among the discarded webbing. A boy at the Cathedral School who picked up a grenade during ▶

❛ Why did my parents and so many others stay on in Shanghai, risking their families' lives? ❜

The End of My War *(continued)*

◄ another outing lost his hand when it exploded. Later, to his credit, he became a champion swimmer.

The Japanese controlled the Shanghai suburbs, and on the way to school I passed through their military checkpoints. By now, in 1940, I owned my first bicycle, and on the pretext of visiting the Kendal-Wards I began to take long rides around the city, pedalling through the confused traffic and avoiding the huge French trams. Sometimes I reached the Bund, and watched the Japanese cruiser *Idzumo* and the British and American gunboats, HMS *Petrel* and USS *Wake*. The amiable British tommies manning their sand-bagged emplacements often invited me to join them, getting me to clean their rifles with their pull-throughs and giving me their regimental cap badges.

As I moved through the checkpoints I was even more drawn to the Japanese soldiers. Many were ruthlessly brutal to the Chinese farmers and rickshaw coolies trying to enter the International Settlement, and in my mind I can still see an hysterical peasant woman near the Avenue Joffre tram terminal, screaming over her bayoneted husband as he died between the wheels of the passing Lincolns and Studebakers. I knew that the Japanese soldiers were brave, and I hoped the British tommies would never have to fight them. But the Japanese had a strain of melancholy that I admired, a quality not much in evidence among the party-going Europeans and Americans whom my parents knew.

By 1941 everyone was aware of the larger

conflict that would soon break out. In my school classroom there were empty desks, as families left Shanghai for the safety of Hong Kong and Singapore. The steamers leaving the Bund were crowded with Europeans turning their backs on the city. Once when I cycled to a friend's home in the Avenue Foch I found his apartment abandoned to the wind, unwanted possessions scattered across the beds. Reality, I was fast learning, was little more than a stage set whose actors and scenery could vanish overnight.

Why did my parents and so many others stay on in Shanghai, risking their families' lives? They knew of the Rape of Nanking, when 20,000 Chinese civilians were butchered by deranged Japanese soldiers. They had seen for themselves how cruelly the Japanese treated the Chinese peasants in the countryside around Shanghai, the casual rapes and executions.

In part they stayed because Shanghai was now their home, where they had made successful lives for themselves away from the Depression-ridden England of the 1930s. Others were missionaries and teachers, who had committed themselves to helping the Chinese people. Together they took for granted that they would be protected by British and American power. Even though Britain was then losing the war against Germany, even after Dunkirk and the fall of France, everyone assumed that the Japanese would be no match for the British Empire and the Royal Navy.

Britain, we knew, possessed the impregnable fortress of Singapore, and a ▶

> ❛ They took for granted that they would be protected by British and American power . . . Japanese pilots had bad eyesight and wore glasses, and their gimcrack planes would be no match for the Spitfires and Hurricanes. ❜

The End of My War *(continued)*

◀ huge battle-fleet. Japanese pilots had bad eyesight and wore glasses, and their gimcrack planes would be no match for the Spitfires and Hurricanes. Over their drinks at the Country Club people boasted that the war against Japan would be over in weeks, or a month at the outside.

These arrogant assumptions were put to the test on December 7 1941, when the Japanese carrier planes attacked Pearl Harbor. In Shanghai, across the International Date Line, it was already Monday, December 8. I was lying in bed, reading my Bible in preparation for that morning's scripture exam, when I heard tanks clanking down Amherst Avenue as the Japanese began their seizure of the International Settlement.

My father and mother raced around the house in a panic, followed by the chattering and excited servants. I watched them fling clothes into suitcases. Fearful of the Reverend Matthews, the martinet who was my headmaster, I pleaded to be driven to school, but my father silenced me with the most wonderful words a child can hear: 'Jamie, there'll be no more school and no more exams, not for a very long time.'

Already I was beginning to think that the war might be a good thing.

The Japanese took control of the International Settlement, and the uneasy peace of military occupation followed. A few Britons in senior administrative posts were hunted down and imprisoned, but the thousands of British and European residents were left to themselves, their morale shattered by the sinking of the *Repulse* and the *Prince of Wales*, two huge battleships sent north from Singapore without air cover.

The little men squinting through their glasses proved to be brilliant torpedo-bomber pilots. Hong Kong soon fell, and the Singapore garrison surrendered even though it outnumbered the Japanese forces by three to one. So was nailed down the coffin of the British Empire, though the corpse was the only one not to know it was dead, and continued to kick for too many years to come.

The myth of European invincibility had died, something that an eleven-year-old brought up on G.A. Henty and tales of derring-do on the north-west frontier found hard to accept. The British Empire was based on bluff, in many ways a brilliant one, but that bluff had been called.

Throughout 1942 life in Shanghai gradually wound itself down. Cars were confiscated, and my father cycled to his office. Allied nationals wore numbered armbands. British companies still carried on their business, but the directors worked in tandem with Japanese supervisors. The time of parties was over. Having outgrown my bicycle, I rollerskated to school, which to my annoyance had reopened, as if the Reverend Matthews was unaware that the war had begun.

Meanwhile the Japanese were constructing a network of internment camps around Shanghai for the British, Dutch and Belgian civilians. In the early months of 1943 came the Ballard family's turn. Our staging post ▶

> ❛ Throughout 1942 life in Shanghai gradually wound itself down. Cars were confiscated, and my father cycled to his office . . . Having outgrown my bicycle, I rollerskated to school. ❜

The End of My War *(continued)*

◄ was the Columbia Country Club in the Great Western Road, and I remember it crammed with people and their suitcases, many of the women in fur coats, sitting like refugees around the swimming pool. Soon we were driven away to the coming years of captivity, and so, in many ways, began my real life.

Lunghua Camp, in the open countryside to the south of Shanghai, occupied the site of a Chinese teacher-training college. Classrooms became dormitories, wooden barrack huts housed the unmarried women, and the staff bungalows served as the quarters for the guards and commandant.

The Lunghua district, with its countless creeks and canals, was notorious as a mosquito-infested area, and soon the first cases of malaria broke out. In the humid summer heat everyone moved in a dull, sweaty daze. Our food, for the first year, consisted of grey sweet potatoes, boiled rice, a coarse brown bread and occasional dice-sized pieces of gristly meat. Rooms and corridors were a jumble of suitcases and trunks, and sheets hanging over lines of string soon converted the open dormitories into a maze of tiny cubicles. Once the 2000 internees had settled in, life in Lunghua was dominated by the overheated summers and freezing winters, by stench, noise and boredom.

I was enthralled. Like most British children in pre-war Shanghai, I had met few adult males other than my father's friends. Within a few weeks, as I roamed around the camp, chess set under my arm, I was soon on good terms with dozens of men. Architects, lawyers, engineers and plant managers, they were bored enough to play a game of chess and dispense a little cynical wisdom to an impressionable young ear.

As a family of four, the Ballards were assigned one of the forty small rooms in G block, so cramped that during the day my father propped his mattress against the wall and set up a card-table from which we could eat our meals. I had been brought up by servants and was fascinated to find myself living, eating and sleeping within an arm's reach of my parents, like the impoverished Chinese families I had seen during my cycle rides around the Shanghai slums.

But my parents must have found their talkative and hyperactive son an immense trial, and were glad to see me anywhere other than their poky room. I roved around the camp, sitting in on bridge and poker games, curious to know how people were adapting to internment. Many of the British in Shanghai had been intoxicated for years, moving through the day from office to lunch to dinner and nightclub in a haze of dry martinis. Sober for the first time, they lost weight and began to read, rekindled old interests and organized drama societies and lecture evenings.

In retrospect, I realize that internment helped people to discover unknown sides to themselves. They conserved their emotions, and kept a careful inventory of hopes and feelings. I often found that taciturn or quick-tempered people could be surprisingly generous, and that some of the ▶

6 As a family of four, the Ballards were assigned one of the forty small rooms ... My parents must have found their talkative and hyperactive son an immense trial, and were glad to see me anywhere other than their poky room. 9

The End of My War *(continued)*

◄ missionaries who had devoted their lives to the Chinese peasantry could show a curious strain of selfishness.

A few chronic idlers refused to work, but most people buckled down to their assigned tasks. The internees ran the camp, cooking the rations and maintaining the septic tanks and water supply. A school opened for the children, a blessed relief for their parents and a valuable punitive weapon for the Japanese. After an escape attempt or any infringement of the rules they would close the school and impose a day-long curfew, forcing the parents to cope with their bored and restless offspring.

Still intrigued by the Japanese, I soon met some of the guards. Hanging around their bungalows, I realized that they were also imprisoned in Lunghua. The younger soldiers invited me into their bare and unfurnished rooms. They strapped me into their kendo armour and taught me to fence, a whirl of wooden swords that usually sent me back to G block dazed, head ringing from a dozen blows.

They were friendly to me while the war went well for Japan, but when the tide turned after the Battle of Midway conditions in the camp began to worsen. Winters in the unheated cement buildings seemed arctic. A few Red Cross supplies arrived, overalls and shoes with soles cut from motor-car tyres. Our rations fell. The rice and cracked wheat, an animal feedstuff I found especially tasty, were little more than warehouse sweepings, filled with nails and dead insects. We pushed hundreds of weevils to the edges of our plates, until my father decreed that we needed the protein and would henceforth eat the weevils.

He and I tended a small garden plot, hoisting buckets of excrement from the G block septic tank to fertilize the beds. All over the camp cucumber frames rose from the carefully tilled soil. Tomatoes and melons supplemented our diet, but by 1944 I had long forgotten the taste of meat, milk, butter and sugar.

By the last year of the war I was aware of a certain estrangement between my parents and myself. We had seen too much of each other, and they had none of the levers that parents can pull, no presents to give, no treats to withhold. Lunghua camp was a huge slum, and as in all slums the teenage boys ran wild. I sympathize now with the parents in English sink-estates who are criticized for failing to control their children.

Our rations continued to fall, and the American bombing raids on the Japanese airfield next to the camp provoked the guards into senseless acts of brutality. Mr Hyashi, a former diplomat who was the camp commandant, was no longer able to control the soldiers. But he was a decent man, and after the war my father flew down to Hong Kong and testified in his defence at the war crimes trials. Justly, Hyashi was acquitted.

VJ Day, everywhere else in the world, lasted for twenty-four hours, but in the countryside around Lunghua it seemed to go on for days. The war-clocks had stopped. At last the first American warships moored ▶

6 Many of the British in Shanghai had been intoxicated for years, moving through the day from office to lunch to dinner and nightclub in a haze of dry martinis. Sober for the first time, they lost weight and began to read, rekindled old interests and organized drama societies and lecture evenings. 9

The End of My War *(continued)*

◄ opposite the Bund, and their forces took control of Shanghai. The city swiftly became its old self, its bars and brothels eager for business. Gangs of whores roamed the streets in the backs of pedicabs, chasing the American servicemen in their jeeps.

The Ballard family left Lunghua a week after the ceasefire, but I often returned to the camp, hitching rides from passing American trucks. I still felt that Lunghua was my real home. I had come to puberty there, and developed the beginnings of an adult mind. I had seen adults under stress, a valuable education I would never have received in peacetime Shanghai.

I now knew, as my parents revealed when we returned to Amherst Avenue, of the extreme danger we had faced. They had heard from Hyashi that in the autumn of 1945 the Japanese military intended to close Lunghua and march us up-country. There, far from the European neutrals in Shanghai, they would have killed us before preparing to face the expected American landings at the mouth of the Yangtse.

American power had saved our lives, above all the atomic bombs dropped on Hiroshima and Nagasaki. Not only our lives had been spared, but those of millions of Asian civilians and, just as likely, millions of Japanese in the home islands. I find wholly baffling the widespread belief today that the dropping of the Hiroshima and Nagasaki bombs was an immoral act, even possibly a war crime to rank with Nazi genocide.

During their long advance across the Pacific, the American armies liberated only one large capital city, Manila. A month of ferocious fighting left 6000 Americans dead, 20,000 Japanese and over 100,000 Filipinos, many of them senselessly slaughtered, a total greater than those who died at Hiroshima.

How many more would have died if the Americans and British had been forced to fight for Singapore, Saigon, Hong Kong and Shanghai? Huge Japanese armies were falling back to the mouth of the Yangtse and would have turned Shanghai into a vast death-ground. The human costs of invading Japan became clear during the fierce struggle for Okinawa, an island close to Japan, when nearly 200,000 Japanese were killed, most of them civilians.

Some historians claim that the war was virtually over, and that the Japanese leaders, seeing their wasted cities and the total collapse of the country's infrastructure, would have surrendered without the atom-bomb attacks. But this ignores one all-important factor – the Japanese soldier. Countless times he had shown that as long as he had a rifle or a grenade he would fight to the end. The only infrastructure the Japanese infantryman needed was his own courage, and there is no reason to believe that he would have fought less tenaciously for his homeland than for a coral atoll thousands of miles away.

The claims that Hiroshima and Nagasaki constitute an American war crime have had an unfortunate effect on the Japanese, confirming their belief that they were the victims of the war rather than the aggressors. As a nation the Japanese have never faced ▶

6 In retrospect, I realize that internment helped people to discover unknown sides to themselves. They conserved their emotions, and kept a careful inventory of hopes and feelings. 9

The End of My War *(continued)*

◄ up to the atrocities they committed, and are unlikely to do so as long as we bend our heads in shame before the memories of Hiroshima and Nagasaki.

The argument that atomic weapons, by virtue of the genetic damage they cause to the future generations, belong to a special category of evil, seems to me to be equally misguided. The genetic consequences of a rifle bullet through the heart are even more catastrophic, for the victim's genes go nowhere except the grave and his descendants are not even born.

In 1992, nearly fifty years after entering Lunghua camp, I returned for the first time. To my surprise, everything was as I remembered it, though the barrack huts had gone, and the former camp was now a Chinese high school. The children were on holiday, and I was able to visit my old room. Standing between the bunks, I knew that this was where I had been happiest and most at home, despite being a prisoner living under the threat of an early death.

But to survive war, especially as a civilian, one needs to accept the rules it imposes and even, as I did, learn to welcome it.

This article first appeared in the Sunday Times *in 1995.* ■

Have You Read?
Other titles by J.G. Ballard

Miracles of Life
Miracles of Life reveals the events of J.G.
Ballard's fascinating, disorientating and
singular life: from the deprivations and
unexpected freedoms of a Japanese prison
camp to his return to a Britain physically and
psychologically crippled by war, from the
social changes of the 1960s to the adjustment
to life after the premature loss of his wife. This
is both a captivating account of the
experiences that have shaped this writer's
extraordinary vision, and an enthralling
narrative of an entirely remarkable life.

Kingdom Come
Richard Pearson, unemployed advertising
executive, arrives in Brooklands, a motorway
town on the M25. Weeks earlier, his father
was fatally wounded in its vast shopping
mall. But as Richard delves into events he
begins to suspect that there is a more sinister
element lurking behind its pristine façade.

The Kindness of Women
This second autobiographical work from
Ballard continues where *Empire of the Sun*
left off. Tracing Jim's life as he moves from
Shanghai to England, and from adolescence
to middle age, it is an unsparingly honest
account of suburban bliss, domestic tragedy
and sexual experimentation. ▶

Have You Read? *(continued)*

◀ *The Drowned World*
In Ballard's first full novel, inspired in part
by his memories of Shanghai, London is a
city inundated by a primeval swamp.

The Drought
Water. Man's most precious commodity is a
luxury of the past in this compelling early
novel from Ballard. And while the
remorseless sun beats down on Dr Charles
Ransom and the remaining inhabitants of
Mount Royal, civilization begins to crack . . .

Collected Short Stories
This volume offers an unparalleled chance to
explore his complete shorter œuvre and
marvel at both his development as a writer
and his mastery of the form.

Crash
Ballard's controversial cult novel,
subsequently made into an equally
controversial film by David Cronenberg, was
originally published in 1973 but it has lost
none of its potency. Vaughan, a TV scientist
turned nightmare angel of the highways,
craves the ultimate erotic atrocity: a union of
blood, semen and engine fluid in a head-on
smash with Elizabeth Taylor.

High Rise
Within the concealing walls of an elegant
forty-storey tower block, the affluent tenants
are hell-bent on an orgy of destruction. In
Ballard's visionary novel, human society slips
into violent reverse as the inhabitants of the

high rise, driven by primal urges, recreate a world ruled by the laws of the jungle.

Millennium People
While searching for the truth behind the Heathrow bomb that killed his ex-wife, psychologist David Markham infiltrates a shadowy protest group based in the comfortable enclave of Chelsea Marina. He finds that these middle-class revolutionaries are intent on destroying everything they've worked so hard for.

FIND OUT MORE

WATCH

Empire of the Sun
With a screenplay by Tom Stoppard, and starring a young Christian Bale as Jim, Steven Spielberg's 1987 adaptation has the grace and grandeur of a David Lean epic and, perhaps more importantly, the author's wholehearted seal of approval.

The Sun
Described by Ballard himself as resembling 'a dream-like newsreel filmed by a secret camera deep in the emperor's bunker' and as a film that 'brilliantly sums up all the dilemmas that surround war and peace' Alexander Sokurov's film offers a remarkable portrait of the Japanese Emperor Hirohito and compellingly details the closing events of the war in Asia.

SURF

www.jgballard.com

If You Liked This, Why Not Try More From *The Perennial Collection*

Naked Lunch The Restored Text
William Burroughs

Since 1959, when it was first published, Naked Lunch has been one of the most important works of the twentieth century. Told by an Ivy-educated narcotics addict, it is the story of his flight south from New York to 'Interzone', a drug-and-sex-soaked retreat in Tangiers where ambiguous Good and enticing Evil vie for the human soul.

'A rollercoaster ride through hell, a safari to the strangest people of the strangest planet – ourselves. Sit back and gorge yourself on this feast of a novel'   JG BALLARD

The Lover
Maguerite Duras

THE SENSATIONAL INTERNATIONAL BESTSELLER
WINNER OF PRIX GONCOURT

Saigon, 1930s: a poor French girl meets the elegant son of a wealthy Chinese family. Soon they are lovers, locked into a private world of passion and intensity that defies all the conventions of their society. This is an unforgettable portrayal of the incandescent relationship between the lovers and of the hate that slowly tears the girl's family apart.

A Thousand Acres
Jane Smiley

Larry Cook's farm is the largest in his county in Iowa, a tribute to his hard work and single-mindedness. Proud and possessive, his sudden decision to retire and hand over the farm to his three daughters is disarmingly uncharacteristic. When the youngest has misgivings he cuts her out – a decision that causes chaos.

'Powerful, poignant, intimate and involving'
New York Times

The Kitchen God's Wife
Amy Tan

Winnie Louis and Helen Kwong have kept each other's secrets since they met as young brides in the 1930s. Now Helen decides to unburden herself of everything and an angry Winnie realises she must be the first to tell her daughter Pearl about her past – about her childhood in China, the happy and desperate events that brought them to America, and the terrible truth even Helen does not know.

'Tan achieves what I want every novelist to achieve: she made me happy, she made me sad, made me think and made me learn'
MARGARET FORSTER